Ladies' Delight

❦

"Zola overwhelms us with an abundance of description that
oscillates between fantastical lyricism and meticulous
realism, with plenty of rather wry psychological
analysis to hold the two poles together."
Tim Parks

"I consider Zola's books among the very
best of the present time."
Vincent Van Gogh

"To enjoy Zola at his best, you have to read one of the great
novels, in which a whole panorama emerges,
as in the work of one of those highly realistic
nineteenth-century painters."
A.N. Wilson

"Nothing gets a crowd going like sex and shopping. Émile Zola
was one of the first to describe this new consumerist
link in his novel *Ladies' Delight*."
The Times

"Perhaps the most famous novel about shopping is Émile Zola's
Ladies' Delight... For Zola, the department store was a
metaphor for the triumph of capitalism... but he
also saw it as the place where women were duped
and enslaved into the new habit of consumerism."
The Guardian

ONEWORLD CLASSICS

Ladies' Delight

Émile Zola

Translated by April Fitzlyon

ONEWORLD
CLASSICS

ONEWORLD CLASSICS LTD
London House
243-253 Lower Mortlake Road
Richmond
Surrey TW9 2LL
United Kingdom
www.oneworldclassics.com

Ladies's Delight first published in French as *Au Bonheur des Dames* in 1883
This translation first published by John Calder (Publishers) Ltd in 1957
This revised edition first published by Oneworld Classics Limited in 2008
English Translation © April Fitzlyon, 1957, 2008
Extra material © Larry Duffy, 2008

Printed in Great Britain by Cox & Wyman Ltd, Reading, Berkshire

ISBN: 978-1-84749-048-3

Contents

Émile Zola (1840–1902)

Five-year-old Émile Zola with his parents, Francesco and Émilie

Alexandrine Zola, Émile's wife,
in a painting by Manet

Jeanne Rozerot, Émile's mistress
and mother to his children

Émile Zola's birthplace in Rue Saint-Joseph, Paris (top left), his parents' house in Aix (top right), Zola's villa in Médan (bottom left) and the interior of Zola's apartment on Rue de Bruxelles, Paris (bottom right)

Émile Zola with his children, Denise and Jacques

Émile Zola's famous article 'J'Accuse…!',
on the front page of *L'Aurore*

Cherchant des documents!

A contemporary department store (top left), a caricature of Zola research-
ing *Ladies' Delight* (top right), a floor plan by Zola of his fictional store
(bottom left) and a preliminary outline of the novel (bottom right)

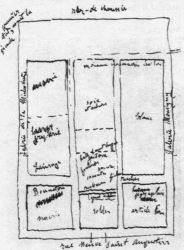

Illustrations from the 1906 Charpentier-Fasquelle edition
of *Ladies' Delight*, depicting scenes from
Chapters 5 (above) and 12 (below)

Ladies' Delight

1

DENISE HAD COME on foot from Saint-Lazare station where, after a night spent on the hard bench of a third-class carriage, she and her two brothers had been set down by a train from Cherbourg. She was holding Pépé's hand, and Jean was following her; they were all three aching from the journey, scared and lost in the midst of the vast city of Paris. Noses in the air, they were looking at the houses, and at each cross-road they asked the way to the Rue de la Michodière where their Uncle Baudu lived. But, just as she was finally emerging into the Place Gaillon, the girl stopped short in surprise.

"Oh!" she said. "Just have a look at that, Jean!"

And there they stood, huddled together, all in black, dressed in the old, worn-out mourning clothes from their father's funeral. She, a meagre twenty-year-old, was carrying a light parcel, while on her other side, her small brother of five was hanging on her arm; her big brother, in the full flower of his magnificent sixteen years, stood looking over her shoulder, his arms dangling.

"Well!" she resumed, after a silence. "There's a shop for you!"

There was, at the corner of the Rue de la Michodière and the Rue Neuve-Saint-Augustin, a drapery shop, the windows of which, on that mild pale October day, were bursting with bright colours. The clock at Saint-Roch was striking eight, only those Parisians who were early risers were about, workers hurrying to their offices, and housewives hurrying to the shops. Two shop assistants, standing on a double ladder outside the door, had just finished hanging up some woollen material, while in the shop window in the Rue Neuve-Saint-Augustin another shop assistant, on hands and knees and with his back turned to them, was daintily folding a piece of blue silk. The shop, as yet void of customers and in which the staff had only just arrived, was buzzing inside like a beehive waking up.

3

"My word!" said Jean. "That beats Valognes... Yours wasn't so fine."

Denise tossed her head. She had spent two years in Valognes, at Cornaille's, the foremost draper in the town; and this shop so suddenly encountered, this building which seemed to her enormous, brought a lump to her throat and held her there, stirred, fascinated, oblivious to everything else. The high door, which cut off the corner of the Place Gaillon, was all of glass, surrounded by intricate decorations loaded with gilding, and reached to the mezzanine floor. Two allegorical figures, two laughing women, their bare bosoms exposed, were unrolling an inscription: AU BONHEUR DES DAMES.* And the shop windows continued beyond, skirting the Rue de la Michodière and the Rue Neuve-Saint-Augustin where, apart from the corner house, they occupied four other houses which had recently been bought and converted, two on the left and two on the right. Seen in perspective, with the show windows on the ground floor and the plate-glass mezzanine-floor windows, behind which all the internal life of the departments was visible, it seemed to her to be an endless vista. Upstairs a girl in a silk dress was sharpening a pencil, while near her two other girls were unfolding some velvet coats.

"*Au Bonheur des Dames*," Jean read out with his romantic laugh – the laugh of a handsome adolescent who had already had an affair with a woman at Valognes. "That's nice, isn't it? That should make people flock here!"

But Denise remained absorbed in front of the display at the main door. There, outside in the street, on the pavement itself, was a cascade of cheap goods, the bait at the entrance, bargains which stopped passers-by. It all fell from above: pieces of woollen material and bunting, merino, cheviot cloth, flannels were falling from the mezzanine floor, floating like flags, with their neutral tones – slate grey, navy blue, olive green – broken up by the white cards of the price tags. To the side, framing the threshold, strips of fur were likewise hanging, straight bands for dress trimmings, the fine ash of squirrel, the pure snow of swansdown, imitation ermine and imitation marten made of rabbit. And below this, on shelves and tables, surrounded by a pile of remnants, there was a profusion of knitted goods being sold for a song, gloves and knitted woollen scarves, hooded capes, cardigans, a regular winter display of variegated colours, mottled, striped, with bleeding stains of red. Denise saw a tartan material at forty-five centimes, strips of American mink at one franc, and mittens at twenty-five centimes. It was a giant fairground spread of hawker's wares, as if the shop were bursting and throwing its surplus into the street.

Uncle Baudu was forgotten. Even Pépé, who had not let go his sister's hand, was staring with wide-open eyes. A carriage forced all three of them to leave the centre of the square; mechanically they went along the Rue Neuve-Saint-Augustin, past the shop windows, stopping again in front of each fresh display. First they were attracted by a complicated arrangement: above, umbrellas, placed obliquely, seemed to be forming the roof of some rustic hut; below, suspended from rods and displaying the rounded outline of calves of the leg, there were silk stockings, some strewn with bunches of roses, others of every hue – black net, red with embroidered clocks, flesh-coloured ones with a satiny texture which had the softness of a blonde woman's skin; lastly, on the backcloth of the shelves, gloves were symmetrically distributed, their fingers elongated, their palms tapering like those of a Byzantine virgin, with the stiff and seemingly adolescent grace of women's clothes which have never been worn. But the last window, above all, held their attention. A display of silks, satins and velvets was blossoming out there, in a supple and shimmering range of the most delicate flower tones; at the summit were the velvets, of deepest black, and as white as curds and whey; lower down were the satins, pinks and blue with bright folds gradually fading into infinitely tender pallors; further down still were the silks, all the colours of the rainbow, pieces of silk rolled up into shells, folded as if round a drawn-in waist, brought to life by the knowing hands of the shop assistants; and, between each motif, between each coloured phrase of the display, there ran a discreet accompaniment, a delicate gathered strand of cream-coloured foulard. And there, in colossal heaps at either end, were the two silks for which the shop held exclusive rights, the Paris-Bonheur and the Cuir d'Or, exceptional wares which were to revolutionize the drapery trade.

"Oh! That faille at five francs sixty!" murmured Denise, amazed at the Paris-Bonheur.

Jean was beginning to feel bored. He stopped a passer-by.

"The Rue de la Michodière, Monsieur?"

When it had been pointed out to him, the first on the right, the three retraced their steps, going round the shop. But, as she was entering the street, Denise was caught again by a shop window where ladies' ready-mades were being displayed. At Cornaille's in Valognes, ready-made clothes had been her speciality. But never had she seen anything like that! She was rooted to the pavement in admiration. In the background a great shawl of Bruges lace, of considerable value, extended like an altar cloth, its two russetty-white wings unfurled; flounces of Alençon lace were strewn as garlands; then there was a lavish, shimmering stream of every kind of lace, Mechlin, Valenciennes, Brussels appliqué, Venetian lace, like a fall of snow. To the right and left, pieces of cloth stood erect in sombre columns, which made the distant tabernacle seem even further away. And there, in that chapel dedicated to the worship of feminine graces, were the clothes: occupying the central position there was a garment quite out of the common, a velvet coat trimmed with silver fox; on one side of it, a silk cloak lined with squirrel; on the other side, a cloth overcoat edged with cock's feathers; and lastly evening wraps in white cashmere, in white quilted silk, trimmed with swansdown or chenille. There was something for every whim, from evening wraps at twenty-nine francs, to the velvet coat which was labelled eighteen hundred francs. The dummies' round bosoms swelled out the material, their ample hips exaggerated the narrowness of the waists, their missing heads were replaced by large tickets with pins stuck through them into the red bunting in the necks; while mirrors on either side of the windows, by a deliberate trick, reflected and multiplied them endlessly, populated the street with these beautiful women who were for sale, and who bore their prices in large figures, in place of their heads.

"They're first rate!" murmured Jean, who could think of no other way of expressing his emotion.

This time he had become motionless again himself, his mouth open. All this luxurious femininity was making him pink with pleasure. He had the beauty of a girl, beauty which he seemed to have stolen from his sister – dazzling skin, curly auburn hair, lips and eyes moist with love. Next to him, in her astonishment Denise looked even thinner, her mouth too large in her long face, her complexion beneath her pale head of hair already tired. And

Pépé, fair too with the fairness of childhood, was pressing even closer to her, as if overcome by an anxious desire for affection, confused and entranced by the beautiful ladies in the shop window. The three fair figures, poorly clad in black – the sad young girl between the pretty child and the superb boy – were so conspicuous and so charming standing there on the pavement that passers-by were turning around and smiling at them.

For some time a fat man with white hair and a big yellowish face, who was standing on the threshold of a shop at the other end of the street, had been looking at them. There he had been standing, his eyes bloodshot, his mouth contracted, beside himself with rage at the displays at the Bonheur des Dames, when the sight of the young girl and her brothers had compounded his exasperation. What were they doing there, those three simpletons, standing gaping at a mountebank's tomfoolery?

"But what about Uncle?" Denise pointed out suddenly, as if waking with a start.

"We are in the Rue de la Michodière," said Jean. "He must live somewhere near here."

They raised their heads and looked about them. Then, just in front of them, above the fat man, they saw a green signboard, its yellow letters discoloured by rain: AU VIEIL ELBEUF, CLOTHS AND FLANNELS – BAUDU (FORMERLY HAUCHECORNE). The house, painted with ancient, mildewed whitewash, and squat in comparison to the big Louis XIV mansions adjacent to it, had only three front windows – and these windows, square and without shutters, were decorated merely with an iron railing, two crossed bars. But of all this bareness, what most struck Denise, whose eyes were still full of the bright displays at the Bonheur des Dames, was the shop on the ground floor, crushed down by a low ceiling, surmounted by a very low mezzanine floor, with prison-like, half-moon-shaped windows. To the right and the left, woodwork of the same colour as the signboard – bottle-green, shaded by time with ochre and pitch – surrounded two deep-set shop windows, black and dusty, in which one could vaguely distinguish bits of material piled up. The door, which was ajar, seemed to open onto the dank gloom of a cellar.

"This is it," said Jean.

"Well, we'd better go in," Denise declared. "Let's go. Come on, Pépé."

Yet they all three faltered, suddenly nervous. When their father had died, a victim of the same fever which had carried off their mother a month earlier, their Uncle Baudu, overwhelmed by this double bereavement, had indeed written to his niece that there would always be room for her in his house if she should ever wish to try her fortune in Paris. But this letter had been written almost a year ago, and the girl now felt sorry that she had left Valognes like that, on the spur of the moment, without warning her uncle. He did not know them at all, for he had never set foot in Valognes again since he had left there, as quite a young man, to become a junior assistant in the draper's shop of Monsieur Hauchecorne, whose daughter he had subsequently married.

"Monsieur Baudu?" Denise inquired, finally bringing herself to speak to the fat man, who was still looking at them, surprised at their behaviour.

"That's me," he answered.

Then, blushing deeply, Denise stammered:

"Oh, thank goodness! I am Denise, and here is Jean and this is Pépé... You see, we did come, Uncle."

Baudu seemed to be stupefied. His big bloodshot eyes wavered in his yellow face, his slow words were confused. It was evident that he had been very far from thinking of this family which had fallen on him out of the blue.

"What's this? What's this? You here!" he repeated several times. "But you were in Valognes! Why aren't you in Valognes?"

In her gentle voice, which was trembling a little, she had to explain to him. After the death of their father, who had squandered every penny he had in his dyeworks, she had mothered the two children. What she had earned at Cornaille's had not been sufficient to feed all three of them. Jean had been working well with a cabinet-maker who mended antique furniture, but he had not received a penny for it. All the same, he had developed a taste for old things, he carved figures in wood; in fact, one day he had found a piece of ivory and had amused himself by making a head out of it which a gentleman who was passing through the town had seen – and it was precisely this gentleman who, by finding a job with an ivory-worker in Paris for Jean, had made them decide to leave Valognes.

"You see, Uncle, Jean will start his apprenticeship as from tomorrow, at his new master's. They don't want any money from me, he will be housed and fed... So I thought that Pépé and I would always be able to manage. We can't be more unhappy than we were at Valognes."

What she did not mention was Jean's amorous escapade, letters written to a very young girl of the local aristocracy, kisses exchanged over a wall – quite a scandal which had made her decide to leave, and she had accompanied her brother to Paris above all in order to watch over him, for she was a prey to maternal fears for this big child, who was so handsome and so gay that all the women adored him.

Uncle Baudu was having difficulty in recovering. He was repeating his questions. Meanwhile, when he had listened to what she told him about her brothers, he addressed her in familiar terms.

"So your father didn't leave you anything? I did think he still had a little left. Oh, I told him often enough in my letters not to take on that dyeworks! He had a good heart, but not an ounce of sense... And you were left with these lads on your hands, you had to feed this little lot!"

His irascible face had lightened, his eyes were no longer bloodshot as when he had been looking at the Bonheur des Dames. Suddenly he noticed that he was barring the door.

"Come along," he said. "Come in, since you've turned up... Come in, it's better than wasting your time looking at nonsense."

And, having directed a last furious scowl at the displays opposite, he made way for the children and went into the shop, calling his wife and daughter as he did so.

"Élisabeth, Geneviève, come along do, here are some people to see you!"

But the gloom of the shop made Denise and the boys hesitate. Blinded by the daylight of the street, they were blinking as if on the verge of some unknown chasm, feeling the ground with their feet with an instinctive fear of some treacherous step. This vague dread drew them together and, keeping even closer to each other, the little boy still clutching the girl's skirts and the big boy behind, they made their entrance gracefully, smiling and nervous. The morning brightness made the black silhouette of their mourning clothes stand out, an oblique light gilded their fair hair.

"Come in, come in," repeated Baudu.

In a few brief sentences, he explained everything to Madame Baudu and her daughter. The former was a little woman riddled with anaemia, white all over, with white hair, white eyes, white lips. Geneviève, in whom her mother's physical deficiency was even more pronounced, had the debility and the colourlessness of a plant grown in the dark. And yet she had a melancholy charm which she owed to her magnificent black hair, miraculously growing out of that miserable flesh.

"Come in," said the two women in their turn. "Welcome!"

And they made Denise sit down behind the counter. Pépé immediately climbed on to his sister's lap, while Jean, leaning against some panelling, kept close to her. They were becoming reassured, were looking at the shop, where their eyes were growing used to the darkness. Now they could see it, its low ceiling blackened with smoke, its oak counters polished with use, its age-old showcases with strong hasps. Bales of dark-coloured goods reached right up to the rafters. The smell of cloth and dyes, a sharp, chemical smell, seemed to be increased tenfold by the dampness of the floorboards. At the back of the shop two male assistants and a girl were putting away lengths of white flannel.

"Perhaps this little man would like to have something to eat?" said Madame Baudu, smiling at Pépé.

"No, thank you," Denise answered, "We had a glass of milk in a café outside the station."

And, as Geneviève was looking at the light parcel she had put on the floor, she added:

"I left our trunk there."

She blushed; she understood that in polite circles people did not turn up out of the blue like that. Already, in the carriage, as soon as the train had left Valognes, she had felt full of regret, and that was why on their arrival she had left the trunk at the station and given the children their breakfast.

"Look here," said Baudu suddenly, "let's be brief and to the point... I did write to you, it's true, but it was a year ago – and you see, my dear, business has not been going at all well for a year..."

He stopped, strangled by an emotion which he did not wish to show. Madame Baudu and Geneviève with a resigned air had lowered their eyes.

"Oh!" he continued. "It's a crisis which will pass. I'm not at all worried... Only, I've reduced my staff, there are only three people now, and the time is certainly not ripe for hiring a fourth. In short, my dear, I can't take you on as I offered to."

Denise was listening to him, startled, very pale. He rubbed it in by adding:

"It wouldn't be worth it, neither for you nor us."

"Very well, Uncle," she finally said bleakly, "I shall try to manage all the same."

The Baudus were not bad people. But they complained of never having had any luck. At the time when their business had been going well they had had to bring up five boys, of whom three had died before they were twenty – the fourth had gone to the bad, the fifth, a captain, had just left for Mexico. They had no one left but Geneviève. Their family had cost them a great deal, and Baudu had completed his own ruin by purchasing a great barn of a house at Rambouillet, his father-in-law's home town. Consequently there was a growing bitterness beneath his fanatical loyalty, which was that of a tradesman of the old school.

"One lets people know," he went on, gradually getting angry at his own hardness. "You could have written to me, I should have replied that you should stay there... To be sure, when I heard of your father's death I said the usual things to you. But you turn up here, without warning... It's very embarrassing."

He was raising his voice, relieving his feelings. His wife and daughter, submissive people that they were, who never made so bold as to interfere, were still looking at the ground. Meanwhile Jean had turned very pale, whereas Denise had clasped the terrified Pépé to her bosom. She let fall two big tears.

"Very well, Uncle," she repeated. "We will go away."

At that he controlled himself. An embarrassed silence reigned. Then he resumed in a surly tone:

"I'm not going to turn you out of the house... Since you're here now, you may as well sleep upstairs this evening. Afterwards we'll see."

At that Madame Baudu and Geneviève understood with a glance that they could go ahead and make arrangements. Everything was settled. There was no need to do anything for Jean. As to Pépé, the best thing for him would be to lodge with

Madame Gras, an old lady who lived on the ground floor of a house in the Rue des Orties, where she took in young children at forty francs a month, full board. Denise declared that she had enough money to pay for the first month. It only remained for her to find a place herself. It would be easy to find her a job in the neighbourhood.

"Wasn't Vinçard looking for a salesgirl?" said Geneviève.

"Why, so he was!" exclaimed Baudu. "We'll go and see him after lunch. We must strike while the iron's hot!"

Not a single customer had come to interrupt this family conclave. The shop remained dark and empty. In the background the two male assistants and the girl continued their task, making whispered, sibilant remarks. However, three ladies did eventually appear, and Denise remained alone for a moment. Heavy-hearted at the thought of their approaching separation, she kissed Pépé who, affectionate as a kitten, was hiding his head without saying a word. When Madame Baudu and Geneviève came back they found him being very good, and Denise assured them that he never made more noise; he would remain silent for whole days on end, living on love. Then, until lunchtime, the three women talked about children, housekeeping, life in Paris and in the provinces, using the short vague sentences of relations who are rather embarrassed at not knowing each other. Jean had gone out on to the doorstep of the shop and, intrigued by the life in the street, he remained there, smiling at the pretty girls who passed.

At ten o'clock a maid appeared. Usually the first meal was served for Baudu, Geneviève and the first assistant. There was a second meal at eleven o'clock for Madame Baudu, the other male assistant and the girl.

"Let's have a bite!" exclaimed the draper, turning towards his niece.

And, as the others were all already seated in the cramped dining room at the back of the shop, he called the first assistant who was lagging behind.

"Colomban!"

The young man apologized, saying he had wanted to finish arranging some flannel. He was a fat lad of twenty-five, stupid but crafty. His honest face, with its big, flabby mouth, had wily eyes.

"For Heaven's sake! There's a time for everything," said Baudu who, squarely installed, was cutting a piece of cold veal with a master's prudence and skill, with a glance weighing up the meagre portions to an ounce.

He served everyone, and even cut some bread. Denise had put Pépé close to her in order to see that he ate properly. But the dark room made her feel uneasy; as she was looking at it she felt a lump in her throat, for she was used to the spacious rooms, bare and light, of her native province. A single window opened onto a little inside courtyard which communicated with the street by means of a dark alley, and this yard, soaking wet and reeking, was like the bottom of a well into which there fell a circle of sinister light. On winter days the gas had to be lit from morning to night. When the weather was good enough for it not to be lit, the effect was even more depressing. It was a moment before Denise's eyes were sufficiently accustomed to the dark to distinguish what was on her plate.

"There's a fellow with a good appetite," Baudu declared, noticing that Jean had polished off his veal. "If he works as much as he eats, he'll be a tough man... But what about you, my dear, you're not eating? And now that we can talk, tell me why you didn't get married at Valognes?"

Denise put down the glass which she was raising to her mouth.

"Oh Uncle, me get married? You don't mean it!... And the little ones?"

She ended up laughing, so quaint did the idea seem to her. In any case, would any man have wanted her, without a penny, as thin as a rake and not, so far, beautiful? No, no, she would never marry, she already had enough with two children.

"You're mistaken," her uncle repeated, "a woman always needs a man. If you'd found a decent young chap you wouldn't have landed on the street in Paris, like gypsies, you and your brothers."

He broke off in order once more to divide, with a parsimony that was nothing if not fair, a dish of bacon and potatoes which the maid was bringing. Then, indicating Geneviève and Colomban with a spoon, he continued:

"Why, those two there will be married in the spring, if the winter season is good."

It was the shop's patriarchal tradition. The founder, Aristide Finet, had given his daughter Désirée to his first assistant, Hauchecorne; he, Baudu, who had arrived in the Rue de la Michodière with seven francs in his pocket, had married old man Hauchecorne's daughter, Élisabeth; and he intended, in his turn, to hand over his daughter Geneviève and the shop to Colomban as soon as business revived. If that would mean having to postpone a marriage which had been decided on three years earlier, he did so from scruple, from stubbornness born of integrity: he had received the business in a prosperous state, he did not wish to hand it over to a son-in-law with fewer customers and when business was uncertain.

Baudu went on talking, introduced Colomban, who came from Rambouillet like Madame Baudu's father; they were even distantly related, in fact. He was a great worker and, for ten years, had been slogging away in the shop and had really earned his promotions! Besides, he wasn't just anybody, his father was that old sinner Colomban, a veterinary surgeon known throughout the Seine-et-Oise, an artist in his own line, but so fond of food that there was nothing he wouldn't eat.

"Thank God!" said the draper in conclusion. "Even if his father does drink and chase skirts, the boy has been able to learn the value of money here."

While he was talking, Denise was studying Colomban and Geneviève. They were sitting next to each other, but they remained there quite calmly, without a blush, without a smile. Since his first day in the shop the young man had been counting on this marriage. He had passed through all the different stages, junior assistant, salaried salesman, had been admitted finally to the confidences and pleasures of the family, and had gone through it all patiently, leading a clockwork-like life and looking on Geneviève as an excellent and honest business deal. The certitude that she would be his prevented him from desiring her. And the girl too had grown accustomed to loving him, but she loved him with all the seriousness of her reserved nature – and although in the tame, regular, every-day existence which she led she did not realize it herself, she loved him with deep passion.

"When people like each other, and when it's possible..." Denise felt forced to say with a smile, in order to be nice.

"Yes, it always ends up like that in the end," declared Colomban, who had not yet said a word, but was slowly munching.

Geneviève, after giving him a long glance, said in her turn:

"People must get on together, afterwards it's plain sailing."

Their fondness for each other had grown up in this ground-floor shop in old Paris. It was like a flower in a cellar. For ten years she had known no one but him, had spent her days beside him, behind the same piles of cloth, in the depths of the shop's gloom; and, morning and evening, they had met again side by side in the cramped dining room, as chilly as a well. They could not have been more lost, more buried, in the depths of the countryside beneath the leaves. Only a doubt, a jealous fear, was to make the girl discover that, from emptiness of heart and boredom of mind, she had given herself for ever in the midst of those conspiring shadows.

Yet Denise thought she noticed a dawning anxiety in the glance which Geneviève had cast at Colomban. Therefore, in a kindly way, she replied:

"Nonsense! When people love each other, they always get on together."

But Baudu was superintending the table with authority. He had distributed slivers of Brie, and in honour of his relatives he ordered a second dessert, a pot of gooseberry preserves – such liberality appeared to surprise Colomban. Pépé, who had been very good until then, behaved badly over the preserves. Jean, whose interest had been aroused by the conversation about marriage, was staring at his cousin Geneviève, whom he considered too lifeless, too pale; deep inside him he was comparing her to a little white rabbit, with black ears and red eyes.

"That's enough chat, we must make room for the others!" the draper concluded, giving the signal to leave the table. "Just because we've allowed ourselves a treat, it's no reason for taking an unfair advantage over everything."

Madame Baudu, the other male assistant, and the girl came and sat down at the table in their turn. Once more Denise remained sitting alone near the door, waiting until her uncle was able to take her to see Vinçard. Pépé was playing at her feet, Jean had taken up his observation post on the doorstep again. And, for almost an hour, she watched what was happening around her. At infrequent intervals customers came into the shop: one lady appeared, then two more. The shop retained its smell of age, its half-light, in which all the way of business of bygone days, good-natured and simple, seemed to be weeping at its neglect. But what fascinated her was the Bonheur des Dames on the other side of the road, for she could see the shop windows through the open door. The sky was still overcast, the mildness brought by rain was warming the air in spite of the season, and in the pale daylight which seemed to be sparsely dusted with sunshine the great shop was coming to life, business was in full swing.

Now Denise had the sensation of a machine working at high pressure, the impetus of which seemed to reach to the very displays themselves. They were no longer the cold shop windows of the morning; now they seemed to be warmed and vibrating with the bustle inside. A crowd was looking at them, women who had stopped were crushing each other in front of the windows. There was a regular mob, made brutal by covetousness. And these passions of the street were giving life to the materials: the laces seemed to be shivering, then subsiding again with an exciting air of mystery, concealing the depths of the shop as they did so; the very pieces of cloth, thick and square, were breathing, exuding a whiff of temptation, while the overcoats were drawing themselves up even more on the lay figures, who themselves were acquiring souls, and the huge velvet coat was billowing out, supple and warm, as if on shoulders of flesh and blood, with heaving breast and quivering hips. But the furnace-like heat with which the shop was ablaze was coming, above all, from the selling, from the bustle of the counters, which could be sensed behind the walls. From there came the continuous rumble of a machine at work, of customers crowding in the departments, bedazzled by the merchandise, then propelled towards the cash desk. And all this regulated, organized with the remorselessness of a machine; a vast horde of women caught in the wheels of an inevitable force.

Since the morning Denise had been undergoing temptation. This shop, to her so vast, which she had seen more people enter in one hour than had visited Cornaille's in six months, dazed and attracted her, and in her desire to penetrate within it there was a vague fear, which made her all the more fascinated. At the same time, her uncle's shop gave her an uneasy feeling. She felt an irrational disdain, an instinctive repugnance for this frigid hideout of old-fashioned methods of business. All the sensations she had passed through, her anxious entry, her relations' sour welcome, the depressing lunch in the dungeon-like darkness, her long wait in the drowsy solitude of the old house in its death throes – all this was combining to form a veiled protest, a passionate desire for life and for light. And, in spite of her kind heart, her eyes always went back to the Bonheur des Dames, as if the salesgirl in her felt a need to take fresh warmth from the blaze of that huge sale.

She let slip a remark:

"They've got plenty of people there, at any rate!"

But she regretted her words when she caught sight of the Baudus nearby. Madame Baudu, who had finished her lunch, was standing up, white as a sheet, her white eyes fixed on the monster, and resigned though she was, she could not see it, could not thus by chance catch sight of it on the other side of the street, without dumb despair making her eyes fill with tears. As to Geneviève, with growing anxiety she was watching Colomban who, not knowing that he was being observed, was looking in rapture at the girls selling coats, whose department was visible behind the mezzanine windows. Baudu, rage on his face, contented himself by saying:

"All is not gold that glitters, you just wait!"

Obviously the family was choking back the surge of resentment which was rising in its throat. A sense of self-respect prevented it from letting itself go so soon in front of the children who had only arrived that morning. In the end, the draper made an effort, and turned round in order to drag himself away from the sight of the selling going on opposite.

"Well," he went on, "let's go and see about Vinçard. Jobs are very sought after, tomorrow it may be too late."

But, before going out, he told the second assistant to go to the station and fetch Denise's trunk. For her part Madame Baudu, to whom the girl had entrusted Pépé, decided that she would take advantage of a free moment by going with the little boy to Madame Gras in the Rue des Orties in order to have a chat with her and come to some agreement. Jean promised his sister that he would not quit the shop.

"It'll only take a couple of minutes," Baudu explained as he was going along the Rue Gaillon with his niece. "Vinçard specializes in silks, and he's still doing some business in that line.

Oh, he has his difficulties, like everyone else, but he's artful and makes both ends meet by being as stingy as can be. But I think he wants to retire, because of his rheumatism."

The shop was in the Rue Neuve-des-Petits-Champs, near the Choiseul Arcade. It was clean and light, smart in an up-to-date way, though small and poorly stocked. Baudu and Denise found Vinçard deep in conference with two gentlemen.

"Don't bother about us," exclaimed the draper. "We're not in a hurry, we'll wait."

And, going tactfully back towards the door he added, bending down to the girl's ear:

"The thin one is at the Bonheur, assistant buyer in the silk department, and the fat one is a manufacturer from Lyons."

Denise gathered that Vinçard was talking up his shop to Robineau, the assistant from the Bonheur des Dames. With a frank air and open manner he was giving his word of honour, with the facility of a man whose style would not be cramped by oaths of that kind. According to him, the shop was a gold mine, and, bursting as he was with rude health, he broke off in order to complain, to whine about his confounded pains which were forcing him to give up making his fortune. But Robineau, highly strung and anxious, was interrupting him impatiently: he knew about the slump which drapers were going through, he quoted a shop specializing in silks which had already been ruined by the proximity of the Bonheur. Vinçard, blazing with anger, raised his voice.

"To be sure! That silly old chump Vabre's crash was inevitable. His wife squandered everything... Besides, here we are more than five hundred yards away, whereas Vabre was right next door to it."

Then Gaujean, the silk manufacturer, broke into the conversation. Once more their voices were lowered. Gaujean was accusing the big stores of ruining the French textile industry; three or four of them were dictating it, were ruling the market, and he insinuated that the only way to fight against them was to encourage small businesses, above all those which specialized, for the future belonged to them. For this reason he was offering very generous credit to Robineau.

"Look how the Bonheur has treated you!" he repeated. "They take no account of services rendered, they're just machines for exploiting the people... They promised you the job of buyer ages ago, and then Bouthemont, who came from outside and had no right to it, got it in the end."

This injustice was still rankling with Robineau. All the same, he was hesitating about setting up in business himself, he explained that the money was not his; his wife had inherited sixty thousand francs, and he was full of scruples about this sum because, so he said, he would rather cut both his hands off on the spot than risk it in bad business.

"No. I have not made up my mind," he concluded at last. "Give me time to think it over, we'll discuss it again."

"As you like," said Vinçard, hiding his disappointment under a good-natured air. "It's not in my own interest to sell. Really, if it wasn't for my rheumatism..."

And, returning to the centre of the shop he said:

"What can I do for you, Monsieur Baudu?"

The draper, who was listening with one ear, introduced Denise, told as much as he thought necessary of her story, said that she had been working in the provinces for two years.

"And, as I hear that you're looking for a good salesgirl..."

Vinçard pretended to be in great despair.

"Oh! That is bad luck! Certainly, I was looking for a salesgirl for over a week. But I've just hired one less than two hours ago."

A silence fell. Denise seemed to be overwhelmed with dismay. Then Robineau, who was looking at her with interest, no doubt touched by her poor appearance, volunteered some information.

"I know that they want someone at our place in the ready-made department."

Baudu could not suppress a heartfelt exclamation.

"At your place! My goodness – no!"

Then he became embarrassed. Denise had blushed all over; never would she dare to go into that huge shop! And the idea of being there filled her with pride.

"Why not?" resumed Robineau, surprised. "On the contrary, it would be an opportunity for her... I'd advise her to go to see Madame Aurélie, the buyer, tomorrow morning. The worst that can happen is that they won't take her."

The draper, in order to hide his inner revulsion, launched into vague phrases: he knew Madame Aurélie, or at any rate her husband, Lhomme, the cashier, a fat man who had had his right arm cut off by an omnibus. Then, abruptly coming back to Denise, he said:

"In any case, it's her affair, not mine... She's quite free..."

And he went out, after saying goodbye to Gaujean and Robineau. Vinçard accompanied him to the door, once more saying how sorry he was. The girl had remained in the middle of the shop, self-conscious, anxious to get fuller information from the shop assistant. But she did not dare, and said goodbye in her turn, adding simply:

"Thank you, Monsieur."

Once in the street, Baudu did not speak to his niece. He was walking fast, forcing her to run, as if carried away by his own thoughts. In the Rue de la Michodière he was about to go into his house when a neighbouring shopkeeper who was standing outside his door made a sign to attract him. Denise stopped to wait for him.

"What is it, Bourras, old chap?" asked the draper.

Bourras was a tall old man, long-haired and bearded, with the head of a prophet and piercing eyes under great bushy eyebrows. He had a walking-stick and umbrella business, did repairs, and even carved handles, a skill which had earned for him in the neighbourhood the renown of an artist. Denise glanced at the shop windows, where umbrellas and walking sticks were lined up in regular ranks. But she looked up, and above all she was astonished by the house: it was a hovel, squashed in between the Bonheur des Dames and a large Louis XIV mansion, pushed, no one could tell how, into the narrow crevice, at the bottom of which its two low storeys were collapsing. Without supports on the right and left it would have fallen down; the slates on its roof were crooked and rotten, its façade scarred with cracks and running with long streaks of iron mould on the half-eaten-away woodwork of the signboard.

"You know, he's written to my landlord about buying the house," said Bourras, looking at the draper intently with his blazing eyes.

Baudu became even paler and hunched his shoulders. There was a silence, the two men remained looking at each other with a serious air.

"One must be prepared for everything," he murmured finally.

At that the old man flew into a passion, shaking his hair and his flowing beard.

"Let him buy the house, he'll pay four times its value for it! But I swear to you that while I'm still alive he shan't have a single stone of it. My lease is for twelve more years... We'll see, we'll see!"

It was a declaration of war. Bourras turned round towards the Bonheur des Dames, which neither of them had named. For an instant Baudu tossed his head in silence; then he crossed the street to go to his house, his legs worn out, repeating only:

"Oh God!... Oh God!"

Denise, who had been listening, followed her uncle. Madame Baudu came in too with Pépé, and she said at once that Madame Gras would take the child whenever they so desired. But Jean had just disappeared, which worried his sister. When he returned, his face alight, talking excitedly about the boulevard, she looked at him in a sad way which made him blush. Their trunk had been brought, and they were to sleep upstairs in the attic.

"By the way, what happened at Vinçard's?" asked Madame Baudu.

The draper told her about his fruitless errand, then added that he had been told about a job for his niece, and, with his arm stretched out towards the Bonheur des Dames in a gesture of contempt, he blurted out the words:

"In there, to be sure!"

The whole family felt hurt about it. In the evening, the first meal was at five o'clock. Denise and the two children once more took their places with Baudu, Geneviève and Colomban. The small dining room was lit by a gas jet and the smell of food was stifling. The meal proceeded in silence. But during the dessert Madame Baudu, who was restless, left the shop to come and sit down behind her niece. And then the wave which had been held up since the morning broke, and they all relieved their feelings by slating the monster.

"It's your own business, you're quite free..." repeated Baudu, first of all. "We don't want to influence you... Only, if you knew what sort of place it is!..."

In broken sentences he told her the story of Octave Mouret. Nothing but luck! A lad from the Midi who had turned up in Paris possessing all the attractive audacity of an adventurer, and from the very next day there had been nothing but affairs with women, an endless exploitation of women, a scandal, which the neighbourhood was still talking about, when he had been caught red-handed; then his sudden and inexplicable conquest of Madame Hédouin, who had brought him the Bonheur des Dames.

"Poor Caroline!" Madame Baudu interrupted. "I was distantly related to her. Ah! If she had lived things would have been different. She wouldn't have allowed us to be murdered... And it was he who killed her. Yes, on his building site! One morning, when she was looking at the work, she fell into a hole. Three days later she died. She, who'd never had a day's illness, who was so healthy, so beautiful! There's some of her blood beneath the stones of that shop!"

With her pale, trembling hand she pointed through the walls towards the great shop. Denise, who was listening as one listens to a fairy tale, shivered slightly. The fear, which since that morning she had been feeling at the roots of the temptation being brought to bear on her, came, perhaps, from the blood of that woman whom she seemed now to see in the red cement of the basement.

"It looks as if it brings him luck," added Madame Baudu without naming Mouret.

But the draper shrugged his shoulders, contemptuous of these old wives' tales. He resumed his story, he explained the situation from the commercial angle. The Bonheur des Dames had been founded in 1822 by the Deleuze brothers. When the eldest died, his daughter Caroline had married the son of a linen manufacturer, Charles Hédouin, and later on, having become a widow, she had married this man Mouret. Through her, therefore, he had acquired a half-share in the shop. Three months after their marriage, her uncle Deleuze had in his turn died, without children; so that, when Caroline had left her bones in the foundations, this man Mouret had become sole heir, sole proprietor of the Bonheur. Nothing but luck!

"A man with ideas, a dangerous troublemaker who'll turn the whole neighbourhood topsy-turvy if he's allowed to!" Baudu went on. "I think Caroline, who was a bit romantic too, must have been taken in by the gentleman's absurd plans... In short, he prevailed on her to buy the house on the left, then the house on the right — and he himself, when he was left on his own, bought two others, so that the shop has gone on growing, gone on growing to such an extent that it threatens to eat us all up now!"

His words were addressed to Denise, but he was speaking for his own benefit, brooding over this story which obsessed him, in order to justify himself. When alone with his family he was an irascible, violent man, his fists always clenched. Madame Baudu was immobile where she sat, no longer taking part in the conversation; Geneviève and Colomban, their eyes lowered, were absent-mindedly collecting and eating crumbs. It was so hot, so stifling in the small room that Pépé had fallen asleep on the table, and even Jean's eyes were closing.

"You wait!" Baudu went on, seized with sudden rage. "Those mountebanks will break their necks! I know that Mouret is going through a difficult time. I know he is. He's had to put all his profits into his mad schemes of expansion and advertisement. What's more, he's taken it into his head to persuade most of his staff to invest their money in his business. So he hasn't a penny now, and if a miracle doesn't occur, if he doesn't manage to triple his sales, as he hopes, you'll see what a crash there'll be! Ah! I'm not a spiteful man, but on that day I'll put out the flags, word of honour!"

He continued in a revengeful voice; one would have thought that the slighted honour of the trade could only be restored by the fall of the Bonheur. Had the like ever been seen before? A draper's shop which sold everything! A real bazaar! And a fine staff they had, too: a crowd of country bumpkins who shunted things about as if they were in a station, who treated the goods and the customers like parcels, dropping their employer or being dropped by him for a word – no affection, no morals, no art! And suddenly he called Colomban to witness: of course he, Colomban, brought up in the good old school, knew the slow, sure way in which one attained to the real subtleties, to the tricks of the trade. The art was not to sell a lot, but to sell at a high price. And then Colomban could also mention how he'd been treated, how he'd become a member of the family, nursed when he was ill, his things laundered and mended, looked after paternally – in a word: loved.

"Of course!" Colomban repeated after each of his employer's shouts.

"You're the last, my boy," said Baudu finally, with emotion. "After you it won't be like that any more... You're my only consolation, for if a scramble like that is what they call business nowadays, I don't understand a thing, I'd rather quit."

Geneviève, her head leaning towards her shoulder as if her thick head of black hair was too heavy for her pale forehead, was scrutinizing the smiling shop assistant, and in her look there was a suspicion, a desire to see if Colomban, prey to a sense of remorse, would not blush at such panegyrics. But, as if he was used to the old tradesman's act, he maintained his calm straightforwardness, his bland air, and the wily crease on his lips.

However, Baudu was shouting more loudly, accusing the bazaar opposite, those savages who were massacring each other in their struggle for existence, of going so far as to destroy the family. He quoted as an example their neighbours in the countryside, the Lhommes, mother, father and son, all three employed in that hole, people with no home life, always out, only eating at home on Sundays, nothing but a hotel and restaurant life! To be sure, his own dining room was not large, one could even have done with a bit more light and air – but at least his life was centred there, and there he had lived surrounded by the love of his family. As he spoke his eyes travelled round the little room, and he was seized with a fit of trembling at the idea, which he refused to acknowledge, that the savages could one day, if they succeeded in killing his business, dislodge him from this nook where, with his wife and daughter on either side of him, he felt warm. In spite of the air of assurance which he put on while foretelling the final crash, deep in his heart he was full of terror; he did really feel that the neighbourhood would be overrun, gradually devoured.

"I'm not saying this to put you off," he resumed, trying to be calm. "If it's in your interest to get a job there, I shall be the first to say: 'Go there.'"

"Yes, I'm sure, Uncle," murmured Denise, bewildered; in the midst of all this emotion her desire to be at the Bonheur des Dames was growing.

He had placed his elbows on the table, and was wearing her out with his stare.

"But come, you've been in the trade, tell me, is it sense for a plain draper's shop to start selling everything under the sun? In the old days, when trade was honest, drapery meant materials, and nothing else. Nowadays their only idea is to ride roughshod over their neighbours and to eat up everything... That's what the neighbourhood is complaining about, for the little shops are beginning to suffer terribly. This man Mouret is ruining them... Why! Bédoré and his sister, in the hosiery shop in the Rue Gaillon, have already lost half their customers. At Mademoiselle Tatin's, the lingerie shop in the Choiseul Arcade, they've reached the point of lowering prices, competing in cheapness. And the effect of this scourge, this plague, makes itself felt as far as the Rue Neuve-des-Petits-Champs, where I have been told that the Vanpouille brothers, the furriers, can't hold out. Eh? Drapers who sell furs, it's too silly! Another idea of Mouret's!"

"And the gloves," said Madame Baudu, "isn't it scandalous? He's had the nerve to create a glove department! Yesterday, when I was going along the Rue Neuve-Saint-Augustin, Quinette was standing by his door looking so depressed that I didn't dare ask him if business was good."

"And umbrellas," Baudu went on. "Really, that beats everything! Bourras is convinced that Mouret simply wanted to ruin him; for after all, what sense does it make, umbrellas and materials together? But Bourras is tough, he won't let himself be done in. We'll have the last laugh one of these days."

He talked about other shopkeepers, reviewed the whole neighbourhood. Occasionally he would let out a confession: if Vinçard was trying to sell, they might as well all pack their bags, for Vinçard was like a rat leaving a sinking ship. Then immediately he would contradict himself, he would dream of an alliance, a league of little retailers to hold out against the colossus. For some time now, with restless hands and his mouth twisted with a nervous twitch, he had been hesitating to talk about himself. Finally, he took the plunge.

"So far as I'm concerned, up till now I haven't had much to complain about. Oh! He has done me some harm, the scoundrel! But so far he only keeps cloth for women, light cloth for dresses and heavier cloth for coats. People always come to me to buy things for men, special types of velvet, liveries – not to mention flannels and duffels, of which I really challenge him to have such a wide assortment. Only he plagues me, he thinks he makes my blood boil because he's put his drapery department there, opposite. You've seen his display, haven't you? He always plants his most beautiful dresses there, set in a framework of lengths of cloth, a real circus parade to catch the girls... Honest to God! I'd blush to use such methods. The Vieil Elbeuf has been famous for almost a hundred years, and it doesn't need booby traps like that at its door. So long as I live, the shop will stay the same as it was when I got it, with its four sample pieces of cloth on the right and on the left, and nothing else!"

His emotion was spreading to the rest of the family. After a silence, Geneviève ventured to say something:

"Our customers are fond of us, Papa. We must remain hopeful... Only today Madame Desforges and Madame de Boves were here, and I'm expecting Madame Marty to look at some flannels."

"As for me," Colomban declared, "I got an order from Madame Bourdelais yesterday. It's true that she told me about an English tweed, the same as ours it seems, but priced fifty centimes cheaper opposite."

"And to think," said Madame Baudu in her tired voice, "that we knew that shop opposite when it was no bigger than a pocket handkerchief! Yes really, my dear Denise, when the Deleuzes founded it, it only had one window in the Rue Neuve-Saint-Augustin – a proper cupboard it was, where a couple of pieces of chintz were jammed together with three of calico... One couldn't turn round in the shop, it was so small... At that time the Vieil Elbeuf, which had existed for over sixty years, was already just as you see it today... Ah! It's all changed, greatly changed!"

She was shaking her head, her slow phrases told of the drama of her life. Born at the Vieil Elbeuf, she loved it even down to its damp stones, she lived only for it and because of it; in bygone days she had been full of pride for this shop, which had been the largest, the most thriving business in the neighbourhood. She had had the continual pain of seeing the rival shop gradually growing, at first despised, then equal in importance, then surpassing it, menacing it. For her it was an ever-open wound, she was dying of the Vieil Elbeuf's humiliation; she, like it, was still living from force of impetus, but she well knew that the shop's death throes would be her own too, that on the day when the shop closed down she would be finished.

Silence reigned. Baudu was beating a tattoo with his fingertips on the oilcloth. He felt weary, almost sorry at having yet once more relieved his feelings like that. Indeed, all the members of the family, their eyes vacant, in a state of despondency, were still turning over in their minds the bitter events of their history. Luck had never smiled on them. The children had been reared, fortune was on the way, when suddenly competition had brought ruin. And there was also the house at Rambouillet, the country house to which, for ten years, the draper had been dreaming of retiring, a bargain he called it, an ancient shack which he was obliged continually to repair, which he had reluctantly decided to let, and for which the tenants neglected to pay rent. His last profits were being spent on it. Meticulously honest as he was, with his dogged adherence to the old ways, it was the only vice he had ever had.

"Now then," he suddenly declared, "we must make way for the others at the table... What a lot of useless talk!"

This acted like a charm. The gas jet was hissing in the dead, stifling air of the little room. Everyone got up with a start, breaking the gloomy silence. Pépé, however, was sleeping so soundly that they laid him down on some pieces of thick flannel. Jean, yawning, had already gone back to the front door.

"To cut the matter short, you do what you like," Baudu repeated once more to his niece. "We're just telling you the facts, that's all. But it's your own business."

His gaze was pressing, he was waiting for a decisive answer. Denise, who instead of being turned against the Bonheur des Dames as a result of these stories, was more fascinated by it than ever, kept her air of calmness and sweetness, which had its roots in an obstinate Norman will. She was content to reply: "We'll see, Uncle."

And she talked of going to bed early with the children, for they were all three very tired. But it was only just striking six, and she was quite pleased to stay in the shop a moment or two longer. Night had fallen; when she reached the street it was dark, soaked with fine, dense rain which had been falling since sunset. A surprise greeted her: a few moments had sufficed for the carriageway to be pitted with puddles, for the gutters to be running with dirty water, for thick, trampled-on mud to make the pavements sticky, and beneath the heavy downpour nothing could be seen but a confused procession of umbrellas jostling each other, swelling out like great gloomy wings in the darkness. She drew back at first, struck by the cold and the badly lit shop, lugubrious at that time of night, making her feel even more depressed. A damp draught, the very breath of that ancient neighbourhood, was coming from the street; it seemed as if the trickling water from the umbrellas was flowing right up to the counters, that the pavement with its mud and its puddles was invading the antiquated ground floor, white with saltpetre rot, and was putting the finishing touches to its mildewed state. It was a real glimpse of old Paris, sodden through, and it made her shiver with woebegone surprise at finding the great city so glacial and so ugly.

But, on the other side of the road, the broad ranks of gas burners at the Bonheur des Dames were lit. And she drew nearer, once more attracted and seemingly warmed by this centre of blazing light. The machine was still humming, still active, letting off steam in a final roar, while the salesmen were folding up the materials and the cashiers counting their takings. Through mirrors dimmed with vapour a vague profusion of lights was visible, the confused interior of a factory. Behind the curtain of rain which was falling this vision, remote, blurred, looked like some giant stokehold, in which the black shadows of the stokers could be seen moving against the red fire of the furnaces. The shop windows were drowning, one could no longer distinguish anything opposite but a snow of lace, the white of which was heightened by frosted glass footlights, and against the background of the chapel, the coats were bursting with energy, the great velvet overcoat trimmed with silver fox was displaying the curved outline of a headless woman, running through the downpour to some festivity in the unknown of the Parisian night.

Denise, yielding to temptation, had come as far as the door without noticing the spurt of raindrops which was soaking her. At this time of night, with its furnace-like glare, the Bonheur des Dames won her over finally and completely. In the great town, dark and silent under the rain, in this Paris of which she knew nothing, it was burning like a beacon, it alone seemed to be the light and the life of the city. She stood there dreaming of her future, of hard work to bring up the children, and of other things too – she did not know what – remote things which made her tremble with desire and fear. The thought of the dead woman under the foundations came back to her; she was afraid, she thought that she could see the lights bleeding; then the whiteness of the lace soothed her, a hope was rising in her heart, a real certainty of joy. The flying spray of rain was cooling her hands and calming within her the fever of her journey.

"That's Bourras," said a voice behind her back.

She leant forwards and caught sight of Bourras, standing motionless at the end of the street in front of the shop window in which, that morning, she had noticed a whole ingenious construction made from umbrellas and walking sticks. The tall old man had slipped out in the dark to feast his eyes on this triumphal display; his expression was heart-rending, he did not even notice the rain beating on his bare head, making his white hair drip.

"He is silly," the voice remarked, "he'll catch his death of cold."

Then, turning round, Denise perceived that she once more had the Baudus behind her. In spite of themselves, like Bourras whom they thought silly, they always came back there in the end, to this scene which was breaking their hearts. They had a mania for suffering. Geneviève, very pale, had noticed that Colomban was watching the shadows of the salesgirls passing the windows on the mezzanine floor, and while Baudu was choking with suppressed malice, Madame Baudu's eyes had silently filled with tears.

"You are going to go there tomorrow, aren't you?" the draper asked finally, tormented with uncertainty, and in any case sensing full well that his niece had been conquered like the rest.

She hesitated, then said gently:

"Yes, Uncle, unless it would vex you too much."

2

NEXT DAY, at half-past seven, Denise was standing outside the Bonheur des Dames. She wanted to call there before taking Jean to his employer, who lived a long way away, at the top of the Faubourg du Temple. But being used to early rising, she had been in too much of a hurry to get up: the shop assistants were only just arriving and, afraid of looking ridiculous, filled with shyness, she stopped to mark time for a moment in the Place Gaillon.

A cold wind which was blowing had already dried the pavement. From every street, lit by the pale early-morning light beneath an ashen sky, shop assistants were busily emerging, the collars of their overcoats turned up, their hands in their pockets, caught unawares by this first nip of winter. Most of them slipped in alone and were swallowed up in the depths of the shop without addressing a word or even a glance to their colleagues striding along all round them; others were walking in twos or threes, talking quickly, taking up the whole width of the pavement; and all, with an identical gesture, threw their cigarette or cigar into the gutter before entering.

Denise noticed that several of these gentlemen stared at her in passing. At that her timidity increased, she no longer felt that she had the strength to follow them, she resolved to go in herself only when the procession should have come to an end – she blushed at the idea of being jostled in the doorway in the midst of all those men. But the procession continued, and in order to escape the glances she slowly walked round the square. When she came back she found a big lad, pale and ungainly, planted in front of the Bonheur des Dames; he too appeared to have been waiting there for a quarter of an hour.

"Excuse me, Mademoiselle," he asked her finally in a stammering voice, "I thought perhaps you might be a salesgirl in the shop?"

She was so overcome at being spoken to by this unknown young man that at first she did not reply.

"Because, you see," he went on, getting even more confused, "I thought I might see if they wouldn't take me on, and you might have been able to give me some information."

He was just as shy as she was, and was taking the plunge first because he sensed that she, like him, was quaking.

'I would have, with pleasure," she replied at last, "but I'm no further advanced than you are, I've come here to apply, too."

"Oh, I see," he said, completely disconcerted.

And they blushed deeply, faced with their common shyness for an instant, touched by the affinity of their positions, yet not daring to wish each other good luck out loud. Then, as neither said anything more, and they were both feeling more and more uncomfortable, they separated awkwardly and began to wait again, each in his own place, a few steps away from the other.

The shop assistants were still going in. Now Denise could hear them joking when they passed close to her, giving her a sideways glance as they did so. Her embarrassment at thus making an exhibition of herself was growing, and she was on the point of deciding to take half an hour's walk in the neighbourhood, when the sight of a young man who was coming quickly along the Rue Port-Mahon detained her a moment longer. Obviously he must have been the head of a department, for all the shop assistants were greeting him. He was tall, with fair skin and a well-kept beard, and his eyes, which were the colour of old gold, as soft as velvet, fell on her for a moment as he was crossing the square. He was already going into the shop, indifferent, while she remained standing there motionless, deeply disturbed by his glance, filled with a strange emotion in which there was more uneasiness than charm. Fear was gripping her, and no mistake; she started to walk slowly down the Rue Gaillon, then the Rue Saint-Roch, waiting for her courage to come back.

It was not just the head of a department, it was Octave Mouret himself. He had not slept that night for, on leaving a party at a stockbroker's, he had gone to have dinner with a friend and two women he had picked up backstage in a small theatre. His buttoned-up overcoat hid his evening dress and his white tie. He went briskly up to his room, washed his face and changed, and by the time he went to sit down at his desk in his office on the ground floor he was hale and hearty, eyes bright, skin fresh, quite ready for work, just as if he had had ten hours' sleep. The office, vast, furnished in old oak and hung with green rep, had as its only ornament a portrait of that same Madame Hédouin of whom the neighbourhood was still talking. Since her death Octave remembered her affectionately, and was grateful to her memory for the fortune which she had showered on him when she married him. And so, before setting about signing the bills which had been placed on his blotter, he gave the portrait the smile of a happy man. After all, when his escapades as a young widower were over, when he left the bedchambers where he was led astray by the need for pleasure, did he not always return to work in her presence in the end?

Someone knocked and, without waiting, a young man came in; he was tall and spare, with thin lips, a very pointed nose and

very well turned out, with sleek hair in which strands of grey
were already beginning to show. Mouret had looked up; then,
going on signing his papers, he said:

"Did you sleep well, Bourdoncle?"

"Very well, thank you," replied the young man, who was
strutting about, quite at home.

Bourdoncle, the son of a poor farmer from the vicinity of
Limoges, had started work at the Bonheur des Dames at the
same time as Mouret in the old days when the shop had been at
the corner of the Place Gaillon. Very intelligent, very much on
the alert, it had seemed then as if he would easily supersede his
companion, who was less serious-minded, who was dilatory in
many ways, who appeared to be thoughtless and had disquieting
affairs with women – but he did not have the same streak of
genius as the ardent Provençal, nor his daring, nor his triumphant
charm. Indeed, with the instinct of a prudent man, he had bowed
to him submissively, and had done so without a struggle from
the very beginning. When Mouret had advised his assistants to
invest their money in the shop, Bourdoncle had been one of the
first to do so, even entrusting an unexpected legacy from an aunt
to him, and little by little, after working his way up through all
the ranks, salesman, assistant buyer in the silk department, then
buyer there, he had become one of the owner's lieutenants, the
one of whom he was fondest and whom he listened to the most,
one of the six men with money invested in the shop who helped
him to run the Bonheur des Dames, forming something rather
like a council of ministers under an absolute monarch. Each
of them looked after a province. Bourdoncle was in charge of
general supervision.

"What about you?" he resumed. "Did you sleep well?"

When Mouret had replied that he had not been to bed he
shook his head, murmuring:

"Doesn't do your health any good."

"Why not?" said the other gaily. "I'm less tired than you are,
old chap. You're eyes are bunged up with sleep, you're getting
dull from being too good... Go and have some fun, it'll stir up
your ideas!"

They always had the same friendly argument. In the past,
Bourdoncle had beaten his mistresses, because, so he said, they
prevented him from sleeping. Now he professed to hate women,

having no doubt outside assignations which he did not talk about, so little importance did they play in his life, and contenting himself in the shop with exploiting the customers, with the utmost contempt for their frivolity in ruining themselves for ridiculous clothes. Mouret, on the contrary, who was prone to going into raptures over women, was entranced and affectionate in their presence, and was always being carried away by new loves – and his amorous affairs were a kind of advertisement for his sales; it seemed as if he was embracing the whole sex in the same caress, the better to dazzle it and hold it at his mercy.

"I saw Madame Desforges last night," he resumed. "She was enchanting at the ball."

"It wasn't with her that you had supper afterwards?" asked his colleague.

Mouret exclaimed in protest:

"Oh, what an idea! She's very respectable, my dear fellow... No, I had supper with Héloïse, the little girl from the Folies*... She's a silly little goose, but so amusing!"

He took another bundle of bills and went on signing them. Bourdoncle was still strutting about. He went and glanced through the high window panes at the Rue Neuve-Saint-Augustin, then came back saying:

"You know, they'll revenge themselves."

"Who will?" asked Mouret, who was not listening.

"Why, the women, of course."

At that Mouret brightened up; he allowed his fundamental brutality to show through his air of sensual adoration. With a shrug of his shoulders he seemed to declare that he would throw all the women away like empty sacks on the day when they had finished helping him to build up his fortune. Bourdoncle, with his cold manner, was obstinately repeating:

"They'll revenge themselves. There'll be one who'll revenge the others, there's sure to be."

"Don't you be worrying!" shouted Mouret, exaggerating his Provençal accent. "That one's not yet born, my lad. And if she does come, you know..."

He had raised his pen, was brandishing it, and pointed it into space as if he wished to pierce an invisible heart with a knife. His colleague started pacing up and down again, giving in, as always, to the superiority of his boss, whose genius, full of defects though it was, nevertheless disconcerted him. He who was so precise, so logical, devoid of passion, incapable of slipping, could still understand the feminine side of success, Paris yielding in a kiss to the boldest man.

Silence reigned. Nothing could be heard but Mouret's pen. Then, in answer to the short questions which were put to him, Bourdoncle gave him information about the big sale of new winter goods, which was to take place on the following Monday. It was a very important affair, the shop was gambling its fortune on it, for the rumours going round the neighbourhood had a foundation of truth: Mouret had plunged into speculation like a poet, with such ostentation, with such a desire for the colossal, that it seemed as if everything must crumble away beneath him. There existed in him a new sort of business sense, a kind of commercial imagination which had worried Madame Hédouin in the past, and which now still sometimes dismayed those concerned, in spite of some initial success. The director was blamed behind his back for going too fast; he was accused of having dangerously increased the size of the shop without being able to count on a sufficient increase in customers; people were, above all, afraid when they saw him stake all the money in the till on a gamble, loading up the counters with a pile of goods without keeping a penny in reserve. Thus, for the forthcoming sale, after having paid out considerable sums to the builders, the entire capital was tied up; yet once more it was a question of victory or death. And being a man adored by women who felt he could not be played false, in the midst of all this anxiety he kept up his triumphant gaiety, his certainty of earning millions. When Bourdoncle ventured to express fears about the undue development of departments of which the turnover was still unsatisfactory, Mouret gave a splendid, confident laugh, exclaiming as he did so:

"Don't worry, old chap, the shop is too small!"

His companion seemed to be flabbergasted, seized with fear which he no longer tried to hide. The shop too small! A draper's shop with nineteen departments and with four hundred and three employees!

"But there's no doubt," Mouret went on, "we shall be forced to expand before eighteen months are out... I'm thinking of it seriously. Last night Madame Desforges promised to introduce me to somebody at her house tomorrow... Well, we'll talk about it when the idea's ripe."

And, having finished signing the bills, he got up and came and gave his colleague, who was recovering with difficulty, some friendly taps on the shoulder. This terror which the prudent people surrounding him felt amused him. In one of the outbursts of sudden frankness with which he sometimes overwhelmed his intimates, he declared that basically he was more Jewish than all the Jews in the world: he had it from his father, a great big cheery fellow who knew the value of money, whom he resembled both physically and in character, and if he had got his streak of excitable imagination from his mother it was, perhaps, his most obvious asset, for he was aware of the invincible force of his charm in daring everything.

"You know very well that we'll follow you to the end," said Bourdoncle finally.

Then, before going down into the shop for their usual glance round, the two of them settled some more details. They examined a sample of a little counterfoil book which Mouret had just come up with for sales invoices. Having noticed that the larger the commission an assistant received, the faster obsolete goods and junk were snapped up, he had based a new sales method on this observation. He now gave his salesmen an interest in the sale of all goods, he gave them a percentage on the smallest bit of material, the smallest thing which they sold; this was a device which had caused a revolution in drapery by creating a struggle for existence between the assistants, from which it was the employers who benefited. This struggle, moreover, had become in his hands a favourite formula, a principle of organization which he constantly applied. He unleashed passions, brought different forces face to face, let the strong devour the weak and was growing fat as a result of this battle of interests. The sample counterfoil book was approved: at the top, on the counterfoil and on the piece to be torn off, the name of the department and the assistant's number were printed; then, also repeated on each side, there were columns for yardage, a description of goods, prices; the salesman had merely to sign the bill before handing it over to the cashier. In this way, checking was extremely simple, the bills given by the cash desk to the counting house simply had to be compared with the counterfoils kept by the assistants. Each week the latter were thus able to get their percentage and their commission, without any possible mistake.

"We shan't be robbed so much," observed Bourdoncle with satisfaction. "That was an excellent idea of yours."

"And I thought of something else last night," Mouret explained. "Yes, last night at that supper... I'd like to give the counting-house staff a small bonus for every mistake they find in the sales counterfoils, when they check them... You see, we shall be certain then that they won't overlook a single one, they'll be more likely to invent them."

And he began to laugh, while his companion looked at him with an air of admiration. This new way of applying the struggle for existence enchanted him, he had a genius for administrative machinery and dreamt of organizing the shop in such a way as to exploit other people's appetites in order peacefully and completely to satisfy his own. When one wants to make people work their hardest, and even get a bit of honesty out of them, he would often say, one must first bring them up against their own needs.

"Well, let's go down," Mouret resumed. "We must deal with this sale... The silk arrived yesterday, didn't it? And Bouthemont should be at the reception office."

Bourdoncle followed him. The reception department was in the basement, on the Rue Neuve-Saint-Augustin side. There, level with the pavement, was a glazed porch where the lorries discharged the goods. These were weighed, then tipped down a rapid chute, the oak and ironwork of which were shining, polished by the friction of bales and cases. Everything which arrived went in through this yawning trapdoor; things were being swallowed up all the time, a cascade of materials was falling with the roar of a river. During big sales, above all, the chute would discharge an endless flow into the basement – silks from Lyons, woollens from England, linens from Flanders, calicoes from Alsace, prints from Rouen – and sometimes the lorries had to queue up; as they flowed down, the packets made a dull sound at the bottom of the hole, like a stone thrown into deep water.

As he was passing, Mouret stopped for a moment in front of the chute. It was working, queues of packing cases were going down it on their own, the men whose hands were pushing them from above invisible, and they seemed to be rushing along by themselves, streaming like rain from some spring higher up. Then some bales appeared, turning round and round like rolled pebbles. Mouret was watching, without saying a word. But this deluge of goods falling into this shop, this flood releasing thousands of francs in a minute, lit a brief light in his limpid eyes. Never before had he been so clearly aware of the battle joined. It was a question of launching this deluge of goods all over Paris. He did not say a word, but went on with his tour of inspection.

In the grey daylight which was coming through the broad ventilators a gang of men was receiving consignments, while others were unnailing packing cases and opening bales in the presence of section managers. The depths of this cellar, of this basement where cast-iron pillars held up the counter-arches and where the bare walls were cemented, were filled with the bustle of a shipyard.

"You've got it all, Bouthemont?" asked Mouret, going up to a young man with broad shoulders who was in the process of checking the contents of a packing case.

"Yes, it should all be there," the latter answered. "But it will take me the whole of the morning to count it."

The section manager ran his eye over an invoice; he was standing before a large counter, on which one of his salesmen was depositing the lengths of silk which he was taking out of the packing case one by one. Behind them, other counters were lined up, also littered with goods which a whole tribe of assistants was examining. There was a general unpacking, a seeming disorder of materials which were being examined, turned over, ticketed, in the midst of a buzz of voices.

Bouthemont, who was becoming famous there, had the round face of a cheerful good sort, with an inky black beard and fine brown eyes. A native of Montpellier, fond of revelling and uproarious, he was a mediocre salesman – but as a buyer he had no equal. He had been sent to Paris by his father, who had a draper's shop in Montpellier, and when the old man thought that his lad had learnt enough to succeed him in the business, he had absolutely refused to go back home; from then on a rivalry had grown up between father and son, the former entirely absorbed in his small provincial trade, indignant at seeing a mere assistant earning three times as much as he did himself, and the latter joking about the old man's routines, making a lot of noise about his earnings and turning the shop topsy-turvy every time he went there. Like the other section managers he earned, apart from his three-thousand-francs fixed salary, a percentage on sales. The people of Montpellier, surprised and impressed, gave it out that the Bouthemont boy had, in the preceding year, pocketed nearly fifteen thousand francs – and this was only a beginning; people predicted to his exasperated father that this figure would increase even more.

Meanwhile, Bourdoncle had picked up one of the lengths of silk, and was examining its texture with the attentive air of a man who knows his business. It was a piece of faille with a blue-and-silver selvedge, the famous Paris-Bonheur with which Mouret was counting on striking a decisive blow.

"It really is good," murmured his colleague.

"And above all, it produces an effect of being better than it is," said Bouthemont. "No one but Dumonteil can make it for us… On my last trip, when I got annoyed with Gaujean, he said he was quite willing to put a hundred looms on making this pattern, but he insisted on twenty-five centimes more per yard."

Almost every month Bouthemont would go to visit the factories, spending days in Lyons, staying in the best hotels and with instructions that money was no object when negotiating with manufacturers. Moreover, he enjoyed absolute freedom, he bought as he thought fit, providing that each year he increased the turnover of his department by a ratio agreed in advance, and it was, in fact, on this increase that he received his percentage of interest. In short, his position at the Bonheur des Dames, like that of all his colleagues the section managers, was that of a specialized merchant in a group of different trades, a kind of vast city of commerce.

"Well, it's decided then," he went on. "We'll price it at five francs sixty… You know that that's scarcely the purchase price."

"Yes, yes, five francs sixty," said Mouret briskly, "and if I was on my own, I'd sell it at a loss."

The section manager laughed heartily.

"Oh! As far as I'm concerned I'd be delighted. That would triple sales, and as my only interest is to get big takings…"

But Bourdoncle remained serious and tight-lipped. He received his percentage on the total profits, and it was not in his interest to bring prices down. The supervision which he carried out consisted precisely in watching the price tags to see that Bouthemont did not yield only to the desire to increase the sales figures and sell at too small a profit. Besides, he was once more seized by his old misgivings when faced with publicity schemes which he did not understand. He ventured to show his distaste, by saying:

"If we sell at five francs sixty it's just as if we were selling it at a loss, as our expenses must be deducted, and they're considerable... Anywhere else they'd sell it at seven francs."

At that Mouret lost his temper. He banged the flat of his hand on the silk and shouted irritably:

"Yes, I know, and that's just why I want to give it away to our customers... Really, my good chap, you'll never understand women. Can't you see that they'll fall on this silk!"

"Doubtless," interrupted his associate, persisting, "and the more they fall on it, the more we shall lose."

"We'll lose a few centimes on these goods, I'll grant you. And after? It won't be such a calamity if we attract all the women here and hold them at our mercy, fascinated, their heads turned at the sight of our piles of goods, emptying their purses without counting! It's everything, old fellow, to excite their interest, and for that one must have an article that delights, that's epoch-making. After that you can sell the other goods just as dearly as they do anywhere else, women will think they pay less for them at your shop. For example, our Cuir-d'Or, that taffeta at seven francs fifty, which is on sale everywhere at that price, will also seem to be an extraordinary bargain, and be sufficient to make good the losses of the Paris-Bonheur. You'll see, you'll see!"

He was waxing eloquent.

"Don't you understand! I want the Paris-Bonheur to revolutionize the market in a week. It's our lucky stroke, and it's what's going to save us and float us. People won't talk about anything else, the blue-and-silver selvedge will be known from one end of France to the other... And you'll hear the groan of fury from our competitors. The small traders will lose some more of their feathers over it. They're done for, all those old clothes dealers dying of rheumatism in their cellars!"

The assistants who were checking the consignment stood round their employer, listening and smiling. He liked talking and being in the right. Once more, Bourdoncle gave in. In the meantime the packing case had been emptied, two men were unnailing another one.

Then Bouthemont said: "But the manufacturers aren't a bit pleased! They're furious with you at Lyons, they claim that your cheap sales are ruining them. You know that Gaujean has definitely declared war against me. Yes, he's sworn to give the small shops long credit rather than accept my prices."

Mouret shrugged his shoulders.

"If Gaujean isn't sensible," he replied, "Gaujean will be left high and dry... What are they complaining of? We pay them immediately, we take everything they manufacture, the least they can do is to work for less... And anyway, the public benefits, that's enough."

The assistant was emptying the second packing case, while Bouthemont had gone back to checking the pieces of material against the invoice. Next, another assistant, at the end of the counter, was marking the price on them and, the checking finished, the invoice signed by the section manager had to be sent up to the central counting house. For an instant longer Mouret watched this work, all the activity surrounding the unpacking of the goods, which were piling up and threatening to swamp the basement; then, without saying another word, he went away with the air of a captain satisfied with his troops, followed by Bourdoncle.

Slowly the two of them went through the basement. At intervals ventilators were shedding a pale light, and in the depths of dark corners, along the narrow corridors, gas jets were continually burning. Leading off these corridors were the stockrooms, vaults shut off with a hoarding, where the different departments stowed away their surplus goods. As he passed, the director gave a glance at the heating installation, which was to be lit on Monday for the first time, and at the small firemen's post which was guarding a giant gas meter enclosed in an iron cage. The kitchen and the dining rooms, old cellars transformed into small rooms, were on the left, towards the corner of Place Gaillon. Finally, at the other end of the basement, he came to the dispatch department. Parcels which customers did not carry away themselves were sent down there, sorted on tables, put into pigeonholes which represented the different districts of Paris; then they were sent up a large staircase which came out just opposite the Vieil Elbeuf and were put into vehicles which were parked near the pavement. With the usual mechanical efficiency of the Bonheur des Dames, this staircase in the Rue de la Michodière disgorged without respite the goods which had been swallowed up by the chute in Rue Neuve-Saint-Augustin, after they had passed, upstairs, through the gearwheels of the various departments.

"Campion," said Mouret to the man in charge of the dispatch department, an ex-sergeant with a thin face, "why were six pairs of sheets which a lady bought yesterday at two o'clock not delivered by the evening?"

"Where does the lady live?" the employee asked.

"In the Rue de Rivoli, at the corner of the Rue d'Alger, Madame Desforges."

At that early hour the sorting tables were bare, the pigeonholes contained nothing but a few parcels left over from the day before. While Campion, after having consulted a register, rummaged among these parcels, Bourdoncle was looking at Mouret, thinking that the fiendish man knew everything, attended to everything, even while sitting at the tables of all-night restaurants and in his mistresses' bedrooms. Finally, the head of the dispatch department discovered the mistake: the cash desk had given a wrong number, and the parcel had been returned.

"Which cash desk dealt with it?" asked Mouret. "What? Number 10, you say…"

And, turning round once more to his associate, he said:

"Cash desk 10, that's Albert, isn't it?… We'll go and have a word with him."

But, before going round the shop, he wanted to go upstairs to the forwarding department, which occupied several rooms on the second floor. It was there that all the orders from the provinces and from abroad were received, and every morning he went there to look at the correspondence. For two years this correspondence had been growing daily. The department, which had at first kept about ten employees busy, now already needed more than thirty. Some were opening the letters, others were reading them, sitting at each side of the same table; still others were sorting the letters, giving each one a serial number which was repeated on a pigeonhole; then, when the letters had been distributed to the different departments, as the departments sent up the goods, so they were put into these pigeonholes according to the serial number. It remained only to check the goods and pack them up in a neighbouring room, where a team of workmen nailed and tied things up from morning till night.

Mouret asked his usual question.

"How many letters this morning, Levasseur?"

"Five hundred and thirty-four, sir," answered the man in charge. "After Monday's sales announcement, I was afraid we wouldn't have enough staff. We found it very difficult to manage yesterday."

Bourdoncle was nodding his head with satisfaction. He had not been expecting five hundred and thirty-four letters on a Tuesday. Round the table employees were slitting letters open and reading, with a continuous sound of crumpled paper, while in front of the pigeonholes the coming and going of goods was beginning. This was one of the most complicated and extensive departments of the shop: those in it lived in a perpetual fever, for the orders of the morning had, according to regulations, all to be dispatched by the evening.

"You'll be given the staff you need, Levasseur," Mouret answered finally; he had seen with a glance what a good state the department was in. "As you know, when there's work we don't refuse the staff."

Upstairs, in the attics, were the rooms where the salesgirls slept. But he went downstairs again, and into the central counting house which was situated near his office. It was a room shut off by a glass partition with a brass pay desk in it, and in which an enormous safe fixed to the wall was visible. There, two cashiers co-ordinated the takings which each evening Lhomme, the chief sales cashier, brought up to them, and they then dealt with expenses, paid manufacturers, the staff, all the little world living in the shop. The counting house communicated with another small room, lined with green files, where ten employees checked the invoices. Next came yet another office, the debit office: there six young men, bent over black desks, with piles of registers behind them, drew up accounts of the salesmen's percentages by collating the retail bills. This section, which was quite new, was running badly.

Mouret and Bourdoncle had passed through the counting house and the checking office. When they went into the other office the young men who were laughing, their noses in the air, had a shock of surprise. Then Mouret, without reprimanding them, explained the system of the small bonus he had thought of paying them for every error they discovered in the sales bills, and when he had left the room the employees, no longer laughing, and looking as if they had been whipped, set to work enthusiastically, hunting for mistakes.

On the ground floor, in the shop, Mouret went straight to No. 10 cash desk, where Albert Lhomme was polishing his nails while waiting for customers. People generally spoke of "the Lhomme dynasty" since Madame Aurélie, the buyer in the ready-made department, after having pushed her husband into the job of chief cashier, had succeeded in obtaining a retail cash desk for her son, a large lad, pale and depraved, who could never stay anywhere, and who caused her the most acute anxiety. But faced with the young man, Mouret stood aside: he felt it repugnant to impair his charm by doing police work; both from preference and as part of his tactics he kept to his role of benevolent god. Lightly, with his elbow, he touched Bourdoncle, the key man, to whom he usually entrusted executions.

"Monsieur Albert," said the latter severely, "you've again taken down an address wrong, the parcel has come back... It's intolerable."

The cashier felt obliged to defend himself, and called the porter who had done up the parcel as a witness. This porter, Joseph by name, also belonged to the Lhomme dynasty as he was Albert's foster-brother, and he owed his job to Madame Aurélie's influence. As the young man was trying to get him to say it was the customer who had made the mistake, he was stuttering, twisting the little goatee which made his scarred face seem longer, torn between his conscience as an old soldier and his gratitude to his protectors.

"Leave Joseph alone, for goodness's sake," Bourdoncle shouted finally. "And please, don't say any more... Oh! You're lucky that we value your mother's good work!"

But, at that moment, Lhomme hastened towards them. From his own cash desk near the door he could see his son's, which was in the glove department. Already white-haired, grown heavy from his sedentary life, he had a soft, unobtrusive face which seemed to be worn away by the reflection of the money which he was ceaselessly counting. The fact that he had had an arm amputated did not hinder him a whit in his task, and people even went out of curiosity to see him checking the takings, so swiftly did the notes and coins slide through his left hand, the only one which remained to him. The son of a tax collector in Chablis, he had turned up in Paris as bookkeeper to a wine merchant in the Port-aux-Vins. Then he had married the daughter of a small Alsatian tailor, the caretaker of the house where he was living in the Rue Cuvier, and from that day on he had been under the thumb of his wife, whose commercial abilities filled him with respect. She earned more than twelve thousand francs in the ready-made department, whereas he had a fixed salary of only five thousand francs. And his respect for a wife who could bring such sums into the family extended to his son as well, for he came from her.

"What's the matter?" he murmured. "Albert has made a mistake?"

At that, Mouret reappeared on the scene to play the part of the good prince, as was his custom. When Bourdoncle had made himself feared, Mouret would take care of his own popularity.

"A stupid mistake," he murmured. "My dear Lhomme, your Albert is a scatterbrain who really should take example from you."

Then, changing the conversation and making himself even more agreeable, he said:

"What about the concert the other day?... Did you have a good seat?"

A blush spread over the old cashier's pale cheeks. Music was his only vice, a secret vice which he indulged in alone, haunting the theatres, concerts, auditions; in spite of his amputated arm he played the horn, thanks to an ingenious system of clamps, and since Madame Lhomme hated noise, in the evening he would wrap his instrument up in a cloth, and was nevertheless roused to ecstasies by the strangely muffled sounds which he extracted from it. In the inevitable confusion of his home he had made an oasis of music for himself. Apart from his admiration for his wife, he was concerned with nothing but this, and the money in the cash desk.

"A very good seat," he answered, his eyes shining. "It was really too kind of you, Monsieur."

Mouret, who took a personal delight in satisfying people's passions, sometimes gave Lhomme tickets which ladies who were patrons of the arts had pressed on him. And he finally won him over completely by saying:

"Ah! Beethoven, ah! Mozart... What music!"

Without waiting for a reply he moved off and caught up with Bourdoncle, who was already going round the departments. In the central hall, an interior courtyard which had been covered with a glass roof, were the silks. First they went along the gallery on the Rue Neuve-Saint-Augustin side, which was filled from one end to the other with household linen. Nothing abnormal struck them, they passed through slowly amid respectful assistants. Then they turned into the printed-cotton-goods and hosiery section, where the same order reigned. But, in the woollen department, which ran the length of the gallery coming back at right angles to the Rue de la Michodière, Bourdoncle, on catching sight of a young man sitting on a counter and looking worn out after a sleepless night, once more assumed his role of chief executioner; the young man, Liénard by name, the son of a rich linen-draper in Angers, hung his head while receiving the reprimand, his only fear being, in the life of indolence, thoughtlessness and pleasure which he led, that he might be called back to the provinces by his father. From then on admonishments fell thick as hail, the Rue de la Michodière gallery bearing the brunt of the storm: in the drapery department one of those salesmen who received board and lodging but no salary, one of those who were starting their careers and who slept in their departments, had come in after eleven o'clock; in the haberdashery the assistant buyer had just been caught in the depths of the basement, finishing a cigarette. And in the glove department, above all, the tempest broke over the head of one of the few Parisians in the shop, who was known as Handsome Mignot; he was the illegitimate son of a lady who taught the harp but had come down in the world; his crime was that he had made a scene in the canteen by complaining about the food. He tried to explain that there were three meal services, one at half-past nine, one at half-past ten and one at half-past eleven, and that as he went to the third service, he always had the dregs of the sauce and helpings of leftover bits.

"What's this? The food is not good?" asked Mouret innocently, opening his mouth at last.

He only gave one franc fifty per head per day to the chef, a real terror from Auvergne, who nevertheless still found it possible to line his own pockets, and the food really was abominable. But Bourdoncle shrugged his shoulders: a chef who had to serve four hundred lunches and four hundred dinners, even in three batches, could scarcely linger over the refinements of his art.

"Never mind," the good-natured director went on, "I want all our employees to have healthy food and plenty of it... I shall speak to the chef about it."

Mignot's complaint was shelved. Then, back at their point of departure, standing near the door among the umbrellas and ties, Mouret and Bourdoncle received a report from one of the four shopwalkers who supervised the shop. Old Jouve, a retired captain who had been decorated at Constantine, still a handsome man with a large sensual nose and majestically bald, told them of a salesman who, at a simple remonstrance from him, had called him "an old dodderer" – and the salesman was immediately dismissed.

Meanwhile, the shop was still empty of customers. Only local housewives were going through the deserted galleries. At the door, the inspector who clocked in the staff had just closed his book and was making a separate list of those who were late. This was the moment when the salesmen took up their positions in their departments, which porters had been sweeping and dusting since five o'clock. Each one put his hat and overcoat away, stifling a yawn as he did so, still looking pale with sleep. Some were exchanging a word, looking about them, seemingly stretching themselves prior to another day's work; others, without hurrying, were drawing back the green baize with which, on the evening before, they had covered the goods which they had previously folded up; and the symmetrically arranged piles of material were appearing, the whole shop was clean and tidy, with tranquil brilliance in the gay early-morning light, waiting for the scrimmage of selling once more to choke and somehow to make it smaller beneath an avalanche of linen, cloth, silk and lace.

In the sharp light of the central hall, at the silk counter, two young men were talking in a low voice. One of them, small and attractive, sturdy-looking and with a pink complexion, was trying to blend different-coloured silks for an indoor display. His name was Hutin, and he was the son of a café proprietor in Yvetot; in eighteen months he had succeeded in becoming one of the principal salesmen, and he had done so by means of a pliability of character, a continuous servile flattery, which hid beneath it a ravenous appetite, a desire to eat up everything, devour the world without even being hungry, just for sheer pleasure.

"Listen, Favier, I'd have hit him if I'd been you, honestly!" he was saying to the other, a big morose-looking lad, dried-up and sallow, who had been born in Besançon of a family of dyers and who, though devoid of charm, hid a disquieting strength of will beneath a reserved manner.

"It doesn't get you anywhere, hitting people," he murmured phlegmatically. "It's better to wait."

They were both talking about Robineau, who was in charge of the assistants while the head of the department was in the basement. Hutin was secretly undermining the assistant buyer, whose job he wished to have. Already, in order to hurt his feelings and make him leave, when the job of first salesman which Robineau had been promised had fallen vacant, he had devised the plan of bringing Bouthemont in from outside. However, Robineau was holding his own, and there was now an unending battle between them. Hutin dreamt of setting the whole department against him, of getting rid of him by dint of ill will and small irritations. What is more, he was carrying out his operations with his pleasant manner, mainly inciting Favier to rebellion, for he was the salesman next to him in seniority, and seemed content to let himself be led, although he would suddenly show reserve through which a whole, silently waged private campaign was discernible.

"Sh! Seventeen!" he said sharply to his colleague, in order to warn him with this time-honoured exclamation of the approach of Mouret and Bourdoncle.

These two were indeed going through the hall, continuing their inspection. They stopped, and asked Robineau for some information about a stock of velvet piled up in boxes which were cluttering up a table. And, when the latter replied that there was no room, Mouret exclaimed with a smile:

"I told you so, Bourdoncle, the shop is too small! One day we shall have to pull down the walls as far as the Rue de Choiseul! You'll see what a crush there'll be next Monday!"

While he was on the subject, he again questioned Robineau and gave him orders concerning the sale for which all the departments were preparing. But, for several minutes, while continuing to talk he had been watching Hutin, who was lingering behind in order to put some blue silks next to grey and yellow silks, and then standing back to see how the colours blended. Suddenly Mouret intervened.

"But why do you try to make it easy on the eye?" he said. "Don't be afraid, blind them... Here! Some red! Some green! Some yellow!"

He had taken up the pieces of material, was scattering them, crushing them, making dazzling combinations with them. Everyone agreed that the director was the best window-dresser in Paris, a revolutionary window-dresser, as a matter of fact, who had founded the school of the brutal and gigantic in the art of display. He wanted avalanches, seemingly fallen at random from disembowelled shelves, and he wanted them blazing with the most flamboyant colours, contrasting brightly with one another. He used to say that on leaving the shop the customer's eyes should ache. Hutin, who, on the contrary, belonged to the classic school of symmetry and melodious effect achieved by shading, watched him lighting this conflagration of materials in the middle of a table without indulging in the slightest criticism, but with his lips pursed in the wry expression of an artist whose convictions were hurt by such an orgy.

"There!" exclaimed Mouret, when he had finished. "And leave it there... You tell me if it catches any women on Monday!"

Just as he was rejoining Bourdoncle and Robineau, a woman was coming in their direction; she remained for a few seconds rooted to the spot, breathless at the sight of the display. It was Denise. She had been hesitating for almost an hour out in the street, the victim of a terrible attack of shyness, and had at last just made up her mind to come in. But she was losing her head to such an extent that she could not understand even the simplest explanations; the assistants of whom she stammeringly enquired for Madame Aurélie pointed out the mezzanine staircase to her in vain; she would thank them, then turn left if she had been told to turn right. Thus for ten minutes she had been scouring the ground floor, going from department to department, surrounded by the ill-natured curiosity and sullen indifference of the salesmen. She felt a desire to run away and, at the same time, a need to admire everything which was holding her back.

She was so lost and small inside the monster, inside the machine, and although it was still idle, she was terrified that she would be caught in its motion which was already beginning to make the walls quake. And the thought of the shop at the Vieil Elbeuf, dark and narrow, made this vast shop appear even bigger to her, made her see it gilded with light like a town, with its monuments, its squares, its streets, in which it seemed as if she would never be able to find her way.

She had not so far dared to venture into the silk hall, of which the high glazed ceiling, sumptuous counters and churchlike atmosphere alarmed her. Then, when she had at last gone in there in order to escape from the laughter of the salesmen in the household-linen department, she had suddenly stumbled straight into Mouret's display, and in spite of being scared, the woman in her was aroused by it and, her cheeks suddenly flushed, she was oblivious of herself as she watched the blazing conflagration of silks.

"Why!" said Hutin crudely in Favier's ear, "It's the fool from the Place Gaillon."

Mouret, while pretending to listen to Bourdoncle and Robineau, was in his heart of hearts flattered by this poor girl's surprise, just as a duchess may be stirred by the brutal look of desire of a passing carter. But Denise had raised her eyes, and she was even more confused when she recognized the young man she took to be the head of a department. She fancied that he was looking at her sternly. Then, no longer knowing how to get away, completely distraught, she once again approached the first assistant she saw, Favier, who was close to her.

"Madame Aurélie, please?"

Favier, unobliging, was content to reply curtly:

"On the mezzanine floor."

And Denise, in a hurry to get away from all those men staring at her, thanked him and was once more turning back to the staircase, when Hutin gave way naturally to his gallant instincts. He had called her a tart, but it was with his kindly air of a handsome salesman that he stopped her.

"No, this way, Mademoiselle... If you would be so good as to..."

He even took a few steps in front of her, conducted her to the foot of the stairs which were in the left-hand corner of the hall.

There he bowed slightly, and smiled at her with the smile he gave to all women.

"Upstairs, turn left... The ready-made department is opposite."

This tender politeness moved Denise deeply. It was as if some brotherly assistance was being given her. She had raised her eyes, she was gazing at Hutin, and everything about him touched her, his handsome face, his smiling glance which allayed her fear, his voice which seemed to her of a consoling sweetness. Her heart swelled with gratitude, she showed her friendship in the few disconnected words which her emotion enabled her to stammer out.

"You're too kind... Please don't trouble... Thank you so much, Monsieur..."

Hutin was already rejoining Favier, to whom he was saying under his breath, in a crude tone:

"She's pretty skinny, isn't she!"

Upstairs, the girl found the ready-made department straight away. It was a vast room surrounded by high cupboards of carved oak, and with plate-glass windows facing the Rue de la Michodière. Five or six women, in silk dresses and very stylish-looking with their back hair curled and their crinolines sweeping behind them, were bustling about there, chatting as they did so. One of them, tall and thin, with too long a head, looking like a runaway horse, was leaning up against a cupboard, as if she was already tired out.

"Madame Aurélie?" Denise repeated.

The saleswoman looked at her, with an air of disdain for her poor get-up, without replying; then, speaking to one of her companions, a short girl with an unhealthy, pasty complexion, she asked in an artless, wearied manner:

"Mademoiselle Vadon, do you know where the buyer is?"

The other girl, who was in the process of arranging long cloaks in order of size, did not even take the trouble to look up.

"No, Mademoiselle Prunaire, I don't know," she said in an artificial way.

A silence ensued. Denise remained motionless, and no one took any notice of her. However, after having waited a moment she plucked up her courage sufficiently to ask a fresh question.

"Do you think that Madame Aurélie will be back soon?"

Then the assistant buyer of the department, a thin, ugly woman whom she had not noticed, a widow with a prominent chin and coarse hair, called to her from a cupboard where she was checking price tags:

"You must wait, if you want to talk to Madame Aurélie in person."

And, questioning another salesgirl, she added:

"Isn't she in the reception office?"

"No, Madame Frédéric, I don't think so," the girl replied. "She didn't say anything, she can't be far away."

Thus informed, Denise remained standing. There were, indeed, a few chairs for customers but, as no one told her to sit down, she did not dare take one in spite of her confusion, which was making her legs feel as if they were breaking. It was clear that these young ladies had sensed her to be a salesgirl coming to apply for a job, and they were staring at her out of the corners of their eyes, stripping her naked, without benevolence, with the veiled hostility of people seated at table who do not like moving up to make room for those outside who are hungry. Her embarrassment grew; taking small steps she crossed the room and went to look out into the street in order not to lose face. Just opposite her the Vieil Elbeuf with its mildewed frontage and its dead shop windows, seen thus from the luxury and from the life in which she now found herself, seemed to her so ugly, so wretched, that at last her heart was wrung with something akin to remorse.

"I say," whispered tall Mademoiselle Prunaire to short Mademoiselle Vadon, "have you seen her boots?"

"And what about her dress!" the other was murmuring.

Her eyes were still on the street, Denise felt herself being devoured. But she was without anger, she had not thought either of them beautiful, neither the tall one with her bun of red hair hanging down her horselike neck, nor the short one with a sour-milk complexion which made her flat and seemingly boneless face look flabby. Clara Prunaire, daughter of a clog-maker in the Vivet forest, had been seduced by the menservants at the Château de Mareuil, where the Countess used to employ her to do the mending; she had subsequently come from a shop at Langres to Paris, where she was now revenging herself on other men for the kicks with which in the past old man Prunaire had bruised her

51

back. Marguerite Vadon had been born in Grenoble, where her family owned a cloth business; she had had to be sent off to the Bonheur des Dames in order to hush up a slip she had made, a child conceived by accident; she was now behaving herself very well, and was eventually to return home to run her parents' shop and marry a cousin who was waiting for her.

"Anyway," Clara resumed in a low voice, "that's someone who won't cut much ice here!"

But they stopped talking, for a woman of about forty-five was coming in. It was Madame Aurélie, very stout and laced in to her black silk dress of which the bodice, stretched over the massive curves of her shoulders and bosom, shone like a breastplate. Below her black hair parted in the middle she had large, motionless eyes, a stern mouth, broad, rather pendulous cheeks; from the augustness of her position as chief buyer her face was acquiring the puffiness of the bloated mask of some Caesar.

"Mademoiselle Vadon," she said in an irritated voice, "why didn't you put the model of the close-fitting coat back in the workroom yesterday?"

"There was an alteration to be made, Madame," the saleswoman replied, "and it was Madame Frédéric who kept it back."

At that the assistant buyer took the model from a cupboard, and the altercation continued. When Madame Aurélie thought she had to defend her authority, everything bowed before her. Extremely vain – to the point of not wishing to be called by her name of Lhomme, which annoyed her, and of not owning up to the fact that her father, whom she spoke of as a tailor in a shop, was really just a doorkeeper – she was good-natured only to those girls who were pliable and affectionate, lost in admiration for her. In the past, in the dressmaking business which she had tried to establish herself, she had become embittered, ceaselessly dogged by bad luck, exasperated by feeling that she was made for affluence and yet achieved nothing but failure – and nowadays still, even after her success at the Bonheur des Dames where she was earning twelve thousand francs a year, it seemed as if she still had a grudge against the world, and she was hard on beginners just as, in the beginning, life had been hard on her.

"That's enough chat!" she finally said tartly. "You've no more sense than the others, Madame Frédéric... Have the alteration done straight away!"

During this discussion Denise had stopped looking at the street. She thought this woman was probably Madame Aurélie but, alarmed by her voice raised in anger, she remained standing there, still waiting. The saleswomen, delighted at having set the buyer and assistant buyer of the department at loggerheads, had gone back to their tasks with an air of complete indifference. Several minutes passed, no one had the kindness to extricate the girl from her embarrassment. In the end, it was Madame Aurélie herself who noticed her and who, surprised at seeing her standing there motionless, asked her what she wanted.

"Madame Aurélie, please?"

"I am Madame Aurélie."

Denise's mouth was dry, her hands were cold, she was seized again with one of her old childhood fears, when she had been terrified she might be whipped. She stammered out her request, then had to begin it afresh in order to make it intelligible. Madame Aurélie looked at her with her large, motionless eyes, and not a single fold of her imperial mask deigned to unbend.

"How old are you, then?"

"I'm twenty, Madame."

"What do you mean, twenty? You don't look as if you're more than sixteen!"

Once more, the saleswomen were looking up. Denise hastened to add:

"Oh, I'm very strong!"

Madame Aurélie shrugged her broad shoulders. Then she declared:

"Oh well, I don't mind putting down your name. We put down the names of those who apply... Mademoiselle Prunaire, give me the register."

It was not found at once; it seemed that Jouve, one of the shopwalkers, had it. Just as Clara, the tall girl, was going to fetch it, Mouret arrived, still followed by Bourdoncle. They were completing their tour of the mezzanine floor, they had been through the laces, the shawls, the furs, the furniture, the underwear, and were finishing up with the ready-made department. Madame Aurélie moved to one side, spoke to them for a moment about an order for coats which she hoped to give one of the big Parisian contractors; usually she bought directly, and on her own responsibility, but for important purchases she preferred to consult the management. Next, Bourdoncle told her about her son Albert's latest careless lapse, at which she appeared to be in despair – that child would be the death of her; it could at least be said of his father, even if he wasn't strong, that he did behave well. The whole Lhomme dynasty, of which she was the undisputed head, sometimes gave her a great deal of trouble.

Meanwhile Mouret, surprised at seeing Denise again, bent down to ask Madame Aurélie what the girl was doing there; when the buyer replied that she had come to apply for a job as a saleswoman, Bourdoncle, with his contempt for women, was flabbergasted at such pretension.

"Nonsense!" he murmured. "It's a joke! She's too ugly."

"It must be admitted there's nothing very beautiful about her," said Mouret, not daring to defend her, although he still felt touched by her ecstasy downstairs when she had been looking at the display.

The register was brought, and Madame Aurélie came back towards Denise. The latter certainly did not make a good impression. She was very clean, in her skimpy black woollen dress; they did not dwell on her poor get-up, as uniform, the regulation silk dress, was provided, but she seemed to be very starved-looking, and her face was sad. Without insisting on the girls being beautiful, for selling they wanted them to be attractive, and beneath the stares of all those ladies and gentlemen who were studying her, weighing her like a mare being haggled over by peasants at a fair, Denise finally lost the remnants of her self-possession.

"Your name?" asked the buyer, pen in hand, ready to write on the end of a counter.

"Denise Baudu, Madame."

"Your age?"

"Twenty and four months."

And she repeated, venturing to look up at Mouret as she did so, at the man she took to be the head of a department whom she kept on meeting, and whose presence perturbed her.

"I don't look it, but I'm very tough."

People smiled. Bourdoncle was studying his nails with impatience. Her words, what is more, fell in the middle of a discouraging silence.

"In what shop have you worked in Paris?" the buyer resumed.

"But Madame, I've just come from Valognes."

This was a fresh disaster. Usually, the Bonheur des Dames stipulated that its saleswomen should have worked for a year in one of the small shops in Paris. Hearing that, Denise was in despair, and if it had not been for the children she would have left straight away in order to bring the useless interrogation to an end.

"Where did you work at Valognes?"

"At Cornaille's."

Mouret let slip a remark: "I know it, it's a good firm."

Usually he never intervened in the hiring of personnel, as the heads of departments were responsible for their own staff. But, with his sensitive flair for women, he felt a hidden charm in this girl, a force of grace and tenderness of which she herself was unaware. The good reputation of the shop in which an applicant had started work carried much weight; often it was the deciding factor in engaging someone. Madame Aurélie went on in a gentler voice:

"And why did you leave Cornaille's?"

"For family reasons," Denise replied, blushing. "We have lost our parents, I had to follow my brothers... In any case, here's a testimonial."

It was excellent. She was beginning to have hopes again, when a final question caused her embarrassment.

"Have you any other references in Paris? Where are you living?"

"At my uncle's," she murmured hesitating to name him, fearing that they would never want the niece of a competitor. "At my Uncle Baudu's, over there, opposite."

At that Mouret intervened a second time.

"What's that? You're Baudu's niece! Did Baudu send you here?"

"Oh no, sir!"

And then she could not help laughing, so peculiar did the idea seem to her. She was transfigured. She grew pink, and the smile on her rather large mouth seemed to light up her whole face. Her grey eyes took on a tender light, adorable dimples appeared in her cheeks, even her fair hair seemed to be soaring with the admirable and courageous gaiety of her whole being.

"Why, she's pretty!" said Mouret in a low voice to Bourdoncle.

With a gesture of boredom his associate refused to concur. Clara had pursed her lips, while Marguerite was turning her back. Only Madame Aurélie nodded her head in approval at Mouret when he continued:

"Your uncle should have brought you himself, his recommendation would have been sufficient. They say he bears us a grudge. We are more broad-minded, and if he can't employ his niece in his own shop, well, we'll show him that his niece had only to knock on our door to be taken in. Tell him that I'm still very fond of him, it's not me he should blame, but the new business conditions. And tell him that he'll succeed in ruining himself if he persists in all those ridiculous, old-fashioned ideas."

Denise became quite pale again. It was Mouret. No one had pronounced his name, but he himself had shown who he was, and she guessed it now, she understood why this young man had caused her such emotion in the street, in the silk department and again now. This emotion, in which she could divine nothing, was weighing more and more heavily on her heart, like a burden that was too heavy. All the stories told her by her uncle came back in her memory, enlarging Mouret, surrounding him with a legend, establishing him as the master of the terrible machine which since the morning had been holding her in the iron teeth of its gearwheels. And, behind his handsome head with his well-kept beard, with his eyes the colour of tarnished gold, she saw the dead woman, that Madame Hédouin with whose blood the stones of the shop had been sealed. Then the cold feeling of the day before seized her once more, and she believed she was simply frightened of him.

Meanwhile, Madame Aurélie was closing the register. Only one saleswoman was needed, and ten applications had already been entered. But her desire to please her employer was too great for her to hesitate. The application would still go through the usual channels, Jouve, the shopwalker, would make enquiries and draw up a report, and the buyer would take a decision.

"Very well, Mademoiselle," she said majestically, in order to retain her authority. "We will write to you."

Embarrassment held Denise rooted there for a moment longer. Surrounded by all those people, she did not know how to get away. Finally, she thanked Madame Aurélie, and when she had to pass in front of Mouret and Bourdoncle she said goodbye to them. They did not even return her greeting for, in any case, they were no longer thinking about her, but were examining the model coat with Madame Frédéric. Clara looked at Marguerite and made a gesture of annoyance, as if predicting that the new salesgirl would not have a very good time in the department. No doubt Denise felt this indifference and malice behind her back, for she went down the staircase with the same uneasiness with which she had ascended it, a prey to strange qualms, wondering whether she should be in despair or delighted at having come. Could she count on the job? In her anxiety, which had prevented her from understanding clearly, she was once more beginning to have her doubts about it. Of all her sensations, two were persisting and gradually effacing the others: the impression made on her by Mouret, so deep as to make her afraid, and then Hutin's kindness, the only pleasure she had had that morning, a memory of charming gentleness which was filling her with gratitude. When she went through the shop in order to go out she looked for the young man, happy at the thought of thanking him once more with a look, and when she did not see him, she felt sad.

"Well Mademoiselle, have you been successful?" a voice tinged with emotion asked her when she finally reached the street.

She turned round and recognized the big, pale, ungainly lad who had spoken to her in the morning. He too was coming out of the Bonheur des Dames, and he appeared to be even more scared than she was, completely bewildered by the interrogation he had just been through.

"Goodness! I've no idea, Monsieur," she replied.

"You're in the same boat as me, then. What a way they've got of looking at you and speaking to you in there! I was trying for the lace department, I've been at Crèvecœur's, in the Rue du Mail."

They were once more standing facing each other and, not knowing how to take their leave, they began to blush. Then the young man, shy to excess, in order to say something ventured to ask her in his awkward, kind way:

"What is your name, Mademoiselle?"

"Denise Baudu."

"I'm called Henri Deloche."

They were smiling now. Yielding to the affinity of their positions, they held out their hands to each other.

"Good luck!"

"Yes, good luck!"

3

E VERY SATURDAY, from four to six, Madame Desforges served tea and cakes to those of her close friends who might wish to come and see her. The flat was on the third floor, at the corner of the Rue de Rivoli and the Rue d'Alger, and the windows of the two drawing rooms looked out over the Tuileries gardens.

On that particular Saturday, as a servant was about to show him into the large drawing room, it so happened that Mouret, from the anteroom and through a door which had been left open, caught sight of Madame Desforges crossing the small drawing room. On seeing him she had stopped, and he went in that way, greeting her in a formal manner. Then, when the servant had shut the door again, he hurriedly seized the young woman's hand and kissed it tenderly.

"Be careful! There are people there!" she said in a whisper, pointing towards the door of the large drawing room. "I went to fetch this fan to show them."

And, with the tip of a fan, she gaily gave him a little tap on his face. She was dark and rather buxom, with large, jealous eyes. He, still holding her hand, asked:

"Will he come?"

"Yes, of course," she replied. "I have his word."

They were both talking about Baron Hartmann, director of the Crédit Immobilier. Madame Desforge's father had been an important civil servant; she was the widow of a stockbroker who had left her a fortune – a fortune which some people denied existed, while others exaggerated it. It was rumoured that even while her husband was alive she had shown her gratitude to Baron Hartmann, whose advice, as an important financier, had been useful to the family, and later on, after her husband's death, the liaison must probably have continued, though always discreetly, without imprudence or scandal. Madame Desforges always avoided notoriety; in the upper-middle class into which she had been born everyone received her. Even now, when the passion of the banker, a sceptical and shrewd man, was turning into a purely fatherly affection, if she did venture to have lovers on whom he turned a blind eye, she exercised such delicate restraint and tact in her love affairs and her knowledge of the world was so skilfully applied that appearances were kept up and no one would have dared to question her virtue out loud. Having met Mouret at the house of some mutual friends, she had at first detested him; then later she had yielded to him, as if carried away by the sudden passion with which he was besieging her. He was manoeuvring in order to get a hold over the Baron through her, and in the meantime she was gradually really falling deeply in love with him, she adored him with the violence of a woman already thirty-five years old, but who only admitted to twenty-nine, for she was in despair at the thought that he was younger, and terrified of losing him.

"Does he know about it?" he went on.

"No, you explain the business to him yourself, sir," she answered, no longer addressing him in familiar terms.

She was looking at him, she was thinking to herself that if he used her influence with the Baron like that, while pretending to consider him simply as an old friend of hers, he must not know anything. But he was still holding her hand, he was calling her his kind Henriette, and she felt her heart melting. Silently, she offered her lips to him, pressed them against his; then, in a low voice, she said:

"Sh! They're waiting for me... Follow me in."

Idle voices, muffled by the hangings, were coming from the large drawing room. She pushed the double door and, leaving it wide open, she handed the fan to one of the four ladies who were sitting in the middle of the room.

"Look, here it is," she said. "I didn't know where it was, my maid would never have found it."

And, turning round, she added gaily:

"Do come in, Monsieur Mouret, come through the small drawing room. It won't be so ceremonious."

Mouret bowed to the ladies, whom he already knew. The drawing room – with its Louis XVI furniture which was upholstered with brocade decorated with nosegays, with its gilded bronzes, its huge green plants – had a tender feminine intimacy about it in spite of its high ceiling, and through the two windows the chestnut trees in the Tuileries gardens could be seen, their leaves being swept away by the October wind.

"Why, this Chantilly lace isn't bad at all!" exclaimed Madame Bourdelais, who was holding the fan.

She was a small, fair woman of thirty, with a little, delicately shaped nose and bright eyes, one of Henriette's school friends, who had married an assistant undersecretary in the Ministry of Finance. She was a member of an old middle-class family, and ran her house and her three children with dispatch, good grace and an exquisite flair for the practical side of life.

"And you paid twenty-five francs for the piece?" she resumed, examining every stitch of the lace. "You say you got it in Luc, from a local craftswoman? No, no, it isn't expensive. But then you had to have it mounted."

"Yes, of course," Madame Desforges replied. "The mount cost me two hundred francs."

At that Madame Bourdelais began to laugh. So that was what Henriette called a bargain! Two hundred francs for a simple ivory mount, with a monogram on it! And all for a bit of Chantilly lace on which she had economized five francs! One could find fans like that already mounted for a hundred and twenty francs. She named a shop in the Rue Poissonière.

Meanwhile, the fan was being handed round by the ladies. Madame Guibal scarcely gave it a glance. She was tall and thin, red-headed, her face suffused with indifference through which there sometimes showed in her grey eyes, beneath her air of detachment, the terrible pangs of egotism. She was never seen in the company of her husband, a well-known lawyer at the Palais de Justice, who on his side, so it was said, led the free life and was entirely immersed in his briefs and his pleasures.

"Oh," she murmured as she passed the fan to Madame de Boves, "I don't suppose I've bought more than a couple in my life. One is always given too many of them."

The Countess replied in a subtly ironic voice:

"You *are* lucky, my dear, to have an attentive husband!"

And she leant towards her daughter, a tall girl of twenty and a half:

"Just look at the monogram, Blanche. What lovely work! It must have been the monogram which put up the price of the mount like that."

Madame de Boves was just over forty. She was a fine woman, with the build of a goddess, She had a big face with regular features and wide, sleepy eyes; her husband, Inspector-General of Stud Farms, had married her for her beauty. She appeared to be deeply stirred by the delicacy of the monogram, as if she was overwhelmed by desire, the emotion of which made her blanch. And suddenly she said:

"Tell us what you think, Monsieur Mouret. Is it too expensive, two hundred francs for this mount?"

Mouret had remained standing in the midst of the five women, smiling, taking an interest in what was interesting them. He picked up the fan, and examined it, and he was about to give an opinion when the servant opened the door, saying:

"Madame Marty."

A thin woman, ugly, pitted by smallpox, dressed with involved elegance, came in. She was ageless, her thirty-five years looked like forty or thirty, depending on the nervous fever which was driving her. A red leather bag, with which she had not parted outside, was hanging from her right hand.

"My dear," she said to Henriette, "forgive me for coming with my bag... Just fancy, on my way to see you I went in to the Bonheur, and as I've been extravagant again, I didn't want to leave this downstairs in my cab, in case it got stolen."

But she had just caught sight of Mouret, and went on, laughing:

"Ah! Monsieur, I didn't say that to boost you up, for I didn't know you were here... You really have got some wonderful lace at the moment."

This drew attention away from the fan, which the young man put down on a pedestal table. Now the ladies were full of curiosity to see what Madame Marty had bought. She was known for her passion for spending, her inability to resist temptation, strictly virtuous though she was, and incapable of yielding to a lover; no sooner was she faced with a tiny bit of ribbon than she would let herself go and the flesh was conquered. The daughter of a minor civil servant, she was now ruining her husband, the fifth-form teacher in the Lycée Bonaparte who, in order to provide for the family's ever-increasing budget, had to double the salary of six thousand francs which he received by giving private lessons. She did not open her bag, but was holding it tightly on her lap, while talking about her daughter Valentine, who was fourteen years old and one of her most expensive indulgences, for she dressed her like herself in all the latest fashions, which irresistibly fascinated her.

"You know," she explained, "this winter, dresses for girls are trimmed with narrow lace... Of course, when I saw some very pretty Valenciennes..."

Finally, she brought herself to open the bag. The ladies were craning their necks forwards when, in the silence which had fallen, the anteroom bell could be heard.

"It's my husband," stammered Madame Marty, full of confusion. "He must have come to fetch me on his way back from the Bonaparte."

She had quickly shut the bag, and with an instinctive movement she made it disappear under her chair. All the ladies began to laugh. Then she blushed at her haste, took the bag back onto her lap, saying that men never understood, and that there was no necessity for them to know anything about such things.

"Monsieur de Boves, Monsieur de Vallagnosc," the servant announced.

This was a surprise. Madame de Boves herself had not been sure her husband would come. The latter, a handsome man, with moustaches and an imperial, who walked with the stiff military bearing favoured by the Tuileries, kissed the hand of Madame Desforges whom he had known as a girl in her father's house. He stood aside so that the other visitor, a tall pale lad with an anaemically distinguished look, could in his turn greet the mistress of the house. But the conversation was scarcely starting up again when two slight exclamations were uttered.

"What! It's you, Paul!"

"Why! Octave!"

Mouret and Vallagnosc were shaking hands. It was Madame Desforges's turn to show surprise. So they knew each other? Yes, indeed, they had grown up together, at a school in Plassans, and it was pure chance that they had never met at her house before.

Still hand in hand they went into the small drawing room, joking as they did so, just as the servant was bringing the tea, a

Chinese service on a silver tray, which he placed near Madame Desforges in the centre of a marble pedestal table with light brass beading on it. The ladies were drawing close together, talking more loudly, entirely absorbed in endless, interlacing words, while Monsieur de Boves, standing behind them, from time to time bent towards them to say a word, with the courtly politeness of a handsome official. The huge room, so elegantly and gaily furnished, was made even gayer by these chattering voices mingled with laughter.

"Well, Paul, old man!" repeated Mouret.

He was sitting close to Vallagnosc, on a settee. By themselves at the far end of the small drawing room – a very elegant boudoir hung with buttercup-coloured silk – out of earshot, and with the ladies only visible to them through the wide-open door, they sat face to face guffawing and slapping each other on the knee. The whole of their youth was reawakening, the old college at Plassans with its two courtyards, and the refectory where they used to eat such a lot of cod, and the dormitories where the pillows used to fly from bed to bed as soon as the master was snoring. Paul, member of an old parliamentary family of ruined and stand-offish minor aristocracy, had been good at his books, always first, always being quoted as an example by the teacher, who had foretold a most brilliant future for him; whereas Octave, slack and happy at the bottom of the class, had wasted away amongst the dunces, employing all his energies on violent pleasures outside school. In spite of their different natures, a close comradeship had nevertheless made them inseparable until they had got through their matriculation examination, one with distinction, the other only just scraping through after two unfortunate attempts. Then life had separated them, and they were meeting again, already altered and aged, after an interval of ten years.

"Tell me now," Mouret asked, "what's happening to you?"

"Oh, nothing's happening to me."

In spite of his joy at their meeting, Vallagnosc still retained his tired and disillusioned manner and, as his friend, surprised, was pressing him, saying:

"Yes, but you must do something after all... What do you do?"

He replied: "Nothing."

63

Octave began to laugh. Nothing was not enough. Sentence by sentence, in the end he extracted Paul's story from him – the usual story of boys without money who think they owe it to their social position to remain in the liberal professions and who bury themselves under their conceited mediocrity – lucky, what is more, if they do not die of starvation in spite of their desks being full of diplomas. He had followed the family tradition and read law; after that he had gone on being supported by his mother, a widow, who already did not know how to marry off her two daughters. He had finally begun to feel ashamed and, leaving the three women to live in discomfort on the remains of their money, he had taken up a minor post in the Ministry of the Interior, where he had buried himself like a mole in its earth.

"And what do you earn?" Mouret resumed.

"Three thousand francs."

"Why, it's a pittance! Poor old chap, I feel really sorry for you... Why! You were so brainy as a boy, you used to lick us all! And they only give you three thousand francs, when they've had you mouldering there for five years! No, it's not fair."

He broke off and came back to his own case.

"I've said goodbye to them myself... You know what I've become?"

"Yes," said Vallagnosc. "I was told that you'd gone into business. You own that big shop on the Place Gaillon, don't you?"

"That's it... calico, old chap!"

Mouret had raised his head, and he slapped him on the knee again; with the hearty gaiety of a cheerful fellow with no shame about the trade which was making him rich, he repeated:

"Calico, masses of it! My goodness, do you remember, I never caught on at their ideas, although deep down I never thought I was any stupider than anyone else. When I'd passed my baccalaureate to please my family, I could quite well have become a lawyer or a doctor like the others, but professions like that frightened me – one sees so many people at the end of their tether in them... So, by God! I threw my bonnet over the windmill – oh! with no regret! – and I took a header into business."

Vallagnosc was smiling with an air of embarrassment. Finally he murmured:

"It's true that your baccalaureate can't be of much use to you for selling calico."

"Goodness!" replied Mouret blithely, "all I ask is that it shouldn't hinder me... And you know, when you've got your feet entangled in a thing like that, it's not so easy to shake it off. You go through life at the pace of a tortoise, while the others, those who are barefoot, run like hares."

Then, noticing that his friend seemed to be pained, he took his hands in his, and went on:

"Come, I don't want to hurt you, but admit that your diplomas haven't satisfied any of your needs... Do you know, the head of my silk department will get more than twelve thousand francs this year? Yes, really! A lad of very sound intelligence, who never got beyond spelling and the four rules... The ordinary salesmen, at my place, make three to four thousand francs, more than you earn yourself – and their education didn't cost what yours did, they were not launched into the world with a signed promise that they would conquer it... Of course, earning money isn't everything. Only, between the poor devils with a smattering of learning who clutter up the professions without being able to eat their fill in them and the practical lads, equipped for life, who know their trade backwards, upon my word! I wouldn't hesitate, I'm for the latter against the former, I think fellows like that understand their epoch pretty well!"

His voice had become excited; Henriette, who was serving tea, had looked round. When he saw her smile at the end of the large drawing room and also noticed two other ladies listening, he was the first to laugh at his own words.

"Anyway, old chap, any counter-jumper who's just beginning has a hope of becoming a millionaire nowadays."

Vallagnosc was leaning back indolently on the sofa. He had half-closed his eyes, in an attitude of fatigue and disdain, in which a touch of affectation added to the real effeteness of his breed.

"Pooh!" he murmured, "Life's not worth so much trouble. Nothing's any fun."

And as Mouret, shocked, was looking at him with an air of surprise, he added:

"Everything happens, and nothing happens. One may as well sit and twiddle one's thumbs!"

Then he went on to express his pessimism, to speak of the pettinesses and the frustrations of existence. At one time he had dreamt of literature, and as a result of associating with poets he had been left with a feeling of universal hopelessness. In the end he always came back to the uselessness of effort, the boredom of hours all equally empty and the ultimate stupidity of the world. Pleasures did not come off, and he did not even get any joy out of doing wrong.

"Now tell me, do you enjoy yourself?" he asked finally. Mouret had reached a state of dazed indignation. He exclaimed:

"What? Do I enjoy myself? Ah! Now what's this nonsense you're telling me? You've got to that point, have you, old fellow? To be sure I enjoy myself, and even when things go wrong, because then I'm furious at seeing them go wrong. I'm an enthusiast, I am. I don't take life calmly, and perhaps that's just why I'm interested in it."

He glanced into the drawing room and lowered his voice.

"Oh! Some women have really been an awful nuisance to me, that I confess. But, when I've got one, I stick to her, damn it! And it doesn't always fail, and I don't give my share to anyone else, I assure you... But it isn't only a question of women, for whom I don't give a damn, actually. You see, it's a question of wanting something and acting, it's a question of creating, really... You get an idea, you fight for it, you knock it into people's heads with a hammer, you watch it grow and carry all before it... Ah! Yes, old chap, I enjoy myself!"

All the joy of action, all the gaiety of existence rang in his words. He repeated that he was a man of his own time. Really, people would have to be deformed, they must have something wrong with their brains and limbs to decline to get on with the job at a time when there was such wide scope for work, when the whole century was pressing towards the future. And he jeered at the hopeless, the disillusioned, the pessimists, all those invalids of budding knowledge who in the midst of the immense contemporary building yard put on the tearful airs of poets or the supercilious looks of sceptics. Yawning with boredom at other people's work was a fine part to play, a really proper and intelligent one indeed!

"It's my only pleasure, to yawn at other people," said Vallagnosc, smiling in his cold way.

At this, Mouret's passion subsided. He became affectionate once more.

"Ah! You're just the same old Paul, always paradoxical! We haven't met again in order to quarrel, have we? Everyone has his own ideas, fortunately. But I must show you my machine in full swing, you'll see that it isn't really so silly... Come now, tell me your news. Your mother and sisters are well, I hope? And weren't you going to get married at Plassans, about six months ago?"

A sudden movement on de Vallagnosc's part made him stop short, and, as the latter had searched the drawing room with an anxious look, he too turned round and saw that Mademoiselle de Boves had her eyes glued on them. Tall and buxom, Blanche was like her mother; only, in her case, her whole face was already putting on flesh and her features were coarse, blown out by unhealthy fat. Paul, in reply to a discreet question, said that nothing had happened so far; perhaps nothing would happen, even. He had met the girl at Madame Desforges's house, which he had visited frequently in the past winter, but where he now only rarely made an appearance, which explained why he had not met Octave there. The Boves had invited him in their turn, and he was particularly fond of the father, who had once been something of a bon viveur, but had now retired and worked in the civil service. They had, moreover, no money: Madame de Boves had brought her husband nothing but her Junoesque beauty, the family was living on a last, hypothetical farm, the slim income from which was fortunately supplemented by the nine thousand francs which the Count received as Inspector General of Stud Farms. The ladies, mother and daughter, were kept very short of money by the Count, who was still a prey to amorous bouts away from home, and they were sometimes reduced to remaking their dresses themselves.

"Then why marry her?" Mouret asked simply.

"Goodness! One must bring these things to a conclusion, after all," said Vallagnosc, with a tired movement of his eyelids. "And then, we have prospects, we are waiting for an aunt to die soon."

Mouret was still staring at Monsieur de Boves, who was sitting near Madame Guibal and, with the amorous laugh of a man on the warpath, paying her marked attention, Octave turned towards his friend and winked in such a significant way that the latter added:

"No, not her... Not yet, at any rate... The unfortunate thing is that his work takes him all over France, to different stud farms, and so he always has pretexts for disappearing. Last month, when his wife thought he was in Perpignan, he was living in an hotel buried in an out-of-the-way district of Paris, in the company of a piano instructress."

There was a silence. Then the young man who, in his turn, was watching the Count's attentions to Madame Guibal, went on in an undertone:

"My goodness, you're right... Especially as they say that the dear lady is not at all unsociable. There's a very funny story about her and an officer... But do look at him! Isn't he comic, hypnotizing her out of the corner of his eye! There's the old France for you, my friend! I simply adore that man, and if I marry his daughter he'll really be able to say that I did it for his sake!"

Mouret was laughing, very amused. He questioned Vallagnosc afresh, and when he heard that the original idea of a marriage between him and Blanche had come from Madame Desforges, he thought the story even funnier. Dear kind Henriette took a widow's pleasure in marrying people off; so much so that when she had settled the daughters, she would sometimes let the fathers choose their mistresses from her circle, but this was done in such a natural and becoming way that society never found any food for scandal in it. And when this happened Mouret, who loved her with the love of an active, hurried man used to calculating his caresses, would then forget all his ulterior motives of seduction, and have feelings of purely comradely friendship for her.

Just then she appeared at the door of the small drawing room followed by an old man of about sixty, whose entrance the two friends had not noticed. Now and again the ladies' voices would become shrill, and the light tinkle of spoons in china teacups formed an accompaniment to them; from time to time, in the middle of a short silence, the sound of a saucer being put down too roughly on the marble of the pedestal table could be heard. A sudden ray from the setting sun, which was just appearing at the edge of a large cloud, was gilding the tops of the chestnut trees in the garden and coming through the windows in reddish-gold dust, illuminating the brocade and the brass work of the furniture with its fire.

"This way, my dear Baron," Madame Desforges was saying. "May I introduce Monsieur Octave Mouret, who very much wishes to tell you how much he admires you."

And, turning towards Octave, she added:

"Monsieur le Baron Hartmann."

The old man's lips were shrewdly twisted in a smile. He was a small, vigorous-looking man, with the large head typical of people from Alsace and with a heavy face which, at the slightest pucker of his mouth, at the lightest flicker of his eyelids, would light up with a flash of intelligence. For a fortnight he had been resisting Henriette's wish, for it was she who had been begging for this interview; it was not that he felt particularly jealous, for being a man of the world he was resigned to playing a father's part, but this was the third of Henriette's male friends she had introduced to him and he was rather afraid, in the long run, of appearing ridiculous. Therefore, as he approached Octave, he had the discreet smile of a rich protector who, though willing to be charming, does not consent to be fooled.

"Oh Monsieur," Mouret was saying, with his Provençal enthusiasm, "that last deal of the Crédit Immobilier was really remarkable! You'll never believe how happy and proud I am to shake hands with you."

"Too kind, Monsieur, too kind," the Baron repeated, still smiling.

With her limpid eyes Henriette was watching them without embarrassment. She remained between the two of them, raising her pretty head, looking from one to the other; wearing a lace dress which exposed her slender wrists and neck, she looked as if she was delighted to see them getting on so well.

"Gentlemen," she said in the end, "I'll leave you to talk."

Then, turning towards Paul, who had risen to his feet, she added:

"Would you like a cup of tea, Monsieur de Vallagnosc?"

"With pleasure, Madame."

And they both went back to the drawing room.

When Mouret had resumed his place on the sofa beside Baron Hartmann, he launched into further panegyrics about the transactions of the Crédit Immobilier. Then he broached a subject which he had very much at heart, he spoke of the new road, the extension of the Rue Réaumur, of which a section was about to be opened between the Place de la Bourse and the Place de l'Opéra, under the name of the Rue du Dix-Décembre. It had been declared available for public purposes eighteen months ago, the expropriation committee had just been appointed, the whole district was passionately excited about this enormous space, worried about the period of construction and taking an interest in the condemned houses. Mouret had been looking forward to this work for almost three years, firstly because he foresaw that business would be brisker as a result, and then because he had ambitions of expansion to which he dared not admit out loud, so greatly were his dreams extending. As the Rue du Dix-Décembre was going to cross the Rue de Choiseul and the Rue de la Michodière, he visualized the Bonheur des Dames over-running the whole block of houses surrounded by these streets and by the Rue Neuve-Saint-Augustin, and he was already imagining it with the façade of a palace on the new thoroughfare, dominating and ruling the conquered city. From this had sprung his keen desire to meet Baron Hartmann, for he had heard that the Crédit Immobilier, by an agreement with the authorities, had contracted to open up the Rue du Dix-Décembre and to build it, on condition that it was granted the ownership of the territory bordering on the new street.

"Really?" he was repeating, trying to put on an ingenuous air. "You're handing over a ready-made street to them, with drains, and pavements and gaslights? And the territory skirting it is enough to compensate you? Oh, that's odd, very odd!"

Finally he came to the ticklish question. He had found out that the Crédit Immobilier was secretly buying up houses in the same block as the Bonheur des Dames, not only those which were due to fall under the pickaxes of the demolition squads, but others too, those which were to remain standing. And he scented in this a plan for some future building scheme; he was very worried about the expansion on which he had set his heart, filled with fear at the idea of one day coming up against a powerful company owning premises which it would certainly not abandon. It was, in fact, this fear which had made him decide to establish a bond between the Baron and himself as soon as possible, the agreeable bond of a woman which, between men passionate by nature, can be such a close one. Doubtless, he could have seen the financier in his office, in order to discuss at his leisure the big deal which he wanted to propose to him. But he felt himself to be stronger in Henriette's house, he knew how much the possession of a mistress in common brings people together and softens them.

For them both to be in her house, in the midst of her beloved perfume, to have her near to win them over with a smile, seemed to him to make success a certainty.

"Haven't you bought what used to be the Duvillard town house, that old building which joins on to me?" he finally asked bluntly.

Baron Hartmann hesitated for a moment, and then denied it. But looking him straight in the face, Mouret began to laugh, and the part he played from then on was that of a good-natured young man, wearing his heart on his sleeve and straight in business.

"Look here, Monsieur le Baron, since I've had the unexpected honour of meeting you, I must make a confession... Oh! I'm not asking you to tell me your secrets. Only, I'm going to confide mine to you, for I'm sure I couldn't put them in wiser hands... Besides, I need your advice, I've been trying to pluck up courage to go and see you for a long time."

He did, indeed, make a confession, he told of his first steps in business, he did not even hide the financial crisis which, in the midst of his triumph, he was passing through. Everything came out, the gradual expansions, the profits continually ploughed back into the business, the sums contributed by employees, the shop risking its very existence at each successive sale in which the whole capital was staked as if on a hand of cards. Nevertheless, it was not for money that he was asking, for he had a fanatical faith in his customers. His ambition was growing, he was proposing to the Baron a partnership, in which the Crédit Immobilier would provide the colossal palace of which he dreamt, whereas he, on his side, would give his genius and the business goodwill already established. They would estimate the value of either party's contribution, nothing seemed easier to him to put into effect.

"What are you going to do with your building sites and premises?" he asked insistently. "You probably have an idea. But I'm quite certain your idea is not as good as mine... Just think about it. We'll build a shopping arcade on the sites, we'll demolish or convert the buildings, and we'll open the most enormous shops in Paris, a bazaar which will make millions."

Then he allowed this heartfelt cry to escape him:

"Oh! If only I could manage without you! But you hold everything now. And then, I should never get the necessary loans... Come now, we must reach an agreement, it would be a crime not to."

"How you do let yourself go, my dear sir," Baron Hartmann contented himself with replying. "What imagination!"

He was shaking his head, he went on smiling, determined not to repay confidences by confidences. The Crédit Immobilier's plan was to create, in the Rue du Dix-Décembre, a rival to the Grand Hotel, a luxurious establishment with a central position which would attract foreigners. In any case, since the hotel would only occupy the sites bordering on the street, the Baron could very well have welcomed Mouret's idea all the same and negotiated for the remaining block of houses, which was still a very vast area. But he had financed two of Henriette's friends already, he was getting rather tired of his performance as an accommodating protector. And then, in spite of his passion for dispatch which made him open his purse to every intelligent and courageous young man, Mouret's streak of business genius surprised him more than it attracted him. Was not this gigantic shop a fantastic, rash speculation? Was it not courting certain ruin to wish thus to expand the drapery trade beyond all bounds? In short, he did not believe in it, he was refusing.

"No doubt, the idea has its attraction," he said, "only it's the idea of a poet... Where would you find the customers to fill a cathedral like that?"

Mouret looked at him for a moment in silence, as if stunned by his refusal. Was it possible? A man with a flair like that, who could smell out money at every level! And suddenly he made a gesture of great eloquence, he pointed to the ladies in the drawing room, exclaiming:

"The customers? Why, there they are!"

The sun was fading, the reddish-gold dust had become nothing but a pale glimmer, bidding farewell and dying away in the silk of the hangings and the panels of the furniture. With the approach of dusk a sense of intimacy was flooding the large room with warm mellowness. While M. de Boves and Paul de Vallagnosc were chatting in front of one of the windows, their eyes lost in the distance of the garden, the ladies had drawn closer together, and were forming a close circle of skirts in the centre of the room, from which laughter was ascending, as well as whispered remarks, eager questions and answers, the very essence of woman's passion for spending and for clothes. They were discussing fashions, Madame de Boves was describing a ball dress.

"First of all, an underskirt of mauve silk, and then, over it flounces of old Alençon lace, thirty centimetres deep—"

"Oh! If I may say so," Madame Marty interrupted. "Some women have all the luck!"

Baron Hartmann, who had followed Mouret's gesture, was looking at the ladies through the wide open door. And he was listening to them with half an ear, while the younger man, inflamed with the desire to convince him further, was confiding in him, explaining how the new kind of drapery business worked. It now depended on a quick turnover of capital, which had to be converted into goods as many times as possible within twelve months. Thus, in the present year, his initial capital of only five hundred thousand francs had produced a turnover of two million francs. And that was a mere nothing which could be multiplied tenfold, for he felt sure that in some departments of his shop he could eventually get his capital back fifteen or twenty times over.

"You see, Monsieur le Baron, that's the whole technique of it. It's quite simple, once one's thought of it. We don't need a large amount of working capital. All we want is to get rid very quickly of the goods we have bought, in order to replace them by something else, thus making the capital earn its interest every time we do it. Like this we can be content with a small profit; as our general expenses reach the enormous figure of sixteen per cent, and we never deduct more than twenty-per-cent profit on stock, it means there's a profit of four per cent at the most, but if the stock is considerable and continually renewed this will end up making millions... You understand, don't you? It's quite obvious."

The Baron shook his head once more. He, who had in his time welcomed the most audacious schemes, and whose boldness at the time when gas lighting was a novelty was still talked about, remained apprehensive and obstinate.

"I quite understand," he replied. "You sell cheaply in order to sell a lot and you sell a lot in order to sell cheaply... only, you must sell, and I repeat my question: to whom will you sell? How do you hope to maintain such colossal sales?"

A sudden burst of voices coming from the drawing room cut short Mouret's explanations. Madame Guibal was saying she would have preferred the flounces of old Alençon lace to be only at the front of the dress.

"But, my dear," Madame de Boves was saying, "the front was covered with it too. I've never seen any finer."

"Why! You give me an idea," Madame Desforges went on, "I have a few yards of Alençon already... I must look for some more to make a trimming."

And the voices dropped again, became only a murmur. Figures were bandied about, a regular haggling was going on and was arousing desires, the ladies were buying lace by the handful.

"Ah!" said Mouret in the end, when he could speak. "You can sell as much as you like when you know how to sell! Therein lies our success."

Then, with his Provençal zest, his enthusiastic phrases conjuring up pictures, he described the new kind of business at work. First, its strength was multiplied tenfold by accumulation, by all the goods being gathered together at one point, supporting and boosting each other; there was never a slack period, seasonable goods were always kept and, as she went from counter to counter, the customer found herself snared, would buy here some material, there some thread, a coat somewhere else, set herself up in clothes, then get caught by unforeseen attractions, yield to the need for all that is useless and pretty. Next, he extolled the system of marked prices. The great revolution in drapery had started from this bright idea. If old-fashioned business, small trade, was in its death throes, it was because it could not keep up the struggle for low prices, which had been inaugurated by the system of marking prices on goods. Now competition was taking place under the public's very eyes, people had only to walk past the shop windows to ascertain prices, and every shop was reducing them, content with the smallest possible profit; there was no cheating, no attempts at making money planned well in advance over a material sold at double its value, but ready sales, a regular profit of a certain percentage on all goods, a fortune put into the smooth running of a sale, its scope the larger because it took place in full view of the public. Wasn't this an astonishing creation? It was throwing the market into confusion, it was transforming Paris, for it was based on the very flesh and blood of Woman.

"I've got the women, I don't care a damn about anything else!" he said, in a brutal admission wrung from him by passion.

Baron Hartmann seemed moved by this exclamation. His smile was losing its touch of irony and, gradually won over by the young man's faith, he was looking at him, beginning to have an affection for him.

"Sh!" he murmured paternally. "They'll hear you."

But the ladies were now all talking at the same time, so excited that they were no longer even listening to each other. Madame de Boves was concluding her description of the evening dress, a tunic of mauve silk, draped and caught back by knots of lace, the bodice cut very low, and with more knots of lace on the shoulders.

"You'll see," she was saying, "I'll have a bodice like that made with a satin—"

"You know," Madame Bourdelais was interrupting, "I wanted some velvet. Oh! it was such a bargain!"

Madame Marty was asking:

"Well, how much was the silk?"

Then all the voices replied at the same time. Madame Guibal, Henriette, Blanche were hard at it, measuring, cutting, squandering. Materials were being looted, shops ransacked. The women's lust for luxury was running riot as they dreamt of dresses, coveted them, feeling so happy in the world of clothes that they lived immersed in it, as they did in the warm air necessary to their existence.

Meanwhile Mouret had glanced towards the drawing room. And, in a few phrases spoken into Baron Hartmann's ear, as if he was telling him confidences of an amorous nature such as men sometimes venture to make when they are alone, he finished explaining the technique of modern big business to him. At last he came to something more important than all the facts already given, of supreme importance, indeed: he spoke of the exploitation of women. Everything else led up to it, the capital ceaselessly renewed, the system of piling up goods, the low prices which attracted people, the marked prices which reassured them. It was women the shops were wrangling over in rivalry, it was women they caught in the everlasting snare of their bargains, after they had dazed them with their displays. They had awoken new desires in their weak flesh, they were an immense temptation to which they inevitably yielded, succumbing in the first place to purchases for the house, then won over by coquetry, finally completely enslaved. By increasing sales tenfold, by making luxury democratic, shops were becoming a terrible agency for spending; inspired as they were by the extravagances of fashion, which were growing ever more expensive, they were causing havoc in homes. And if, when she was in the shops, the woman was queen, adulated and humoured in her weaknesses, surrounded with attentions, she reigned there as amorous queen whose subjects trade on her, and who pays for every whim with a drop of her own blood. Beneath the very charm of his gallantry, Mouret allowed the brutality of a Jew selling women by the pound to show through; he was building a temple to Woman, making a legion of shop assistants burn incense before her, creating the rites of a new cult; he thought only of her, ceaselessly trying to devise even greater enticements – and behind her back, when he had emptied her pockets and wrecked her nerves, he was full of the secret contempt of a man to whom a mistress has just committed the folly of yielding.

"Get the women," he said to the Baron in a low voice, giving an impudent laugh as he did so, "and you'll sell the world!"

Now the Baron understood. A few sentences had sufficed, he guessed the rest, and such gallant exploitation excited him, roused memories of his dissolute past. He gave a flicker of his eyelids with an air of understanding, he was ending up by admiring the inventor of this technique for devouring women. It was very good. He made the same remark as Bourdoncle, a remark prompted by his long experience:

"You know, they'll revenge themselves."

But Mouret shrugged his shoulders, in a movement of crushing disdain. All women belonged to him, were his chattels, and he belonged to none of them. When he had extracted his fortune and his pleasure from them, he would throw them on the rubbish heap for those who could still make a living out of them. He had the calculated disdain of a southerner and of a speculator.

"Well, sir," he asked in conclusion, "are you on my side? Does the business of the building sites seem possible to you?"

The Baron, half won over, nevertheless hesitated to commit himself like that, still felt a doubt about the charm which was gradually having an effect on him. He was about to reply evasively, when an urgent summons from the ladies saved him the trouble. In the midst of idle laughter voices were calling:

"Monsieur Mouret!"

And since the latter, annoyed at being interrupted, was pretending not to hear, Madame de Boves, who had been standing up for a moment, came to the door of the small drawing room.

"They are calling for you, Monsieur Mouret... It's not at all chivalrous of you to bury yourself in a corner to talk business."

At that, he made up his mind, and with such an obvious good grace and air of delight that the Baron was filled with admiration. They both stood up, and went into the large drawing room.

"Here I am. I'm at your service, ladies," he said as he went in, a smile on his lips.

A hubbub of triumph greeted him. He had to move further forwards, the ladies made a place for him in their midst. The sun had just set behind the trees in the garden, daylight was fading, a delicate shadow was gradually flooding the vast room. It was the affecting hour of twilight, that moment of discreet voluptuousness in Parisian houses when the light in the street is dying and the lamps are still being lit in the butler's pantry. Monsieur de Boves and Vallagnosc, still standing in front of the window, were casting a pool of shadow on the carpet; while, motionless in the last ray of light coming from the other window, there stood Monsieur Marty, who had come in discreetly a few minutes earlier, and was displaying his thin profile, his skimpy, clean frock coat, and his face grown pale from teaching and made even more distressed-looking by the ladies' conversation about dresses.

"That sale is going to be next Monday, isn't it?" Madame Marty was just asking.

"But of course, Madame," Mouret replied in a flutelike voice, an actor's voice which he affected when speaking to women.

Then Henriette interposed.

"You know, we're all going... They say you're preparing marvels."

"Oh! Marvels!" he murmured with an air of modest self-complacency. "I only try to be worthy of your patronage."

They were bombarding him with questions. Madame Bourdelais, Madame Guibal, Blanche too, wanted to know all about it.

"Come now, give us some details," Madame de Boves was repeating insistently. "You're making us die of curiosity!"

They were surrounding him, when Henriette noticed that he had not yet had a cup of tea. At that there was consternation; four of them began to serve him, but only on condition that he would reply to them afterwards. Henriette was pouring out, Madame Marty was holding the cup, while Madame de Boves and Madame Bourdelais were wrangling for the honour of putting in the sugar. Then, when he had refused to sit down and had started to drink his tea slowly, standing in their midst, they all drew closer, imprisoning him within the closed circle of their skirts. Heads raised and eyes shining, they were smiling at him.

"Your silk, your Paris-Bonheur, which all the newspapers are talking about?" Madame Marty went on impatiently.

"Oh!" he replied, "an exceptional article, a coarse faille, supple and strong... You'll see it, ladies. And you'll only find it in our shop, for we have bought the exclusive rights."

"Really! A beautiful silk at five francs sixty!" said Madame Bourdelais, in raptures. "It's unbelievable!"

Since the launching of the advertisements, this silk had been occupying a considerable place in their daily life. They discussed it and were looking forward to it, tormented by desire and doubt. And, beneath the chattering curiosity with which they were overwhelming the young man, each one's individual temperament as a customer was discernible: Madame Marty, carried away by her mania for spending, taking everything from the Bonheur des Dames without making any choice, simply buying at random from the displays; Madame Guibal walking round the shop for hours without ever making a purchase, happy and satisfied by merely feasting her eyes; Madame de Boves, short of money, everlastingly tortured by too great a desire, bearing a grudge against the goods which she could not take away; Madame Bourdelais, with the flair of a wise and practical middle-class woman, going straight to the bargains, using the big shops with such housewifely acumen, calmly and without losing her head, that she did really save money there; finally Henriette who, extremely well-dressed as she was, bought only certain articles there – her gloves, some hosiery, all her household linen.

"We have other materials which are amazingly inexpensive and yet sumptuous," Mouret was continuing in his melodious voice.

"For example, I recommend our Cuir-d'Or to you, a taffeta with an incomparable sheen... Amongst the fancy silks there are some charming patterns, designs chosen from thousands of others by our buyer, and for velvets, you will find an extremely rich collection of shades... I warn you that a lot of cloth will be worn this year. You will see our matelassés, our cheviots..."

They were no longer interrupting him, but were drawing in even closer in their circle, their lips slightly parted in a vague smile, their faces close together and craning forwards, as if their whole being was yearning towards their tempter. Their eyes were growing dim, a slight shiver was running over the napes of their necks. And, in the midst of the heady scents which were rising from their hair, he maintained the composure of a conqueror. Between each sentence he went on taking little sips of tea, the perfume of which cooled down those other, more pungent scents, in which there was a touch of musk.

Baron Hartmann, who had not taken his eyes off him, felt his admiration mounting before charm which had such self-possession and force that it could make sport with women like that, without succumbing to the intoxicating scents which they exude.

"So cloth will be worn," resumed Madame Marty, whose passion for clothes was lighting up her haggard face. "I must go and have a look."

Madame Bourdelais, who was keeping a clear head, said in her turn:

"Your remnant sale is on Thursday, isn't it? I shall wait, I've all my little ones to clothe."

And, turning her delicate fair head towards the mistress of the house, she said:

"You still get your dresses from Sauveur, don't you?"

"Why, yes!" Henriette replied, "Sauveur is very expensive, but she's the only person in Paris who knows how to make the bodice of a dress... And then, whatever Monsieur Mouret may say, she has the prettiest designs, designs which one doesn't see anywhere else. I personally can't bear to meet my dress on every woman's back."

Mouret at first gave a discreet smile. Then he hinted that Madame Sauveur bought her materials at his shop; doubtless, she took certain designs, for which she secured the exclusive rights, direct from the manufacturers, but for black silk goods, for example, she kept her eyes open for bargains at the Bonheur des Dames, and bought considerable supplies which she later disposed of at two or three times the price.

"For instance, I'm quite certain that she'll send someone to snap up our Paris-Bonheur. Why should she go and pay more for this silk at the factory than she would pay in our shop? Honestly! We're selling it at a loss."

This dealt the ladies a final blow. The idea of getting goods sold at a loss aroused in them the ruthlessness of Woman, whose pleasure in purchasing is doubled when she thinks she is robbing the shopkeeper. He knew that they were incapable of resisting low prices.

"But we sell everything for a song!" he exclaimed gaily, picking up Madame Desforges's fan, which had remained on the pedestal table behind him, as he did so. "Look! Here's this fan... How much did you say it cost?"

"Twenty-five francs for the Chantilly, and two hundred for the mount," said Henriette.

"Well, the Chantilly isn't expensive. All the same, we have the same one for eighteen francs... As to the mount, my dear lady, it's an abominable theft, I wouldn't dare to sell one like that for more than ninety francs."

"That's just what I said," exclaimed Madame Bourdelais.

"Ninety francs!" murmured Madame de Boves. "One must really be penniless to do without!"

She had picked up the fan again and, with her daughter Blanche was once more examining it; on her large, regular face, in her wide, sleepy eyes, her pent-up and hopeless desire for a whim which she would not be able to satisfy was mounting. Then, for a second time, the fan was passed round by the ladies, to the accompaniment of remarks and exclamations. In the meantime Monsieur de Boves and Vallagnosc had left the window. The former came back and took up his position once more behind Madame Guibal, his gaze delving into her corsage while he nevertheless maintained his decorous, haughty manner, while the young man was bending down towards Blanche, trying to think of something nice to say.

"It's a bit depressing, don't you think, this white frame with black lace?"

"Oh!" she replied quite seriously, without a blush colouring her puffy face. "I've seen one in mother-of-pearl with white feathers. It was simply virginal!"

Monsieur de Boves, who had doubtless intercepted the agonized look with which his wife was watching the fan, at last put a word in the conversation:

"They break at once, those little contraptions."

"Don't talk to me about it!" Madame Guibal declared with the pout of a beautiful redhead, pretending to be unconcerned. "I'm tired of having mine reglued."

Madame Marty, very excited by the conversation, had for some time been feverishly twisting her red leather bag on her lap. She had not yet been able to show her purchases, she was dying to display them with a kind of sensual urge. Suddenly she forgot all about her husband, opened her bag, and took out a few yards of narrow lace rolled round a card.

"This is the Valenciennes for my daughter," she said. "It's three centimetres wide, isn't it delightful? One franc ninety centimes."

The lace passed from hand to hand. The ladies exclaimed in admiration. Mouret declared that he sold little trimmings like that at the factory price. But Madame Marty had closed her bag again, as if to hide things in it which could not be shown. However, as the Valenciennes was such a success she could not resist the desire to take out a handkerchief as well.

"There was this handkerchief too... Brussels lace, my dear... Oh! A real find! Twenty francs!"

From then on, the bag was inexhaustible. As she took out each fresh article she was blushing with pleasure, with the modesty of a woman undressing, which made her charmingly embarrassed.

There was a scarf in Spanish lace for thirty francs; she had not wanted it, but the assistant had sworn to her that it was the last and that they were going to go up in price. Next there was a veil in Chantilly – rather dear, fifty francs – if she did not wear it herself she would make something for her daughter with it.

"Goodness! Lace is lovely!" she was repeating with her hysterical laugh. "When I see it I could buy the whole shop."

"And this?" Madame de Boves asked her, examining a remnant of guipure.

"That," she replied, "is for insertion... There are twenty-six yards. You see, it was one franc a yard!"

"Oh!" said Madame Bourdelais, surprised. "What are you going to do with it then?"

"Goodness, I don't know… But it had such an amusing design!"

At that moment, as she looked up, she caught sight opposite her of her terrified husband. He had become even paler, his whole person conveyed the resigned anguish of a poor man who witnesses the wreckage of his hard-earned salary. Each fresh bit of lace was for him a disaster, it meant bitter days swallowed up by teaching, spent in hurrying through the mud to give private lessons, the unceasing struggle of his life resulting in secret poverty, in the hell of a needy household. Faced with the growing alarm of his gaze she tried to retrieve the handkerchief, the veil, the jabot; her hands were fluttering feverishly, she was repeating with little embarrassed laughs:

"You'll have me scolded by my husband… I assure you, dear, I've really been very sensible, for there was a big fichu there at five hundred francs… Oh! It was marvellous!"

"Why didn't you buy it?" said Madame Guibal calmly. "Monsieur Marty is the most generous of men."

The teacher was forced to bow and say that his wife was quite free to do as she pleased. But, at the thought of the danger of the big fichu, an icy shiver had run down his spine, and as Mouret was just at that moment affirming that the new shops were increasing the well-being of middle-class families, he gave him a terrible look, the flash of hatred of a man too timid to murder people.

In any case the ladies had not parted with the lace. They were intoxicating themselves with it. Pieces were being unwound, coming and going from one woman to another, drawing them even closer together, linking them with light strands. Their guilty hands were lingering in their laps, where they could feel the caress of the miraculously fine material. And Mouret was even more tightly imprisoned by them, they were overwhelming him with further questions. As the daylight was continuing to fade, he sometimes had to bend his head down in order to examine a stitch, to point out a design, lightly brushing against their hair with his beard as he did so. But in the soft voluptuousness of dusk, surrounded by the warm odour of their shoulders, beneath the air of rapture which he affected, he nevertheless remained their master. He had something female in him, they felt themselves penetrated and possessed by the delicate understanding which he had for their secret selves and, won over by him, they were quite unconstrained; whereas he was looming up like some despotic king of fashion, brutally lording it over them, sure that from then onwards he had them at his mercy.

"Oh! Monsieur Mouret! Monsieur Mouret!" the whispering, rapturous voices were babbling out of the darkness in the drawing room.

The dying lights of the sky were fading in the brass work of the furniture. The laces alone retained a snowy glint on the dark laps of the ladies who surrounded the young man in a blurred group like the vague kneeling figures of devotees. A last gleam of light was shining on the side of the teapot, the short, bright glimmer of a night light burning in a bedchamber lukewarm with the perfume of tea. But suddenly the servant came in with two lamps and the charm was broken. Light and gay, the drawing room woke up. Madame Marty was putting the lace back in the depths of her little bag; Madame de Boves was eating another rum baba, while Henriette, who had got up, was talking in a low voice with the Baron in one of the window recesses.

"He's charming," said the Baron.

She let slip the unintentional remark of a woman in love: "Yes, isn't he?"

He smiled and looked at her with fatherly indulgence. It was the first time that he felt her conquered to such an extent and, being above suffering over it himself, he felt only compassion at seeing her in the hands of a fine young fellow like that, so loving and yet so completely unfeeling. And so, thinking that he should warn her, he murmured in a joking tone:

"Take care, my dear, he'll eat you up, all of you."

A spark of jealousy lit up Henriette's beautiful eyes. Doubtless she guessed that Mouret had simply made use of her in order to make contact with the Baron. She swore to herself she would make him mad with passion for her, for his love, the love of a busy man, had the facile charm of a song scattered to the winds.

"Oh!" she replied, pretending to joke in her turn. "In the end it's always the lamb that eats the wolf!"

At that the Baron, much intrigued, gave her an encouraging nod. Perhaps she was the woman who would come to revenge the others?

When Mouret, after repeating to Vallagnosc that he wanted to show him his machine in motion, came up to say goodbye, the Baron took him aside in a window recess facing the garden which was now black with darkness. At last he was succumbing to Mouret's charm; faith had come to him when he saw him amongst the ladies. They both talked for a moment in low voices. Then the banker declared:

"Well! I'll look into the matter… If your sale on Monday is as important as you say it will be, then the deal is on."

They shook hands, and Mouret, looking delighted, took his leave, for he did not enjoy his dinner in the evening if he had not first been to have a look at the takings at the Bonheur des Dames.

4

O N THAT PARTICULAR MONDAY, 10th October, a bright victorious sun pierced through the grey storm clouds which, for a week, had been making Paris gloomy. Throughout the night there had still been drizzle, a fine spray making the streets dirty with its moisture, but at daybreak the pavements had been wiped clean by the brisk gusts which were carrying the clouds away, and the blue sky had the limpid gaiety of springtime.

And so, from eight o'clock on, the Bonheur des Dames, in all the glory of its great sale of winter fashions, was blazing in rays of bright sunshine. Flags were waving at the door, woollen goods were flapping in the fresh morning air, enlivening the Place Gaillon with the hubbub of a fairground, and the windows facing the two streets were displaying symphonies of window dressing, the brilliant shades of which were further heightened by the translucence of the glass. It was an orgy of colours, the joy of the street bursting out there, the whole corner was a sumptuous spread openly displayed on which everyone could go and feast his eyes.

But at that time of day not many people were going in; there were only a few hurrying customers, local housewives, women who wished to avoid the afternoon crush. Behind the materials which decked it, one felt the shop was empty, armed and awaiting action, its floors polished and its counters overflowing with goods. The hurried morning crowd scarcely glanced at the shop windows, without slackening pace. In the Rue Neuve-Saint-Augustin and the Place Gaillon, where carriages were to be parked, there were merely two cabs at nine o'clock. Only local inhabitants, above all the small tradesmen, roused by such a display of streamers and plumes, were forming groups in doorways and at street corners, their noses in the air and making plenty of sour comments. Their indignation was aroused by the fact that in the Rue de la Michodière, outside the dispatch office, there stood one of the four carriages which Mouret had just launched on Paris – painted green, picked out with yellow and red, and with highly varnished panels which flashed gold and purple in the sunlight. Once it had been filled with parcels left over from the day before, the carriage which was standing there – with its new and gaudy colour scheme, with the name of the shop blazoned on its front and back and topped in addition by a placard bearing an announcement of the day's sale – finally went off at the trot, pulled by a superb horse. Baudu, standing livid on the threshold of Le Vieil Elbeuf, watched it bowling along as far as the boulevard, carrying the hated name of the Bonheur des Dames all over the town, surrounded by a starlike radiance.

Meanwhile, a few cabs were arriving and lining up. Each time a customer appeared there was a stir among the pageboys lined up beneath the high porch, dressed in a livery consisting of a grey coat and trousers and a yellow-and-red striped waistcoat. Jouve, the shopwalker, the retired captain, was there too, in frock coat and white tie, wearing his medal like a token of integrity of long standing, receiving the ladies with an air of solemn politeness and leaning towards them to show them the way to the departments. Then they would disappear into the lobby, which had been changed into an oriental hall.

No sooner had they passed the door than they were greeted with a surprise, a marvel which enraptured them all. It had been Mouret's idea. He had recently been the first to buy in the Levant, at very favourable terms, a collection of antique and modern carpets, of rare carpets such as until then had only been sold by antique dealers at very high prices, and he was going to flood the market with them, he was letting them go almost at cost price, simply using them as a splendid setting which would attract art connoisseurs to his shop. From the centre of Place

Gaillon one could catch a glimpse of this oriental hall, made entirely of carpets and door curtains, which the porters had hung up under his directions. First of all, on the ceiling, there were stretched carpets from Smyrna, the complicated designs of which stood out on red backgrounds. Then, on all four sides, were hung door curtains: door curtains from Kerman and from Syria, striped with green, yellow and vermilion; door curtains from Diyarbakir, more commonplace, harsher to the touch, like shepherds' tunics; and still more carpets which could be used as hangings, long carpets from Ispahan, from Teheran and Kermanshah, broader carpets from Schoumaka and Madras, a strange blossoming of peonies and palms, imagination running riot in a dream garden. On the ground there were still more carpets, thick fleeces were strewn there; in the centre there was a carpet from Agra, a remarkable specimen with a white background and a broad border of soft blue on which ran purplish embellishments of most exquisite invention; and there were other marvels displayed everywhere, carpets from Mecca with velvet glints, prayer rugs from Dagestan with the symbolic pointed design on them, carpets from Kurdistan strewn with full-blown flowers; finally, in a corner, there was a cascade of cheap rugs, rugs from Geurdis, from Kula and from Kirsehir, all in a heap, priced from fifteen francs upwards. This sumptuous pasha's tent was furnished with armchairs and divans made from camel bags, some scattered with designs of multicoloured lozenges, others covered with naive roses. Turkey, Arabia, Persia, the Indies were there. Palaces had been emptied, mosques and bazaars rifled. In the worn antique carpets tawny gold was the predominating tone, and their faded tints retained a sombre warmth, the smelting of some extinguished furnace, with the beautiful, fired colour of an old master. Visions of the Orient floated beneath the luxury of this barbaric art, in the midst of the strong odour which the old wools had retained from lands of vermin and sun.

In the morning at eight o'clock, when Denise, who was going to start work that very Monday, had crossed the oriental hall, she had been flabbergasted, no longer recognizing the entrance of the shop, her confusion compounded by this harem scene set up at the door. A porter had conducted her through the attics and had handed her over to Madame Cabin, who was in charge of the cleaning and the bedrooms, and who had installed her in No. 7, where her trunk had already been brought. It was a narrow mansard-roofed cell, with a hinged skylight window opening onto the roof and furnished with a small bed, a walnut-wood cupboard, a dressing table and two chairs. Twenty similar rooms led off the convent-like corridor which had been painted yellow, and out of the thirty-five girls in the shop, the twenty who had no home in Paris slept there, while the other fifteen lived out, some of them with fictitious aunts or cousins. Denise immediately took off her skimpy woollen dress, worn thin with brushing and darned on the sleeves, the only one she had brought from Valognes. Then she slipped on the uniform of her department, a black silk dress which had been altered for her and was waiting for her on the bed. The dress was still a little too big, too broad across the shoulders. But she was in such a hurry in her excitement that she did not linger over such details of elegance. She had never worn silk before. When she went downstairs again, all in her Sunday best and ill at ease, she looked at the gleaming skirt, and the loud rustling of the material made her feel ashamed.

Downstairs, as she was entering the department, a quarrel was breaking out. She heard Clara say in a shrill voice:

"I arrived before her, Madame."

"It's not true," Marguerite replied. "She pushed me at the door, but I already had one foot inside the salon."

It was a question of putting their names down on the roster which controlled their turns at selling. The salesgirls wrote down their names on a slate, in the order of their arrival, and each time they had had a customer, they would put down their names again at the bottom of the list. In the end Madame Aurélie took Marguerite's side.

"She's always unfair!" Clara murmured furiously.

But Denise's entrance reconciled the girls. They looked at her, then they smiled. How could anyone really be so dowdy! The girl went awkwardly to put her name down on the roster, in last place. Meanwhile Madame Aurélie was examining her with an anxious pursing of her lips. She could not refrain from saying:

"My dear, two of your size could fit into your dress. It'll have to be taken in... And then, you don't know how to dress yourself. Come here and let me arrange you a bit."

She led her to one of the tall mirrors, which alternated with the solid doors of the cupboards in which the garments were crammed together. The vast room, surrounded by the mirrors and by the carved oak woodwork and decorated with red moquette bearing a big floral design, resembled the commonplace lounge of a hotel which people are continually rushing through. The young ladies completed the resemblance, dressed as they were in the regulation silk, displaying their saleable graces without ever sitting down on the dozen chairs reserved for customers only. Each girl had a large pencil, seemingly plunged into her bosom between the two buttonholes of her bodice, with its point sticking out into the air, and the splash of white of a cashbook could be glimpsed half emerging from a pocket. Several of the girls ventured to wear jewellery, rings, brooches, necklaces, but their pride, the luxury which in the enforced uniformity of their dress they used as a weapon, was their bare heads, the profusion of their hair which, if it was insufficient, was augmented by plaits and chignons, combed, curled and flaunted.

"Now then, pull your belt in front," Madame Aurélie was repeating. "There, now at any rate you haven't got a bulge at the back… And your hair… how can you make such a mess of it! You could make it superb if you wanted to."

It was, indeed, Denise's only beauty. Ash blonde in colour, it reached to her ankles, and when she was doing her hair it got in her way to such an extent that she merely rolled it up in a pile and held it in place with the strong teeth of a horn comb. Clara, very annoyed by this hair, all tied up so askew in its untamed grace, was pretending to laugh at it. She had made a sign to a salesgirl from the lingerie department, a girl with a broad face and a kindly air. The two departments, which were adjacent, were always on hostile terms, but the girls sometimes got together in order to laugh at people.

"Mademoiselle Cugnot, just look at that mane!" repeated Clara, while Marguerite was nudging her with her elbow, also pretending to choke with laughter.

But the girl from the lingerie department was not in a joking mood. She had been watching Denise for a little while, she remembered what she had herself suffered during the first few months in her department.

"Well, and so what?" she said. "Not everyone has a mane like that!"

And she went back to the lingerie department, leaving the other two feeling abashed. Denise, who had overheard, watched her go with a look of gratitude, while Madame Aurélie was giving her a cashbook with her name on it, saying:

"Come now, tomorrow you'll make yourself tidier... And now try to pick up the ways of the shop, wait your turn for selling. Today will be a hard day, it'll give us a chance of judging what you're capable of."

Meanwhile, the department remained deserted, few customers went up to the dress departments at this early hour. Erect and inert, the girls were reserving their strength, preparing for the exertions of the afternoon. And Denise, intimidated by the thought that they were watching her first efforts, sharpened her pencil so as not to lose face; then, imitating the others, she plunged it into her bosom, between the two buttonholes. She was trying to make herself be brave, she must conquer her job. The day before she had been told that she would start work "au pair", in other words without a fixed salary; she would have only a percentage and a commission on the sales she made. But she hoped thus to earn at least twelve hundred francs, for she knew that good saleswomen could make as much as two thousand when they tried. Her budget was planned, a hundred francs a month would enable her to pay Pépé's board and lodging and to provide for Jean, who was not receiving a penny; she herself would be able to buy a few clothes and some underlinen. Only, in order to reach this considerable figure she must prove herself hard-working and strong, not take the ill will around her to heart, stand up for herself and seize her share from her companions if necessary. As she was thus working herself up for the struggle, a tall young man who was passing by the department smiled at her; when she recognized Deloche, who had started work the day before in the lace department, she returned his smile, happy to pick up this friendship again, seeing a good omen in his greeting.

At half-past nine a bell had rung for the first lunch service. Then a fresh peal summoned people to the second lunch. And still the customers did not come. The assistant buyer, Madame Frédéric, who with the surly tenseness of a widow took pleasure in gloomy thoughts, was swearing curtly that the day was lost; they would not see more than a couple of souls, they might as well close the cupboards and go home; this prediction made the moon face of Marguerite, who was very grasping, become gloomy, whereas Clara, like a runaway horse, was already dreaming of an outing to the woods at Verrières if the shop were to collapse. As to Madame Aurélie, she was walking about the empty department silent and grave, wearing her Caesar's mask, like a general who bears the responsibility for victory or defeat.

At about eleven o'clock a few ladies put in an appearance. Denise's turn to sell was coming. Just at that moment a customer was announced.

"That fat woman from the provinces, you know," murmured Marguerite.

She was a woman of forty-five who came to Paris from time to time from the depths of a distant county. There, for months, she saved up her pennies; then no sooner had she left the train than she would drop in at the Bonheur des Dames and spend it all. She rarely bought anything by post, for she wanted to see things, she took joy in touching the goods, she even went so far as to buy up stocks of needles which, she said, cost the earth in her small town. The whole shop knew her, knew that she was called Madame Boutarel, and that she lived in Albi, without caring any more about either her circumstances or indeed her existence.

"How are you, Madame?" Madame Aurélie, who had advanced, asked graciously. "And what can we do for you? Someone will help you immediately."

Then, turning round, she called:

"Mesdemoiselles!"

Denise was coming forwards, but Clara had made a dash. Usually she was lazy about selling, not caring about money as she earned more, and with less effort, outside. But the idea of cheating the new arrival out of a good customer was spurring her on.

"Excuse me, it's my turn," said Denise indignantly.

With a severe look Madame Aurélie motioned her aside, murmuring as she did so:

"There are no turns, I am the only person who gives orders here. Wait till you know something before serving regular customers."

The girl retired, and as tears were coming into her eyes and she wished to hide her over-sensitiveness, she turned her back, standing in front of the plate-glass windows and pretending to look at the street. Were they going to prevent her from selling? Would they all conspire like that to take away important sales from her? Fears for the future were seizing her, she felt herself crushed between all the different interests at play. And yielding to the bitterness of her abandonment, with her forehead against the cold glass, she was looking at the Vieil Elbeuf opposite, and feeling that she should have begged her uncle to keep her; perhaps he wished himself to go back on his decision, for he had seemed to her very upset the day before. Now she was quite alone in this huge shop where no one loved her, where she felt hurt and lost. Pépé and Jean, who had never left her side, were living with strangers; it was a wrench, and the two big tears which she was holding back were making the street dance in a mist.

Meanwhile, as she stood there, voices were buzzing behind her.

"This one makes me all bunched up," Madame Boutarel was saying.

"Madame is mistaken," Clara was repeating. "The shoulders fit perfectly... Unless Madame would rather have a pelisse than a coat."

Denise gave a start. A hand had been placed on her arm, Madame Aurélie was summoning her severely.

"What's this! You're not doing anything now, you're watching the passers-by? Oh, that won't do at all!"

"But as you won't let me sell, Madame—"

"There's other work for you, Mademoiselle. Begin at the beginning... Do the folding."

In order to satisfy the few customers who had arrived, the cupboards had already had to be turned upside down, and the two long oak tables, on the left and right of the salon, were littered with a jumble of coats, pelisses, cloaks, clothes of every size and in every material. Without replying, Denise set about sorting them, folding them carefully, and putting them away in the cupboards. It was the humblest job for beginners. She did not protest any more, knowing that passive obedience was demanded of her, biding her time until the buyer should agree to allow her to sell, as her original intention had seemed to have been. And she was still folding when Mouret appeared. It was a shock for her; she blushed, and thinking that he was going to speak to her, she once more felt herself overcome by her strange fear. But he did not even see her, he no longer remembered the little girl whom he had backed up because of the charming fleeting impression she had made on him.

"Madame Aurélie!" he called in a curt voice.

He was a little pale, but his eyes were clear and resolute all the same. On going round the departments he had just discovered that they were empty, and in spite of his obstinate faith in luck, the possibility of defeat had suddenly loomed up. Of course, it was scarcely eleven o'clock; he knew from experience that the crowd never arrived before the afternoon. Only certain symptoms were worrying him: at other sales there had been some activity from the morning onwards, and on top of that he could not even see any of those hatless women, local customers, who used to drop in on him as neighbours. Like all great captains when joining battle, he had been overcome by a moment of superstitious weakness, in spite his habitual man-of-action disposition. It would not be a success, he was lost, and he could not have said why: he thought he could read his defeat on the very faces of the ladies who were passing.

At that moment Madame Boutarel, who always bought things, was departing, saying as she did so:

"No, you haven't anything I like... I'll see, I'll think about it."

Mouret watched her go. And, as Madame Aurélie was hastening towards him at his summons, he took her aside; they exchanged a few rapid words. She made a gesture of regret, she was obviously replying that the sale was not warming up. For a moment they remained facing each other, overcome with the kind of doubt which generals hide from their troops. Then he said out aloud, with a gallant air:

"If you need any staff, take a girl from the workroom... She would be some help to you, after all."

He went on with his inspection, in despair. Since the morning he had been avoiding Bourdoncle, whose anxious remarks irritated him. As he was leaving the lingerie department, where the sale was going even worse, he ran into him and had to endure Bourdoncle expressing his fears. Then, with a brutality which even his important employees were not spared in black moments, he told him straight out to go to the devil.

"Shut up, can't you! Everything is all right... I shall end up by kicking all the milksops out into the street."

Standing alone, Mouret planted himself beside the hall balustrade. From there he dominated the shop, for he had the mezzanine departments around him and was looking down into the ground-floor departments. Upstairs, the emptiness seemed heart-breaking to him: in the lace department an old lady was having all the boxes ransacked without buying anything; while in the lingerie department three good-for-nothing girls were taking their time over choosing ninety-centime collars. Downstairs, beneath the covered arcades, in shafts of light coming from the street, he noticed that the customers were beginning to be more numerous. It was a slow procession with wide gaps in it, a stroll past the counters; women in jackets were crowding round the haberdashery, the hosiery, but there was hardly anyone in the household-linen or woollen-goods departments. The pageboys, in their green uniform with shining brass buttons, arms dangling, were waiting for people to arrive. From time to time a shopwalker would pass by with a ceremonious air, stiff in his white tie. But it was, above all, the deathly peace of the hall which made Mouret's heart ache; the daylight was falling on it from above through a roof of frosted glass, filtered into diffused white dust suspended over the silk department, which seemed to be sleeping in the midst of the cold silence of a chapel. Only the footsteps of an assistant, whispered words, the rustle of a skirt passing by, made light sounds there, muffled by the warmth from the central heating. However, carriages were arriving: the sound of the horses suddenly coming to a standstill could be heard; then doors would be slammed to again. A distant hubbub was coming from the street – a hubbub of the curious jostling each other opposite the shop windows, of hackney cabs parking in the Place Gaillon, all the sounds of a crowd drawing nearer... But Mouret, seeing the idle cashiers leaning back behind their cash-desk windows, and the table for parcels, with their boxes of string and their quires of blue paper, remaining bare, was furious with himself for being afraid, and thought he could feel the great shop slowing down to a standstill and growing cold beneath his feet.

"I say, Favier," murmured Hutin, "look at the boss, up there... He doesn't look very happy!"

"What a rotten hole this is!" Favier replied. "To think that I haven't sold a thing yet!"

Both of them, while keeping on the lookout for customers, were thus whispering short phrases without looking at each other. The other salesmen of the department were in the process of piling up lengths of Paris-Bonheur, under Robineau's orders, while Bouthemont, deep in conference with a thin young woman, was seemingly taking an important order in undertones. Around them the silks, on elegant, frail shelves, folded up in long sheaths of cream-coloured paper, were piled up like strange-looking pamphlets. And the fancy silks littering the counters, the moiré fabrics, the satins, the velvets, seemed like flower beds of mown blooms, a whole harvest of delicate and costly materials. It was the department of elegance, a veritable drawing room, in which the goods were so ethereal that they seemed no more than a luxurious furnishing.

"I must have a hundred francs for Sunday," Hutin resumed. "If I don't make at least my twelve francs a day, I'm done for... I was counting on this sale of theirs."

"By Jove! A hundred francs, that's a bit stiff," said Favier. "I only want fifty or sixty... So you treat yourself to smart women, do you?"

"Oh no, old chap, I don't. You know, I did something silly! I made a bet, and I lost... So I've got to square up with five people, two men and three women... What a damned awful morning this is! I'll sock the first woman that passes for twenty yards of Paris-Bonheur!"

They went on chatting for another moment, they told each other what they had done the day before, and what they hoped to do in a week's time. Favier backed horses, Hutin went in for boating and kept cabaret singers. But the same need for money spurred them both on, they dreamt of nothing but money, they fought for it from Monday to Saturday, and then they spent it all on Sunday. In the shop they were tyrannized by this preoccupation, it was a struggle, a struggle with no respite. And there was that cunning fellow Bouthemont, who had just appropriated for himself the woman sent by Madame Sauveur, that thin woman with whom he was chatting! It would be a splendid deal, two or three dozen lengths of material, for the great dressmaker had a large appetite. And a moment earlier Robineau, too, had taken it into his head to pinch one of Favier's customers!

"Oh! Him! We'll have to get even with him," resumed Hutin, who took advantage of the slightest thing in order to rouse the department against the man whose place he wished to have. "The buyer and assistant buyer aren't meant to sell! Word of honour, old chap, if ever I become assistant buyer, you'll see how kind I'll be to all the rest of you!"

And the whole of his small, Norman person, fat and round, was strenuously exuding an air of bonhomie. Favier could not help giving him a sideways look, but he maintained the impassiveness of a morose man, and was content to reply:

"Yes, I know... So far as I'm concerned, I'd be delighted."

Then, seeing a lady approaching, he added in a lower voice:

"Look out! Here's one for you."

She was a woman with a blotchy complexion, in a yellow hat and a red dress. Hutin immediately scented the sort of woman who would not buy anything. He dropped smartly down behind the counter, pretending to do up the laces of one of his shoes; thus hidden, he murmured:

"Not on your life! Let someone else have her... Thanks very much! And lose my turn!..."

However, Robineau was calling him.

"Whose turn is it, gentlemen? Monsieur Hutin's? Where is Monsieur Hutin?"

And as the latter was obviously not replying, it was the salesman who came after him on the roster who served the blotchy lady. She did, indeed, only require some patterns, together with the prices, and she kept the salesman for more than ten minutes, overwhelming him with questions. But the assistant buyer had seen Hutin stand up again behind the counter. And so when a fresh customer turned up he interposed with a stern air and stopped the young man who was dashing forwards.

"Your turn has gone... I called you, and as you were there behind—"

"But I didn't hear, sir."

"That's enough! Put your name down at the bottom... Come along, Monsieur Favier, it's your turn."

Favier, who was really very amused by the incident, apologized to his friend with a glance. Hutin, his lips pale, had turned his head away. What infuriated him was that it was a customer he knew well, a charming, fair woman who often came to the department and whom the salesmen among themselves called "the pretty lady", although they knew nothing about her, not even her name. She used to buy a great deal, would have it carried to her carriage, and then would disappear. Tall, elegant, dressed with exquisite charm, she appeared to be very rich and from the highest society.

"Well, how was that tart of yours?" Hutin asked Favier, when the latter came back from the cash desk to which he had accompanied the lady.

"A tart?" Favier replied. "No, she looks much too genteel... I should think she must be the wife of a stockbroker or a doctor, well, I don't know, something in that line."

"Oh, go on! She's a tart... It's impossible to tell nowadays, they all have the airs of refined ladies!"

Favier looked at his cashbook.

"It doesn't matter!' he went on, "I've stung her for two hundred and ninety-three francs. That means nearly three francs for me."

Hutin pursed his lips and vented his malice on the cashbooks – another ridiculous invention which was cluttering up their pockets! There was a secret struggle between the two men. Usually Favier pretended to take a back seat, to acknowledge Hutin's superiority, so as to be free to attack him from the rear. And that was why the latter was taking so much to heart the three francs which a salesman whom he did not consider to be of the same calibre as himself had pocketed so easily. Really, what a day! If it went on like that he would not earn enough to treat his guests to soda water. And in the teeth of the battle which was warming up, he was walking round the counters, his tongue hanging out, wanting his share, even jealous of his superior, who was seeing the thin young woman off, repeating to her as he did so:

"Very well, it's settled. Tell her that I'll do my best to obtain favourable rates for her from Monsieur Mouret."

For some time now Mouret had no longer been standing by the hall balustrade on the mezzanine floor. Suddenly he reappeared at the top of the main staircase which led to the ground floor; from there he could still look over the whole shop. The colour was coming back into his face, which seemed larger now that his faith was being reborn again at the sight of the surge of people which little by little was filling the shop. At last the long-awaited rush had come, the afternoon crush of which he had for a moment despaired in his fever of anxiety; all the assistants were at their posts, a last bell had just rung for the end of the third lunch service; the disastrous morning, due no doubt to a downpour at about nine o'clock, could still be made good, for the blue sky of the morning had regained its victorious gaiety once more. Now that the mezzanine departments were coming to life he had to stand back in order to let the ladies pass, as they went upstairs in little groups to the lingerie and gowns; while behind him, in the lace and shawl departments, he could hear big figures being bandied about. But he was reassured above all by the sight of the ground-floor galleries. There was a crush of people in the haberdashery, the household-linen and wool departments were overrun as well, the procession of customers was becoming denser, and almost all of them were wearing hats now, there were only a few bonnets of belated housewives. In the silk hall, under the pale light, ladies had taken off their gloves in order gently to feel pieces of Paris-Bonheur, while talking in low voices. And he could no longer have any doubt about the sounds which were reaching him from outside, the rattle of carriages, the banging of doors, the growing hum of the crowd. Beneath his feet he felt the machine getting underway, warming up and coming to life again, from the cash desks, where there was the clink of gold, to the tables, where the porters were hurrying to pack up the goods, down to the very depths of the basement, where the dispatch department was filling up with parcels being sent down to it and making the shop vibrate with its subterranean rumble. In the midst of the mob Inspector Jouve was walking about solemnly, on the lookout for thieves.

"Why! It's you!" said Mouret suddenly, recognizing Paul de Vallagnosc who was being brought towards him by a pageboy. "No, no, you're not disturbing me… And, in any case, you may as well follow me round if you want to see everything, for today I'm staying on the bridge."

He still had misgivings. There was no doubt that people were coming, but would the sale be the triumph he had hoped for? Nevertheless, he was laughing with Paul and gaily led him away.

"It seems to be warming up a bit," said Hutin to Favier. "But I haven't any luck, some days have a hoodoo on them, honestly!

I've just missed another sale, that wretch didn't buy anything from me."

With his chin he indicated a woman who was leaving and looking with disgust at all the materials as she did so. He wouldn't grow fat on his salary of a thousand francs if he did not sell anything; usually he made seven or eight francs in percentages or commission, which meant that he had, including his salary, an average of about ten francs a day. Favier had never earned more than eight, and here was the clout taking the food out of his very mouth, for he was just selling another dress length. An unresponsive fellow, who had never known how to warm up a customer! It was exasperating!

"The sockers and reelers look as though they're coining money," Favier murmured, referring to the salesmen of the hosiery and haberdashery departments.

But Hutin, who was searching the shop with a look, said suddenly:

"Do you know Madame Desforges, the boss's girlfriend? There… that dark woman in the glove department, the one who is having gloves tried on by Mignot."

He fell silent and then, as if talking to Mignot, from whom he did not take his eyes, he resumed:

"Go on, go on, old fellow, give her fingers a good squeeze, for all the good it may do you! We know all about your conquests, don't we!"

There existed between him and the glove assistant the rivalry of two good-looking men, both of whom pretended to flirt with the customers. Neither of them could in fact boast of any real good fortune; Mignot lived on the myth of a police superintendent's wife who had fallen in love with him, whereas Hutin had really made the conquest in the department of a trimmer who was tired of hanging about the shady hotels of the neighbourhood, but both Mignot and Hutin lied about it, they were only too pleased to let people believe that they had mysterious adventures, trysts made with countesses between purchases.

"You should deal with her yourself," said Favier in his astringent way.

"That's an idea!" Hutin cried. "If she comes here, I'd get round her at the drop of a hat!"

In the glove department there was a whole row of ladies seated in front of the narrow counter which was spread with green velvet and had nickel-plated corners; the smiling assistants were stacking up in front of the customers flat, bright pink boxes, which they were taking out of the counter itself, like the labelled draws of a file case. Mignot, in particular, was leaning forwards with his pretty baby face, and speaking in tender accents, rolling his Rs like the Parisian he was. He had already sold twelve pairs of kid gloves, Bonheur gloves, the shop's speciality, to Madame Desforges. She had next asked for three pairs of suede gloves. And she was now trying some Saxe gloves on, for fear that the size was not right.

"Oh! It's absolutely perfect, Madame!" Mignot was repeating. "Six and three quarters would be too big for a hand like yours."

Half-lying on the counter, he was holding her hand, taking her fingers one by one and sliding the glove on with a long, practised and sustained caress, and he was looking at her as if he expected to see from her face that she was swooning with voluptuous joy. But she, her elbow on the edge of the velvet, her fist raised, handed over her fingers to him with the same tranquil air with which she would give her foot to her maid in order to have her boots buttoned. He was not a man, she made use of him for such intimate services with the familiar contempt she had for those in her employ, without even looking at him.

"I'm not hurting you, Madame?"

She replied in the negative, with a sign of her head.

The smell of Saxe gloves, that smell of deer with a dash of sweetened musk, usually excited her, and she would laugh about it sometimes, she would confess that she had a liking for this ambiguous perfume, which is as if an animal in heat has landed in a woman's powder box. But standing at that commonplace counter she did not smell the gloves, they did not engender any sensual ardour between her and the very ordinary salesman simply doing his job.

"Is there anything else you want, Madame?"

"Nothing, thank you... Would you take that to No. 10 cash desk, for Madame Desforges, you know?..."

Being a regular customer at the shop, she gave her name at a cash desk, and sent each of her purchases there, without having to go there herself with an assistant. When she had left, Mignot winked as he turned towards his neighbour, whom he would have had believe that wonderful things had just taken place.

"She's glovable all over, isn't she?" he murmured crudely.

Meanwhile Madame Desforges was continuing her purchases. She turned to the left, stopped in the household linen department to get some dishcloths; then she went all round, penetrated as far as the woollens at the end of the gallery. As she was pleased with her cook, she wished to give her a dress. The woollen department was overflowing with a dense crowd; all the lower-middle-class women had repaired there and were fingering the materials, absorbed in silent calculations; she had to sit down for a moment. On the shelves were piled thick lengths of material, which with a jerk of their arms the salesmen were taking down, one by one. As a result they were beginning to be quite confused among the swamped counters, where the materials were mingling and overflowing. It was a rising tide of neutral tints, of the muted tones of wool, iron greys, yellowish greys, blue greys, with here and there splashes of colour made by a Scottish plaid, a blood-red background of flannel bursting out. And the white labels of the rolls were like a flight of sparse white snowflakes speckling black earth in December.

Behind a pile of poplin Liénard was joking with a big hatless girl, a local seamstress sent by her employer to stock up with merino cloth. He hated these big sale days which tired out his arms, and since he was largely kept by his father and did not care whether he sold or not, he tried to dodge work, doing just enough to keep him from being thrown out.

"I say, Mademoiselle Fanny," he was saying. "You're always in a hurry... was the checked vicuña a success, the other day? You know, I shall come and get a commission from you."

But the seamstress was making her escape, laughing as she did so, and Liénard found himself facing Madame Desforges, whom he could not help asking:

"What does Madame require?"

She wanted something for a dress, inexpensive but hard-wearing. Liénard, aiming at sparing his arms, for that was his sole concern, manoeuvred so as to make her take one of the materials already unfolded on the counter. There were cashmeres there, serges, vicuñas, he swore to her that nothing finer existed, there was no end to them. But none of them seemed to satisfy her.

She had glimpsed a bluish serge twill on a shelf. So in the end he reluctantly brought himself to get down the serge twill, which she said was too coarse. Next was a cheviot, then materials with diagonal stripes, salt-and-pepper cloth, every variety of woollen material, which she was curious to touch for sheer pleasure, though she had decided in her heart of hearts that she would just buy anything. So the young man was obliged to empty the highest shelves, his shoulders were breaking, the counter had disappeared beneath the silky texture of cashmeres and poplins, the harsh nap of cheviots, and the fluffy down of vicuñas. Every material and every shade was to be seen there. She asked to be shown grenadine and Chambéry gauze without even having the slightest desire to buy any. Then, when she had had enough, she said:

"Oh well! Really, the first is still the best. It's for my cook... Yes, the serge with the little dots, the one at two francs."

And when Liénard, pale with restrained anger, had measured it out, she said:

"Will you take it to No. 10 cash desk... For Madame Desforges."

As she was going away she caught sight of Madame Marty nearby, accompanied by her daughter Valentine, a big, lanky girl of fourteen, forward in manner and already casting the guilty glances of a woman at the goods.

"Why! It's you, my dear?"

"Yes, dear... What a crowd, isn't it?"

"Oh! Don't talk to me about it, it's stifling. What a success! Have you seen the oriental hall?"

"Superb! Amazing!"

And, elbowed and jostled by the growing mass of hard-up women who were falling on the inexpensive woollens, they went into ecstasies over the exhibition of carpets. Next, Madame Marty explained that she was looking for some material for a coat, but she had not made up her mind, she wanted to see some woollen matelassé.

"But just look at it. Maman," murmured Valentine, "it's too common."

"Come to the silks," said Madame Desforges. "We must see their famous Paris-Bonheur."

For a moment Madame Marty hesitated. It would be very expensive, she had so expressly sworn to her husband that she would be sensible! She had been buying for an hour already, a whole batch of articles was following her – a muff and ruching for herself, stockings for her daughter. In the end she said to the assistant who was showing her the matelassé:

"Well, no! I'm going to the silks… None of that is what I'm looking for."

The assistant took the articles and walked ahead of the ladies.

The crowd had reached the silk department too. Above all there was a crush before the interior display arranged by Hutin, to which Mouret had added masterly touches. At the end of the hall, surrounding one of the small cast-iron columns which held up the glass roof, material was streaming down like a bubbling sheet of water, falling from above and broadening out to the floor. First, pale satins and soft silks were gushing out: duchess satins, renaissance satins, in the pearly shades of spring water – light silks as transparent as crystal, Nile green, turquoise, blossom pink, Danube blue. Next came the thicker materials, the marvellous satins, royal satins, in warm shades flowing in rising waves. And at the foot, as if in the basin of a fountain, the heavy materials, the damasks, the brocades, the silks encrusted with pearls and gold, were sleeping on a deep bed of velvets – velvets of all kinds, black, white, coloured, embossed on a background of silk or of satin, their shimmering flecks forming a motionless lake in which glints of the sky and of the countryside seemed to dance. Women pale with desire were leaning over as if to see their reflections. Faced with this unleashed cataract, they all remained standing there, filled with the fear of being caught up in that overflow of luxury and with an irresistible desire to throw themselves into it and be lost.

"Why, so you're here, are you?" said Madame Desforges, on finding Madame Bourdelais installed in front of a counter.

"Ah! Good day to you!" the latter replied, shaking hands with them. "Yes, I came in to have a look."

"It's stupendous, this display, isn't it? A dream… And the oriental hall, have you seen the oriental hall?"

"Yes, yes, extraordinary!"

But beneath this enthusiasm, which was certainly going to be the fashionable attitude of the day, Madame Bourdelais was keeping her composure as a practical housewife. She was carefully examining a piece of Paris-Bonheur, for she had come solely in order to take advantage of the exceptional cheapness of this silk, if she should consider it really good value. Doubtless she was satisfied, for she ordered twenty-five yards, reckoning that she would easily be able to cut a dress for herself and a coat for her little girl out of it.

"What! You're going already?" Madame Desforges resumed. "Come and have a look round with us, do."

"No, thank you, they're expecting me at home... I didn't want to risk bringing the children in a crowd like this."

And she went away preceded by the salesman carrying the twenty-five yards of silk; he conducted her to No. 10 cash desk, where young Albert was quite losing his head in the midst of all the requests for invoices with which he was being besieged. When the salesman could get near, he called out the sale he had made, after having entered it with a pencil stroke on his counterfoil book, and the cashier wrote it down in the register; then it was counter-checked, and the detached page from the counterfoil book was stuck on an iron spike near the receipt stamp.

"A hundred and forty francs," said Albert.

Madame Bourdelais paid and gave her address, for she had come on foot and did not want to have anything to carry. Behind the cash desk Joseph was already holding the silk and was packing it up, and the parcel, thrown into a basket on wheels, was sent down to the dispatch department, into which all the goods from the shop now seemed to be rushing with a noise like a weir.

Meanwhile, the congestion was becoming so great in the silk department that Madame Desforges and Madame Marty were not able to find a free assistant at first. They remained standing, mingling with the crowd of ladies who were looking at the materials, feeling them, remaining there for hours without making up their minds. Everything pointed to a great success above all for the Paris-Bonheur, for one of those waves of enthusiasm, the sudden fever of which sets a fashion in one day, was growing around it. The salesmen were all occupied only in measuring that silk; above the hats the pale light of the unfolded lengths could be seen shimmering, while fingers were moving all the time up and down the oak yard measures hanging from brass shafts; the noise of scissors biting into the material could be heard, and they did so without a pause, as fast as it was unpacked, as if there were not enough arms to satisfy the voracious, outstretched hands of the customers.

"It really isn't bad for five francs sixty," said Madame Desforges, who had succeeded in securing a piece of it from the edge of a table.

Madame Marty and her daughter Valentine were feeling disillusioned. The newspapers had talked about it so much that they had expected something with more body to it, more lustrous. But Bouthemont had just recognized Madame Desforges and, wishing to pay court to a beautiful creature who was reputed to hold the director completely in her power, he was coming towards her with his rather uncouth good nature. What? She was not being served! It was unpardonable! She must be lenient with them, they really didn't know where to look for shame. And he searched for some chairs amidst the surrounding skirts, laughing with his good-natured laugh in which a brutal love of women was discernible, which Henriette did not, apparently, find unattractive.

"I say," murmured Favier as he went to get a roll of velvet from a shelf behind Hutin, "there's Bouthemont doing that special customer of yours."

Hutin had forgotten Madame Desforges, for he was beside himself with rage with an old lady who, having kept him for a quarter of an hour, had just bought a yard of black satin for a corset. During rush hours they no longer kept to the roster, salesmen served customers as they came. He was replying to Madame Boutarel, who was finishing off her afternoon at the Bonheur des Dames, where she had already spent three hours in the morning, when Favier's warning gave him a start. Was he going to miss the director's girlfriend, out of whom he had sworn to make five francs? That would be the crowning piece of bad luck, for he had not so far made three francs for himself, in spite of all the skirts cluttering up the place!

Just then Bouthemont was repeating very loudly:

"Come now, gentlemen, someone this way, please!"

At that Hutin handed Madame Boutarel over to Robineau, who was not doing anything.

"Here you are, Madame, ask the assistant buyer... he'll be able to tell you better than I can."

He made a dash and got the salesman who had accompanied the ladies from the woollens to hand Madame Marty's articles over to him. Nervous excitement must have upset his delicate flair that day. Usually, from his first glance at a woman, he could tell if she would buy, and how much. Then he would dominate the customer, hurrying to get rid of her in order to move on to another, and he would force her to make up her mind by persuading her that he knew what material she wanted better than she did.

"What kind of silk, Madame?" he asked in his most courteous manner.

Madame Desforges was scarcely opening her mouth when he went on:

"I know, I've just what you want."

When the length of Paris-Bonheur had been unfolded on a narrow stretch of counter between piles of other silks, Madame Marty and her daughter drew nearer. Hutin, rather worried, gathered that it was a question of supplying them first of all. Words were being exchanged in undertones, Madame Desforges was advising her friend.

"Oh! There's no question about it," she murmured, "a silk at five francs sixty will never be equal to one at fifteen, or even at ten francs."

"It's very thin," Madame Marty was repeating. "I'm afraid it hasn't got enough body for a coat."

This remark made the salesman intervene. He had the exaggerated politeness of a man who cannot be in the wrong.

"But, Madame, suppleness is one of the qualities of this silk. It does not crease... It's precisely what you need."

Impressed by such assurance, the ladies were silent. They had picked up the material again and were examining it once more when they felt a touch on their shoulders. It was Madame Guibal, who had been walking through the shop at a leisurely pace for an hour already, feasting her eyes on the piled-up riches, without having bought so much as a yard of calico. Yet another outburst of chatter took place on the spot.

"Why! You of all people!"

"Yes, it's me, just a bit knocked about, that's all!"

"Yes, isn't one? What a crowd, one can't get round... What about the oriental hall?"

"Entrancing!"

"My goodness! What a success... Do wait a moment, we'll go upstairs together."

"No thank you, I've just come from there."

Hutin was waiting, hiding his impatience beneath a smile which was never absent from his lips. How much longer were they going to keep him there? Really, women had a nerve, it was just as if they had stolen money out of his very pocket. Finally, Madame Guibal withdrew in order to continue her slow stroll, going round and round the great display of silks with an air of delight.

"If I were you, I'd buy the coat ready-made," said Madame Desforges, coming back to the Paris-Bonheur. "It'll cost you less."

"It's true that what with the trimmings and having it made up..." murmured Madame Marty. "And then one has a selection to choose from."

The three ladies had risen to their feet. Madame Desforges went up to Hutin and resumed:

"Would you kindly conduct us to the ready-made department?"

Unaccustomed to defeats of this kind, he was staggered. What! the dark-haired lady was not buying anything! His instinct had let him down then! He abandoned Madame Marty, and turned all his attention to Henriette, trying out his powers as a good salesman on her.

"And you, Madame, don't you wish to see our satins, our velvets? We have some remarkable bargains."

"No, thank you, another time," she replied calmly, not looking at him any more than she had at Mignot.

Hutin had to pick up Madame Marty's things again and walk ahead of them in order to conduct them to the ready-made department. He had the additional grief of seeing that Robineau was in the process of selling a large quantity of silk to Madame Boutarel. He certainly had lost his good nose and no mistake, he wouldn't make a penny. Beneath his pleasant, polite manner, the rage of a man who has been robbed and devoured by others was embittering him.

"On the first floor, Mesdames," he said, without ceasing to smile.

It was no longer easy to reach the staircase. A compact surge of heads was flowing through the arcades, broadening out into an overflowing river in the centre of the hall. A real commercial battle was developing, the salesmen were holding the multitude of women at their mercy, and were passing them over from one to another, vying with each other for speed. The hour of the tremendous afternoon rush had come, the overheated machine was calling the tune to the customers and extracting money from their very flesh. In the silk department, above all, there was madness in the air, the Paris-Bonheur had attracted such a crowd that for several minutes Hutin could not advance a step. When Henriette, suffocating there, looked up, she glimpsed Mouret at the top of the stairs, for he always came back to the same place from where he could watch the victory. She smiled, hoping that he would come down and extricate her. But he could not even distinguish her in the throng, he was still with Vallagnosc, busy showing him the shop, his face radiant with triumph. By now the commotion inside was muffling the sounds from the street; the rumbling of cabs and the banging of doors could no longer be heard; beyond the huge murmur of the sale there remained nothing but a sensation of the vastness of Paris – a city so vast that it would always be able to supply customers. In the still air, in which the stifling central heating brought out the smell of materials, the hubbub was increasing, composed of every imaginable sound – of the continuous trampling of feet, of the same sentences repeated a hundred times at the counters, of gold ringing on the brass of the cash desks which were being besieged by a scrimmage of purses, of baskets on wheels with their loads of parcels falling without respite into the gaping cellars. In the end everything was becoming intermingled under a fine dust, the divisions between departments were no longer recognizable; over there, the haberdashery seemed swamped; further on, in the household linen, a ray of sunlight coming through the window facing the Rue Neuve-Saint-Augustin was like a golden arrow in the snow; there in the woollen and glove departments, a dense mass of hats and hair was cutting off the far confines of the shop from sight. Even the clothes of the crowd could no longer be seen, only headdresses, gaudy with feathers and ribbons, were floating on the surface; a few men's hats were making black smudges, whereas the pale complexions of the women, tired out and feeling the heat, were acquiring the translucency of camelias. Finally, thanks to some strenuous elbow work, Hutin opened up a pathway for the ladies by walking ahead of them. When she reached the top of the stairs Henriette could no longer find Mouret, who had just plunged Vallagnosc into the very middle of the crowd in order to make him even more dazed, and also because he himself felt overcome with a physical longing to breathe in success. He could feel it there, pressing against his limbs, as if he was holding all his customers in a long embrace, which made him delightfully out of breath.

"To the left, Mesdames," said Hutin in a voice which was still courteous in spite of his growing exasperation.

Upstairs there was the same congestion. Even the furniture department, usually the quietest, was being invaded. The shawls, the furs, the underwear departments were teeming with people. As the ladies were going through the lace department, they once more ran into people they knew. Madame de Boves was there with her daughter Blanche, both deep in the articles which Deloche was showing them. Hutin, parcel in hand, once more had to make a halt.

"Good afternoon! I was just thinking about you."

"And I was looking for you. But how can one possibly find anyone in such a crowd?"

"It's marvellous, isn't it?"

"Dazzling, my dear. We can scarcely stand any longer."

"You're buying things?"

"Oh no! We're just looking. It rests us a bit to sit down."

Madame de Boves who, as a matter of fact, had nothing but her fare home in her purse, was asking for all manner of lace to be taken out of the boxes for the pleasure of seeing and touching it. She had sensed that Deloche was the type of inexperienced salesman, awkward and slow, who dares not resist ladies' whims, she was taking advantage of his scared obligingness and had already kept him for half an hour, asking all the time for fresh articles. The counter was overflowing, she was plunging her hands into the growing cascade of pillow lace, Mechlin lace, valenciennes, Chantilly, her fingers trembling with desire, her face gradually warming up with sensual joy; whereas at her side Blanche, obsessed by the same passion, was very pale, her flesh puffy and flabby.

Meanwhile, the conversation was continuing; Hutin, motionless, awaiting their convenience, could have slapped them.

"Why!" said Madame Marty, "you're looking at scarves and veils just like mine."

It was true; Madame de Boves, who had been tormented by Madame Marty's laces since the preceding Saturday, had not been able to resist the urge at least to touch the same patterns, since owing to the straitened circumstances in which her husband kept her she was unable to take them away. She blushed slightly, and explained that Blanche had wished to see some Spanish-lace scarves. Then she added:

"You're going to the ready-made clothes... Very well! We'll see you later. Shall we meet in the oriental hall?"

"All right, in the oriental hall... It's wonderful, isn't it?"

They took leave of each other, going into raptures as they did so in the midst of the congestion caused by a sale of inexpensive insertions and small trimmings. Deloche, happy to have something to do, had started emptying the boxes for mother and daughter once more. And slowly, among the groups crowded all along the counters, Jouve the shopwalker was walking with his military gait, flaunting his medal, watching over those precious, choice goods which could so easily be hidden in the depths of a sleeve. As he passed behind Madame de Boves he cast a quick glance at her feverish hands, surprised at seeing her with her arms plunged in such a cascade of lace.

"To the right, Madame," said Hutin, setting off once more.

He was beside himself. As if it wasn't enough to make him miss a sale downstairs! Now they were holding him up at every turning! His irritation was, above all, full of the resentment felt by departments selling material against those selling manufactured goods; they were continually at daggers drawn, wrangling over customers, cheating each other out of their percentages and commissions. Those in the silk department, more even than those in the woollen materials, were maddened when they had to conduct to the ready-made clothes department a lady who had finally decided to buy a coat after having asked to see taffetas and failles.

"Mademoiselle Vadon!" said Hutin, when he finally reached the counter, in a voice which was becoming annoyed.

But she passed by without taking any notice, absorbed by a sale which she was hurrying to finish. The room was full, a queue of people was going through it at one end, entering and leaving it by the doors of the lace and lingerie departments, which faced each other, whilst in the background customers who had taken off their outdoor things were trying on clothes, arching their backs in front of the looking glasses. The red moquette muffled the sound of footsteps, the shrill, remote voice of the ground floor was dying away, there was nothing but a discreet murmur, the warmth of a drawing room made oppressive by a whole mob of women.

"Mademoiselle Prunaire!" cried Hutin.

And since she did not stop either, he added inaudibly between his teeth:

"You old monkeys!"

He certainly wasted no love on them; his legs were aching from going upstairs to bring them customers, and he was furious about the earnings which he accused them of taking out of his pocket in this way. It was a secret struggle, in which the girls showed just as much asperity as he did, and in their common weariness, always on their feet as they were, dead to the flesh, the sexes disappeared and nothing remained but opposing interests inflamed by the fever of business.

"Well, isn't there anyone here?" Hutin asked.

Then he caught sight of Denise. She had been busy unfolding things since the morning, she had only been allowed to deal with a few unlikely sales, which in any case she had failed to bring off. When he recognized her, busy clearing an enormous pile of clothes off a table, he ran to fetch her.

"Here, Mademoiselle, do serve these ladies who are waiting."

He quickly put Madame Marty's things, which he was sick of carrying about, into her arms. His smile was coming back, and there was in it the secret malice of an experienced salesman with a shrewd idea of the trouble he was going to cause both the ladies and the girl. Meanwhile, the latter was quite overcome by the prospect of this unexpected sale. For the second time he was appearing like some unknown friend, brotherly and affectionate, always waiting in the background to come to her assistance. Her eyes shone with gratitude; with a lingering glance she watched him go, elbowing his way out in order to get back to his department as quickly as possible.

"I would like to see some coats," said Madame Marty.

Denise questioned her. What kind of coat? But the customer did not know, had no idea, she just wanted to see what models the shop had. And the girl, already very tired, deafened by the crowd, lost her head; she had never served anyone but the rare customers in Valognes; she did not yet know how many models there were, or where they were kept in the cupboards. She was taking an endless time to comply with the request of the two friends, who were growing impatient, when Madame Aurélie caught sight of Madame Desforges, of whose liaison she was presumably aware, for she hastened to come and ask:

"Are these ladies being attended to?"

"Yes, by the young lady who is looking for something over there," Henriette replied. "But she doesn't seem to know very much about it, she can't find anything."

At that, the buyer finally paralysed Denise completely by going and saying to her in a low voice:

"You see yourself that you don't know a thing. Don't interfere, please."

And she called out:

"Mademoiselle Vadon, coats please!"

She stayed there while Marguerite was showing the models. With the customers the latter affected a curtly polite voice, the disagreeable attitude of a girl clad in silk, used to rubbing shoulders with the smartest people, yet jealous and resentful of them without even realizing it herself. When she heard Madame Marty say that she did not wish to spend more than two hundred francs, she pursed her lips in pity. Oh, Madame should spend more than that, it would be impossible for Madame to find anything decent for two hundred francs! And she threw down the common coats onto a counter with a gesture as if to say: "You see what trash they are!" Madame Marty did not dare tell her that she liked them. She leant across to whisper into Madame Desforges's ear:

"I say, don't you prefer being served by men? One feels more at ease."

Finally Marguerite brought a silk coat trimmed with jet, which she treated with respect. Madame Aurélie summoned Denise.

"Do something to help, can't you? Put this on."

Denise, her heart stricken, despairing of ever succeeding in the shop, had remained motionless, her arms dangling. Obviously they were going to give her notice, the children would starve.

The hubbub of the crowd buzzed in her head, she felt herself swaying, her muscles were aching from having lifted armfuls of clothes, a real navvy's job which she had never done before. Nevertheless, she had to obey, she had to let Marguerite drape the coat over her, as if on a dummy.

"Stand straight," said Madame Aurélie.

But almost immediately Denise was forgotten. Mouret was just coming in with Vallagnosc and Bourdoncle; he was greeting the ladies, being complimented by them on his magnificent display of winter fashions. Inevitably there were exclamations of delight about the oriental salon. Vallagnosc, who was just completing his stroll round the counters, was more surprised than admiring; with the apathy of a pessimist he was thinking that it was after all nothing but a lot of linen all at once. As to Bourdoncle, forgetting that he was on the staff, he too was congratulating the chief, so that his doubts and anxious nagging of the morning might be forgotten.

"Yes, yes, it's going quite well, I'm pleased," Mouret, radiant, was repeating, replying to Henriette's tender glances with a smile. "But I mustn't interrupt you, Mesdames."

At that, all eyes went back to Denise again. She was abandoning herself to Marguerite, who was making her turn slowly round.

"Mmmm? What do you think about it?" Madame Marty asked Madame Desforges.

The latter, as supreme arbiter of fashion, settled the question:

"It's not bad, and the shape is original... Only, it seems to me that it's rather clumsy at the waist."

"Oh!" Madame Aurélie intervened. "You should see it on Madame herself... You see, it doesn't look anything on Mademoiselle, who is not at all well upholstered... Stand up straight, do, Mademoiselle, give it its full value."

People smiled. Denise had become very pale. She was overwhelmed with shame at being thus treated like a machine which people were freely examining and joking about. Madame Desforges, feeling antipathy to a temperament opposed to her own, irritated by the girl's gentle face, added spitefully:

"It would probably look better if Mademoiselle's dress wasn't so loose for her."

And she was looking at Mouret with the mocking look of a Parisian amused by the ridiculous get-up of a girl from the provinces. He felt the amorous caress of this glance, the triumph of a woman proud of her beauty and her artistry. And so, in gratitude for being adored, in spite of the goodwill he felt towards Denise, whose secret charm was casting its spell over his susceptible nature, he felt obliged to jeer in his turn.

"And then, she should have combed her hair," he murmured.

It was the last straw. The director was condescending to smile, all the girls burst into fits of laughter. Marguerite hazarded the slight chuckle of a refined girl controlling herself; Clara had abandoned a sale in order to have a good laugh at her ease; even the salesgirls from the lingerie department had drawn near, attracted by the uproar. As to the ladies, they were joking more discreetly, with an air of worldly understanding. Madame Aurélie's imperial profile alone was unbending, as if the new girl's beautiful, untamed hair and delicate, slender shoulders had cast a slur on the good management of her department. Surrounded by all these people making fun of her, Denise had grown even paler. She felt that violence had been done to her, that, defenceless, she had been stripped naked. What had she done, after all, to deserve being attacked like that for her waist being too small and her bun being too big? But she was hurt above all by the laughter of Mouret and of Madame Desforges, for some instinct had made her aware of their understanding, and some unknown grief was making her heart sink; that lady must be really wicked to attack a poor girl like that who was not saying a word, while he was positively making her blood run cold with a fear which was drowning all her other feelings, so that she could not analyse them. Forsaken like an outcast, her most intimate feminine modesty assailed, sickened by the unfairness, she was choking back the sobs which were rising in her throat.

"You'll see to it that she combs her hair tomorrow, won't you? It's really unseemly!..." the terrifying Bourdoncle was repeating to Madame Aurélie. Full of contempt for her small limbs, he had condemned Denise from the moment she arrived.

At last the buyer came and took the coat off Denise's shoulders, saying in a low voice to her as she did so:

"Well, Mademoiselle! That's a fine beginning. Really, if you wanted to show us what you're capable of... you couldn't have been sillier."

Denise, for fear that the tears might gush from her eyes, hastened to return to the pile of clothes which she was putting back and sorting on a counter. There, at any rate, she was lost in the crowd, tiredness was preventing her from thinking. But she noticed that the salesgirl from the lingerie department, who already that morning had defended her, was close to her. The latter had just witnessed the scene; she murmured into her ear:

"My dear, you mustn't be so sensitive. Go on, choke them back, otherwise you'll be made to shed a lot more... You know, I'm from Chartres. Pauline Cugnot's my name, and my parents back home are millers... Well, they'd have eaten me up here at the beginning if I hadn't kept my end up... Come on, be brave! Give me your hand, we'll have a nice chat when you feel like it."

The hand which was being held out only made Denise feel twice as upset. She shook it furtively, and hastened to carry away a heavy load of overcoats, afraid of doing something wrong again, of being scolded if it became known that she had a friend.

Meanwhile Madame Aurélie herself had just placed the coat on Madame Marty's shoulders, and everyone was exclaiming: Oh! How lovely! It's charming! It immediately begins to look as if it has some shape... Madame Desforges declared that they would never find anything better. Greetings were exchanged, Mouret took his leave, whereas Vallagnosc had caught sight of Madame de Boves in the lace department with her daughter, and hastened to offer her his arm. Marguerite, standing at one of the mezzanine-floor cash desks, was already calling out the various purchases made by Madame Marty, who paid, and gave orders that the parcel should be taken to her carriage. Madame Desforges had found all her things again at No. 10 cash desk. Then the ladies met once more in the oriental hall. They were leaving, but they did so in a burst of voluble admiration. Even Madame Guibal was waxing enthusiastic.

"Oh, it's delightful! One feels one's actually there!"

"Yes, a real harem, isn't it? And not expensive!"

"Look at the ones from Smyrna, ah! Those from Smyrna! What shades, what delicacy!"

"And that one from Kurdistan, look there! A Delacroix!"*

Slowly, the crowd was diminishing. Peals of bells, at hourly intervals, had already rung for the first two evening meals; the third was about to be served, and in the departments, which were gradually being deserted, there just remained a few belated customers whose passion for spending had made them forget the time. From outside only the rattle of the last cabs could be heard through the muffled voice of Paris, the snore of a replete ogre digesting the linens and cloths, the silks and the laces, with which people had been stuffing him since the morning, Inside, in the blaze of the gas jets which, burning in the dusk, had illuminated the crowning commotion of the sale, it was like a battlefield still hot from the massacre of materials. The salesmen, worn out with tiredness, were camping amidst the havoc of their cash desks and counters, which looked as if they had been wrecked by the raging blast of a hurricane. The ground-floor galleries were obstructed by a rout of chairs which made it difficult to get round them; in the glove department one had to step over a barricade of boxes, piled up round Mignot; in the woollens it was impossible to get through at all, Liénard was dozing on a sea of materials in which some half-destroyed stacks of cloth were still standing, like ruined houses swamped by an overflowing river; further along, the white linen had snowed all over the ground, one stumbled against ice floes of table napkins, one walked on the soft flakes of handkerchiefs. Upstairs in the mezzanine departments the havoc was the same; furs littered the floor, ready-made clothes were heaped up like the trench coats of out-of-combat soldiers; the laces and underclothes, unfolded, creased, thrown down at random, looked as if a multitude of women had undressed there haphazard in a wave of desire; while downstairs, in the depths of the shop, the dispatch service, working full blast, was still disgorging the parcels with which it was bursting, and which were being carried away by the delivery vans in a final movement of the superheated machine. But there had been a mass onslaught of customers above all in the silk department, there they had made a clean sweep, one could walk there quite easily, the hall was bare, the whole colossal stock of Paris-Bonheur had just been slashed to bits, swept away, as if by a horde of ravenous locusts. In the midst of this void Hutin and Favier, out of breath from the struggle, were turning the pages of their cashbooks, calculating their percentages. Favier had made fifteen francs for himself, whereas Hutin, who had not been able to make more than thirteen, had been beaten that day, and was furious at his bad luck. Their eyes were lighting up with acquisitive passion, and around them the whole of the rest of the shop was also making calculations, burning with the same fever, with the brutal gaiety of nights of carnage.

"Well, Bourdoncle!" shouted Mouret. "Are you still worried?"

He had come back once more to his favourite post, at the top of the mezzanine staircase by the balustrade, and at the sight of the massacre of materials spread out below him, he gave a victorious laugh. His fears of the morning, that moment of unpardonable weakness which no one would ever know about, had given him a flashy hankering for triumph. So in the end the campaign had been won, the small tradespeople of the neighbourhood reduced to shreds, Baron Hartmann, with his millions and his building sites, conquered. As he was watching the cashiers bent over their ledgers, adding up the long columns of figures, as he listened to the tinkle of gold falling through their fingers into brass bowls, he could already see the Bonheur des Dames growing beyond all measure, its hall expanding, its arcades being extended as far as the Rue du Dix-Décembre.

"And aren't you now convinced," he resumed, "that the shop is too small? We could have sold twice as much."

Bourdoncle was eating humble pie and was, what is more, delighted at having been in the wrong. But then they saw a sight which made them serious again; Lhomme, chief sales cashier, had just collected together the individual takings from each cash desk as he did every evening; after having added them up, he used to inscribe the total takings on a sheet of paper which he put on his spike file, and he would then carry the takings, in a wallet and bags, according to the nature of the currency, up to the counting house. On that particular day gold and silver predominated; he slowly climbed the staircase, carrying three enormous bags. As he had lost his right arm, which was amputated at the elbow, he hugged them to his chest with his left arm, holding one of them in place with his chin, to prevent it sliding off. His heavy breathing could be heard from afar as he went along, overladen and haughty, amid the respectful shop assistants.

"How much, Lhomme?" asked Mouret.

"Eighty thousand, seven hundred and forty-two francs, ten centimes!"

A laugh of pleasure shook the Bonheur des Dames. News of the figure was spreading. It was the biggest figure ever attained so far by a draper's shop in one day.

That evening, as Denise went up to bed, she leant against the walls of the narrow corridor beneath the zinc roofing. Once inside her room and the door closed, she flung herself upon the bed, her feet were hurting her so much. For a long time she stared vacantly at the dressing table, at the cupboard, at the whole room which had the bareness of a hotel bedroom. So that was where she was going to live, and her first horrible, endless day loomed up before her. She would never have had the courage to go through it again. Then she noticed that she was still dressed in silk; her uniform overwhelmed her, and before unpacking her trunk she had a childish desire to put on her old woollen dress, which had remained on the back of a chair. But when she was once more dressed in her own poor garment, she was overcome with emotion, and the sobs which she had been holding back since the morning suddenly burst in a flood of bitter tears. She had fallen back on the bed again, and was weeping at the thought of the two children, and she went on weeping, without having the strength to take off her shoes, drunk with weariness and sorrow.

5

THE NEXT DAY Denise had scarcely been in the department for half an hour when Madame Aurélie said to her in a curt voice:

"Mademoiselle, you're wanted in the head office."

The girl found Mouret alone, sitting in the great office hung with green rep. He had just remembered "Touslehead", as Bourdoncle called her, and although he was usually reluctant to play a policeman's part, he had had the idea of summoning her to give her a bit of a jolt, in case she was still looking dowdy like a girl from the provinces. The day before, in spite of the joke he had made, his self-esteem had been wounded when the smartness of one of his salesgirls had been discussed in front of Madame Desforges. His feelings were confused, a mixture of sympathy and anger.

"Mademoiselle," he began, "we took you out of consideration for your uncle, and you must not put us to the painful necessity..."

But he stopped. Opposite him, on the other side of the desk, Denise was standing erect, solemn and pale. Her silk dress was no longer too big, but hugging her rounded figure, moulding the pure lines of her girlish shoulders, and if her hair, knotted in thick braids, still remained untamed, she was at least trying to control it. She had fallen asleep fully clothed, all her tears spent, and on waking at about four o'clock she had felt ashamed of her attack of hysterical self-pity. She had immediately set about taking in the dress, and had spent an hour in front of the narrow mirror, combing her hair, without being able to smooth it down as she would have liked.

"Oh! Thank goodness," murmured Mouret. "You're better this morning... Only, those locks of yours are still real little devils!"

He had got up, he came to put her hair to rights with the same familiar gesture as Madame Aurélie when she had tried to arrange it the day before.

"There! You should tuck that one behind the ear... The bun is too high up."

She was not saying a word, offering no resistance as he tidied her. In spite of her vow to be brave, when she had reached the office she had felt cold all over, convinced she had been summoned to be given notice. And Mouret's obvious kindness did not reassure her, she still dreaded him, she still felt an uneasiness when close to him, which she explained as a very natural confusion in the presence of a powerful man on whom her future depended. When he saw how she was trembling as his hands brushed against the nape of her neck he regretted his gesture of kindness, for the one thing he was afraid of was losing his authority.

"Well, Mademoiselle," he resumed, once more putting the desk between them, "try to pay attention to your appearance. You're no longer in Valognes, study our Parisian girls... If your uncle's name was enough to open the doors of our shop to you, I should like to believe that you will live up to what you yourself seemed to me to promise. Unfortunately, not everyone here shares my opinion... So now you've been warned, haven't you? Don't prove me wrong."

He was treating her like a child, with more pity than kindness, his curiosity about the feminine sex merely awakened by the exciting woman he could sense developing in this poor, puny child. And while he was lecturing her, she, having caught sight of the portrait of Madame Hédouin whose handsome face with regular features was smiling gravely in its gold frame, felt herself seized with a tremor once more, in spite of the encouraging things he was saying to her. It was the dead lady, the one whom the neighbourhood accused him of having killed so as to found the shop on her lifeblood.

Mouret was still talking.

"You may go," he said finally, and he went on writing without getting up.

She went, and in the corridor she gave a sigh of profound relief.

From that day on Denise showed the stuff of which she was made. Beneath her attacks of sensitivity her common sense was always there, the fact of being weak and alone made her brave, and she carried on gaily with the task which she had set herself. She made no fuss; she went straight ahead to her goal taking no notice of obstacles, and she did so simply and naturally, for this invincible gentleness was at the very roots of her nature.

In the first place she had to overcome terrible hardships in the department. The parcels of clothes made her arms ache to such an extent that during the first six weeks she would cry out as she turned over in the night, aching in every limb, her shoulders black and blue. But her shoes caused her even more suffering, for they were heavy shoes she had brought from Valognes, and lack of money prevented her from replacing them by light boots. She was always standing, walking about from morning to night, scolded if she was caught leaning up against the woodwork for a minute, and her feet, the small feet of a little girl, were swollen and felt as if they were being pulped in instruments of torture; her heels throbbed with inflammation, the soles of her feet were covered with blisters, the peeling skin of which stuck to her stockings. Subsequently the health of her whole body was impaired, her limbs and organs were strained by the exhaustion of her legs, she had sudden disorders of a feminine nature which her pallor betrayed. And yet she, who was so thin and looked so fragile, stood up to it, while many salesgirls were forced to leave the drapery business because they contracted occupational diseases. When she was reaching breaking point, worn out by work which would have made men succumb, she kept going, smiling and erect, because she suffered with a good grace and was obstinately courageous.

Next, she was tortured because the department was against her. Surreptitious persecution by her companions was added to her physical sufferings. In spite of being patient and gentle for two months, she had not so far disarmed them. There was nothing but wounding words and cruel tricks, and she was cold-shouldered in a way which, needing affection as she did, wounded her to the quick. She had been teased for a long time about her unfortunate first day; the words "clogs" and "gollywog" went the rounds, girls who failed to make a sale were "sent to Valognes", in a word she was considered the duffer of the counter. When later on, once she was familiar with the workings of the shop, she proved herself to be a remarkable saleswoman, there was indignant amazement, and from then on the girls conspired never to let her have a worthwhile customer. Marguerite and Clara pursued her with instinctive hatred, joining forces so as not to be destroyed by this newcomer, for although they pretended to have contempt for her, they really feared her. As to Madame Aurélie, she was hurt by the girl's proud reserve, by the fact that she did not hang round her with an air of admiration; so she abandoned Denise to the spite of girls whom she particularly liked, court favourites who were always sucking up to her, busy buttering her up with the endless flattery which her strong, authoritarian personality needed to make it blossom out. For a time the assistant buyer, Madame Frédéric, seemed not to enter into the plot, but it must have been an oversight, for as soon as she realized the difficulties she might get into because of her good manners, she turned out to be just as unkind. Then Denise was completely forsaken, they were all dead against "Touslehead", who lived in a perpetual state of war, and in spite of all her courage it was only with difficulty that she succeeded in keeping her place in the department.

Nowadays this was her life: she had to smile, put on a gallant, affable manner and be clad in a silk dress which did not even belong to her and, ill-fed and ill-treated as she was, she suffered agonies of fatigue, in continual fear of being brutally dismissed. Her room was her only sanctuary, the sole place where she would still give way to tears when she had suffered too much during the day. But when the zinc roof became covered with December snow it made the room terribly cold; she had to curl up in bed, put all her clothes on top of her, and cry under the blanket so as not to get her face chapped from the frost. Mouret no longer even spoke to her. When during working hours she caught sight of Bourdoncle's stern gaze she would begin to tremble, for she sensed in him a natural enemy who would never forgive her the slightest lapse. In the midst of this universal hostility, she was surprised by the strange benevolence of Inspector Jouve: if he found her on her own he would smile to her, try to say something agreeable; twice he had saved her from being reprimanded, although she showed him no gratitude for having done so, for she felt more perturbed than touched by his protection.

One evening, after dinner, when the girls were tidying the cupboards, Joseph came to tell Denise that a young man was asking for her downstairs. Very apprehensive, Denise went down.

"Why!" said Clara, "so Touslehead has a lover, has she?"

"He must be in a bad way..." said Marguerite.

Downstairs in the doorway Denise found her brother Jean. She had absolutely forbidden him to call at the shop like that, as it created a very bad impression. But he seemed so beside himself that she did not dare scold him; he had no cap and was panting from having run there from the Faubourg du Temple.

"Have you got ten francs?" he blurted out. "Give me ten francs or I'm a lost man."

The big scallywag looked so funny, with his handsome girl's face and his blond hair flying in the wind, rapping out this melodramatic phrase, that if his request for money had not caused her such agonies, she would have smiled.

"What do you mean, ten francs?" she murmured. "What on earth's the matter?"

He blushed and explained that he had met a friend's sister. Denise, to whom he had communicated his embarrassment, silenced him – she did not need to know more. Twice before he had already come running to her for similar loans, but the first time it had only been a question of one franc twenty-five centimes, and the second time one franc fifty. He was always getting involved with women.

"I can't give you ten francs," she went on. "I haven't paid for Pépé this month yet, and I've only just got enough money. There'll be scarcely enough left over for me to buy myself some boots, which I need very badly… Really, Jean, you aren't a bit reasonable. It's too bad."

"Then, I'm lost," he repeated, with a tragic gesture. "Listen, Sis: she's tall and dark, we went to a café with her brother, and I had no idea that the drinks…"

She had to interrupt him again, and as the tears were filling her beloved scatterbrain's eyes, she took a ten-franc coin out of her purse and slipped it into his hand. Immediately he began to laugh.

"I knew you would… But, word of honour! From now on, I'll never ask again! I'd have to be a proper scoundrel to do that."

He went on his way once more, after having kissed her violently on the cheek. Inside the shop, employees were watching with surprise.

That night, Denise slept badly. Since she had started work at the Bonheur des Dames, money had been a bitter worry to her. She was still there "au pair", with no regular salary, and as the girls in the department prevented her from selling, she could only just manage to pay for Pépé's board and lodging thanks to the few unimportant customers they handed over to her. She suffered dire poverty – poverty in a silk dress. Often she had to sit up all night looking after her skimpy wardrobe, mending her underwear, darning her nightdresses which were in ribbons, not to mention her shoes which she had patched just as skilfully as a cobbler would have done. She risked washing things in her basin. But her old woollen dress worried her above all, for she had no other, and was forced to put it on again each evening when she took off the uniform silk dress, and that wore it out terribly; a spot on it put her in a fever, the slightest tear was a catastrophe. And she had nothing for herself; not a penny with which to buy the trifles a woman needs: she had had to wait a fortnight before she could renew her stock of needles and thread. And so it was a disaster when Jean suddenly turned up with his stories of love affairs and wrecked her budget. Every franc he took made a great gap in it. As to finding ten francs the next day, there was not the slightest hope that she would do so. Until daybreak she had nightmares of Pépé being thrown into the street, while she lifted up the paving stones with her bruised fingers to see if there was any money underneath.

And it so happened that on the next day she had to smile, to play the part of a smart well-dressed girl. Some regular customers came to the department, and Madame Aurélie called her several times and made her put on coats in order to show the new styles. And while she was posing in the way prescribed by fashion plates, she was thinking about the forty francs for Pépé's board and lodging which she had promised to pay that evening. She could very well do without the boots that month, but even if she added those four francs, saved up centime by centime, to the thirty francs she had left, that would only make thirty-four francs – and where could she get six francs from to complete the sum? Her heart was in agonies of distress at the very thought.

"You'll notice that the shoulders are loose," Madame Aurélie was saying. "It's very smart, and also very comfortable... Mademoiselle can cross her arms."

"Oh yes, certainly!" Denise was repeating, keeping up a pleasant manner, "One doesn't know one has it on... Madame will be very pleased with it."

She was now reproaching herself for having gone to fetch Pépé from Madame Gras's one Sunday in order to take him for a walk in the Champs-Elysées. The poor little thing went out with her so rarely! But it had meant buying him some gingerbread and a spade, and then taking him to see Punch and Judy, and in no time she had spent one franc forty-five. Really, Jean did not give the little boy a thought when he was up to his tricks. And in the end she had to bear the brunt of it all.

"Of course, if Madame does not care for it..." the buyer was saying. "Here, Mademoiselle! Put on the cloak, so that Madame can judge!"

Denise was walking along taking mincing steps with the cloak on her shoulders, saying as she did so:

"This one has more warmth in it... It's the latest fashion."

Beneath her professional good nature, she was thus racking her brains, trying to think where she could get some money. The other girls, who were rushed off their feet, let her make a big sale, but it was Tuesday; there were four days to wait before she would get her week's pay. After dinner she resolved to put off her visit to Madame Gras till next day. She would make an excuse, say that she had been detained, and by that time she might perhaps have got the six francs.

As Denise avoided spending anything at all, she went to bed early. What could she do in the streets, without any money, shy as she was and still worried by the great city, where she was only familiar with the streets neighbouring on the shop? After having ventured as far as the Palais-Royal to get some air, she would go back quickly, shut herself in her room, and set about sewing or washing clothes. Along the whole length of the corridor off which the rooms led there was barrack-like promiscuity; there were girls who were often none too fastidious, gossiping over slop pails and dirty linen, acerbity being worked off in continuous bickerings and reconciliations. Moreover, the girls were forbidden to go upstairs during the daytime; they did not live there, they just spent the night there, going back in the evening only at the last minute, and escaping from there in the morning still only half-awake after a rapid wash, and the draught which ceaselessly swept through the corridor, the fatigue of thirteen hours' work which made them throw themselves panting on their beds, made the attics seem more like an inn through which there passed a stampede of exhausted, peevish travellers. Denise had no friend. Of all the girls only one, Pauline Cugnot, showed her any kindness, and in any case, as the ready-made and lingerie departments, which were next door to each other, were in open warfare, so far the two salesgirls' nascent friendship had had to be limited to occasional words exchanged on the run. Pauline did occupy the room on the right of Denise's, but as she used to disappear at the end of the meal and not come back before eleven, the latter only heard her going to bed, but never met her outside working hours.

On that particular night, Denise had resigned herself to playing cobbler again. She was holding her shoes, examining them, seeing how she could make them last out until the end of the month. Finally, she had made up her mind to sew the soles on again with a strong needle, as they were threatening to leave the uppers. In the meantime, a collar and some cuffs were soaking in the basin, full of soapy water.

Every evening she heard the same sounds, girls coming in one by one, short whispered conversations, laughter, sometimes quarrels. Then the beds would creak and yawns would be heard, and deep sleep would descend on the rooms. Her left-hand neighbour talked in her sleep, which had frightened her at first. Perhaps others, like her, stayed up in spite of the rule, in order to mend things, but they must have taken the same precautions as she did, slowing up her movements and avoiding the slightest noise, for nothing but a chilling silence came from the closed doors.

Eleven o'clock had already struck ten minutes ago when a sound of footsteps made her raise her head. Another girl coming back late! And hearing the door next to hers open, she recognized Pauline. Then she was dumbfounded: the girl from the lingerie department was quietly retracing her footsteps and knocking on her door.

"Hurry up, it's me."

Girls were forbidden to visit each other in their rooms. Therefore Denise unlocked the door quietly in case her neighbour was caught by Madame Cabin, who kept watch to see that the rules were strictly observed.

"Was she there?" she asked, shutting the door again.

"Who? Madame Cabin?" said Pauline, "It's not her I'm afraid of… So long as I've got a franc to give her!"

Then she added:

"I've wanted a chat with you for a long time. It's impossible downstairs… And then, you looked so miserable this evening at dinner!"

Denise was thanking her, asking her to sit down, touched by her good-natured manner. But she was in such confusion as a result of this unexpected visit that she was still holding the shoe which she was sewing together, and Pauline's eyes fell on it. She shook her head, looked around her and caught sight of the collar and cuffs in the basin.

"You poor thing, I thought as much," she went on. "Don't worry! I know what it's like. At the beginning, when I'd just come from Chartres and my old dad didn't send me a penny, I washed a good few chemises, I can tell you. Yes, yes, my chemises even! I had two of them, and you'd always have found one of them soaking."

She had sat down, out of breath from running. Her broad face, with small lively eyes and a big, kindly mouth, had a certain charm, in spite of the features being coarse. And suddenly, without any transition, she told Denise all about herself; how she had spent her youth at a mill, how her father had been ruined by a lawsuit and she had been sent to Paris with twenty francs in her pocket to make her fortune; then, how she had started as a salesgirl, first in a shop in the Batignolles district, then at the Bonheur des Dames, how terrible it had been at the beginning, all the injuries and privations she had suffered; and finally she told about the life she was leading at the moment, how she earned two hundred francs a month, what her pleasures were, how she let her days pass, heedless of the morrow. On her dark-blue cloth dress, nipped in stylishly at the waist, there shone some jewellery – a brooch, a watch chain; beneath her velvet toque, adorned with a big grey feather, she was all smiles.

Denise, shoe in hand, had become very red in the face. She was trying to blurt out an explanation.

"Don't worry, I've been through it too!…" Pauline kept on repeating. "Look, I'm older than you, I'm twenty-six, though I don't look it… Tell me all about your little troubles."

In the face of this friendliness so candidly proffered, Denise gave in. In her petticoat and with an old shawl tied round her shoulders she sat down beside Pauline who was all dressed up, and they started to have a good heart-to-heart talk. It was freezing in the room, the cold seemed to seep into it through the attic walls, bare as a prison, but the girls did not notice that their fingers were numbed, they were absorbed in their confidences. Little by little, Denise opened up to her, talked about Jean and Pépé, said how much the question of money tormented her, and from that they both went on to attack the girls in the ready-made department. Pauline was relieving her feelings.

"Oh! What beastly cats they are! If only they behaved in a decent, friendly way you could make over a hundred francs for yourself."

"Everyone has a grudge against me, and I don't know why," Denise was saying, overcome with tears. "For instance, Monsieur Bourdoncle is always on the lookout to catch me doing something wrong, as if I got on his nerves. There's no one but old Jouve…"

The other interrupted her.

"What, that old ass, the shopwalker? Oh! don't you trust him, my dear… You want to be careful of men with big noses like that, you know! It's all very well for him to show off his medal like that, there's a story about him that's supposed to have happened in our department, in the lingerie… But what a child you are to take it all to heart like that! How awful it is to be so sensitive!

To be sure, what's happening to you happens to everyone: you're just being given a bit of a welcome!"

She seized her hands and kissed her, carried away by her kind heart. The money question, however, was more serious. Certainly the poor girl could not support her two brothers, pay for the little one's board and lodging and buy treats for the big one's mistresses, out of a few uncertain francs which the other girls did not want, for it was to be feared that she would not be given a salary before business revived in March.

"Listen, you can't go on like that much longer..." said Pauline. "If I was you I'd..."

But a noise coming from the corridor silenced her. Perhaps it was Marguerite, who was suspected of walking about in her nightdress in order to spy on the others and see if they were sleeping. Pauline, who was still clasping her friend's hands, looked at her for a moment in silence, straining her ears. Then she began again in a very low voice, with an air of gentle conviction.

"If I was in your place I'd get someone."

"What do you mean, get someone?" murmured Denise, without at first understanding.

When she did understand, she took her hands away, quite stupefied. This advice embarrassed her, for it was an idea which had never occurred to her, and she could see no advantage in it.

"Oh, no!" she replied simply.

"Well, then," Pauline continued, "you'll never be able to manage, you mark my words! The figures speak for themselves – forty francs for the little one, five francs or so every now and then for the big boy – and then you, you really can't always go about like a beggar, with shoes that the girls make jokes about; yes, really, your shoes do you harm. It would really be much better to take someone."

"No." Denise repeated.

"Well, you really are silly, you know... One has to do it, my dear, and it's so natural! We've all been through it. Now take me – I was "au pair" like you. Didn't have a cent. Of course, one is lodged and fed, but then one has to have clothes, and then it's impossible to be without a penny, shut up in your room counting the flies on the window. So really, one has to let oneself go in the end..."

She spoke of her first lover, a solicitor's clerk whom she had met during an outing at Meudon. After him, she had taken up with a post-office employee. And now, since autumn, she had been keeping company with a salesman employed at the Bon Marché, a very nice young chap, at whose place she spent all her free time. She never had more than one lover at a time, what is more. She was a decent girl, and would become indignant at the mention of the sort of girls who gave themselves to the first person they met.

"It isn't as if I'm telling you to misbehave yourself, after all," she went on sharply. "For example, I wouldn't like to be seen in the company of that Clara of yours, for fear people might accuse me of carrying on like she does. But when one lives with someone quietly, and has nothing with which to reproach oneself... Does that really seem wicked to you, then?"

"No," replied Denise. "It just isn't my line, that's all."

There was a fresh silence. They were smiling at each other, both moved by this whispered conversation in the icy little room.

"And then, one would have to like someone first," she went on, her cheeks pink.

Pauline was surprised, then in the end she laughed and kissed Denise once more, saying: "But dearie, people meet and take to each other! Aren't you funny? No one's going to force you... Look, would you like Baugé to take us somewhere in the country on Sunday? He'd bring one of his friends."

"No," Denise repeated, gently obstinate.

At that Pauline did not insist any further. Every girl was free to do as she wished. She had said what she had said from kindness of heart, for it made her really sad to see a friend in such difficulties. And as it was almost midnight, she stood up to leave. But before doing so she forced Denise to accept the six francs which she needed, begging her not to worry about it, and only to pay them back when she should be earning more.

"Now," she added, "put out your candle, so they can't see which door is opening... You can light it again afterwards."

When the candle was out they shook hands once more, and Pauline slipped out quietly and went back to her room leaving no sound but the swish of her skirt behind her in the silence, as the other little rooms slept, overwhelmed with fatigue.

Before going to bed, Denise wanted to finish sewing up her shoe and do her washing. As the night wore on, the cold was becoming more acute. But she did not feel it, the conversation she had just had had stirred up her blood. She was not at all shocked, she felt that people were quite at liberty to arrange their lives as they thought best when they were alone in the world, and free. She had never been a slave to ideas, it was simply her common sense and healthy nature which made her live the clean life which she led. In the end, towards one o'clock she went to bed. No, there was no one whom she loved, so what was the good of upsetting her life, spoiling the maternal devotion she had dedicated to her two brothers? And yet she did not fall asleep, warm shivers were running over the nape of her neck, insomnia was making indistinct forms pass before her closed eyes, forms which vanished in the night.

From then on, Denise took an interest in the love affairs in her department. Except during heavy rush hours, the girls there thought about men all the time. Gossip would go the rounds, stories of intrigues would amuse the girls for a whole week on end. Clara was a scandal, for she was kept by three men, so it was said, not to mention the queue of casual lovers which she trailed behind her; she only stayed on at the shop – where she worked as little as possible, for she was contemptuous of money which she could earn more agreeably elsewhere – in order to cover herself in the eyes of her family, for she lived in perpetual terror of old Monsieur Prunaire, who used to threaten to turn up in Paris and give her a good beating with a clog. Marguerite, on the contrary, behaved well, she was not known to have a lover; this caused some surprise, for everyone knew about the scrape she had got into, how she had come to Paris in order to hush up her confinement; how had she managed to have her child if she was so chaste? Some said it was just a fluke, adding that she now was keeping herself for her cousin in Grenoble. The girls also made fun of Madame Frédéric, crediting her with discreet relationships with important people; the truth was that they knew nothing about her love affairs; she would disappear in the evening with the sullenness of a widow, looking as if she was in a hurry, but no one knew where she was rushing. As to Madame Aurélie's passions, the cravings she was alleged to have for docile young men were certainly an invention; discontented salesgirls made up stories like that for a laugh. Perhaps, in the past, the chief buyer had had too maternal a feeling for one of her son's friends, but nowadays, in the ready-made department she was a woman with a responsible position, no longer interested in such childlike things. In the evening, when the girls flocked out in a stampede, nine out of ten of them had lovers waiting at the door; in the Place Gaillon, all along the Rue de la Michodière and the Rue Neuve-Saint-Augustin, there were groups of motionless men on sentry guard, watching out of the corner of their eyes, and when the procession began, each one would hold out his arm and lead his girl away, and they would go off, chatting as they went, with truly marital equanimity.

But it was the discovery of Colomban's secret that disquieted Denise most of all. She could see him at all hours on the other side of the road, on the threshold of the Vieil Elbeuf, always gazing upwards with his eyes fixed on the girls in the ready-made department. When he felt that she was watching him he would blush and turn his head away, as if he feared that the girl would betray him to her cousin Geneviève, although the Baudus and their niece had had nothing to do with each other since the latter joined the Bonheur des Dames. She had thought at first that, judging from his bashful air of a despairing lover, he was in love with Marguerite, who behaved well and lived in the shop and was not an easy prey. Then when she found out for certain that the shop assistant's passionate glances were addressed to Clara, she was flabbergasted. He had been standing there on the pavement opposite like that for months, aflame with passion, without plucking up courage to make an avowal – and all that for a loose girl, living in the Rue Louis-le-Grand, whom he could have accosted any evening before she went off, always on the arm of a different man! Clara herself did not appear to be aware of the conquest she had made. Denise's discovery filled her with a painful emotion. Was love really as silly as that? Why! This lad, who had real happiness within easy reach, was spoiling his life, worshipping a street woman as if she was a saint! And from that day on, every time she caught sight of Geneviève's pale, sickly profile behind the greenish windows of the Vieil Elbeuf, her heart ached.

Denise would daydream in the evenings as she watched the girls going off with their lovers. Those who did not sleep at the

Bonheur des Dames would disappear until the next day, and when they returned to their departments they would bring with them clinging to their skirts the smell of the outside world, all the disquieting unknown. And sometimes the girl would give an answering smile to the friendly nod with which she was greeted by Pauline, for whom Baugé always waited regularly from half-past eight onwards, standing at the corner by the Gaillon fountain. Denise was usually the last to leave, and when she had had a surreptitious walk around, always alone, she would be the first to come in again; then she would either work or go to bed, her head in a dream, full of curiosity about Parisian life, of which she knew nothing. She did not, indeed, envy the other girls, she was happy in her solitude, in her unsociable life in which she shut herself away as if in a sanctuary, but she would sometimes be carried away by her imagination, she tried to guess at things, conjuring up pictures of the pleasures which were always being described in her presence – cafés, restaurants, Sundays spent on the water and in pleasure gardens. And after all this she was left spiritually worn out, filled with desire mingled with lassitude; she would feel as if she was already satiated with these amusements, which she had never tasted.

However, there was not much time for dangerous daydreams in her hard-worked existence. In the shop, worn out as they were by thirteen hours' work, no one thought about love between salesmen and saleswomen at all. If the continuous battle for money had not already wiped out the difference between the sexes, the everlasting scrimmage, which kept their minds busy and made their backs ache, would have been sufficient to kill all desire. In spite of the rivalries and friendships between men and women, the everlasting jostling between department and department, only a few rare love affairs were known to have taken place. All those who worked there had become nothing but cogs, caught up by the impetus of the machine, surrendering their personalities, merely adding their strength to the mighty common whole of the phalanstery. It was only outside that private lives began again, with the sudden flare-up of reawakening passions.

Nevertheless, one day Denise did see Albert Lhomme, the buyer's son, walking through the department several times with an air of indifference, and then slipping a note into the hand of a girl in the lingerie department. The winter off-season, lasting from December to February, was approaching, and there were slack times, hours she spent standing and looking far away at the other end of the shop, waiting for customers. The salesgirls in the ready-made department were on friendly terms above all with the salesmen in the neighbouring lace department, although their enforced intimacy never went beyond jokes exchanged in low voices. The assistant buyer in the lace department was a bit of a wag, who used to pester Clara with salacious confidences just for a laugh, although he was really so little interested in her that he did not even try to meet her again outside. This was the kind of relationship which existed between departments, between men and girls; there were understanding glances, words which they alone understood, sometimes conversations on the sly, with backs half-turned and pensive airs in order to put the terrifying Bourdoncle off the scent. As to Deloche, for a long time he contented himself with smiling at Denise; then, plucking up his courage, he murmured a word of friendship to her when he bumped into her. On the day when she caught sight of Madame Aurélie's son giving a note to the girl from the lingerie department, Deloche, feeling a need to take an interest in her, and not being able to think of anything to say, just asked her if she had had a good lunch. He, too, saw the white smudge of the letter; he looked at the girl, and they both blushed at this intrigue brought to a head in front of them.

But, in the midst of these warm breezes which were gradually awakening the woman in her, Denise still kept her childlike tranquillity. Only when she met Hutin did her heart beat faster. And that, in her eyes, was merely gratitude, she thought that she was just touched by the young man's politeness. He could not bring a customer to the department without her becoming flustered. Several times, coming back from a cash desk, she found herself going a roundabout way, going through the silk department quite unnecessarily, with a lump in her throat from emotion. One afternoon she found Mouret there, and he seemed to watch her go with a smile. He no longer took any notice of her, and only said a word to her from time to time in order to give her advice about the way she dressed herself and to chaff her for being a tomboy, an untamed creature with something boyish about her, whom he would never be able to make into a girl with style, in spite of his experience as a Don Juan; he would even laugh about it, he condescended to tease her, without admitting to himself how much this little salesgirl, whose hair looked so funny, disquieted him. Faced with his silent smile, Denise trembled as if she had done something wrong. Did he know then why she was going through the silk department, when she herself could not have explained what made her go out of her way like that?

Hutin, however, did not appear to notice the girl's grateful glances at all. The shopgirls were not his type, he pretended to despise them, at the same time boasting more than ever about the extraordinary adventures he had with customers: at his counter a baroness had been smitten with love at first sight for him, and an architect's wife had fallen into his arms one day when he had gone to her house about an error in yardage. This Norman bragging merely covered up the fact that he picked up girls in bars and music halls. Like all the young gentlemen in the drapery business, he had a mania for spending, and would go through the whole week in his department struggling with the avidity of a miser with the sole desire of throwing his money to the winds, on racecourses, in restaurants and at dances on Sunday; he never saved anything, never put anything by, his earnings were squandered as soon as he received them, he was absolutely heedless of the morrow. Favier did not join these parties. He and Hutin, who were so intimate in the shop, would say goodbye to each other at the door and not exchange another word; many of the salesmen, in continual contact with each other, would become strangers like that as soon as they set foot in the street, knowing nothing of each other's lives. Hutin's crony was Liénard. They both lived in the same hotel, the Hôtel de Smyrne in the Rue Sainte-Anne, a gloomy house inhabited entirely by shop assistants. In the morning they came to work together; then, in the evening, the first to finish tidying up his counter would go and wait for the other at the Café Saint-Roch in the Rue Saint-Roch, a little café in which the shop assistants from the Bonheur des Dames usually congregated, and where they brawled and drank, playing cards in the pipe smoke. Often they would stay on there till almost one o'clock, when the exhausted owner of the establishment would throw them out. Moreover, for about a month now they had been spending three evenings a week in the depths of a low music hall in Montmartre; they used to take their friends there and were making a reputation for Mademoiselle Laure, the hefty songstress who performed there and who was Hutin's latest conquest; they encouraged her gifts with such violent bangings of their canes and with such a din that the police had already had to intervene on two occasions.

Thus the winter passed, and at last Denise obtained a fixed salary of three hundred francs. It was high time; her heavy shoes were falling to pieces. In the last month she even avoided going out so as not to finish them off at one go.

"My goodness, Mademoiselle, you do make a noise with your shoes!" Madame Aurélie frequently repeated in an irritated way. "It's unbearable... What have you got on your feet?"

The day when Denise came down wearing light fabric boots for which she had paid five francs, Marguerite and Clara voiced their astonishment under their breath, but loud enough to be heard:

"Why! Touslehead has left off her clogs!" said one of them.

"Ah! Well," said the other, "it must have been a wrench... They'd belonged to her mother."

There was, what is more, a general uprising against Denise. The department had finally discovered her friendship with Pauline, and considered her liking for a salesgirl of an enemy department as defiance. The girls talked of treason, accusing her of going next door and repeating whatever they said. The war between the ready-made and lingerie departments acquired a fresh violence as a result, never had it raged with such force; the words exchanged were as hard as bullets, and one evening someone even slapped someone else's face behind some boxes of chemises. Perhaps this long-standing quarrel had originated because the girls in the lingerie department wore woollen dresses, whereas the ready-made-department girls were clad in silk; in any case, the lingerie girls would put on the shocked expressions of decent girls when speaking of their neighbours; and the facts proved them right, the silk seemed to have a noticeable influence on the ready-made-department girls' licentiousness. Clara was treated with contempt because of her flock of lovers, even Marguerite was twitted about her child, while Madame Frédéric was accused of hidden passions. And all on account of Denise!

"Mesdemoiselles, control yourselves, no ugly words, please!" Madame Aurélie would say gravely, in the midst of the angry passions unleashed in her little world. "Show them who you are!"

She preferred to keep aloof. As she confessed one day, in reply to a question from Mouret, none of the girls were worth much, there was nothing to choose between them. But she suddenly began to take a passionate interest when she learnt from Bourdoncle's own mouth that he had just found her son kissing a girl from the lingerie department in the depths of the basement – the salesgirl to whom the young man had been passing letters. It was outrageous, and she accused the girl from the lingerie point blank of having made Albert fall into a trap; yes, a plot had been hatched against her; after making certain that her department was above reproach, people were trying to disgrace her by ruining a mere child with no experience. She only made such a fuss in order to confuse the issue, for she had no illusions about her son, she knew him to be capable of anything. At one time the affair looked as if it might become serious, for Mignot, the glover, became involved. He was Albert's friend, and when the latter sent his mistresses to him, hatless girls who spent hours ransacking the cardboard boxes, he would give them preferential treatment; there was, moreover, a story about some suede gloves given to the girl in the lingerie department, in which no one had the last word. In the end the scandal was hushed up out of consideration for the buyer in the ready-made department, whom even Mouret treated with respect. A week later Bourdoncle simply found some pretext for dismissing the salesgirl guilty of having allowed herself to be kissed. The management might turn a blind eye to the terrible dissipation which went on outside, but it would not tolerate the slightest bawdiness inside the shop.

It was Denise who suffered from the incident. Madame Aurélie, fully informed about it though she was, harboured a secret grudge against her; she had seen her laughing with Pauline, she suspected insolence, gossip about her son's love affairs. And so she made the girl even more isolated in the department than she had been before. For some time she had been planning to take the girls to spend a Sunday at Rignolles, near Rambouillet, where she had bought a property out of the first hundred thousand francs she had saved, and suddenly she made up her mind to do so; it would be a way of punishing Denise, of openly cold-shouldering her. Everyone except the latter was invited. A fortnight beforehand, the department talked of nothing but this excursion; the girls would look at the sky, warm with May sunshine, and were already planning how they would spend every moment of the day, and looking forward to all manner of pleasures, such as donkeys, milk and brown bread. And there would only be women, which made it even more amusing! Madame Aurélie usually killed time on her days off like that, by going for walks with other ladies, for she was so unused to being at home with her family, and felt so ill at ease, so out of place on the rare evenings when she could dine at home with her husband and son, that she preferred, even on those evenings, to abandon her family and go and dine in a restaurant. Lhomme would go his own way too, delighted to pick up his bachelor existence again, and Albert, relieved, would go off whoremongering; they were so unaccustomed to being at home, and got so much on each other's nerves and bored each other on Sundays that all three of them did no more than pass through their flat as if it was a public hotel where one spends the night. So far as the trip to Rambouillet was concerned, Madame Aurélie simply declared that propriety forbade Albert taking part in it, and that it would be tactful of his father if he refused to come – an announcement which delighted both men. Meanwhile, the happy day was approaching, the girls were forever discussing it, talking about clothes they were preparing, as if they were setting out on a six months' journey, while Denise, pale and silent at being left out, had to listen to them.

"Don't they make you mad, eh?" Pauline said to her one morning. "I'd have my own back on them, if I was you! They're having a good time, I'd have a good time too, honest I would!... Come with us on Sunday, Baugé is taking me to Joinville."

"No, thank you," the girl replied, with calm obstinacy.

"But why? Are you still afraid someone will take you by force?"

And Pauline had a good laugh. Denise smiled in her turn. She knew quite well how things happened: it was on a party of that sort that all the girls had met their first lovers, friends brought along as if by chance, and she did not want that.

"Look," Pauline went on, "I swear to you that Baugé won't bring anyone with him. There'll be just the three of us... I'm certainly not going to marry you off if you don't like the idea."

Denise was hesitating, tortured by such desire that her cheeks were flushing. Since her companions had started showing off about the country pleasures they were going to have, she had been feeling stifled, overwhelmed with a longing for the open sky, dreaming of tall grasses which would reach to her shoulders, of giant trees the shadows of which would flow over her like fresh water. Her childhood, spent in the lush greenery of the Cotentin, was reawakening with a yearning for sunshine.

"Yes, all right," she said finally.

Everything was arranged. Baugé was to come and fetch the girls at eight o'clock in the Place Gaillon; from there they would go by cab to the station at Vincennes. Denise, whose salary of twenty-five francs was swallowed up each month by the children, had only been able to freshen up her old black woollen dress by trimming it with a checked poplin binding, and she had made herself a bonnet-shaped hat, covered with silk and trimmed with a blue ribbon. Thus simply dressed, she looked very young, like a little girl who had grown too quickly; she had the neatness of the poor, and was a little ashamed and embarrassed by the overflowing profusion of her hair, bursting out from under her hat. Pauline, on the contrary, was sporting a silk spring dress with violet and white stripes, a matching toque laden with feathers, and was wearing jewellery round her neck and on her hands with all the flashiness of a prosperous shopgirl. It was as if she was getting her own back for the week by wearing silk on Sundays, although she was condemned to wearing wool in her department, whereas Denise, who spent Monday to Saturday in her silk uniform, put on her shabby, threadbare woollen dress again on Sundays.

"There's Baugé," said Pauline, pointing out a tall youth standing near the fountain.

She introduced her lover, and Denise immediately felt at ease, for he was so obviously a decent sort. Baugé, enormous, with the slow strength of an ox at the plough, had a long, Flemish face, in which his vacant eyes laughed with childish puerility. Born in Dunkerque, the younger son of a grocer, he had come to Paris after being virtually turned out by his father and brother, who considered him excessively stupid. Nevertheless, at the Bon Marché he was earning three thousand five hundred francs. He was stupid, but very clever about linens. Women found him agreeable.

"What about the cab?" asked Pauline.

They had to walk as far as the boulevard. There was already warmth in the sunshine, the lovely May morning was smiling on the paving stones of the streets, and there was not a cloud in the sky; the blue air, as transparent as crystal, was full of gaiety. Denise's lips were half open with an involuntary smile; she was breathing deeply, she felt that her chest was emerging from six months' suffocation. At last she no longer felt the stuffiness, the heavy stones of the Bonheur des Dames on top of her! So she really had a whole day in the open country before her! It was like new health, infinite joy into which she was entering with the fresh sensations of a child. In the cab, however, she looked away, embarrassed, when Pauline planted a large kiss on her lover's lips.

"Why!" she said, her head still turned towards the window. "There's Monsieur Lhomme, over there... How he's walking!"

"He's got his French horn with him," added Pauline, who had leant across. "He really is a bit cracked! It almost looks as if he's dashing to meet someone."

Lhomme, his instrument case under his arm, was indeed rushing along by the gymnasium, his nose in the air, laughing to himself with pleasure at the idea of the treat which he was anticipating. He was going to spend the day at the home of a friend, a flautist in one of the small theatres where amateurs played chamber music from breakfast time onwards on Sundays.

"At eight o'clock! What an enthusiast he is!" Pauline went on. "And you know, Madame Aurélie and all her set must have taken the six-twenty-five train to Rambouillet... You can bet husband and wife won't meet."

The two girls talked about the trip to Rambouillet. They did not hope it would rain on the others, because then they would get it in the neck too, but if a cloud could break through there without the splashes coming as far as Joinville, it would be rather fun all the same. Then they pitched into Clara, a bungler who didn't know how to spend the money of the men who kept her; didn't she use to buy three pairs of boots at a time, boots which she threw away the next day after having cut them with scissors because her feet were covered with swellings? In any case, the girls in the drapery business had no more sense than the men: they squandered everything, never saved a penny, two and three hundred francs a month went on frills and furbelows, and on sweets.

"But he only has one arm!" said Baugé suddenly. "How does he play the horn?"

He had not taken his eyes off Lhomme. Then Pauline, who sometimes took advantage of his innocence, told him that the cashier supported the instrument against the wall – and he quite believed her, thinking it a very ingenious idea. And then when she, filled with remorse, explained to him how Lhomme adapted a system of pincers to his stump which he then used like a hand, he tossed his head, seized with suspicion, declaring that they couldn't make him swallow that.

"You're too silly!" she said laughing. "Never mind, I love you all the same."

The cab bowled along, they arrived at Vincennes station just in time for a train. It was Baugé who paid, but Denise had declared that she intended to pay her share of the expenses; they would settle up in the evening. They got into the second class, all the carriages were buzzing with gaiety. At Nogent a wedding party left the train amid laughter. Finally, they got out at Joinville and went to the island straight away to order lunch, and there they stayed, on the bank beneath the tall poplars which border the Marne. It was cold in the shade, a sharp breeze was blowing in the sunshine, intensifying in the distance, on the other bank, the limpid purity of the open country, with cultivated fields unfolding. Denise was lingering behind Pauline and her lover, who were walking with their arms round each other's waists; she had picked a handful of buttercups, and was watching the water flow past, happy, although her heart would sink and she hung her head when Baugé leant across to kiss the nape of his sweetheart's neck. Tears came into her eyes. And yet, she was not unhappy. What made her choke back her tears like that, and why did the vast countryside, where she had looked forward to such carefree happiness, fill her with a vague regret of which she could not have named the cause?

Later, during lunch, Pauline's rollicking laughter made her head swim. The latter, who adored the suburbs with the passion of a bohemian used to living in gaslight and the stuffy air of crowds, had wanted to lunch outside in an arbour, in spite of the freshness of the wind. She was amused by the sudden gusts which made the tablecloth flap, she thought the arbour, still bare of leaves, was fun, with its freshly painted trellis, the lozenges of which were silhouetted on the tablecloth. What is more, she was devouring her food with the hungry greed of a girl who, being badly fed in the shop, gave herself indigestion with the things she liked when she was outside it; it was her vice, all her money went on that, on cakes, on indigestible things, on little dishes sampled freely during her spare time. As Denise seemed to have had enough eggs, fried fish and chicken sauté, she restrained herself and did not dare order strawberries, a fruit which was still expensive, for fear of making the bill too big.

"Now what are we going to do?" asked Baugé, when the coffee was served.

Usually, in the afternoon, he and Pauline went back to Paris for dinner and would finish their day at the theatre. But at Denise's wish they decided that they would stay at Joinville; it would be amusing, they would give themselves a surfeit of the country. And all the afternoon they walked the fields. For a moment they discussed the idea of a trip in a boat, then they abandoned it; Baugé rowed too badly. But their dawdling, along paths taken at random, took them back along the banks of the Marne all the same; they were watching with interest the life of the river, the fleets of skiffs and rowing boats, the teams of oarsmen who populated it. The sun was sinking, they were going back towards Joinville, when two skiffs going downstream and racing each other exchanged a volley of abuse, in which the repeated cries of 'pub-crawlers' and 'counter-jumpers' predominated.

"Why!" said Pauline, "it's Monsieur Hutin!"

"Yes," said Baugé, his hand against the sun, "I recognize the mahogany skiff… The other skiff must be manned with a team of students."

And he explained the old enmity which often set students and commercial employees at loggerheads. On hearing Hutin's name pronounced, Denise had stopped walking; and with set eyes she was following the slender craft, looking for the young man amidst the scullers without being able to pick out anything but the white splash of colour made by two women, of whom one, sitting at the tiller, had a red hat. The voices were lost in the roar of the river.

"Into the water with them, the pub-crawlers!"

"Into the water with them, into the water with them, the counter-jumpers!"

In the evening they went back to the restaurant on the island. But it had become too cold outside; they had to eat in one of the two inside rooms, where the dampness of winter was still soaking the tablecloths through with the chilliness of wet washing. From six o'clock on there were not enough tables, the hikers were hurrying, trying to find a place, and all the time the waiters were bringing chairs and benches, putting plates closer together, cramming people in. It was stifling now, they had to open the windows. Outside the daylight was fading, a greenish dusk was falling from the poplars, and so quickly that the restaurant owner, ill-equipped for such meals, having no lamps, had to have a candle put on each table. The noise – laughs, calls, the clash of china – was deafening; in the draught from the windows the candles were taking fright and guttering; while moths were beating their wings in the air warmed by the smell of food and cut through by little icy blasts.

"They aren't half having fun, aren't they?" Pauline was saying, deep in a fish stew which she declared was wonderful.

She leant over in order to add:

"Haven't you noticed Monsieur Albert over there?"

It was indeed the younger Lhomme, surrounded by three dubious-looking women, an old lady in a yellow hat with the low appearance of a procuress and two girls under age, little girls of about thirteen or fourteen, with swaying hips and embarrassingly insolent. He, already very drunk, was banging his glass on the table and talking of thrashing the waiter if he did not bring some liqueurs immediately.

"Oh, well!" Pauline went on. "There's a family for you! The mother at Rambouillet, the father in Paris and the son in Joinville... They won't tread on each other's toes!"

Denise, who detested noise, was nevertheless smiling, tasting the joy of no longer thinking in the midst of such an uproar. But suddenly, in the neighbouring room, there was a burst of voices which drowned all others. There were yells, which must have been followed by blows, for pushes and the crash of chairs could be heard, a real struggle in which the shouts from the river were recurring:

"Into the water with them, the counter-jumpers!"

"Into the water with them, into the water with them, the pub-crawlers!"

And, when the inn-keeper's gruff voice had calmed the battle, Hutin suddenly appeared. In a red pullover, a cap back to front on the back of his head, he had the big girl in white who had been at the tiller, on his arm; she, in order to wear the skiff's colours, had planted a tuft of poppies behind her ear. Clamour and applause greeted their entrance; and he was radiant; he threw out his chest as he swayed along with a nautical roll, flaunting a bruise on his cheek caused by a blow he had received, all puffed up with pride. Behind them followed the team. A table was taken by assault, the din became tremendous.

"It seems," Baugé explained, after listening to the conversations behind him, "it seems that the students recognized Hutin's woman, who used to live in the neighbourhood, and is now singing in a music hall in Montmartre. And then they came to blows over her... They never pay women, those students don't."

"In any case," said Pauline, with a supercilious air, "she's frightfully ugly, that one is, with her carroty hair... Honestly, I don't know where Monsieur Hutin gets them, but each one's worse than the last."

Denise had grown pale. She was filled with an icy cold, as if her heart's blood had been drained away drop by drop. Already, on the river bank, at the sight of the swift skiff, she had felt the first shiver, and now she could no longer have any doubt that girl was really with Hutin. She had a lump in her throat, her hands were trembling, she was no longer eating.

"What's the matter with you?" her friend asked.

"Nothing," she stammered, "it's rather hot."

But Hutin was at a neighbouring table, and when he caught sight of Baugé, whom he knew, he started a conversation in a piercing voice in order to go on holding the attention of the room.

"I say," he shouted, "are you still chaste at the Bon Marché?"

"Not so much as all that," the other replied, very red in the face.

"Go on with you! They only take virgins, and they've got a confessional permanently attached to the shop for salesmen who look at them... A shop where marriages are arranged... No thanks!"

There was laughter. Liénard, who was a member of the team, added:

"It's not like it is at the Louvre... They've got a midwife attached to the gown department there. Word of honour!"

The gaiety was redoubled. Pauline herself was bursting with laughter, so amusing did the idea of the midwife seem to her. But Baugé was still vexed by the jokes about his shop's innocence. Suddenly he burst out:

"Don't tell me you're so well off at the Bonheur des Dames! Kicked out for the slightest word, and a boss who looks as if he picks up the customers!"

Hutin was no longer listening to him, but was launching into a panegyric about the Place Clichy. He knew a girl there who was so respectable that women shopping didn't dare speak to her for fear of humiliating her. Then he drew his plate closer, and told how he had made a hundred and fifteen francs during the week. Oh! It had been a marvellous week, Favier left behind with fifty-two francs, the whole roster beaten – and one could see that, couldn't one? He was blowing his money, he would not go to bed until he had got rid of the whole hundred and fifteen francs. Then, since he was getting tipsy, he went for Robineau, that whippersnapper of an assistant buyer, who pretended to keep aloof to such an extent that he did not wish to walk with one of his salesmen in the street.

"Shut up," said Liénard, "you talk too much, old chap."

The heat had increased, the candles were guttering onto the tablecloths stained with wine and through the open windows, when the noise made by the diners suddenly subsided, a distant, long-drawn-out voice was audible, the voice of the river and of the tall poplars which were falling asleep in the peaceful night. Seeing that Denise, dead white, her chin convulsed with the tears she was holding back, was not feeling better, Baugé had just asked for the bill, but the waiter did not reappear, and Denise had to go on suffering Hutin's verbal outbursts. Now he was saying that he was smarter than Liénard, because Liénard simply squandered his father's money, whereas he squandered money that he had earned, the fruits of his intelligence. In the end Baugé paid the bill and the two women went out.

"There's a girl from the Louvre," murmured Pauline in the outer room, looking at a tall thin girl who was putting on her coat.

"You don't know her, you can't tell," said the young man.

"Nonsense! Look at the way she drapes herself! Midwife's department, I'm sure! She ought to be pleased, if she's heard!"

They were outside. Denise gave a sigh of relief. She had thought she would die in that suffocating heat, in the middle of all that shouting, and she still attributed her faintness to the lack of air. Now she could breathe. Coolness was descending from the starry sky. As the two girls were leaving the restaurant garden, a timid voice murmured in the shadows:

"Good evening, Mesdemoiselles."

It was Deloche. They had not seen him at the back of the outer room, where he had been dining alone, after having come from Paris on foot for the sake of the walk. When she recognized his friendly voice Denise, who was feeling wretched, automatically yielded to the need for support.

"Monsieur Deloche, you're coming back with us," she said. "Give me your arm."

Pauline and Baugé were already walking ahead. They were surprised. They had not thought it would happen like that, and with that boy too. However, as they still had an hour before catching the train, they went right to the end of the island, walking along the bank beneath the tall trees, and from time to time they turned round murmuring:

"Where can they be? Ah! They're here… It's funny, all the same."

At first Denise and Deloche had remained silent. Slowly the hubbub of the restaurant was dying away, was acquiring a musical sweetness in the depths of the night, and still feverish from that furnace, the candles of which were one by one being extinguished behind the leaves, they were advancing further into the coldness of the trees. It was as if a wall of darkness was facing them, a mass of shadow so dense that they could not even distinguish the pale track of the footpath. Yet they were treading softly and fearlessly. Then their eyes became accustomed to the dark, to the left they could see the trunks of the poplars, like sombre columns supporting the domes of their branches, covered with stars, while to the right the water in the dark had, at times, the gloss of a mirror of pewter. The wind was dropping, they could hear nothing but the flow of the river.

"I am pleased I met you," Deloche, who was the first to bring himself to speak, stammered out finally. "You don't know what pleasure you are giving me by consenting to take a walk with me."

And after a great many embarrassed words, with the darkness helping him, he ventured to say that he loved her. He had been wanting to write to her about it for a long time, and she would never have known it perhaps but for that beautiful, conspiring night, but for the water singing and the trees covering them with the curtain of their shade. Yet, she made no reply, she was still walking, her arm in his, with the same air of suffering. He was trying to see her face when he heard a muffled sob.

"Oh! My God!" he went on. "You're crying, Mademoiselle, you're crying... Have I vexed you?"

"No, no," she murmured.

She was trying to hold back her tears, but could not do so. During dinner already she had thought her heart would burst, and now in the darkness she let herself go, sobs were choking her at the thought that, had Hutin been in Deloche's place, speaking to her lovingly like that, she would have been powerless to resist. This avowal, which she was at last making to herself, filled her with confusion. Shame was burning her face as if, beneath those very trees, she had fallen into the arms of that young man who was showing off in public with tarts.

"I didn't want to offend you," repeated Deloche, who was on the verge of tears.

"No, listen," she said in a voice which was still trembling. "I'm not at all angry with you. Only, I beg of you not to talk to me any more as you have just done... What you ask is impossible. Oh! You're a good fellow, I'll be glad to be your friend, but nothing more... Your friend, you understand!"

He was trembling. After taking a few steps in silence, he blurted out:

"The long and short of it is you don't love me?"

And since she was trying not to distress him by brutally saying "No" outright, he continued in a gentle, heart-broken voice:

"In any case, I expected it... I've never had any luck, I know that I can never be happy. At home they used to beat me. In Paris I've always been a whipping boy. You see, when one doesn't know how to steal other people's mistresses, and when one is clumsy enough not to make as much money as they do, well, one might as well go off and die in some hole or other straight away... Oh!

Don't worry, I won't annoy you any more. And as to loving you, you can't prevent me, can you? I'll love you without expecting anything in return, like an animal... That's how it is, everything goes west, that's my lot in life."

In his turn he wept. She comforted him, and as they were pouring out their hearts in a friendly way, they learnt that they both came from the same part of the world, she from Valognes, he from Bricquebec, thirteen kilometres away. It was a new link between them. His father, a badly-off minor law-court official who was morbidly jealous, used to thrash him, saying he was not his child, exasperated by his long, pale face and his flaxen hair, which he said were not in the family. From that they went on to talk about the great pastures surrounded by quickset hedges, the overgrown paths which disappeared beneath the elms, the roadways turfed at either side like the avenue in a park. Around them the night was growing lighter, they could distinguish the rushes by the river, the lacework of the shady trees, black against the flickering stars, and they began to feel soothed; they forgot their troubles, drawn together in comradeship by their misfortune.

"Well?" Pauline asked Denise brightly, taking her aside when they reached the station.

From her friend's smile and tone of tender curiosity, the girl understood. She became very red as she replied:

"Of course not, my dear! I told you that I didn't want to, didn't I? He comes from my part of the world. We were talking about Valognes."

Pauline and Baugé felt perplexed, their ideas were upset, they no longer knew what to believe. Deloche left them in the Place de la Bastille; like all the young men who received no salary, he slept in the shop, where he had to be by eleven o'clock. Not wishing to go back with him Denise, who had been given a theatre pass, accepted an invitation to accompany Pauline to Baugé's house. In order to be nearer to his mistress he had come to live in the Rue Saint-Roch. They took a cab, and Denise was dumbfounded when, on the way, she learnt that her friend was going to spend the night with the young man. There was nothing easier, one gave five francs to Madame Cabin, all the girls did it. Baugé did the honours of his room, which was furnished with old Empire-style furniture sent him by his father. When Denise talked of settling up, he became cross and then in the end accepted the fifteen francs sixty which she had put on the chest of drawers, but then he wanted to give her a cup of tea, and after struggling with a kettle and spirit lamp, he was obliged to go down again to buy some sugar. Midnight was striking when he filled the cups.

Denise kept on saying: "I must be going."

And Pauline would reply: "Wait a bit... The theatres don't shut up so early."

In that bachelor room Denise felt awkward. She had seen her friend undress as far as her petticoat and corsets, and she was watching her prepare the bed, opening it, patting the high pillows with her bare arms, and this little bit of housework, done in her presence in preparation for a night of love, upset her, made her feel ashamed, by reawakening in her wounded heart the memory of Hutin. Days spent like that were not at all wholesome. Finally, at a quarter past midnight, she left them. But she left in embarrassment when, in reply to her innocently wishing them a good night, Pauline thoughtlessly exclaimed:

"Thanks, it *will* be a good night!"

The separate entrance which led to Mouret's flat and to the staff bedrooms was in the Rue Neuve-Saint-Augustin. Madame Cabin would open the door and then have a look to check who was coming in. The lobby was feebly lit by a night light, Denise stood in its glimmer, hesitating, seized with misgiving, for as she had rounded the corner of the street she had seen the door close on the vague shadow of a man. It must have been the director, coming back from a party, and the idea that he was there in the dark, waiting for her perhaps, caused her one of those strange fears with which he still threw her into confusion without any good reason. Someone moved on the first floor, boots were squeaking. At that, she lost her head; she pushed a door which led into the shop and which was left open for the night-watch patrols. She found herself in the cotton-goods department.

"My goodness! What shall I do?" she stammered out in her emotion.

The idea came to her that there existed upstairs another communicating door leading to the bedrooms. Only that meant going through the whole shop. She preferred to make the journey, in spite of the darkness which flooded the galleries. Not a gas jet was burning; there were only oil lamps hooked

onto the branches of the chandeliers at infrequent intervals, and
these scattered lights, like yellow spots, their rays consumed by
the night, resembled the lanterns hung in mines. Great shadows
were floating about; one could hardly distinguish the heaps
of merchandise, which were acquiring terrifying outlines of
crumbling columns, crouching beasts, lurking thieves. The heavy
silence, broken by distant breathing, was intensifying this gloom
even more. Nevertheless, she found her bearings: the household
linen was making a pale streak on her left, like houses in a street
which take on a blue light under a summer sky; she wanted to
go straight across the hall, but she bumped into some piles of
calico and decided it would be safer to go through the hosiery,
and then the woollens. When she got there she was alarmed by
a noise like thunder, the sonorous snoring of Joseph, the porter,
who was sleeping behind the mourning goods. She sped into the
hall, which was lit with twilight coming through its glazed roof;
it seemed to have grown larger, full of the nocturnal terror which
churches have, its cash desks immobile, and the outlines of its
big measuring sticks forming inverted crosses. Now she was in
full flight. In the haberdashery and glove departments she once
more almost stepped over some of the duty porters, and she only
felt saved when she finally found the staircase. But upstairs by the
ready-made department she was seized with terror on catching
sight of a lantern, its winking eye walking along; it was a watch
patrol, two firemen in the process of registering on the indicator
dials that they had passed through there. For a minute she did
not understand, she watched them going from the shawls to the
furniture, then on to the underwear, terrified by their strange
manoeuvres, by the grating of the key, by the iron doors which
were clanging to with a murderous noise. When they drew near
she went and took refuge in the depths of the lace department,
but the sudden call of a voice made her leave it immediately
again, and reach the communicating door at the run. She had
recognized Deloche's voice, he slept in his department on a small
iron bed which he put up himself every evening; he was not yet
asleep but, his eyes still open, was reliving the pleasant hours he
had spent that evening.

"What! It's you, Mademoiselle!" said Mouret, whom Denise
found facing her on the staircase, a little pocket lamp in his
hand.

She stammered, tried to explain that she had just been to fetch something from her department. But he was not at all cross, he was looking at her in his paternal and at the same time inquisitive way.

"You had a theatre pass then, did you?"

"Yes, Monsieur."

"And did you enjoy yourself? Which theatre did you go to?"

"I went to the country, Monsieur."

That made him laugh. Then he asked, stressing the words:

"By yourself?"

"No, Monsieur, with a girl friend," she replied, her cheeks crimson with shame at the thought which no doubt had occurred to him.

At that he was silent. But he was still looking at her as she stood there in her little black dress, her hat trimmed with a single blue ribbon. Would this little wildflower end up by being a pretty girl? She smelt sweet from her trip in the fresh air, she looked charming, with her lovely hair in frightened array all over her forehead. And he who had for six months been treating her as a child, he who, yielding to the ideas of a man of experience, to a malicious fancy to find out how a woman might develop and go astray in Paris, would sometimes give her advice – he was laughing no longer, but was experiencing an indefinable feeling of surprise and fear, mingled with affection. Doubtless, it was a lover who was making her become so much more attractive. At this thought, he felt as if a favourite bird with which he had been playing had just pecked him and drawn blood.

"Goodnight, Monsieur," murmured Denise, continuing on her way upstairs without waiting.

He did not reply, but watched her disappear. Then he went back to his own room.

6

WHEN THE SUMMER SLACK SEASON CAME, a gust of panic blew through the Bonheur des Dames. Everyone was in terror of dismissal, of the mass discharges with which the management was making a clean sweep of the shop, now empty of customers during the heat of July and August.

Each morning, while making his tour of inspection with Bour-doncle, Mouret would take aside the heads of departments, whom he had urged to take on more salesmen than they needed during the winter, so that sales should not suffer, at the risk of having to weed out their personnel later on. Now it was a question of cutting down costs by turning one third of the shop assistants, the weak ones who let themselves be devoured by the strong, into the street.

"Come now," he was saying, "you've got some there who are no use to you... We really can't keep them on just to stand about like that with their arms dangling."

And if the head of the department should hesitate, not knowing whom to sacrifice, he would say:

"You must make do, six salesmen are all you need... You can take on some more in October, there are enough of them hanging about the streets!"

It was Bourdoncle, in any case, who dealt with executions. He had a dreadful way of saying through his thin lips, "Proceed to the pay desk!" – words which fell like the blows of an axe. He made anything a pretext for clearing the ground. He would invent misdeeds, he would take advantage of the very slightest carelessness. "You were sitting down, Monsieur: proceed to the pay desk!" "You're answering back, I believe: proceed to the pay desk!" "Your shoes are not polished: proceed to the pay desk!" Even the brave were trembling at the massacre he left in his wake. Then, as this technique did not work quickly enough, he devised a trap in which without effort in a few days he garrotted the number of salesmen condemned in advance. From eight o'clock on he stood in the entrance door, watch in hand: and if they were three minutes late his relentless "Proceed to the pay desk!" axed the out-of-breath young men. The job was done quickly and efficiently.

"You there, you look awful!"' he ended up by saying one day to a poor devil whose crooked nose got on his nerves. "Proceed to the pay desk!"

Favoured employees were given a fortnight's holiday, during which they were not paid; this was a more humane way of cutting down costs. In any case, under the lash of necessity and habit, salesmen took their precarious position for granted. Ever since their arrival in Paris they had been knocking about the place, beginning their apprenticeship in one shop, finishing it in another, they were dismissed or left of their own accord on the spur of the moment, as chance and their interests dictated. The factory was at a standstill, so the workmen's bread and butter had been discontinued, and this took place with the unfeeling motion of a machine, the useless cog was calmly thrown aside, like an iron wheel to which no gratitude is felt for services rendered. So much the worse for those who did not know how to carve out a share for themselves!

Nowadays the departments were talking of nothing else. Each day fresh stories went the rounds. The names of salesmen who had been dismissed were mentioned in the same way as during an epidemic one counts the dead. The shawl and woollen departments, in particular, suffered severely: seven assistants disappeared from there in a week. Next, a drama threw the lingerie department into confusion; there a customer felt queasy and accused the girl who was serving her of having eaten garlic; the salesgirl was dismissed on the spot, although, badly fed and always as hungry as she was, she had simply been finishing off a store of crusts at the counter. At the slightest complaint from customers the management proved inexorable; no excuse was accepted, the employee was always wrong, and had to disappear like a defective tool which harmed the good sales mechanism, while his colleagues hung their heads and did not even try to defend him. In the panic which was spreading everyone trembled with fear for himself; one day, when Mignot in spite of the rule was taking out a parcel under his overcoat, he was almost caught and immediately thought himself in the street; Liénard, whose laziness was a byword, owed it to his father's position in the drapery trade that he was not sacked one afternoon when Bourdoncle found him sleeping upright, propped between two piles of English velvet. Above all the Lhommes were worried, for they daily expected the dismissal of their son Albert; the way he kept his cash desk was causing great dissatisfaction, women came there and distracted his attention, and Madame Aurélie was twice obliged to intercede with the management.

Meanwhile, in the midst of the clean sweep which was being made, Denise was in such danger that she lived in constant fear of a catastrophe. In vain was she brave, in vain did she struggle with all her cheerfulness and good sense not to give way to attacks of sensitivity; as soon as she closed the door of her room tears would blind her, she was in despair at the thought of finding herself in the street, on bad terms with her uncle, not knowing where to go, without any savings and with two children on her hands. The feelings she had experienced in the first weeks were coming to life again, she felt she was a grain of millet beneath a powerful millstone, and she was filled with downhearted forlornness at feeling herself of so little importance in that huge machine, which would crush her with its calm indifference. It was impossible to have any illusions: if one of the salesgirls from the ready-made department was to be dismissed, she was the obvious choice. No doubt, during the trip to Rambouillet the girls had stirred up Madame Aurélie against her, for since then the latter had been treating her with an air of severity in which there was something akin to spite. In any case, she had not been forgiven for going to Joinville, for they considered that to have been rebellion, a means of flouting the whole department by conspicuously keeping company outside the shop with a girl from an enemy camp. Never had Denise suffered so much in her department, and now she was despairing of ever winning it over.

"Oh, don't take any notice of them!" Pauline would say. "They just give themselves airs, the silly gooses!"

But it was precisely their ladylike ways which intimidated the girl. From daily rubbing shoulders with rich customers almost all the salesgirls acquired airs and graces, and ended up by forming a vague class floating between the working and middle classes, and often beneath their dress sense, beneath the manners and phrases which they had picked up, there was nothing but a sham education, picked up from reading cheap newspapers, from tirades in the theatre and from all the follies of the moment in the Paris streets.

"You know, Touslehead has got a child!" Clara said one day as she came into the department.

There was some astonishment, so she went on:

"But I tell you I saw her yesterday taking the kid for a walk! She must stable it somewhere."

Two days later, on returning from dinner, Marguerite volunteered a fresh piece of news.

"Here's a nice thing, I've just seen Touslehead's lover... Just imagine, a workman! Yes, a dirty little workman, with yellow hair, who was watching her through the windows."

From then on it was an accepted fact; Denise had a lover who was a navvy, and she was hiding her child somewhere in the neighbourhood. They bombarded her with spiteful innuendoes. The first time she grasped what they meant she became very pale at the monstrousness of such conjectures. It was abominable, she wanted to exonerate herself and blurted out:

"But they're my brothers!"

"Oh, her brothers!" said Clara, in a scoffing voice.

Madame Aurélie was obliged to intervene.

"Be quiet, Mesdemoiselles, you'd do better to change these price tags... Mademoiselle Baudu is perfectly at liberty to behave badly outside the shop. If only she worked while she's here, at least!"

This curt defence was a condemnation. The girl, as flabbergasted as if she had been accused of a crime, tried vainly to explain the facts. People laughed and shrugged their shoulders, and this wounded her to the quick. When the rumour spread, Deloche was so indignant that he talked of boxing the ears of the girls in the ready-made department, and it was only the fear of compromising her that held him back. Since the evening at Joinville his love for her was submissive, his friendship almost religious, as he showed by gazing at her like a faithful dog. No one must suspect their affection, for people would have laughed at them, but that did not prevent him from dreaming of acts of sudden violence, of blows of revenge if ever anyone should attack her in his presence.

In the end Denise did not reply to them any more. It was too odious, no one would believe her. When one of the girls ventured to make a fresh hint, she merely looked at her steadily, in a sad, calm manner. In any case, she had other troubles, material anxieties, which were worrying her much more. Jean still was not being sensible, he was always badgering her with requests for money. Hardly a week passed without her receiving some story from him, four pages long, and when the shop postman handed over these letters written in big, passionate handwriting to her she would hasten to hide them in her pocket, for the salesgirls made great play of laughing about them, whilst chanting broad jokes as they did so. Then, having invented a pretext for going to decipher the letters at the other end of the shop, she would be overwhelmed with fears; she felt that poor Jean was ruined. She would swallow all his fibs about extraordinary amorous adventures, and her ignorance of such things made her exaggerate the dangers even more. Now it was forty centimes in order to extricate him from a woman's jealousy, now five francs, now six francs to redress the honour of a poor girl whose father would kill him otherwise. And so, as her salary and percentages were insufficient, she had had the idea of looking for a little extra work apart from her job. She had confided in Robineau, whom she had continued to find likeable ever since their first meeting at Vinçard's, and he had obtained for her some neckties to be knotted at twenty-five centimes the dozen. In the evening between nine o'clock and one she could sew six dozen of them, which earned her one franc fifty, from which a candle at twenty centimes had to be deducted. But this one franc twenty a day kept Jean; she did not complain about the lack of sleep, and would have considered herself very happy had not a catastrophe yet once more upset her budget. At the end of the second fortnight, when she went to see the woman through whom she obtained the neckties, she found the door closed; the woman was insolvent, bankrupt, which meant that Denise lost eighteen francs thirty centimes, a considerable sum on which she had been absolutely counting for a week. All her troubles in the department paled before this disaster.

"You look sad," said Pauline, whom she met in the furniture department. "Tell me, do you need anything?"

But Denise already owed her friend twelve francs. Trying to smile, she replied:

"No, thank you... I slept badly, that's all."

It was the twentieth of July, at the very height of the panic about dismissals. Out of the four hundred employees, Bourdoncle had already got rid of fifty, and there was a rumour of fresh executions. However, she gave no thought to the ominous signs in the air, she was completely obsessed by the distress caused by a fresh adventure of Jean's which was even more alarming than its predecessors. That day he needed fifteen francs, the dispatch of which alone could save him from the vengeance of a deceived husband. The day before she had received a first letter propounding the drama; then in rapid succession two other letters had arrived, and in the last one above all, which she had just been finishing when Pauline had met her, Jean announced that he would die that evening if he did not receive the fifteen francs. She was racking her brains. She could not take it out of Pépé's board and lodging, for she had paid that two days ago. All her misfortunes were coming at the same time, for she had hoped to get her eighteen francs thirty centimes back through Robineau, who would perhaps be able to find the woman again who had supplied the neckties – but Robineau, having obtained two weeks' leave, had not returned the day before as had been expected.

Meanwhile Pauline was still questioning her in a friendly way. When the two of them met like that, at the end of one of the out-of-the-way departments, they would chat for a few minutes, keeping on the lookout as they did so. Suddenly the girl from the lingerie made as if to escape; she had just caught sight of the white tie of a shopwalker who was coming out of the shawl department.

"Oh no, it's old Jouve," she murmured, reassured. "I don't know why the old man laughs like that when he sees us together... If I was you I'd be afraid, he's much too nice to you. A mangy old dog whose day's done and who still thinks he's talking to his troops."

Indeed, old Jouve was detested by all the salesmen because his supervision was so strict. More than half the dismissals were based on reports made by him. His large red nose – the nose of a one-time captain and bon viveur – became human only in the departments staffed by women.

"Why should I be afraid?" asked Denise.

"Why," replied Pauline, laughing, "he may expect you to show gratitude... Several of the girls have to humour him."

Jouve had moved away, pretending not to see them, and they could hear him pitching into a salesman in the lace department who was guilty of looking at a horse which had fallen down in the Rue Neuve-Saint-Augustin.

"By the way," Pauline went on, "weren't you looking for Monsieur Robineau yesterday? He's back."

Denise thought she was saved.

"Thanks, then I'll go all the way round the silk department..."

It can't be helped! They sent me upstairs to the workroom to fetch a knife."

They separated. With a busy look, as if she was running from cash desk to cash desk checking up on some error, the girl reached the staircase and went down into the hall. It was a quarter to ten, the bell had just gone for the first meal service. A sultry sun was warming the glazed roof, and in spite of the grey linen blinds the heat was beating down in the still air. Now and then a cool breath would arise from the floors, which the porters were sprinkling with a thin trickle of water. Somnolence, a summer siesta, reigned in the emptiness stretching between the departments, which were like chapels filled with sleeping darkness after the final Mass. Nonchalant salesmen were standing about, a few customers were going through the galleries, crossing the hall with the abandoned gait of women tortured by the sun.

As Denise was going downstairs Favier was just measuring out the material for a dress in fine pink-spotted silk for Madame Boutarel, who had arrived the day before from the south. Since the beginning of the month the provinces were supplying customers; one saw nothing but dowdy women, yellow shawls, green skirts, a mass invasion from the country. The apathetic shop assistants were no longer even smiling. Favier accompanied Madame Boutarel to the haberdashery, and when he reappeared he said to Hutin:

"Yesterday they were all from Auvergne, today they're all from Provence... They give me a headache."

But Hutin made a dash forwards, it was his turn, and he had recognized "the pretty lady", the charming fair woman whom the department described in that way, for they knew nothing about her, not even her name! They all used to smile at her, not a week passed without her coming into the Bonheur, always alone. This time she had with her a little boy of four or five, and they chatted about this.

"So she's married, is she?" asked Favier, when Hutin came back from the cash desk where he had had thirty yards of duchess satin debited.

"Maybe," the latter replied, "although the kid doesn't prove a thing. He might belong to a friend... What is certain is that she must have been crying. Oh, she was frightfully sad, and her eyes were red!"

Silence reigned. The two salesmen were looking vaguely into the far confines of the shop. Then Favier resumed in a slow voice:

"If she's married, perhaps her husband has been clouting her."

"Perhaps," Hutin repeated. "Unless it was a lover who's left her in the lurch."

And after a fresh silence he concluded:

"As if I cared, anyway!"

At that moment, Denise was going through the silk department, slackening her pace and looking about her in order to find Robineau. She did not see him, so went into the household-linen gallery, then through the silk department a second time. The two salesmen had noticed her stratagem.

"Here she is again, that skinny girl!" murmured Hutin.

"She's looking for Robineau," said Favier. "I don't know what they're cooking up together. Oh, certainly nothing amusing, Robineau is too silly about that sort of thing... They say he got her some work, knotting ties... What a business, eh?"

Hutin was contemplating doing something ill-natured. When Denise passed close by him he stopped her, saying:

"Is it me you're looking for?"

She became very red. Since the evening at Joinville she had not dared read what was in her heart, for there was a clash of confused feelings in it. She kept on seeing him again in her memory, with the redheaded girl, and if she still trembled in his presence it was perhaps from uneasiness. Had she ever loved him? Did she love him still? She had no desire to probe into these thoughts which distressed her.

"No, Monsieur," she replied, confused.

Then Hutin took advantage of her embarrassment to make fun of her.

"Do you wish to be served? Favier, do serve Robineau to Mademoiselle."

She looked at him intently, with the same calm, sad gaze with which she used to greet the girls' wounding remarks. Oh, how unkind he was, attacking her just as the others did! And it seemed as if something was rent within her, as if a last bond was breaking. There was such suffering in her face that Favier, not very soft-hearted by nature, nevertheless came to her help.

"Monsieur Robineau is in the stockroom," he said. "He's sure to be back for lunch... If you want to speak to him, you'll find him here this afternoon."

Denise thanked him, and went upstairs again to the ready-made department, where Madame Aurélie was waiting for her in cold fury. What! She had been gone for half an hour! Where had she been? Not in the workroom, to be sure? The girl hung her head, thinking how misfortune was dogging her. If Robineau did not come back, all was lost. She was planning to go downstairs again, all the same.

In the silk department, Robineau's return had set off a whole revolution. The department had been hoping that he would be so sick of the trouble people made for him all the time that he would not come back, and indeed at one time, as he was under constant pressure from Vinçard, who wanted to transfer his business to him, he had almost taken it. Hutin's underhand activities, the mine which, for many months, he had been digging out under the assistant buyer's feet, was on the point of exploding at last. During Robineau's leave, Hutin, as senior salesman, had deputized for him, and had done his utmost to injure his reputation in the eyes of his superiors, and to install himself in his place by being overzealous; he discovered and exposed small irregularities, he submitted plans for improvement, he thought out new designs. Moreover, everyone in the department, from the newcomer dreaming of becoming a salesman to the senior salesman coveting Robineau's job, had only one fixed idea – to dislodge their comrade senior to them in order to move up a grade, to devour him if he should become an obstacle – and it was as if this struggle of desires, this pressure of one against another, was the very thing which made the machine run smoothly, which whipped up sales and ignited that blaze of success which astounded Paris. After Hutin, there was Favier, and then after Favier there were others, in a queue. The sound of people loudly licking their lips could be heard. Robineau was condemned, everyone was already carrying away a bone. Therefore, when the assistant buyer reappeared, there was general grousing. The question had to be settled once and for all, and the attitude of the salesmen had seemed so menacing to the head of the department that he had just sent Robineau to the stockroom in order to give the management time to come to a decision.

"If they keep him on we'd all rather leave," Hutin was declaring.

This business was upsetting Bouthemont, whose gayness was ill adapted to an internal worry of this sort. It grieved him no longer to see anything but glum faces around him. Nevertheless, he wished to be fair.

"Come now, leave him alone, he's not doing you any harm."

But there was an outburst of protest.

"What d'you mean, he's not doing us any harm? He's an unbearable person, always nervy and so stuck-up that he'd run you over as soon as look at you!"

This was the great grudge the department had against him. As well as having the nerves of a woman, Robineau had an overbearing manner and was touchy in a way they could not bear. At least twenty anecdotes were told about him, from how he had made a poor young fellow ill to how he had humiliated customers with his cutting remarks.

"Well, gentlemen," said Bouthemont, "I can't do anything myself... I've spoken to the management about it, and I'm going to discuss it with them in a moment or two."

The bell was going for the second meal, the sound of it was coming up from the basement, distant and muffled in the dead air of the shop. Hutin and Favier went downstairs. From every department salesmen were arriving one by one, in disorder, crowding downstairs at the entrance to the kitchen corridor, a damp corridor always lit by gas jets. Without laughter, without speaking, the herd was hurrying there, surrounded by the growing noise of crockery and a strong smell of food. Then, at the end of the corridor, there was a sudden halt at a hatch. And there a cook, surrounded by piles of plates and armed with forks and spoons which he was plunging into copper pans, was distributing the helpings. When he stood aside, beyond his stomach draped in white the blazing kitchen could be seen.

"Oh, damn it!" Hutin murmured, consulting the menu which was written on a blackboard above the hatch. "Beef with mustard sauce or skate... They never give us a roast in this dump! All their stews and fish don't keep body and soul together..."

The fish, moreover, was despised by most people, for the pan remained full. All the same, Favier took the skate. Behind him Hutin bent down, saying:

"Beef with mustard sauce."

With a mechanical gesture the cook speared a piece of meat and then poured a spoonful of sauce over it, and Hutin, choking at the scorching blast he had received in his face from the hatch, had scarcely carried off his helping when already behind him the words "Beef with mustard sauce", "Beef with mustard sauce" were succeeding each other like litanies, while the cook was spearing bits of meat without respite and pouring sauce over them with the rapid and rhythmic movement of a well-regulated clock.

"This skate of theirs is cold," declared Favier, whose hand could feel no warmth from it.

They were all moving off now, arms stretched out, holding their plates straight, afraid of bumping into each other. Ten paces further on was the bar, another hatch with a shining pewter counter on which the portions of wine were set out in small bottles with no corks, still damp from rinsing. Each one received one of these bottles in his empty hand as he passed, and after that, heavily laden, he would repair to his table with a serious air, watching his balance.

Hutin was grumbling under his breath.

"What a walk, with all this crockery!"

The table which Favier and he shared was at the end of the corridor, in the last dining room. All the dining rooms were the same, they had once been cellars four by five yards broad, and had been plastered with cement and fitted up as refectories, but the damp was ruining the paint, the yellow walls were blotched with greenish spots, and from the narrow ventilation shaft, opening on the street at pavement level, the daylight which fell was livid, with vague shadows of passers-by ceaselessly going through it. In July and December alike it was stifling there in the hot steam, laden with nauseating smells which wafted from the neighbouring kitchen.

Hutin was the first to go in. On the table, which was fixed to the wall at one end and covered with oilcloth, there was nothing to indicate the places but glasses and knives and forks. Piles of spare plates stood at each end, whilst in the middle there lay a large loaf stuck with a knife, handle in air. Hutin disentangled himself from his bottle and put down his plate; then, after having taken his table napkin from the bottom of a shelf, which was the only decoration on the walls, he sat down with a sigh.

"I certainly am hungry!" he murmured.

"It's always the same," said Favier, installing himself on his left. "When one's starving, there's nothing to eat."

The table was rapidly filling up. It was laid for twenty-two people. At first there was nothing but a violent din of forks, the guzzling of a lot of hearty young men whose stomachs were hollow from thirteen hours' daily hard work. In the early days the assistants, who had an hour for their meal, had been allowed to go and have their coffee outside, so they used quickly to eat their lunch in twenty minutes, being in a hurry to reach the street. But that had stirred them up too much, they had come back inattentive, with their minds not on their work, and the management had decided that they should no longer go out, but that they should pay fifteen centimes extra for a cup of coffee if they wanted one. So now they dawdled over the meal, not at all anxious to go back to their departments before it was time to do so. Many of them were reading a newspaper, folded and propped against their bottle as they bolted down huge mouthfuls. Others, once they had taken the edge off their hunger, were talking rowdily, always coming back to the eternal subjects of the bad food, the money they earned, what they had done last Sunday and what they were going to do next Sunday.

"I say, what about that chap Robineau of yours?" a salesman asked Hutin.

All the departments were taking an interest in the silk department's struggle against its assistant buyer. The question was discussed every day until midnight at the Café Saint-Roch. Hutin, who was struggling with his bit of beef, was content to reply:

"Well, he's back, Robineau is."

Then suddenly losing his temper:

"Damn it all, they've given me donkey! It really is disgusting, honestly it is!"

"You shouldn't complain!" said Favier. "Look at me, I was stupid enough to take skate... It's gone bad!"

They were all talking at once, complaining and joking. At a corner of the table, against the wall, Deloche was eating in silence. He was cursed with an inordinate appetite which he had never been able to satisfy, and as he earned too little to buy himself extras, he would cut himself slices of bread, and devour the least tempting dishes greedily. As a result, they were all making fun of him, shouting:

"Favier, pass your skate to Deloche... He likes it like that."

"And your meat, Hutin: Deloche wants it for his pudding."

The poor lad shrugged his shoulders and did not even reply. It was not his fault if he was famished. Besides, the others might despise the food, but they were stuffing themselves with it all the same.

But a faint whistle silenced them. This signalled the presence of Mouret and Bourdoncle in the corridor. For some time now the complaints of the staff had been such that the management had taken to coming down to judge the quality of the food for itself. Out of the thirty centimes per head per day which the cook received, he had to pay everything – provisions, coal, gas, staff – and the management was naively astonished when the results were not very good. That very morning each department had chosen a salesman as delegate, and Mignot and Liénard had undertaken to speak for their colleagues. Therefore, in the sudden silence, they strained their ears, listening to the voices which could be heard coming from the neighbouring room, which Mouret and Bourdoncle had just entered. The latter was declaring that the beef was excellent, and Mignot, infuriated by this calm assurance, was repeating: "Chew it and see," while Liénard, tackling the skate, was saying sweetly: "But it stinks, Monsieur!" Then Mouret launched forth into cordial phrases: he would do everything for the well-being of his employees, he was a father to them, he would rather eat dry bread himself than let them be badly fed.

"I promise you I will go into the question," he finally concluded, raising his voice so that he could be heard from one end of the corridor to the other.

The management's inquiry was over, the noise of forks recommenced. Hutin murmured:

"Yes, if you count on that you can wait till the cows come home!... Oh! They don't stint their kind words. If you want promises, you can have as many as you like. They feed us on old boots and kick us out like dogs!"

The salesman who had already questioned him repeated:

"About Robineau... you were saying?..."

But the clatter of crockery drowned his voice. The assistants changed their plates themselves, and to the left and right the piles were diminishing. A kitchen hand was bringing some large tin platters, and Hutin exclaimed:

"A gratin of rice, that's the end!"

"Let's have a pennyworth of glue!" said Favier, helping himself.

Some liked it, others found it too tacky. And those who were reading remained silent, deep in the serial story in their papers, not even knowing what they were eating. They were all mopping their brows, the small narrow cellar was filling up with murky fumes, while all the time, like black stripes, the shadows of passers-by were running across the tablecloth.

"Pass the bread to Deloche," shouted a wag.

Each one would cut himself a slice and then replunge the knife right up to the hilt in the crust, and the bread was going round the table all the time.

"Who'll have my rice in exchange for his dessert?" asked Hutin.

When he had concluded the deal with a small, thin man, he tried to sell his wine as well, but no one wanted it, they thought it execrable.

"Well, I was telling you that Robineau is back," he went on, in the midst of cross-currents of laughter and conversations. "Oh! It's a sad business about him… D'you know, he leads the salesgirls astray! Yes, he gets neckties for them to knot!"

"Be quiet!" murmured Favier. "Look at them passing sentence on him!"

Out of the corner of his eye he was looking at Bouthemont, who was walking between Mouret and Bourdoncle in the corridor; they were all three of them absorbed and talking animatedly in low voices. The dining room for section managers and their deputies happened to be just opposite. When Bouthemont had seen Mouret passing by he had risen from the table, having finished, and was telling him about all the trouble in his department, and how perplexed he was about it. The other two were listening to him, so far refusing to sacrifice Robineau, who was a first-class salesman and had been there since Madame Hédouin's day. But when he came to the story of the neckties, Bourdoncle lost his temper. The fellow must be mad to act as a go-between for giving the salesgirls extra work. The shop paid the girls quite highly enough for their time; if they worked at night on their own account it was obvious that they would do less work during the day in the shop; therefore they were robbing it, they were risking their health, which did not belong to them. The night was made for sleeping, they must all sleep, or else they would be kicked out!

"Things are hotting up," Hutin remarked.

Each time the three men walked slowly past the dining room the assistants were on the look out for them, and would comment on their slightest gestures. It made them forget their rice gratin, in which a cashier had just found a trouser button.

"I heard the word 'necktie'," said Favier. "And did you see Bourdoncle's face, and how he suddenly went pale?"

Mouret, meanwhile, was sharing the latter's indignation. A salesgirl reduced to working at night seemed to him to be an attack against the very structure of the Bonheur. Which of them could be such a silly ninny that she could not support herself on her profits from sales? But when Bouthemont named Denise he calmed down and found excuses for her. Ah yes! That little thing! She was not very handy yet, and she had dependants, so he had been assured. Bourdoncle interrupted him, declaring that she must be dismissed on the spot. They would never make anything of a plain Jane like that, he had always said so; he seemed to be satisfying a personal grudge. At that, Mouret became embarrassed and pretended to laugh. My goodness! What a hard man he was! Couldn't it be forgiven for once? They would summon the culprit and give her a scolding. The long and short of it was that Robineau was in the wrong, for being a senior assistant and knowing the ways of the shop he should have stopped her from doing it.

"My word! Now the boss is laughing!" said Favier in astonishment, as the group went past the door again.

"Good Lord!" swore Hutin. "If they persist in saddling us with that Robineau of theirs, we'll give them something to laugh about!"

Bourdoncle was looking Mouret straight in the face. Then he merely made a gesture of contempt, as much as to say that he understood at last, and that it was idiotic. Bouthemont had resumed his complaints: the salesmen were threatening to leave, and there were some excellent ones amongst them. But what appeared to make more impression on the gentlemen was a rumour of friendly relations between Robineau and Gaujean: the latter, so it was said, was urging the buyer to set up his own business in the neighbourhood, and was offering him the most generous credit in order to bring down the Bonheur des Dames. There was a silence. Ah! So Robineau was dreaming of battle! Mouret had become serious; he pretended to be scornful, he avoided taking a decision, as if the affair was of no importance. They would see, he would speak to him. And he went on at once to joke with Bouthemont, whose father had arrived two days earlier from his little shop in Montpellier and had almost choked with amazement and indignation when he arrived in the enormous hall where his son reigned. They were still laughing about the old fellow who, when he had recovered his meridional self-possession, had set about disparaging everything, maintaining that the drapery trade would finish up in the street.

"Here comes Robineau now," murmured the section manager. "I sent him to the stockroom in order to avoid an unfortunate clash... Forgive me if I insist, but things have got to such a pitch that something must be done."

Robineau, who was coming in, was indeed passing them, and went to his table, greeting them as he did so.

Mouret merely repeated:

"All right, we'll see about it."

They left. Hutin and Favier were still waiting for them. When they did not see them reappear, they let off steam. Was the management now going to come down to each meal like that to count how many mouthfuls they had? Fine fun it would be if they couldn't even be free while they were eating! The truth of the matter was that they had just seen Robineau coming in again, and the governor's good humour was making them worry about the outcome of the struggle which they had set in motion. They lowered their voices, thinking up new ways of annoying him.

"But I'm starving!" Hutin continued out loud. "You leave the table even hungrier than you were!"

He had, nevertheless, eaten two portions of preserves, his own and the one he had exchanged for his helping of rice. Suddenly he exclaimed:

"Damn it all! I'll stump up for an extra helping! Victor, bring me a third portion of preserves!"

The waiter was finishing serving the puddings. Then he brought the coffee, and those who took it gave him their fifteen centimes on the spot. Some of the salesmen left and were dawdling along the corridor, looking for dark corners in which to smoke a cigarette. Others remained behind, drooping over the table cluttered up with greasy plates. They were rolling pellets of bread, going back over the same stories again and again, in the midst of the smell of burnt fat which they no longer noticed and the heat of a Turkish bath which turned their ears red. The walls were oozing with moisture, slow asphyxiation was descending from the mouldy ceiling. Deloche, stuffed full of bread, was digesting in silence, looking up at the ventilator; every day after lunch it was his relaxation thus to watch the feet of the passers-by who were hurrying along quickly on the pavement level – feet cut off at the ankle, heavy shoes, elegant high boots, dainty women's ankle boots, a continual coming and going of live feet, devoid of bodies and heads. On rainy days it was very dirty.

"What! Already!" cried Hutin.

A bell was ringing at the end of the corridor, they had to give up their places to the third meal service. The waiters were coming to wash the oilcloth with buckets of tepid water and big sponges. The dining rooms were slowly emptying, the salesmen were going back to their departments again, dawdling all the way up the stairs. And in the kitchen the cook had once more taken his place between the pans of beef, skate and sauce, armed with his spoons and forks, ready once more to fill the plates with the rhythmic movement of a well-regulated clock.

As Hutin and Favier were lagging behind they saw Denise coming downstairs.

"Monsieur Robineau is back, Mademoiselle," said the senior salesman, with mocking politeness.

"He is lunching," the other added. "But if it's too urgent, you can go in."

Denise went on going downstairs without answering, without looking round. However, when she passed the dining room for section managers and their assistants she could not help glancing in. Robineau was indeed there. She would try to speak to him in the afternoon, and she went on down the corridor to reach her table, which was at the other end.

The women ate separately, in two rooms reserved for them. Denise went into the first room. It was also an old cellar transformed into a refectory, but it had been fitted up more comfortably. On the oval table in the centre the fifteen places were laid further apart, and the wine was in carafes; a dish of skate and a dish of beef with mustard sauce occupied either end of the table. Waiters in white aprons were serving the ladies, which relieved them of the disagreeable necessity of fetching their helpings themselves from the hatch. The management had considered this to be more seemly.

"So you've been all round, have you?" asked Pauline, who was already seated and was cutting herself some bread.

"Yes," Denise replied, blushing, "I was accompanying a customer."

She was lying. Clara nudged the elbow of the salesgirl sitting next to her. What was the matter with Touslehead that day? She really was very queer. She kept on getting letters from her lover in rapid succession; then she was running round the shop like a lost soul, making pretexts of errands in the workroom without even going there. There was certainly something going on. So Clara spoke of a horrible drama which was filling the newspapers, and as she did so went on eating her skate with no distaste, with the unconcern of a girl who had in the past been fed on rancid bacon.

"Have you read about that man who cut his mistress's head off with the stroke of a razor?"

"Of course!" remarked a little assistant from the lingerie department with a gentle, delicate face. "He found her with another man. He was quite right!"

But Pauline protested. What! Just because you didn't love a man any longer he'd have the right to slit your throat! Really, what an idea! And breaking off and turning to the waiter, she said:

"Pierre, you know I just can't stomach the beef... Do ask them to make me something specially – an omelette, eh? And a runny one, if possible!"

As she always had some titbits in her pocket she took out some chocolate drops and set about munching them with her bread while she waited.

"It certainly isn't much fun, a man like that," Clara resumed. "And there are a lot of jealous men about! Only the other day there was a workman who threw his wife down a well."

She was not taking her eyes off Denise, and seeing her grow pale she thought she had guessed what was the matter. Obviously, the little goody-goody was terrified of being hit by her lover, to whom she was probably being unfaithful. It would be funny if he were to come right into the shop to hunt her out, as she seemed to fear. But the conversation was changing, a salesgirl was telling them how to take marks out of velvet. Next they talked about a play at the Gaité, in which some sweet little girls danced even better than grown-ups. Pauline, momentarily saddened by the sight of her omelette, which was overcooked, brightened up again when she found that it was not too bad after all.

"Do pass me the wine," she said to Denise. "You ought to order yourself an omelette."

"Oh! The beef's enough for me," replied the girl who, so as not to spend anything, used to keep to the food provided by the shop, no matter how repulsive it was.

When the waiter brought the rice gratin the girls protested. They had left it the week before, and they had hoped that it would not reappear again. Denise, absent-minded and worried about Jean as a result of Clara's stories, was the only one to eat it; they were all watching her with an air of disgust. There was an orgy of extra dishes, the girls filled themselves up with preserves. In any case, it was considered elegant to do so, to pay for their food with their own money.

"You know, the gentlemen have complained," said the fragile-looking girl from the lingerie department, "and the management has promised—"

She was interrupted with laughter, they no longer talked of anything but the management. They all had coffee, except Denise who could not stand it, so she said. They lingered over their cups, the girls from the lingerie department dressed with lower-middle-class simplicity in wool, those from the ready-made department in silk, their table napkins tucked under their chins so as not to get marks on their dresses, like ladies who had gone down to eat in the servants' hall with their maids. They had opened the skylight of the ventilator in order to let out the stifling, reeking air, but they had to shut it again at once, for the wheels of cabs seemed to be going across the table.

"Sh!" breathed Pauline. "Here's that old fool!"

It was Inspector Jouve. He was fond of prowling about like that, in the girls' direction, towards the end of meals. In any case, he had to supervise their dining rooms. He would come in, eyes smiling, and go round the table; sometimes even he would chat with them, would ask if they had enjoyed their meal. But, as he both made them uneasy and bored them, they would all hasten to run away. Although the bell had not yet gone, Clara was the first to disappear; others followed her. Soon no one but Denise and Pauline remained. The latter, having drunk her coffee, was finishing up her chocolate drops.

"Well!" she said as she stood up, "I'm going to send a waiter to fetch me some oranges... Are you coming?"

"In a moment," answered Denise, who was nibbling a crust, determined to be the last to remain so that she could tackle Robineau when she went upstairs again.

However, once alone with Jouve she had an uneasy feeling, and, thwarted in her purpose, she finally left the table. But seeing her go towards the door, he barred her way:

"Mademoiselle Baudu..."

He was standing before her, smiling with a paternal air. His thick grey moustaches and close-cropped hair made him look military decorum personified, and he was puffing out his chest, on which his medal ribbon was displayed.

"What is it, Monsieur Jouve?" she asked, reassured.

"I saw you again this morning, talking upstairs, behind the carpets. You know it's against the rules, and if I was to report it... she's very fond of you, your friend Pauline, isn't she?"

His moustache bristled, his enormous nose, the shrewd hooked nose of a person with the desires of a bull, was aflame.

"What are you up to, the two of you, loving each other like that, eh?"

Denise, without understanding, began to feel uneasy again. He was coming too close, he was speaking right in her face.

"It's true, we were chatting, Monsieur Jouve," she stammered. "But there's nothing very bad about chatting a little... You're very kind to me, thank you all the same..."

"I ought not be kind to you," he said. "Justice, that's the only thing I recognize... Only, you're so nice that..."

He was moving even closer. At that she was really frightened. Pauline's words came back to her, she remembered the stories that were going round, of salesgirls terrorized by old Jouve, having to buy his goodwill. In the shop, it must be added, he was content with small liberties, he would gently tap the cheeks of obliging girls with his swollen fingers, he would take their hands, then keep them in his as if he had forgotten them. It all remained paternal, and he would only let the bull loose outside, if they consented to take bread and butter with him at his place in the Rue des Moineaux.

"Leave me alone," murmured the girl, drawing back.

"Come now," he was saying, "you're not going to be shy with a friend who's always good to you... Be a nice girl, come and have a cup of tea and a slice of bread and butter this evening. It's kindly meant."

She was struggling now.

"No! No!"

The dining room remained empty, the waiter had not re-appeared. Jouve, keeping his ears open for the sound of footsteps, gave a quick glance around and, very excited, he departed from his usual behaviour, went beyond his paternal familiarities and tried to kiss her on the neck.

"Little wretch, little silly... How can one be so silly with hair like this? Do come tonight, just for fun."

But she was in a panic, in terrified disgust at the approach of that ardent face, whose breath she could feel. Suddenly she gave him a push with such an effort that he swayed and almost fell onto the table. Fortunately a chair caught him, but the impact bowled over a carafe of wine, bespattering his white tie and soaking his red ribbon. And there he remained, not wiping himself, choking with rage at such brutality. What! When he wasn't expecting it, wasn't even trying hard and was simply giving way to his kind nature!

"Ah! Mademoiselle, you'll be sorry for this, upon my word!"

Denise had fled. The bell was just ringing, and, flustered, still trembling, she forgot about Robineau and went up to her department. Then she no longer dared go down again. As the sun warmed the Place Gaillon side of the shop in the afternoon, it was stifling in the salons on the mezzanine floor in spite of the blinds. Some customers came, and although they did not buy anything, the girls were bathed in perspiration as a result. The whole department was yawning, watched by Madame Aurélie's large and somnolent eyes. Finally, towards three o'clock, seeing the buyer drop off to sleep, Denise quietly slipped off and resumed her trip round the shop, trying to look busy. In order to put the curious off the scent she did not go straight down to the silk department; first she made as if she had business in the lace department, she approached Deloche, and asked him for some information; then on the ground floor she went through the cottons, and was going into the neckties when a start of surprise made her stop short. Jean was facing her.

"What! You?" she murmured, quite pale.

He still had on his working overalls and was bareheaded, his fair hair in disorder and curling over his girlish skin. Standing before a case full of narrow black ties, he seemed to be deep in reflection.

"What are you doing here?" she went on.

"Why," he replied, "I was waiting for you! You forbade me to come so I came in all the same, but I haven't said a word to anyone. Oh, you needn't worry! Pretend you don't know me if you like."

Some salesmen were already looking at them with a surprised air. Jean lowered his voice.

"You know, she wanted to come with me. Yes, she's in the square, by the fountain... Give me the fifteen francs quickly, or we're done for, as sure as eggs is eggs!"

At this, Denise became very agitated. People were laughing derisively, were listening to what was going on. As there was a staircase to the basement at the back of the tie department, she pushed her brother towards it and made him quickly go down it. Once downstairs he went on with his story, embarrassed, racking his brains for facts, afraid of not being believed.

"Money's nothing to her. She's too refined... and as for her husband, well! He doesn't care a damn about fifteen francs! He wouldn't give his wife permission for a million... a glue manufacturer, did I tell you? They're very high-class people... No, it's for a scoundrel, a friend of hers who saw us – and you see, if I don't give him fifteen francs, this evening..."

"Shut up," murmured Denise. "Later... go ahead, walk on, do!"

They had gone down into the dispatch department. The slack season was sending the vast cellar to sleep, under the pallid light from the ventilators. It was cold there, silence was descending from the roof. But all the same a boy was taking the few parcels for the Madeleine district from one of the compartments, and on the big sorting table Campion, the head of the department, was sitting and swinging his legs, with his eyes wide open.

Jean was starting off again:

"The husband, who has a big knife..."

"Go on, do!" Denise repeated, still pushing him.

They went down one of the narrow corridors, where the gas always burned. To the right and left, in the depths of dark cellars, the reserve stocks were making piles of shadows behind the hoardings. Finally she stopped by one of these wattle screens. Doubtless no one would come, but it was forbidden, and she gave a shudder.

"If that scoundrel talks," Jean went on, "the husband who has a big knife..."

"Where do you think I can get fifteen francs from?" Denise burst out in despair. "Can't you really be sensible? Such funny things keep on happening to you all the time!"

He smote his breast. In all his romantic inventions, he himself did not know what the precise truth was. He simply dramatized his financial requirements, and at the root of it there was always some pressing necessity.

"I swear on everything I hold most sacred that this time it's really true... I was holding her like this, and she was kissing me..."

Once more she told him to be quiet; tortured, at the end of her tether, she lost her temper.

"I don't want to hear about it. Keep your bad behaviour to yourself. It's too disgusting, d'you understand? And you pester me every week, I'm killing myself to keep you supplied with francs. Yes, I sit up all night... Not to mention the fact that you are taking the bread out of your brother's mouth."

Jean stood gaping, his face pale. What! It was disgusting? And he did not understand; ever since his childhood he had treated his sister as a friend, it seemed quite natural to open his heart to her. He was choking above all at hearing that she sat up all night. The idea that he was killing her and squandering Pépé's share overwhelmed him to such an extent that he began to cry.

"You're right, I'm a rotter," he exclaimed. "But it isn't disgusting, really. On the contrary, and that's why one goes on doing it... You see, this one is twenty years old already. She thought she'd make fun of me because I'm only just seventeen... My goodness! I'm furious with myself! I could hit myself!"

He had taken her hands, he was kissing them, wetting them with tears.

"Give me the fifteen francs, it'll be the last time, I swear to you... Or else, no! Don't give me anything, I'd rather die. If the husband murders me it'll be good riddance for you."

And as she too was crying, he had a twinge of remorse.

"I say that, but really, I don't know. Perhaps he doesn't want to kill anyone... We'll manage, I promise you, Sis. Come on, goodbye, I'm off."

But a sound of footsteps at the end of the corridor alarmed them. She pulled him over by the stores again, into a dark corner. For a moment they could no longer hear anything but the hiss of a gas jet near them. Then the footsteps approached and, craning her neck, she recognized Inspector Jouve, who in his stiff way had just entered the corridor. Was it by chance that he was going that way? Or had some other supervisor, on duty at the door, tipped him off? She was seized with such fear that she lost her head, and she pushed Jean out of the dark hole where they were hiding and drove him in front of her, mumbling as she did so:

"Get out! Get out!"

They were both racing away, hearing as they did so the breath of old Jouve at their heels, for he had also started to run. They crossed through the dispatch department again and arrived at the foot of a stairway, the glazed well hole of which opened on to the Rue de la Michodière.

"Get out!" repeated Denise. "Get out! If I can I'll send you the fifteen francs all the same."

Jean, dazed, made his escape. The shopwalker who was just coming up, out of breath, caught sight only of a bit of white overall and some fair curls blown about by the wind in the street. He recovered his breath for a moment in order to regain his correct bearing. He had a brand-new white necktie, taken from the lingerie department, and its knot, which was very wide, was shining like snow.

"Well, that's a nice thing, Mademoiselle," he said, his lips trembling. "Yes, it's a nice thing, a very nice thing... If you think that I'm going to tolerate nice things like that in the basement..."

And he went on pursuing her with this word, while she went upstairs again to the shop, her throat choked with emotion, without being able to think of anything to say in her own defence. Now she was bitterly regretting that she had run. Why hadn't she explained her conduct, pointed out her brother? Again everyone would suppose the worst, and no matter how she might swear that it was untrue, they would not believe her. Yet once more she forgot Robineau and went straight back to the department.

Without waiting, Jouve went to the management to make his report. But the porter on duty told him that the director was with Monsieur Bourdoncle and Monsieur Robineau; the three of them had been talking for a quarter of an hour. The door, moreover, was half open; Mouret could be heard gaily asking the assistant if he had had a good holiday, there was not the slightest question of a dismissal – on the contrary, the conversation was about certain measures to be taken in the department.

"Do you want something, Monsieur Jouve?" shouted Mouret. "Do come in!"

But some instinct forewarned the shopwalker. As Bourdoncle had left the room, Jouve preferred to tell the whole story to him. Slowly they went along the shawl gallery, walking side by side, one leaning forwards and speaking in a very low voice, the other listening, not a line of his hard face allowing his impressions to be seen.

"Very well," the latter said in the end.

And as they had arrived outside the ready-made department, he went into it. At that moment Madame Aurélie was losing her temper with Denise. Where had she been now? Madame Aurélie presumed that she wouldn't say that she had gone up to the workroom this time! Really, these continual vanishings could not be tolerated any longer.

"Madame Aurélie," called Bourdoncle.

He was making up his mind to force the issue, he did not want to consult Mouret, for fear that he might be weak. The buyer advanced, and once more the story was related in undertones. The whole department was waiting, scenting a catastrophe.

Finally Madame Aurélie turned round with a grave air.

"Mademoiselle Baudu..."

Her bloated imperial mask had the inexorable immobility of omnipotence.

"Proceed to the pay desk!"

The terrible sentence rang out very loudly through the department, which was then empty of customers. Denise had remained erect and white, holding her breath. Then in a broken voice she stammered:

"Me! Me! But why? What have I done?"

Bourdoncle replied harshly that she was quite well aware what she had done and would do well not to press for an explanation – and he spoke of the neckties, and said that it would be a fine thing if all the girls were to meet men in the basement.

"But it's my brother!" she cried, with the heart-rending anger of an outraged virgin.

Marguerite and Clara started to laugh, while Madame Frédéric, usually so discreet, was also shaking her head with an air of incredulity. Always saying it was her brother! It really was very silly! Then Denise looked at them all; at Bourdoncle, who from the first moment had not wanted her; at Jouve, who had stayed there to give evidence, and from whom she could not expect any justice; and then at the girls, whose hearts she had not been able to melt in spite of nine months' smiling courage, those girls who were delighted to push her out at last. What was the good of struggling? Why try to foist herself on them when no one liked her? And she went away without saying another word, she did not even cast a last glance at the salon where she had struggled for so long.

But as soon as she was alone by the hall balustrade, her heart was wrung with a keener pain. No one liked her, and at the sudden thought of Mouret all her resignation left her. No! She could not accept a dismissal like that. Perhaps he would believe that dirty story about an assignation with a man in the depths of the cellars. This idea tortured her with shame, with an anguish such as she had never experienced until then. She wanted to go and find him, she would explain things to him, just so that he would know, for she did not mind leaving once he knew the truth. And her old fear, the chill which froze her in his presence, suddenly broke out in a passionate need to see him and not to leave the shop without swearing to him that she had never belonged to another man.

It was almost five o'clock; in the cool evening air the shop was coming to life a little. Quickly she set off towards the director's office. But when she was outside the door she was once more overwhelmed with hopeless sadness. She was tongue-tied, the weight of existence was once more crushing her. He would not believe her, he would laugh like the others – and this fear made her lose heart. It was all over, she would be better off alone, out of sight, dead. And so, without even letting Deloche and Pauline know, she went at once to the pay desk.

"Mademoiselle," said the clerk, "you've got twenty-two days, that makes eighteen francs seventy, to which seven francs percentage and bonus must be added... That's what you made it, isn't it?"

"Yes, Monsieur... Thank you."

And Denise was just going away with her money when she did, at last, meet Robineau. He had already heard of her dismissal and promised to try to get in touch with the woman through whom he had obtained the ties. He was comforting her in a whisper, carried away with anger. What an existence! To be at the continual mercy of a whim! To be thrown out from one moment to the next, without even being able to insist on the full month's wages! Denise went upstairs to inform Madame Cabin that she would try to send someone for her trunk during the course of the evening. Five o'clock was striking when she found herself on the pavement in the Place Gaillon, dazed in the midst of the cabs and the crowd.

That very evening, when Robineau was going home, he received a letter from the management informing him in four lines that, for reasons of an administrative nature, they would be forced to dispense with his services. He had been in the shop for seven years, that very afternoon he had been talking to those gentlemen; it was a staggering blow. Hutin and Favier were celebrating victory in the silk department just as boisterously as Marguerite and Clara were exulting in the ready-made department. Good riddance! Clean sweeps make room! Only Deloche and Pauline, when they met as they went through the crowd in the departments, exchanged heart-broken words, regretting Denise, who had been so gentle and so upright.

"Ah," the young man would say, "if ever she should make good anywhere else, I wish she'd come back here to show all those good-for-nothings a thing or two!"

It was Bourdoncle who bore the brunt of Mouret's violent reaction to the affair. When the latter heard of Denise's dismissal he became extremely angry. Usually he had very little to do with the staff, but this time he affected to consider that there had been an encroachment of power, an attempt to evade his authority. Was he no longer the master, by any chance, for people to take it on themselves to give orders? Everything must pass through his hands, absolutely everything, and he would break anyone who resisted him like a straw. Then when, in a nervous torment which he was unable to hide, he had made personal inquiries, he lost his temper again. The poor girl had not been lying; it really was her brother, Campion had fully recognized him. So why should she be dismissed? He even talked of taking her on again.

Meanwhile Bourdoncle, strong with passive resistance, bent his back beneath the storm. He was studying Mouret. Finally, one day when he saw that he was calmer, he ventured to say, in a special tone of voice:

"It's better for everyone that she's gone."

Mouret became embarrassed, his face flushed.

"Upon my word," he answered, laughing, "perhaps you're right... Let's get down and have a look at the sales. It's picking up, we made nearly a hundred thousand francs yesterday."

7

FOR A MOMENT Denise had remained dazed on the pavement in the sunshine which, at five o'clock, was still scorching. July was warming the gutters, Paris was bathed in its chalky summer light full of blinding reflections. And the catastrophe had been so sudden, she had been pushed out so roughly, that she was mechanically turning over the twenty-five francs seventy centimes in her pocket, while wondering where to go and what to do.

A whole queue of cabs prevented her from leaving the pavement by the Bonheur des Dames. When she was able to venture between the wheels, she crossed the Place Gaillon as if she wanted to go to the Rue Louis-le-Grand; then she changed her mind and went towards the Rue Saint-Roch. But she still had no plan, for she stopped at the corner of the Rue Neuve-des-Petits-Champs which, after having looked about her in an irresolute way, she finally took. When she saw the Choiseul arcade she went down it, found herself in the Rue Monsigny without knowing how she had got there, and ended up again in the Rue Neuve-Saint-Augustin. Her ears were filled with buzzing, and the thought of her trunk came back to her at the sight of a street porter, but where could she have it taken to, and why all that difficulty when only an hour earlier she had still had a bed in which to sleep that night?

Then, looking up at the houses, she began to examine the windows. Placards succeeded each other. She saw them confusedly, continually overwhelmed afresh as she was by the internal commotion which was shaking her to the roots. Was it possible? Alone, from one minute to the next, lost in this huge unknown city, unprotected, penniless! Yet she had to eat and sleep all the same. The streets succeeded each other, the Rue des Moulins, the Rue Saint-Anne. She scoured the neighbourhood, retracing her footsteps, always coming back to the only square which she knew well. Suddenly she was dumbfounded, she was once more outside the Bonheur des Dames, and in order to escape from this obsession she plunged into the Rue de la Michodière.

Fortunately Baudu was not at his doorway; behind its dark window panes the Vieil Elbeuf seemed dead. She would never have dared to go to her uncle's, for he affected to have nothing to do with her any longer and, in the misfortune which he had predicted would befall her, she did not want to be a burden to him. But on the other side of the street a yellow placard caught her eye: FURNISHED ROOM TO LET. The house looked so poor that it was the first one which did not intimidate her. Then she recognized it, with its two low storeys, with its rust-coloured front, squeezed in between the Bonheur des Dames and what had once been the Duvillard mansion. On the threshold of the umbrella shop old Bourras, long-haired and bearded like a prophet, with spectacles on his nose, was examining the ivory of a walking-stick knob. He rented the whole house, and sublet the two upper storeys furnished in order to help pay his rent.

"You have a room to let, Monsieur?" asked Denise, obeying an instinctive urge.

He raised his large eyes covered with thick eyebrows, surprised at seeing her. All those girls were known to him. And after looking at her clean little dress and decent appearance, he replied:

"It's not for the likes of you."

"How much is it, then?" Denise went on.

"Fifteen francs a month."

At that, she asked to see it. In the narrow shop, as he was still staring at her with an astonished air, she told him how she had left the Bonheur and of her desire not to be an embarrassment to her uncle. Finally the old man went to fetch a key from the room at the back of the shop, a dark room where he cooked and slept; beyond it, behind a dusty window pane, the greenish light of an internal courtyard, scarcely two yards wide, could be seen.

"I'll go first so you won't fall," said Bourras in the damp passageway which skirted the shop.

He stumbled against a step and went up, multiplying his warnings. Careful! The banisters were against the wall, there was a hole at the corner, sometimes tenants left their dustbins on the stairs. Denise, in total darkness, could distinguish nothing, but could only feel the chilliness of the old, damp plasterwork. However, on the first floor, a small pane opening onto the courtyard enabled her to see vaguely, as if from the depths of a stagnant pond, the warped staircase, the walls black with filth, the cracked and peeling doors.

"If only one of these rooms was free!" Bourras went on. "You'd be fine there... But they're always occupied by ladies."

On the second floor the light increased, illuminating the stairs of the dwelling with a garish pallor. A baker's apprentice occupied the first room, and it was the other, at the back, which was vacant. When Bourras had opened the door he had to remain on the landing so that Denise could have space to inspect the room. The bed, in the corner by the door, left just enough space for one person to pass. At the end of the room there was a little walnut-wood chest of drawers, a table of black pinewood and two chairs. Tenants who did a little cooking used to kneel down in front of the fireplace, where there was a clay oven.

"Upon my word!" the old man was saying. "It's not grand, but the window's gay, you can see the people in the street."

And as Denise was looking with surprise at the corner of the ceiling above the bed, where a lady who had made a brief stay there had written her name "Ernestine" by moving a candle flame along, he added good-naturedly:

"If one were to repair it, one would never be able to make both ends meet... Well, it's all I've got."

"It'll suit me very well," the girl declared.

She paid for a month in advance, asked for the linen, a pair of sheets and two towels, and made her bed without waiting, happy, relieved to know where she would spend the night. An hour later she had sent someone to fetch her trunk and she had settled in.

During the first two months she suffered terrible privations. Being unable to pay for Pépé's board and lodging any longer, she had taken him back to live with her, and he slept on an old easy chair lent by Bourras. She needed exactly one franc fifty a day, including the rent, providing she herself lived on dry bread so as to give a little meat to the child. For the first fortnight things did not go too badly; she had started off with ten francs, then she had the good luck to find the woman again who had let her have the ties, who paid her the eighteen francs thirty she owed her. But after that she was completely destitute. In vain did she apply to shops, in the Place Clichy, at the Bon Marché, at the Louvre; everywhere the off season was stopping business, they told her to come back in the autumn, more than five thousand shop assistants, dismissed like her, were tramping the streets without work. Then she tried to get some small odd jobs – only in her ignorance of Paris she did not know where to apply: she accepted ungrateful tasks and did not even always get paid for them. Some evenings she would make Pépé dine alone on soup, telling him that she had already eaten outside, and she would go to bed, her head buzzing, fed by nothing but the fever which was making her hands burn. When Jean turned up in the midst of this poverty he would call himself a scoundrel with such despairing violence that she was obliged to lie to him; often she would still find a way to slip him a couple of francs to prove to him that she had something put aside. She never wept in front of the children. On Sundays when she was able to cook a bit of veal in the fireplace, kneeling on the floor, the narrow room would echo with the gaiety of children heedless of existence. Then Jean would go back to his work, Pépé would fall asleep and she would pass a hideous night, in agonies for the morrow.

Other fears kept her awake, too. The two ladies on the first floor used to receive visitors very late, and sometimes a man would make a mistake, come upstairs and bang with his fists on her door. As Bourras had calmly told her not to reply, she used to bury her head under her pillow to escape from the oaths. Then her neighbour, the baker, had wanted to have a bit of fun. He only came back in the morning, and would lie in wait for her when she went to fetch her water; he even made holes in the dividing wall and watched her washing her face, which forced her to hang her clothes all along the wall. But she suffered even more from being pestered in the street, from the continual obsession of passers-by. She could not go down to buy a candle in those muddy streets, where the dissolute living of old neighbourhoods prowled about, without hearing an eager whistle or crude words of lust behind her, and encouraged by the house's sordid aspect, men followed her right to the end of the dark passageway. Why on earth had she not got a lover? That surprised people, seemed ridiculous. She would have to succumb one day. She would not have been able to explain herself how she managed to resist under the threat of hunger and surrounded by the heady desires with which the air about her was laden.

One evening Denise did not even have any bread for Pépé's soup, when a gentleman wearing a medal started to follow her. Outside the passageway he became brutal, and she, revolted and disgusted, slammed the door in his face. Then, upstairs, she sat down, her hands shaking. The little boy was asleep. What should she reply to him if he should wake up and ask her for something to eat? And yet she had only to have consented, her poverty would have been at an end, she would have had money, dresses and a fine room. It was easy, they said everyone did it in the end, because in Paris a woman could live on what she earned. But her whole being revolted against it, she felt no indignation against others for giving in, but merely an aversion to anything dirty or senseless. She looked at life in a logical, wise and courageous way.

She would often examine her thoughts in this strain. An old ballad would go through her head, about a sailor's fiancée whose love protected her from the perils of waiting for him. At Valognes she used to hum the sentimental refrain while looking at the empty street. Had she too love in her heart for someone which enabled her to be so brave? She still dreamt uneasily of Hutin. Each day she saw him pass beneath her window. Now that he was assistant buyer he walked alone, surrounded by the respect of the ordinary salesmen. Never did he raise his head, and she believed that it was the young man's vanity which made her suffer, and would watch him without fear of being caught. And as soon as she caught sight of Mouret, who also went by every evening, she would begin to tremble, and would quickly hide, her heart beating. There was no need for him to know where she was living, and she was ashamed of the house, she was grieved at what he might think of her, even though they might never meet again.

In any case, Denise was still living in the bustle of the Bonheur des Dames. Only a wall separated her room from her old department, and from the morning onwards she would relive her days there, she could sense the crowd growing with the increasing hum of selling. The slightest sounds would shake the old hovel clinging on to the giant's side; it beat with that enormous pulse. Besides, Denise could not avoid sometimes meeting people. Twice she found herself face to face with Pauline who, grieved to know that she was badly off, offered to help her. She had even been obliged to lie in order to avoid her friend coming to see her or having to go and visit her one Sunday at Baugé's place. But it was more difficult to keep Deloche's hopeless affection at bay; he kept on the lookout for her, was aware of all her worries, waited for her in doorways. One evening he had wanted to lend her thirty francs – his brother's savings, so he said, very red in the face. And these meetings made her miss the shop all the time, made her take part in the internal life which was going on there as if she had never left it.

No one ever came up to Denise's room. One afternoon she was surprised to hear a knock on the door. It was Colomban. She stood up to receive him. He, very embarrassed, first stammeringly asked her about herself and spoke of the Vieil Elbeuf. Perhaps her Uncle Baudu, regretting his hardness, had sent him, for Baudu still did not even greet his niece when he saw her, although he could not have been unaware of the poverty in which she was living. But when she questioned the shop assistant outright, he appeared to be even more embarrassed: no, no, it was not his employer who had sent him – and in the end he mentioned Clara, he just wanted to talk about Clara. Little by little he became braver, asked for advice, thinking that Denise could further his cause with her one-time colleague. She vainly tried to discourage him, reproaching him for making Geneviève unhappy just for a heartless trollop. He came back another day, he acquired the habit of coming to see her. This was enough to satisfy his timid passion, he would endlessly begin the same conversation all over again, trembling with joy at being with a woman who had been in close contact with Clara. And as a result Denise participated even more in life at the Bonheur des Dames.

It was towards the end of September that the girl experienced really dire poverty. Pépé had fallen ill, with a disquietingly heavy cold which worried her. He should have been fed on beef tea, but she did not even have any bread. One day when, feeling vanquished, she was sobbing in one of those fits of black despair which make girls take to the streets or throw themselves into the Seine, old Bourras gently knocked at the door. He had brought a loaf and a milk can full of beef tea.

"Here, this is for the little boy!" he said in his gruff way. "Don't cry so loud, it upsets my tenants."

And as she was thanking him in a fresh bout of tears, he added:

"Be quiet, can't you... Come and see me tomorrow. I've got some work for you."

Since the terrible blow which the Bonheur des Dames had struck him by creating an umbrella-and-sunshade department, Bourras no longer employed any staff. In order to reduce costs he did everything himself, cleaning, repairs and sewing. In any case, his customers were diminishing to such an extent that sometimes there was no work to be done. And so when he installed Denise in a corner of his shop the next day he had to invent work for her. After all, he could not let people die in his house.

"You'll have two francs a day," he said. "When you find something better you can drop me."

She was afraid of him, and she finished her work so quickly that he did not know what else to give her to do. There were pieces of silk to be sewn, there was lace to be repaired. For the first few days she did not dare raise her head, it embarrassed her to feel him near her, with his old lion's mane and his hooked nose, his piercing eyes beneath the wiry tufts of his eyebrows. His voice was harsh, his gestures were crazy, and mothers in the neighbourhood would terrify their children by threatening to send for him, as one sends for the police. Yet urchins would never go past his door without shouting out some kind of abuse, which he did not even seem to hear. All his maniacal fury was worked off on the wretches who were dishonouring his craft by selling cheap goods, trash, goods which even dogs wouldn't want to use, as he was wont to say.

Denise would tremble when he shouted furiously to her:

"Art is done for, d'you hear! You can't find a decent handle anywhere. They make bits of stick, but handles, they're finished! Find me a handle and I'll give you twenty francs!"

He had the pride of an artist, there was not a workman in Paris capable of making a handle like the ones he made, both light and at the same time strong. Above all he carved the knobs on them with delightful imagination, always finding fresh subjects – flowers, fruit, animals, heads, executed in a lifelike and spontaneous way. He used nothing but a penknife, and he could be seen for whole days at a stretch, his spectacles on his nose, carving boxwood or ebony.

"A lot of ignoramuses," he would say, "who are satisfied with gluing silk on whalebone! They buy their handles by the gross, ready-made handles... And they can sell as many as they like! You mark my words, art's done for!"

In the end Denise conquered her misgivings. He had wanted Pépé to come down and play in the shop, for he adored children. When the little boy was playing on all fours there was no room to turn round, with her sitting in her corner doing repairs and Bourras by the window carving wood with his penknife. Each day now brought the same tasks and the same conversations. As he worked he would always come back to discussing the Bonheur des Dames again; he would never tire of explaining the stage his terrific duel with it had reached. Since 1845 he had been in that house, for which he had a thirty years' lease at a rent of eighteen hundred francs, and as he made a thousand francs out of his four furnished rooms, the shop cost him eight hundred francs. It was not much, he had no expenses, he could hold out for a long time yet. It sounded, to listen to him, as if there was no doubt of his victory, he would devour the monster.

Suddenly he would break off.

"I ask you, have they got any dogs' heads like that?"

And he would screw up his eyes behind his glasses the better to judge the head he was carving – the head of a mastiff with its lips drawn back and its fangs showing in a growl which was full of life. Pépé, in raptures at the dog, would raise himself up to look at it, leaning his two little arms on the old man's knees.

"So long as I can make both ends meet, I don't care about anything else," the latter would resume, delicately attacking the tongue with the tip of his penknife as he did so. "The rascals have killed my profits, but if I'm not making anything nowadays, all the same I'm not losing anything so far, or at least very little. You see, I'm determined to leave my bones here rather than give in."

He was brandishing his tool, his white hair was blowing about in a gust of anger.

"All the same," Denise would venture to say gently, without looking up from her needle. "If they were to offer you a reasonable sum it would be wiser to accept."

At that his fierce obstinacy would flare up.

"Never! If they held a knife at my throat, I'd say no, by God! I've still got ten years' lease, they won't get the shop until ten years are up, and I'll have to be starving between four empty walls... Twice already they've been here, trying to get round me. They were offering me twelve thousand francs for the business and eighteen thousand francs for the remaining years of the lease, thirty thousand altogether... I wouldn't sell, not for fifty thousand! I've got them, I want to see them lick the dust in front of me!"

"Thirty thousand francs, that's pretty good," Denise would resume. "You could go and set up shop further away... And what if they bought the house?"

Bourras, who was finishing off his mastiff's tongue, was for a moment engrossed, with a childish smile spread vaguely over his face, snowy like God the Father's. Then he started off again.

"The house is in no danger! They were talking of buying it last year, they were offering eighty thousand francs, double what it's worth today. But the landlord, a retired greengrocer, a scoundrel like them, wanted to blackmail them. And in any case they don't trust me, they know very well that I'd be even less likely to give in... No! No! Here I am, here I stay! The Emperor himself with all his cannons wouldn't be able to make me budge!"

Denise did not dare breathe another word. She went on sewing, while between two notches with his knife the old man would let fall further broken phrases: this was only the beginning, later they'd see extraordinary things happen, he'd got ideas which would make a clean sweep of their umbrella department; at the roots of his obstinacy was the muttered rebellion of the small individual manufacturer against the commonplace invasion of cheap store goods.

Pépé had, meanwhile, finally succeeded in climbing onto Bourras's lap. He was holding out impatient hands towards the mastiff's head.

"Give, Monsieur."

"In a minute, darling," the old man would reply in a voice becoming softened with tenderness. "He hasn't any eyes, I must make his eyes now."

And while he was fiddling with one of the eyes, he once more addressed Denise.

"Can you hear them? What a roar they do make next door! That's what exasperates me most of all, honestly! Having them on top of one all the time like that, with their damned music like a steam engine."

It made his little table vibrate, so he said. The whole shop was shaken by it, he would spend his afternoons without a single customer, being jarred by the vibration caused by the crowd squeezing into the Bonheur des Dames. It was a subject upon which he was eternally harping. There they'd had another good day, there was a din on the other side of the wall, the silk department must have made ten thousand francs – or else he was jubilant, the wall had remained unresponsive, a shower of rain had killed the takings. The slightest sounds, the faintest murmurs would thus provide him with endless occasions for comment.

"There! Someone slipped! Oh! If only they could all fall and break their necks! And that, my dear, is some ladies quarrelling. So much the better! So much the better! D'you hear the parcels going down into the basement, eh? It's disgusting!"

It was no use for Denise to argue with him about it, for then he would bitterly remind her of the shameful manner in which she had been dismissed. Then she would have to describe for him for the hundredth time the months she had spent in the ready-made department, her sufferings at the beginning, the small, unhealthy bedrooms, the bad food, the everlasting battle between the salesmen; and thus, from morning till evening, the two of them would talk of nothing but the shop, drinking it in all the time in the very air which they were breathing.

"Give me, Monsieur," Pépé was eagerly repeating, still holding out his hands.

The mastiff's head was finished, Bourras was making it go backwards and forwards with boisterous gaiety.

"Look out, he's going to bite you... There you are, amuse yourself with it, and try not to break it."

Then, once more overwhelmed by his obsession, he would shake his fist at the wall.

"You can push as hard as you like to make the house fall down... But you won't get it, not even if you overrun the whole street!"

Now Denise always had something to eat. She felt deep gratitude to the old shopkeeper, whose kind heart she could sense beneath his violent eccentricities. Nevertheless, she had a keen desire to find work elsewhere, for she saw him inventing little jobs and realized that since his business was collapsing he did not need any staff, and that he employed her out of pure charity. Six months had passed, the winter slack season had just started again. She was losing hope of finding herself a job before March, when one evening in January Deloche, who was lying in wait for her in a doorway, gave her some advice. Why did she not go and apply at Robineau's, for perhaps they needed staff there?

In September Robineau had made up his mind to buy Vinçard's business, although he feared he was endangering his wife's sixty thousand francs by so doing. He had paid forty thousand francs for the silk shop and he was launching out in business with the other twenty thousand. It was not much, but he had Gaujean behind him, who was to support him with long credits. Since his estrangement from the Bonheur des Dames Gaujean had been longing to create competition to the colossus; he believed that victory would be certain if several specialized shops where customers could find a very varied choice of goods could be created in the neighbourhood. It was only the rich manufacturers in Lyons, like Dumonteil, who could meet the requirements of the big shops; they were content to keep their looms busy for them, taking a chance on subsequently making profits by selling to less important shops. But Gaujean was far from being of

Dumonteil's calibre. For many years nothing but a commission agent, he had only had his own looms for five or six years, and he still employed a good many home workers, whom he provided with raw materials and paid a certain amount per yard. In fact, it was this system which, by increasing his manufacturing costs, prevented him from competing with Dumonteil for supplying the Paris-Bonheur. He bore a grudge about this, and saw in Robineau the means for a decisive battle against the cheap drapery stores, which he accused of ruining French manufacturers.

When Denise went to apply for a job she found Madame Robineau alone. She was the daughter of a foreman in the Highways Department, was absolutely ignorant about business matters, and still had the charming awkwardness of a girl brought up as a boarder in a convent in Blois. She was very dark, very pretty, with a gay gentleness about her which gave her great charm. Moreover, she adored her husband and lived only for this love. Denise was just about to leave her name when Robineau came in, and he hired her on the spot, as it so happened that one of his two salesgirls had left him the day before to go to the Bonheur des Dames.

"They don't leave us a single promising person," he said. "Anyway with you I shan't worry, for you're like me, you can't be very fond of them... Come tomorrow."

That evening Denise was at a loss as to how to tell Bourras that she was leaving him. He did in fact say she was ungrateful and lost his temper, and then, when she defended herself with tears in her eyes, giving him to understand that his acts of charity had not taken her in, he became emotional in his turn, stammering that he had plenty of work, that she was abandoning him just at the moment when he was going to bring out a new umbrella which he had invented.

"What about Pépé?" he asked.

The child was Denise's great worry. She did not dare send him back to Madame Gras, and at the same time could not leave him alone in her room, shut in from morning to night.

"Don't worry, I'll keep him," the old man went on. "He's all right in my shop, the little fellow... We'll do the cooking together!"

And as she, afraid of being a nuisance to him, was refusing, he said:

"Good Heavens! You do distrust me... I'm not going to eat him, you know!"

Denise was happier at Robineau's. He paid her very little, sixty francs a month, and gave her nothing but her meals, no interest on sales, as was the custom in old-fashioned shops. But she was treated with great kindness, especially by Madame Robineau, who was always smiling behind the counter. He, nervy and worried, was sometimes inclined to be abrupt. By the time a month had passed Denise belonged to the family, as did the other salesgirl, a little woman who was consumptive and taciturn. The family no longer stood on ceremony with the girls, but talked business during meals in the room at the back of the shop, which opened onto a big courtyard. And it was there, one evening, that it was decided to start a campaign against the Bonheur des Dames.

Gaujean had come to dinner. As soon as the joint, a homely leg of mutton, was served, he had broached the question in the toneless voice, thickened by the Rhône mists, of a man from Lyons.

"It's becoming impossible," he was repeating. "You see, they go to Dumonteil's and have the exclusive rights of a design reserved for themselves and, insisting on a rebate of fifty centimes a yard, they carry off three hundred lengths on the spot. What's more, as they pay with ready cash, they also profit from the eighteen-per-cent discount... often Dumonteil doesn't even make twenty centimes. He works in order to keep his looms busy, for an idle loom is a dying loom... So how can you expect us, with our more limited equipment and above all with our home workers, to keep up the struggle?"

Robineau, pensive, was forgetting to eat.

"Three hundred lengths!" he murmured. "Why, I quake with fear when I take twelve, and with ninety days to pay... They can price it at a franc or two francs cheaper than we can, I've worked out that their list prices are at least fifteen per cent lower compared to ours... That's what kills small tradespeople."

He was in a mood of despondency. His wife, worried, was looking at him tenderly. Business was quite beyond her, she was bewildered by all those figures, and did not understand why one should take on a worry like that when it was so easy to be gay and love each other. Nevertheless, it was enough for her that her husband wished to conquer; she too became full of enthusiasm, and would have been willing to die at her counter.

"But why don't all the manufacturers come to an agreement between themselves?" Robineau went on violently. "They would lay down the law to them, instead of having to submit to it."

Gaujean, who had asked for another slice of mutton, was slowly munching.

"Ah! Why, why... The looms must work, as I told you. When one has weaving being done all over the place, in the Gard, in the Isère, one can't stop work for a day without enormous losses... Then people like me who sometimes employ home workers with ten or fifteen looms, we are more the masters of production from the point of view of stock, whereas the big manufacturers are always obliged to get rid of their stock as quickly as they can on the widest possible market... That's why they do go down on their knees to the big shops. I know three or four of them who quarrel over them, who are willing to lose money in order to obtain their orders. And they make it up on the small shops like yours. Yes, if the big shops keep them going, it's out of you that they make the profits... God knows how the crisis will end!"

"It's odious!" concluded Robineau, who felt better after this cry of rage.

Denise, with her instinctive love for logic and life, was listening in silence. Secretly she was on the side of the big shops. They fell silent, they were eating some bottled green beans; finally she ventured to say gaily:

"Anyway, the public doesn't complain!"

Madame Robineau could not suppress a mild laugh, which displeased her husband and Gaujean. Of course the customers were satisfied since, after all, it was the customers who profited from the reduction in prices. Only, everyone had to live; where would one get if, under the pretext of general well-being, one were to make the consumer fat at the expense of the producer? And an argument started. While pretending to joke, Denise was at the same time producing sound arguments: the middlemen, factory agents, travellers, commission agents, were disappearing – which was an important factor in reducing prices. What is more, the manufacturers could not even exist without the big shops, for as soon as one of them lost their custom, bankruptcy became inevitable. Finally, it was anyway a natural development of business, it was impossible to stop things going the way they were going, when everyone was working for it, whether they liked it or not.

"So you're on the side of the people who kicked you into the street?" Gaujean asked.

Denise became very red. She was surprised herself at the fervour with which she was defending them. What could there be in her heart to make such passion mount within her?

"Goodness, no!" she answered. "I'm probably wrong, you know more about it... I just said what I thought. Prices, instead of being fixed by about fifty shops like they used to be, are fixed nowadays by four or five, which have lowered them, thanks to the power of their capital and the number of their customers... So much the better for the public, that's all!"

Robineau kept his temper. He had become grave, and was looking at the tablecloth. He had often felt the new way of business in the air, this development of which the girl was talking, and he used to wonder, in his clear-sighted moments, why he should want to resist a current of such force, which would carry all before it. Madame Robineau herself, seeing her husband thoughtful, gave a look of approval at Denise, who had relapsed into silence again.

"Look here," Gaujean resumed, "to cut a long story short, all that is just theories... Let's talk about what concerns us."

Following the cheese, the maid had just served preserves and pears. He helped himself to preserves and ate them by the spoonful, with the unconscious greed of a fat man who loved sweet things.

"What you must do is to beat their Paris-Bonheur, which was their great success this year... I've come to an understanding with some of my colleagues in Lyons, and I'm going to make you an exceptional offer, a black silk, a faille, which you'll be able to sell at five francs fifty... They sell theirs at five francs sixty, don't they? Very well! It'll be ten centimes cheaper, and that's enough, you'll sink them."

Robineau's eyes had lit up again. His nerves were always in a turmoil, and he would frequently jump from fear to hope like that.

"Have you got a pattern?" he asked.

When Gaujean had taken a little square of silk from his note-case, he was quite overcome with enthusiasm and exclaimed:

"But it's even finer than the Paris-Bonheur! In any case, it makes more effect, the texture's got more body to it... You're right, we must have a shot at it. Oh, you know I want them at my feet this time, or else I give up!"

Madame Robineau, sharing this enthusiasm, declared that the silk was superb. Even Denise thought they would be successful. Thus the end of the dinner was very gay. They were talking in loud voices, it seemed as if the Bonheur des Dames was already at its last gasp. Gaujean, who was finishing off the jar of preserves, was explaining what enormous sacrifices he and his colleagues were going to impose on themselves in order to supply a material of that kind so cheaply; they would rather ruin themselves over it, for they had sworn to kill the big shops. As the coffee was being brought the gaiety was even more enhanced by the arrival of Vinçard. He had been passing by and had come in to say a word of greeting to his successor.

"Capital!" he exclaimed, feeling the silk. "You'll beat them, I'll be bound! You ought to be very grateful to me, eh? Didn't I tell you that this place was a gold mine?"

He himself had just bought a restaurant at Vincennes. It was a dream of long standing which he had secretly cherished while he was struggling in the silk business, terrified that he would not be able to sell his business before the crash came, and swearing that he would put what little money he had into a business in which one could rob people in comfort. The idea of a restaurant had come to him after a cousin's wedding; stomachs were always good business, for he had been made to pay ten francs for some washing-up water with a few noodles swimming about in it. Faced with the Robineaus, his joy at having saddled them with a bad business of which he had been despairing of ridding himself made his face, with its round eyes and its big, honest mouth, seem even broader.

"And what about your pains?" Madame Robineau asked kindly.

"What's that? My pains?" he murmured, astonished.

"Yes, the rheumatism which made your life a misery here."

He recollected and blushed slightly.

"Oh! I've still got it... However, the country air, you know... Never mind, you've got a splendid bargain. If it hadn't been for my rheumatism I'd have retired with an income of ten thousand francs before ten years were out... Honestly I would have."

A fortnight later the struggle between Robineau and the Bonheur des Dames began. It made news, and for a moment the whole Parisian market was taken up with it. Robineau, using his opponent's own weapons, had advertised in the newspapers. Moreover, he took great trouble with his display, heaped up enormous piles of the celebrated silk in his windows, announced it with huge white placards on which the price of five francs fifty stood out in giant figures. It was this figure which caused a revolution amongst the ladies – ten centimes cheaper than at the Bonheur des Dames, and the silk seemed to be thicker! From the very first day there was a stream of customers: Madame Marty, under the pretext of showing how economical she was, bought a dress which she did not need. Madame Bourdelais said the material was lovely, but she would rather wait, sensing no doubt what was going to happen. And in fact, the next week Mouret made no bones about it and reduced the price of the Paris-Bonheur by twenty centimes, selling it at five francs forty; he had had a lively discussion with Bourdoncle and the others concerned before convincing them that they must agree to take up the glove and risk losing on the purchase price; those twenty centimes meant a dead loss, for the silk was already being sold at cost price. It was a severe blow for Robineau, he had not believed that his rival would lower prices, for such suicidal competitions, such sales at a loss, were as yet unprecedented, and the stream of customers, responding to the lower prices, had immediately flowed back to the Rue Neuve-Saint-Augustin again, while the shop in the Rue Neuve-des-Petits-Champs was emptying. Gaujean rushed up from Lyons, there were anxious confabulations, and in the end a heroic decision was taken: the price of the silk would be reduced, they would let it go at five francs thirty, a price below which no one in their senses would go. The next day Mouret priced his material at five francs twenty. And, from then on, everyone went mad. Robineau replied with five francs fifteen, Mouret changed his price tags to five francs ten. They were both fighting with only five centimes, and each time they made this gift to the public they were losing considerable sums. The customers were all smiles, delighted with this duel, excited by the terrible blows the two shops were giving each other in order to please them. Finally,

Mouret ventured the figure of five francs; his staff was pale, its blood running cold at such defiance of fortune. Robineau, utterly crushed, winded, likewise stopped at five francs, not having the courage to go down any lower. They remained entrenched, face to face, with the wreckage of their goods around them.

But if, on both sides, honour was saved, for Robineau at any rate the situation was becoming critical. The Bonheur des Dames had loans and a sufficient number of customers to enable it to break even; whereas he, backed up only by Gaujean, unable to make good his losses with other wares, was at a low ebb, and every day was slipping a little further down the slope towards bankruptcy. He was perishing as a result of his rashness, in spite of the large numbers of customers which he had gained as a result of the ups and downs of the struggle. One of his secret torments was to see those customers slowly leaving him to go back to the Bonheur des Dames, after all the money he had lost and the efforts he had made in order to win them over.

One day, indeed, his patience deserted him. A customer, Madame de Boves, had come to see his stock of coats, for he had added a ready-made clothes department to the silks which were his speciality. She could not make up her mind, and was complaining of the quality of the materials. Finally, she said:

"Their Paris-Bonheur is much stronger."

Robineau controlled himself, and replied with his salesman-like politeness that she was mistaken, and he was all the more respectful because he was afraid of letting the rebellion within him show.

"Now, just look at the silk this cloak is made of!" she resumed. "It's just like a spider's web... No matter what you may say, Monsieur, their silk at five francs is like leather in comparison to this."

He did not say any more, his face was flushed and his lips set. It so happened that he had had the ingenious idea of buying the silk for his ready-made clothes from his rival. This meant that it was Mouret who was losing over the material, not him. He merely cut the selvedge off it before using it.

"Really, you consider the Paris-Bonheur is thicker?" he murmured.

"Oh, a hundred times thicker!" said Madame de Boves. "There's no comparison."

The unfairness of his customer, who was nevertheless running down his goods, was making his blood boil. And while she was still turning the cloak round with a fastidious air, a little bit of the blue-and-silver selvedge which had escaped the scissors showed under the lining. At that he could not longer control himself, he owned up, throwing discretion to the winds.

"Well, Madame, this silk *is* Paris-Bonheur, I bought it myself. Yes, certainly, look at the selvedge!"

Madame de Boves went away very annoyed. The story got round, and many ladies left him as a result. And in the midst of his downfall, when fear for the morrow seized him, he worried only about his wife, who had been brought up in happy security and was incapable of living in poverty. What would happen to her if, as a result of some catastrophe, they were to find themselves in the street and in debt? It was his fault, he should never have touched her sixty thousand francs. It was she who had to console him. Had not the money been just as much his as hers? He loved her, she did not want anything else, she gave him everything, her heart, her life. In the room at the back of the shop they could be heard kissing. Little by little the pace of the shop became more stable; each month the losses increased relatively slowly, which postponed the fatal issue. Stubborn hope kept them going, they still proclaimed the imminent collapse of the Bonheur des Dames.

"Pooh!" he would say. "After all, we're young, aren't we? The future's ours!"

"And then what does it matter, so long as you did what you wanted to do?" she would go on. "So long as you're happy, I'm happy, my dearest."

Seeing how much they loved each other, Denise became very fond of them. She was apprehensive, she felt the crash was inevitable, but she no longer dared intervene. It was there with them that she finally understood how powerful the new business methods were and became full of enthusiasm for this force which was transforming Paris. Her ideas were becoming more mature, the grace of a woman was emerging from the timid child who had arrived from Valognes. Besides, in spite of her tiredness and lack of money, her life was fairly pleasant. When she had spent the whole day on her feet she had to go home quickly to look after Pépé, whom old Bourras, fortunately, persisted in feeding

– but she had other things to do as well, a shirt to be washed, a blouse to be mended, not to mention the din the little boy made, which made her head split. She never went to bed before midnight. Sunday was the day on which she did all the heavy work: she cleaned out her room, tidied herself up, being often so busy that she had no time to comb her hair before five o'clock. However, she was sensible enough to go out sometimes, taking the child with her for a long excursion on foot in the direction of Neuilly, and once there they would have a treat and drink a glass of milk at a dairy where they were allowed to sit down in the yard. Jean scorned these outings; he would turn up now and then on weekday evenings, then would disappear, saying he had other visits to make. He no longer asked for money, but he would arrive looking so dejected that his sister, worried about him, always had a five-franc piece put aside for him. This was her extravagance.

"Five francs!" Jean would cry each time. "I say! You are sweet! It just so happens that there's the stationer's wife—"

"Shut up," Denise would interrupt him. "I don't want to know."

But he would think she was accusing him of boasting.

"But I tell you she's the stationer's wife... Oh, something really gorgeous!"

Three months passed. The spring was coming round again, Denise refused to go to Joinville once more with Pauline and Baugé. She met them sometimes in the Rue Saint-Roch, when she was leaving Robineau's. At one of these meetings Pauline confided to her that she was perhaps going to marry her lover; it was she who still couldn't make up her mind, they did not at all like married salesgirls at the Bonheur des Dames. This idea of marriage surprised Denise, she did venture to advise her friend. One day Colomban stopped her near the fountain in order to talk to her about Clara, and just at that moment the latter crossed the square; Denise had to make her escape, for he was entreating her to ask her one-time colleague if she would care to marry him. What could be the matter with them all? Why did they all make such a fuss about it? She considered herself very lucky not to be in love with anyone.

"Have you heard the news?" the umbrella merchant said to her one evening as she came in.

"No, Monsieur Bourras."

"Well! The scoundrels have bought the Duvillard house... I'm surrounded!"

He was waving his long arms in a fit of rage which was making his white mane stand on end.

"It's a fishy scheme, and one can't understand a thing!" he resumed. "It seems that the house belonged to the Crédit Immobilier, the chairman of which, Baron Hartmann, had just transferred it to that precious Mouret of ours... Now they've got me on the right, on the left, and behind. Look! Just like I hold this walking-stick knob in my fist – d'you see?"

It was true, the transfer must have been signed the day before. It seemed as if Bourras's little house, squeezed in between the Bonheur des Dames and the Duvillard mansion, clinging on there like a swallow's nest in a crevice in a wall, must immediately be crushed on the day the shop invaded the Duvillard mansion – and this day had come, the colossus was encircling the feeble obstacle, surrounding it with stacks of goods, threatening to swallow it up, to absorb it by the sheer force of its gigantic suction. Bourras was fully aware of the pressure which was making his shop crack. He thought he could see the shop shrinking, the terrible mechanism was roaring to such an extent now that he was afraid of being swallowed up himself, of being sucked through the wall with his umbrellas and walking sticks.

"Can you hear them, eh?" he shouted. "It's as if they were eating the walls! And everywhere there's the same noise of saws cutting into plaster, in my cellar, in my loft... It doesn't matter! Perhaps after all they won't be able to flatten me out like a sheet of paper. I'll stay, even if they make my roof cave in and if the rain falls in my bed in bucketfuls!"

It was this moment that Mouret chose to make fresh proposals to Bourras: the figure was increased, they would buy his business and the lease for fifty thousand francs. This offer redoubled the old man's fury and he refused it with insults. How these scoundrels must be robbing people to pay fifty thousand francs for something which was not worth ten thousand! And he defended his shop like a decent girl defends her virtue, in the name of honour, out of self-respect.

For about a fortnight Denise saw that Bourras was preoccupied. He moved around feverishly, measured the walls of his house, looked at it from the middle of the street with the air of an architect. Then, one morning, some workmen arrived. It was the decisive battle, he had had the rash idea of beating the Bonheur des Dames at its own game by making concessions to modern luxury. Customers who reproached him for his dark shop would certainly come back again when they saw it shining brightly, brand new. First of all the cracks were filled up and the front was distempered; next the woodwork in the shop window was painted light green; he even carried this magnificence so far as to gild the signboard. Three thousand francs, which Bourras had been keeping aside as a last resource, were swallowed up. The neighbourhood, what is more, was in an uproar; people came to gaze at him losing his head in the midst of these riches, unable to pick up his old ways again. Flustered, his long beard and hair streaming behind him, he no longer seemed at home in that gleaming setting, against the pastel background. Now passers-by on the opposite pavement watched him, surprised, as he waved his arms about and carved his handles. And a new fever was gaining a hold on him, he was afraid of making things dirty, he was sinking ever deeper into this luxury business of which he understood nothing.

Meanwhile, like Robineau, Bourras had launched his campaign against the Bonheur des Dames. He had just put his new invention on the market, the frilled umbrella, which was later on to become popular. Moreover, the Bonheur immediately improved the invention. Then the struggle over prices began. He had a model at one franc ninety-five, in zanelle, with a steel frame which, according to the label, would wear for ever. But he hoped above all to beat his rival with his handles, handles of bamboo, of dogwood, of olive wood, of myrtle, of rattan, every imaginable kind of handle. The Bonheur, being less artistic, paid more attention to the materials, boasting of its alpacas and mohairs, its serges and taffetas. It was victorious; the old man repeated in despair that art was done for, that he was reduced to carving handles for pleasure, with no hope of selling them.

"It's my fault!" he cried to Denise. "I shouldn't have had trash like that at one franc ninety-five... That's where new ideas get you. I wanted to follow those ruffians' example, so much the better if I've done for myself as a result!"

July was extremely hot, and Denise felt the heat very much in her small room under the tiles. Therefore, when she left her shop she would fetch Pépé from Bourras and, instead of going up to her room straight away, she would go to the Tuileries gardens for a breath of fresh air until the gates were closed. One evening, as she was walking towards the chestnut trees, she stopped short: she thought she recognized Hutin, a few steps away and walking straight towards her. Then her heart beat violently; it was Mouret, who had dined on the Left Bank and was hastening on foot to Madame Desforges's house. The sudden movement which the girl made to avoid him made him look at her. Night was falling, but he recognized her all the same.

"Is it you, Mademoiselle?"

She did not answer, dazed that he had deigned to stop. He, smiling, was hiding his embarrassment beneath an air of kindly patronage.

"So you're still in Paris?"

"Yes, Monsieur," she said in the end.

She was slowly backing away, endeavouring to say goodbye in order to continue her walk. But he himself retraced his steps, he followed her under the dark shadows of the great chestnut trees. It was cool there; in the distance children were laughing, bowling hoops.

"That's your brother, isn't it?" he questioned her further, his eyes on Pépé.

The latter, intimidated by the extraordinary event of a gentleman being with them, was walking solemnly beside his sister, whose hand he was holding.

"Yes, Monsieur," she replied once more.

She had blushed; she was thinking of the loathsome stories which Marguerite and Clara had invented. No doubt Mouret understood the cause of her blush, for he quickly added:

"Listen, Mademoiselle, I must offer you an apology... Yes, I would like to have told you before how much I regretted the error which was made. You were too lightly accused of misbehaviour... Well, the harm's been done, I just wanted to tell you that everyone in the shop now knows of your love for your brothers..."

He went on, full of a respectful politeness which salesgirls in the Bonheur des Dames were not at all accustomed to receive from him. Denise's confusion had increased, but joy was flooding her heart. So he knew that she had not given herself to anyone! They both remained silent, he stayed close beside her, adjusting his steps to the child's small ones, and beneath the dark shadow of the great trees the sounds of Paris were dying away.

"I can but offer to reinstate you, Mademoiselle," he went on. "Naturally, if you would like to come back to us—"

She interrupted him, refusing with febrile haste.

"I can't Monsieur... Thank you all the same, but I've found work elsewhere."

He was aware of it, he had been told that she was at Robineau's. And calmly, on a footing of equality which was charming, he talked to her about Robineau, giving him his due: a keenly intelligent young man, only too highly strung. It would end up in catastrophe, Gaujean had overburdened him with too big an affair, which would be the end of them both. At that, Denise won over by this familiarity, began to confide in him more, making it clear that in their battle with the small tradespeople she was on the side of the big shops; she grew excited, quoted examples, showed that she knew all about the question and was even full of bold new ideas. Delighted, he listened to her with surprise. He was turning towards her, trying to distinguish her features in the growing dark. She seemed to be just the same still, clad in a simple dress, with a gentle face, but this modest unobtrusiveness gave off a penetrating perfume, and he felt its power. No doubt this little thing had grown accustomed to the air of Paris, and now she was becoming a woman – and she was disturbing, what is more, with her sensible manner and her beautiful hair heavy with passion.

"Since you're on our side," he said, laughing, "why do you stay with our opponents? For example, haven't I been told that you lodge with that man Bourras?"

"And a very worthy man he is," she murmured.

"No, really the old man's dotty, he's a madman who'll force me to reduce him to beggary, when I'd like to get rid of him by paying a fortune! And, what's more, you're not in your proper place there, his house has a bad reputation, he lets to individuals..."

But he felt that the girl was embarrassed, and hastened to add:

"Of course, one can be decent wherever one lives, and in fact there's more merit in being so when one isn't well off."

Once more they took a few steps in silence. Pépé, with the attentive air of a precocious child, seemed to be listening. From time to time he looked up at his sister, whose burning hand shaken by slight quivers surprised him.

"Look here!" Mouret went on gaily, "will you be my ambassador? I had intended to increase my offer even more tomorrow, to make a proposal of eighty thousand francs to Bourras... You speak to him about it first, do tell him he's committing suicide. He may listen to you, because he's fond of you, and you'll be doing him a real service."

"All right!" Denise replied, and she too was smiling. "I'll do as you ask, but I doubt if I'll succeed."

Silence fell again. They had nothing more to say to each other. For a moment he tried to talk about her uncle Baudu; then seeing how ill at ease the girl was, he had to stop. Meanwhile, they were still walking side by side, and they finally came out near the Rue de Rivoli in an avenue where it was still light. Leaving the darkness of the trees was like a sudden awakening. He understood that he could not detain her any longer.

"Goodbye, Mademoiselle."

"Good evening, Monsieur."

But he did not go away. Raising his eyes, he had just caught a glimpse of Madame Desforges's windows lit up in front of him at the corner of the Rue d'Alger, where she was waiting for him. He had turned to look at Denise again, he could see her clearly in the pale dusk: she was a skinny little thing compared to Henriette, why on earth did she warm his heart like that? It was an idiotic whim.

"Here's a little boy who's getting tired," he resumed, in order to say something more. "And you'll really remember, won't you, that our shop is always open to you. You've only to knock on our door, and I'll give you all the compensation you desire... Goodnight, Mademoiselle."

"Goodnight, Monsieur."

When Mouret had left her, Denise went back under the chest-nut trees, into the shady darkness. For a long time she walked aimlessly between the enormous trunks, her face flushed, her head buzzing with confused ideas. Pépé, still hanging on to her hand, was stretching his short legs in order to keep up with her. She had forgotten him. Finally he said:

"You're going too fast, Sis."

Then she sat down on a bench and, being weary, the child fell asleep across her lap. She was holding him, pressing him to her virginal bosom, her eyes far away in the shadowy distance. And when, an hour later, she went slowly back to the Rue de la Michodière, she wore the calm expression of a sensible girl.

"Damn it!" Bourras shouted to her as soon as he caught sight of her. "It's happened... That blackguard Mouret has just bought my house."

He was beside himself, he was battling all by himself in the middle of his shop, with such wild gestures that he was in danger of smashing the windows.

"Oh! The dirty scoundrel! It's the greengrocer who's written to me. And d'you know how much he's sold it for, my house? A hundred and fifty thousand francs, four times more than it's worth! He's another fine robber for you! Just imagine, he used my decorations as a pretext; yes, he pointed out that the house had just been done up like new... When will they stop making an ass of me, I'd like to know!"

The idea that his money, spent on distemper and paint, had been of profit to the greengrocer exasperated him. And now there was Mouret becoming his landlord: he would have to pay him! It was in his house, in the house of his detested rival, that he would be living from now on! Such a thought put the finishing touches to his fury.

"I knew I could hear them digging through the wall... Now they're here, it's just as if they were eating out of my plate!"

And with a blow of his fist on the counter, he shook the whole shop, making the umbrellas and the parasols dance.

Denise, dazed, had not been able to get a word in. She remained motionless, waiting for the storm to subside, while Pépé, who was very weary, was falling asleep on a chair. Finally, when Bourras calmed down a little, she resolved to give him Mouret's message; no doubt the old man was angry, but the very excess of his anger and the hopeless position in which he was might bring about a sudden acceptance.

"It so happens I've just met someone," she began. "Yes, someone from the Bonheur, and someone very well informed... It appears that tomorrow they're going to offer you eighty thousand francs..."

He interrupted her with a terrible roar:

"Eighty thousand francs! Eighty thousand francs! Not for a million now!"

She wanted to reason with him. But the door of the shop opened, and suddenly she drew back, pale and mute. It was her uncle Baudu, with his yellow face looking aged. Bourras seized his neighbour by the coat buttons, and shouted into his face, without letting him say a word, egged on by his presence:

"D'you know what they've got the nerve to offer me? Eighty thousand francs! They've stooped to that, the robbers! They think that I'll sell myself like a tart... Ah! They've bought the house and they think they've got me! Well, it's finished, they won't get it! I might have given in perhaps, but as it belongs to them now, just let them try to get it!"

"So the news is true?" said Baudu in his low voice. "I've been told it was, and I came to find out."

"Eighty thousand francs!" Bourras was repeating. "Why not a hundred thousand? It's all that money which makes me so indignant. Do they think they'll make me commit a piece of knavery, with their money? They won't get it, by God! Never, never, d'you hear?"

Denise broke the silence to say in her calm way:

"They'll get it in nine years' time, when your lease expires."

And despite the presence of her uncle, she entreated the old man to accept. The struggle was becoming impossible, he was fighting against superior forces, he was mad to refuse the fortune which was being offered. But he still refused. In nine years' time, he sincerely hoped he would be dead, so as not to see them get it.

"D'you hear, Monsieur Baudu?" he resumed. "Your niece is on their side, it's her they've told to corrupt me... She's with the scoundrels, word of honour!"

Her uncle, until then, had appeared not to see Denise. He was tossing his head with the surly movement which he affected on the threshold of his shop each time he saw her pass. But he slowly turned round and looked at her. His thick lips were trembling.

"Yes, I know," he answered in a low voice.

He went on looking at her. Denise, moved to the point of tears, found him much changed by grief. He, overwhelmed with secret remorse at not having helped her, was perhaps thinking of the life of poverty which she had lately been through. Then the sight of Pépé, asleep on a chair in the midst of all these outbursts, seemed to soften his heart.

"Denise," he said simply, "do come in tomorrow and have some soup with the little boy. My wife and Geneviève asked me to invite you if I saw you."

She became very red in the face and kissed him. And, as he was leaving, Bourras, pleased about this reconciliation, shouted after him:

"Give her a good spanking, she's not a bad girl... So far as I'm concerned, the house can fall down, they'll find me underneath the stones."

"Our houses are falling down already neighbour," said Baudu with a gloomy air. "And we'll all stay in them."

8

MEANWHILE, the whole neighbourhood was talking about the great thoroughfare which was going to be opened up from the new Opéra to the Bourse, and which was to be called the Rue du Dix-Décembre. Expropriation notices had been served, and two gangs of demolition workers were already attacking the site at each end, one pulling down the old mansions in the Rue Louis-le-Grand, the other knocking down the flimsy walls of the old Vaudeville – and the pickaxes could be heard getting nearer to each other, the Rue de Choiseul and the Rue de la Michodière were passionately concerned about their condemned houses. Before a fortnight was out the breach would make a broad gash through them, full of hubbub and sunshine.

But the neighbourhood was even more agitated by the building work which had been embarked upon at the Bonheur des Dames. There was talk of considerable extensions, of gigantic shops occupying the three frontages of the Rue de la Michodière, the Rue Neuve-Saint-Augustin and the Rue Monsigny. Mouret, it was said, had negotiated with Baron Hartmann, the chairman of the Crédit Immobilier, and was to occupy the whole block of houses, excepting the frontage on the Rue du Dix-Décembre, where the Baron wanted to build a rival to the Grand Hotel. Everywhere the Bonheur was buying up leases, shops were closing, tenants were moving out, and in the empty buildings an army of workmen was starting on the redecorating, beneath clouds of plaster. Alone, in the middle of the upheaval, old Bourras's narrow hovel remained steadfast and intact, obstinately clinging on between the high walls swarming with bricklayers.

When, next day, Denise went with Pépé to her Uncle Baudu's, the street was blocked up by a line of tip carts which were unloading bricks outside what had once been the Duvillard house. Standing on the threshold of his shop, her uncle was watching with a gloomy eye. It seemed as if the Vieil Elbeuf was shrinking as the Bonheur des Dames expanded. The girl thought the window panes looked blacker, even more crushed down by the low mezzanine floor with its round, prison-like bay windows; the damp had further discoloured the old green signboard, the whole front of the house, livid and somehow shrunken, was oozing with anguish.

"Ah, there you are," said Baudu. "Be careful! They'll run you over!"

Inside the shop Denise felt the same tug at her heart strings. On seeing it again it seemed gloomier, more overcome by the somnolence of ruin, empty corners formed gloomy cavities, dust was invading the counters and cash desks, while a smell of cellars and saltpetre was coming from the bales of cloth, which were no longer handled. At the cash desk Madame Baudu and Geneviève sat mute and motionless, as if in some lonely spot where no one would come to disturb them. The mother was hemming dishcloths. The daughter, her hands in her lap, was looking into space.

"Good evening, Aunt," said Denise. "I'm so happy to see you again, and if I have caused you grief, please forgive me."

Madame Baudu, deeply moved, kissed her.

"My dear," she replied, "if that was my only grief, you'd find me much more cheerful!"

"Good evening, Geneviève," Denise went on, and took the initiative in kissing her cousin on the cheek.

The latter seemed to wake up with a start. She returned her kisses, at a loss for something to say. Then the two women picked up Pépé, who was holding out his small arms. The reconciliation was complete.

"Well! It's six o'clock, let's sit down and eat," said Baudu. "Why didn't you bring Jean with you?"

"Well, he should be coming," murmured Denise, embarrassed. "I saw him this morning, and he definitely promised me... Oh!

You mustn't wait for him, his employer must have kept him late."

She feared some extraordinary adventure, and wanted to make excuses for him in advance.

"Well, then let's sit down," her uncle repeated.

Then, turning towards the dark back of the shop, he called: "Colomban, you can have your dinner at the same time as us. No one will come."

Denise had not noticed the shop assistant. Her aunt explained to her that they had had to dismiss the other salesman and the girl. Business was becoming so bad that Colomban was sufficient – and even he spent hours doing nothing, apathetic, dropping off to sleep with his eyes open.

In the dining room the gas was burning, although it was during the long days of summer. Denise gave a slight shiver as she went in, her shoulders caught by the chilliness which the walls were exuding. Once more she saw the round table, the meal laid on the oilcloth, the window getting its air and light from the depths of the stinking alley of the little yard. And these things, like the shop, seemed to her to have become even gloomier, and to be shedding tears.

"Father," said Geneviève, embarrassed on behalf of Denise, "Would you like me to shut the window? It doesn't smell nice."

He was surprised. He could not smell anything.

"Shut the window, if it amuses you," he answered finally, "only we shan't get any air."

It was indeed stifling. The dinner was a family affair, very simple. After the soup, as soon as the maid had served the boiled beef, Baudu inevitably began to talk about the people opposite. At first he was very tolerant and allowed his niece to have a different opinion.

"Goodness me! You're quite free to stick up for those great barracks of shops... Everyone to his own taste, my dear... As being kicked out in that dirty way didn't put you off, it means you must have sound reason for liking them – and if you were to go back there, you know, I wouldn't bear you any ill will at all... Isn't that so? No one here would bear her any ill will."

"Oh, no!" murmured Madame Baudu.

Denise calmly stated her case, mentioning the same reasons as she had at Robineau's: the logical development of trade, the needs of modern times, the magnitude of such new creations and finally the increasing well-being of the public. Baudu, with his round eyes and thick mouth, was listening with a visible mental effort. Then, when she had finished, he shook his head.

"That's all hallucinations. Business is business, you can't get away from it... Oh! I grant you, they're successful, but that's all. For a long time I thought they'd come a cropper; yes, I was expecting it, I was biding my time, d'you remember? Well, no! It seems that nowadays it's the robbers who are making a fortune, while honest folk are dying in the gutter... That's the state we're in, and I'm forced to bow to the facts. And I'm bowing, by God! I'm bowing!"

Repressed rage was gradually rousing him. Suddenly he brandished his fork and said:

"But the Vieil Elbeuf will never make any concessions... D'you hear? I said as much to Bourras: 'Neighbour, you're in league with those charlatans, your daubs of paint are a disgrace.'"

"Do eat," Madame Baudu interrupted, worried at seeing him so worked up.

"Wait, I want my niece to be well acquainted with my motto. Listen to this, my girl: I'm like this jug, I don't budge. They're successful – so much the worse for them! As for me, I protest, that's all!"

The maid was bringing in a piece of roast veal. With trembling hands, he carved it, and he no longer had his sure judgement, the authority with which he had weighed out the helpings. The consciousness of his defeat had deprived him of his former self-assurance, that of a respected employer. Pépé thought his uncle was getting angry, and had to be calmed by being given his dessert, some biscuits which were in front of him, straight away. Then his uncle, lowering his voice, tried to talk of something else. For a moment he discussed the demolition work; he approved of the Rue du Dix-Décembre, the opening up of which would certainly increase business in the neighbourhood. But that again brought him back to the Bonheur des Dames; everything brought him back to it, it was a morbid obsession. They were all smothered with plaster, no one was selling anything any more, now that the carts bringing building materials were blocking up the road. In any case, it would be so big that it would be ridiculous; the customers would lose themselves, they might just as well take over the Halles.* And in spite of his wife's imploring looks, in spite of his own efforts, he went on from the rebuilding to discuss the shop's turnover. Wasn't it inconceivable? In less than four years they had increased it fivefold; their annual takings, formerly eight millions, were approaching the figure of forty million according to the last stock-taking. It was madness, something never before seen, and it was no good struggling against it any longer. They were getting bigger all the time, they now had a thousand employees, they were proclaiming that they had twenty-eight departments. It was above all this figure of twenty-eight departments which made him beside himself. Of course, they must have split some of them into two, but others were completely new: a furniture department for example, and a fancy-goods department. What could one make of that? Fancy goods! Really, those people had no pride, they'd end up by selling fish. While pretending to respect Denise's ideas, her uncle was trying to win her over.

"Frankly, you can't defend them. Can you see me adding a saucepan department to my drapery business, eh? You'd say I was mad... At least admit that you have no respect for them."

The girl merely smiled, embarrassed, understanding how useless sound reasoning was. He went on:

"Well, you're on their side. We won't say any more about it, it's pointless for them to make us fall out again. It would be the last straw to see them coming between me and my family! Go back to them if you want to, but I forbid you to deafen my ears by talking about their affairs any more!"

A silence fell. His former violence was petering out into feverish resignation. As it was stifling in the narrow room, heated by the gas jet, the maid had to open the windows again, and the damp stench from the yard wafted over the table. Some sauté potatoes had appeared. They helped themselves slowly, without a word.

"Why, look at those two," Baudu began again, pointing to Geneviève and Colomban with his knife. "Ask them if they like it, your Bonheur des Dames!"

Side by side, in the accustomed place where they had been meeting twice a day for the past twelve years, Colomban and Geneviève were eating with restraint. They had not said a word. He, exaggerating the stolid good nature of his face, seemed to be hiding, behind his drooping eyelids, the internal fire which was consuming him; whereas she, her head drooping even more under the weight of her hair, seemed to be giving way to despair, as if stricken by some secret suffering.

"Last year was disastrous," Baudu was explaining. "Their marriage just had to be postponed... Go on, just for fun, you just ask them what they think of your friends."

In order to satisfy him, Denise questioned the young people.

"I can't have much love for them," Geneviève replied. "But don't worry, not everyone detests them."

She was looking at Colomban, who was rolling a pellet of bread with an absorbed air. Feeling the girl's eyes were on him, he launched into violent phrases:

"It's a filthy place! They're scoundrels, all of them! In fact, it's a real plague for the neighbourhood!"

"D'you hear what he says, d'you hear what he says?" shouted Baudu, delighted. "That's one person they'll never get! Believe me, you're the last, my boy, there won't be any more like you!"

But Geneviève, her face set and pained, did not take her eyes off Colomban. She was penetrating to his very heart, and he, feeling uncomfortable, was reiterating his abuse with renewed zeal. Facing them, Madame Baudu, anxious and silent, was looking from one to the other as if she had divined that a fresh misfortune was coming from that quarter. For some time her daughter's sadness had been alarming her, she felt that she was dying.

"The shop's on its own," she said in the end, getting up from the table, wishing to put an end to the scene. "Have a look, Colomban, I thought I heard someone."

They had finished, they stood up. Baudu and Colomban went to talk to a commercial traveller who had come to take orders. Madame Baudu led Pépé away to show him some pictures. The maid had quickly cleared the table, and Denise stood lost in thought near the window, looking at the little yard when, turning round, she caught sight of Geneviève, still sitting at her place, her eyes on the oilcloth, which was still damp from the sponge with which it had been wiped.

"Is something the matter?" Denise asked her cousin.

The girl did not answer, but persisted in studying a tear in the oilcloth, as if completely overwhelmed by the thoughts going on inside her. Then she raised her head again painfully, and looked at the face full of sympathy which was leaning towards her. So the others had gone then, had they? What was she doing sitting on that chair? Suddenly she was choked with sobs, her head dropped forwards onto the table again. She was weeping, soaking her sleeve with tears.

"My goodness! What is the matter?" exclaimed Denise, overwhelmed. "Would you like me to call someone?"

Hysterically, Geneviève had seized her by the arm. She held on to it, stammering:

"No, no, no, stay... Oh! So long as Mamma doesn't know! With you I don't mind, but the others... not the others! I didn't mean to do this, I swear to you... It's when I saw I was all alone... Wait a minute, I'm better, I'm not crying any more."

Fresh paroxysms of tears were overwhelming her again, shaking her frail body with great shudders. It seemed as if her piled up black hair was crushing the nape of her neck. While she was rolling her feverish head on her folded arms, a hairpin came undone and her hair flowed down over her neck, burying it beneath its shades. Meanwhile, for fear of attracting attention, Denise was trying to comfort her without making any noise. She unfastened her cousin's dress, and was cut to the heart to see how emaciated and sickly she was: the poor girl had the hollow chest of a child, she had been reduced to the nothingness of a virgin riddled with anaemia. Denise picked up her hair by the handful, that superb hair which seemed to drink away her life; then she tied it up firmly, in order to disentangle her and give her some air.

"Thank you, you are kind," Geneviève was saying. "Oh! I'm not fat, am I? I used to be fatter, and it's all gone... Do up my dress again, Mamma might see my shoulders. I hide them as much as I can... Oh goodness! I'm not well, I'm not well."

However, the paroxysm was abating. She remained on her chair, crushed, staring intently at her cousin. And, after a silence, she asked:

"Tell me the truth: does he love her?"

Denise felt her cheeks going red. She had perfectly well understood that she was referring to Colomban and Clara. But she pretended to be surprised.

"Who d'you mean, dear?"

Geneviève was tossing her head with a sceptical air.

"Please don't lie to me. Do me the favour of making me sure, at least... You must know, I feel you do. Yes, you used to know that woman, and I've seen Colomban following you, talking to you in undertones. He gave you messages for her, didn't he? Oh, for pity's sake, tell me the truth, I swear to you it'll do me good."

Never had Denise been in such a dilemma. Faced with this child who never said a word and yet guessed everything, she lowered her eyes. However, she found sufficient strength to go on deceiving her.

"But it's you that he loves!"

At that Geneviève made a gesture of despair.

"All right, you don't want to say anything... In any case, it doesn't make any difference, I've seen them. He goes out onto the pavement all the time in order to look at her. And she, up there, laughs like anything... Of course they meet outside."

"No, not that, I swear to you!" cried Denise, forgetting herself, carried away by the desire to give her at least that consolation.

The girl took a deep breath. She gave a feeble smile. Then, in the weak voice of a convalescent, she said:

"I would love a glass of water... I'm sorry to bother you. Over there, in the sideboard."

When she had taken the jug, she emptied a big glass at one gulp. With one hand she was holding off Denise, who was afraid that she might do herself some harm.

"No, no, leave me, I'm always thirsty... At night, I get up in order to drink."

There was another silence. Then she went on quietly:

"If only you knew – for ten years I've been accustomed to the idea of this marriage. When I was still wearing short dresses Colomban was already destined for me... And then I can't remember any more how it all happened. From always living together, staying here shut in with each other without ever having any fun together, I must have ended up by thinking him my husband before he actually was. I didn't know if I loved him, I was his wife, that's all... And now he wants to go off with someone else! Oh God! It's breaking my heart! You see, it's pain with which I am unfamiliar. I feel it in my chest and in my head, then it goes all over, it's killing me!"

Tears were coming into her eyes again. Denise, whose own eyes were also growing moist from pity, asked her:

"Does my aunt suspect anything?"

"Yes, Mamma does suspect something, I think… As to Papa, he is too worried, he doesn't know the pain he's causing me by postponing the marriage… Mamma has questioned me several times. It makes her anxious to see me pining. She's never been strong herself, she often says to me: 'You poor dear, I didn't make you very robust.' And then, in these shops one doesn't grow. But she must think I am really getting too thin… Look at my arms, that's not normal, is it?"

With a trembling hand she had taken up the jug again. Her cousin wanted to stop her drinking.

"No, I'm too thirsty, leave me alone."

They could hear Baudu raising his voice. Then, yielding to an impulse of her heart, Denise knelt down and put her arms round Geneviève in a sisterly way. She was kissing her, swearing to her that everything would be all right, that she would marry Colomban, that she would get well and would be happy. Quickly, she stood up again. Her uncle was calling her.

"Come along, Jean is here."

It was indeed Jean, an agitated Jean who had just arrived for dinner. When he was told that it was striking eight, he gaped with astonishment. It couldn't be, he had only just left his employer's. He was teased about it, he had come by way of the forest of Vincennes, no doubt! But as soon as he could get near his sister he whispered to her under his breath:

"It's a little laundress who was taking back her washing… I've got a hired cab outside. Give me five francs."

He went out for a minute and came back to have dinner, for Madame Baudu absolutely refused to let him go away again without at least eating some soup. Geneviève had reappeared, as silent and unobtrusive as ever. Colomban was half dozing behind a counter. The evening slipped by, slowly and sadly, enlivened only by the footsteps of their uncle, who was walking up and down the empty shop. One lone gas jet was burning, the dark shadows were falling from the ceiling in great shovelfuls, like black earth into a grave.

Months passed. Denise would go in almost every day to cheer up Geneviève for a moment. But the melancholy of the Baudus was increasing. The building work going on opposite was a continuous torture which heightened their misfortune. Even when they did have a moment of hope, some unexpected joy, the din of a cart full of bricks, of a stonecutter's saw, or even merely the shout of a bricklayer was enough to spoil it immediately. What is more, it shook the whole neighbourhood. From behind a hoarding which skirted and obstructed the three streets there came a swing of feverish activity. Although the architect was making use of the existing buildings, he was opening them up on all sides in order to convert them, and in the middle, in the gap made by the backyards, he was building a central gallery as vast as a church, which was to open into the Rue Neuve-Saint-Augustin through a main doorway in the centre of the façade. They had at first had great difficulties in building the basements, for they had come across drain seepage, and also made ground full of human bones. Next, the sinking of a well had violently preoccupied the neighbouring houses, a well a hundred metres deep, the output of which was to be five hundred litres a minute. Now the walls were as high as the first floor; scaffolding and wooden towers enclosed the whole island; unceasingly the creaking of windlasses pulling up ashlars could be heard, the sudden unloading of metal plates, the hubbub made by the tribe of workmen, accompanied by the noise of pickaxes and hammers. But what deafened people above all was the jarring noise of machinery; everything worked by steam, the air was rent with piercing whistles; while at the slightest breath of wind a cloud of plaster would take flight and rain down on the neighbouring roofs like snowfall. In despair, the Baudus watched this relentless dust penetrating everywhere, going through the most tightly fitting woodwork, soiling the materials in the shop, even penetrating into their beds – and the idea that, in spite of everything, they were breathing it in, that they would end up by dying of it, was poisoning their existence.

Moreover, the situation was to become even worse. In September the architect, afraid of not being ready in time, decided that work should go on all night. Powerful electric lamps were installed, and there was no longer any end to the movement; gangs succeeded each other, hammers never stopped, machines whistled continually, the din which never diminished seemed to be lifting and scattering the plaster. And then the exasperated Baudus even had to forgo their sleep; they were shaken in their bedroom, no sooner did exhaustion make them drowsy, than the noise turned into nightmares. Then, if they got up barefoot to cool their fever, and went and lifted the curtain, they were appalled by the vision of the Bonheur des Dames blazing away in the darkness, like some colossal forge, forging their ruin. In the midst of the half-built walls, pitted with empty windows, electric lamps were casting broad blue rays of blinding intensity. It would strike two o'clock in the morning, then three, then four o'clock. In its troubled sleep the neighbourhood saw the site enlarged by the lunar brightness, grown colossal and fantastic, crawling with black shadows, with loud-voiced workmen whose silhouettes were gesticulating against the garish white of the new walls.

The small tradespeople of the neighbouring streets had received yet another terrible blow, as Uncle Baudu had foretold they would. Each time the Bonheur des Dames created a new department, there was fresh ruin amongst the shopkeepers round about. The disaster was spreading, even the oldest shops could be heard creaking. Mademoiselle Tatin of the underwear shop in the Choiseul arcade had just been declared bankrupt; Quinette, the glove-maker, could scarcely hold out another six months; the Vanpouilles, the furriers, were obliged to sublet part of their shops; and if Bédoré the hosier and his sister were still holding out in the Rue Gaillon, it was obviously because they were living on what they had saved up in the past. Now fresh cases of ruin were about to be added to those which had been foreseen for a long time: the fancy-goods department was threatening Deslignières, a fat, red-faced man who was the proprietor of a fancy-goods store in the Rue Saint-Roch, while the furniture department was hitting Piot and Rivoire, whose shops dozed in the shade of the Sainte-Anne passageway. There was even fear that the fancy-goods dealer might have a fit of apoplexy, for seeing the Bonheur advertise purses at a reduction of thirty per cent, he was in a constant state of fury. The furniture sellers, who were calmer, pretended to joke about these counter-jumpers who were trying their hands at selling tables and cupboards, but customers were already leaving them, the success of the rival department promised to be tremendous. It was no good, there was nothing for it but to bow the head in resignation; after them others would be swept away, and there was no longer any reason why all the remaining businesses should not be driven from their counters, one after another. One day nothing but the roof of the Bonheur would cover the whole district.

Nowadays, morning and evening, when the thousand employees were going in and leaving, they stretched out in such a long queue in the Place Gaillon that people would stop to look at them, just as one looks at a regiment going by. They congested the pavements for ten minutes, and the shopkeepers standing at their doors would think of their sole assistant, whom they already did not know how to feed. The big shop's last stock-taking, when the turnover had been forty million, had also revolutionized the neighbourhood. The figure had spread from house to house, amidst cries of surprise and rage. Forty million! How could one dream of such a thing? Doubtless with their considerable trade expenses and their system of low prices the net profit was at the most four per cent. But a profit of sixteen hundred thousand francs was still a pretty good sum, one could be content with four per cent when one was dealing with capital of that order. It was said that Mouret's former capital, the initial five hundred thousand francs, increased each year by the total profits – a capital which by now had become four million – had thus been turned into goods over the counters ten times. Robineau, devoting himself to making this calculation after a meal in Denise's presence, remained for a moment overwhelmed, his eyes on his empty plate: she was right, it was this incessant renewal of capital which was the invincible strength of the new way of business. Bourras alone, as arrogant and stupid as a monument, still denied the facts and refused to understand. They were just a band of robbers, and nothing more! Liars! Charlatans, who would be pulled out of the river one fine morning!

The Baudus, however, in spite of their determination not to make any changes in the ways of the Vieil Elbeuf, were trying to keep up with the competition. The customers no longer came to them, so they did their utmost to go to the customers through the intermediary of agents. There was at that time in the Place de Paris an agent who had connections with all the best tailors, and who was the salvation of small shops selling cloth and flannel, if he chose to represent them. Naturally there was a lot of competition to get him, he was becoming an important personality, and Baudu, having beaten him down over the price, had the misfortune of seeing him come to an agreement with the Matignons in the Rue Croix-des-Petits-Champs. He was robbed by two other agents in rapid succession; a third, who was honest, was doing nothing to help him. It was a slow death, there were no jolts, only a continuous slowing-down of business, customers lost one after another. A day came when bills were overdue. Until then, they had been living on the savings of bygone days; from now on they would be in debt. In December, Baudu, terrified by the number of his promissory notes, resigned himself to making the cruellest of sacrifices: he sold his country house at Rambouillet, a house which cost so much money in continual repairs, and for which the tenants had not even paid him rent when he decided to get rid of it. This sale meant the death of the only dream of his life, and his heart bled for it as for the loss of a dear one. He had to accept seventy thousand francs, what is more, for a property which had cost him more than two hundred thousand. He was lucky, indeed, to find the Lhommes, his neighbours, whose desire to add to their property made them decide to buy it. The seventy thousand francs would keep the shop going for a little while longer. In spite of all the setbacks, the idea of a fight was reviving: with organization, perhaps, they now might be able to come through.

On the Sunday on which the Lhommes paid the money, they consented to dine at the Vieil Elbeuf. Madame Aurélie arrived first, they had to wait for the cashier who arrived late and in a fluster, as a result of having spent a whole afternoon making music; while as to young Albert, he accepted the invitation, but did not put in an appearance. It was, in any case, a distressing evening. The Baudus, living without any air in the depths of their narrow dining room, suffered from the blast of wind brought into it by the Lhommes, with their disbanded family and their taste for the free life. Geneviève, who considered Madame Aurélie's imperial demeanour offensive, did not open her mouth; whereas Colomban was admiring the buyer, thrilled at the thought that she reigned over Clara.

That evening, when Madame Baudu was already in bed, Baudu, before joining her, walked up and down the room for a long time. It was mild, the damp weather of a thaw. Outside, in spite of the shut windows and drawn curtains, the roar of the machines on the building site opposite could be heard.

"D'you know what I'm thinking about, Élisabeth?" he said finally. "Well, although those Lhommes are making a lot of money, I'd rather be in my shoes than in theirs... They're successful, it's true. She told us, didn't she, that she's made nearly twenty thousand francs this year, and that enabled her to take my poor old house from me. It doesn't matter! I've no longer got my house, but at least I don't go playing music in one direction while you go gadding about in the other... No, you know, they can't be happy."

He was still suffering deeply from his sacrifice, he felt a grudge against them, the people who had bought his dream from him. When he came close to the bed he bent towards his wife, gesticulating; then, once more back by the window, he was silent for a moment, listening to the din from the building site. Then he started making his old accusations again, his despairing complaints about modern times: such a thing had never been seen before, shop assistants were now earning more than shopkeepers, it was the cashiers who were buying up their employers' estates! As a result, everything was breaking up, the family no longer existed, people lived in hotels instead of supping decently at home. Finally, he ended by prophesying that one day young Albert with his actresses would fritter away the estate at Rambouillet.

Madame Baudu was listening to him, her head upright on the pillow, so pale that her face was the same colour as the linen. She ended by saying gently: "They've paid you."

At last Baudu was silent. He walked up and down for a few seconds, his eyes on the ground. Then he resumed:

"They've paid me, it's true – and after all, their money's as good as any other... It would be funny if we got the shop going again with *that* money. Oh! If only I wasn't so old and tired!"

A long silence reigned. The draper was absorbed by vague plans. Suddenly, looking at the ceiling and without moving her head, his wife spoke:

"Have you noticed your daughter lately?"

"No," he answered.

"Well, she worries me rather... She's growing pale, she seems to be giving way to despair."

Standing by the bed, he was full of surprise.

"Really? But why? If she is ill she should say so. We'll have to get the doctor tomorrow."

Madame Baudu still remained motionless. After a good minute she merely declared in her deliberate way:

"About this marriage with Colomban – I think it would be better to get it over."

He looked at her, then started to walk up and down again. Could his daughter really fall ill on account of the shop assistant? Did she love him to such an extent then, that she could not wait? This was yet another misfortune! It overwhelmed him, particularly as he himself had decided ideas about the marriage. He would never have wished it to take place under the present conditions. Nevertheless, anxiety was softening him.

"Very well," he said finally, "I'll speak to Colomban."

Without saying another word, he continued his walk. Soon his wife's eyes closed, she looked quite white as she slept, as if she was dead. And still he walked up and down. Before going to bed he parted the curtains and glanced out; on the other side of the road the gaping windows of the old Duvillard mansion made holes opening onto the building site, where workmen were moving about in the glare of electric lamps.

The very next day Baudu led Colomban to the end of a narrow part of the shop on the mezzanine floor. He had decided the day before what he would say.

"My boy," he began. "You know that I've sold my house at Rambouillet. That's going to enable us to make a special effort. But first of all I'd like to have a little talk with you."

The young man, who seemed apprehensive about the interview, was waiting awkwardly. His small eyes were blinking in his broad face, and he remained with his mouth open, which in his case was a sign that he was deeply disturbed.

"Now listen to me carefully," the draper resumed. "When old Hauchecorne handed over the Vieil Elbeuf to me, the shop was prosperous; he himself in the past had received it in good condition from old Finet... You know my ideas: I thought I would be committing a mean act if I were to hand on this family trust depleted to my children – and that is why I always put off your marriage to Geneviève. Yes, I was stubborn, I hoped to bring back former prosperity. I wanted to push the books under your nose, saying: 'Look! In the year I joined so much cloth was sold, and this year, the year I leave, ten or twenty thousand francs' worth more of it have been sold... ' In short, it was a vow

I'd made to myself, you see, the very natural desire to prove to myself that the shop had not deteriorated while in my hands. Otherwise I should feel that I'd robbed you."

His voice was choking with emotion. He blew his nose in order to pull himself together, and asked:

"Why don't you say something?"

But Colomban had nothing to say: he shook his head, he was waiting, more and more worried, thinking he had guessed what his employer was getting at. It was marriage as soon as possible. How could he refuse? He would never have the strength to do so. And what about the other woman, she of whom he dreamt at night, his flesh scorched by such passion that he would throw himself on the floor, quite naked, afraid it would kill him!

"At the moment," Baudu continued, "we've got some money, which can be our salvation. The situation is becoming worse every day, but perhaps if we make a supreme effort… Well, I wanted to warn you. We're going to stake everything. If we're beaten, well, that'll be the end of us… Only, I'm sorry to say, my boy, as a result, your marriage will have to be postponed again, for I don't want to plunge you into the fight all on your own. That would be too despicable of me, wouldn't it?"

Colomban, relieved, had sat down on some pieces of duffel. His legs were still shaking. He was afraid that he might show his joy, and was hanging his head, while twirling his thumbs on his lap.

"Why don't you say something?" Baudu repeated.

No, he did not say anything, he could think of nothing to say. So the draper went on with due deliberation:

"I was sure that this would grieve you… Pull yourself together a bit, you mustn't remain crushed like that… Above all, try to understand my position. How can I tie a stone like that round your neck? Instead of leaving you a good business, I might perhaps leave you a bankruptcy. No, only cads indulge in tricks of that sort… Of course, I only desire your happiness, but you'll never make me go against my conscience."

He went on talking in the same strain for a long time, floundering in contradictory phrases, like a man who would have liked his hints to be understood and his hand to be forced. As he had promised his daughter and the shop to Colomban, strict integrity forced him to hand them both over in good condition, without blemishes or debts. Only he was tired, he felt the burden was too heavy for him, a hint of entreaty could be heard breaking through his faltering voice. The words became even more confused on his lips, he was waiting for Colomban to say something, something impulsive prompted by his heart – but it never came.

"Of course I know," he was murmuring, "old people lack fire... With young people things burn up again, they're hot-blooded, it's natural... But, no, no, I can't do it, honestly I can't! If I were to hand over to you now, you'd reproach me later!"

He fell silent, trembling all over, and as the young man was still hanging his head, after a painful silence he asked him for the third time:

"Why don't you say something?"

Finally, without looking at him, Colomban replied:

"There's nothing to say... You're the master, you're wiser than the rest of us. Since you insist, we will wait, we'll try to be sensible."

That was that. Baudu was still hoping that Colomban was going to throw himself into his arms, crying, "Father, you should rest, it's our turn to fight, give us the shop as it is, so that we can perform the miracle of saving it!" Then he looked at him and was overcome with shame; he secretly accused himself of having wanted to dupe his children. The old shopkeeper's mania for honesty was aroused in him; it was this cautious young man who was right, for there are no feelings in business, there are only figures.

"Give me a kiss, my boy," he said in conclusion. "It's settled then, we won't discuss marriage again for a year. We must think about serious things first and foremost."

That evening in their bedroom, when Madame Baudu questioned her husband as to the results of the interview, he had regained his obstinate determination to fight personally to the end. He praised Colomban very highly: a reliable lad, steadfast in his ideas and, what is more, brought up according to sound principles, incapable, for example, of joking with the customers like those country bumpkins at the Bonheur. No, he was honest, he was one of the family, he didn't gamble on the sales as if they were shares on the Stock Exchange.

"Well, when's the wedding going to be?" asked Madame Baudu.

"Later on," he replied. "When I'm in a position to keep my promises."

She made no movement, but merely replied:

"It'll be the death of our girl."

Roused with anger, Baudu controlled himself. It would be the death of him if they went on upsetting him like that all the time! Was it his fault? He loved his daughter, he talked of shedding his blood for her, but all the same he couldn't make the shop do well when it didn't want to any longer. Geneviève should be sensible and have a little patience, until they had better sales. Damn it all! Colomban was staying there, no one would steal him!

"It's incredible!" he went on repeating. "Such a well-brought-up girl!"

Madame Baudu said no more. No doubt she had guessed at the tortures of jealousy which Geneviève was suffering, but she did not dare confide them to her husband. She had always been prevented by a queer, feminine modesty from broaching certain delicate subjects of an emotional nature with him. When he saw that she remained silent, he directed his anger against the people opposite, shaking his fists in the air at the building site where, that night, iron girders were being installed with great blows from a hammer.

Denise was going to go back to work at the Bonheur des Dames again. She realized that the Robineaus, forced to cut down their staff, did not know how to give her notice. The only way they could still keep going was by doing everything themselves; Gaujean, persisting in his feud with the Bonheur, was giving longer credit, and was even promising to find funds for them, but they were beginning to be frightened, they wanted to make an attempt at economy and order. For a fortnight Denise felt that they were ill at ease with her, and she was forced to take the initiative and say that she had a job elsewhere. It was a relief; Madame Robineau, deeply moved, kissed her, swearing that she would always miss her. Then when, in reply to a question, the girl answered that she would go back to Mouret's shop, Robineau went pale.

"You're right," he shouted violently.

It was not so easy to break the news to old Bourras. Nevertheless, Denise had to give him notice, and she dreaded it, for she felt deeply grateful to him. Bourras, in fact was, in a constant state of anger, being right in the middle of the hubbub of the neighbouring building site. Carts with building materials barred the way to his shop; pickaxes were knocking at his walls; everything in his house, all the umbrellas and walking sticks, were dancing to the noise of hammers. It seemed as if the hovel, obstinately remaining in the midst of this demolition work, was going to crack. But what was worst of all was that the architect, in order to connect the shops' existing departments with those which were being installed in the old Duvillard mansion, had had the idea of digging a passage underneath the little house which separated them. This house belonged to Mouret & Co. Ltd and as there was a clause in the lease that the tenant had to agree to repair work being carried out, one fine morning some workmen turned up. At this, Bourras almost had a stroke. Surely it was enough to constrict him on all sides, left, right and centre, without getting him by the feet as well and eating the earth from under him? He had chased the builders away, and was taking the matter to court. Repair work, agreed! But this was a question of making improvements. It was thought in the neighbourhood that he would win his case, though this was by no means certain. Anyway, the case threatened to be a long one, and people were taking a passionate interest in the interminable duel.

On the day when Denise finally plucked up courage to give him notice, it so happened that Bourras was just returning from his lawyer.

"Would you believe it!" he exclaimed. "They say now that the house is unsound, they're trying to make out that the foundations need repairing. Upon my word! They're sick of shaking it with their damned machines. It's not surprising if it's breaking up!"

Then, when the girl had announced to him that she was leaving, and that she was going back to the Bonheur with a salary of a thousand francs, he was so upset that he could only hold his old, trembling hands up to heaven. Emotion had made him sink into a chair.

"You! You too!" he stammered. "Well, there's only me now, there's no one left but me!"

After a silence he asked:

"What about the boy?"

"He'll go back to Madame Gras," Denise replied. "She was very fond of him."

Once more they fell silent. She would have preferred him to have been furious, swearing, banging his fists; the sight of the old man, shaken to the core and crushed, cut her to the heart. But he was gradually recovering, he was starting to shout again.

"A thousand francs, one doesn't turn that down... You'll all go. Go on then, leave me alone. Yes, alone, d'you hear? There's one person who'll never give in... And tell them that I'll win my case, even if I have to put my last shirt on it!"

Denise was not leaving Robineau until the end of the month. She had seen Mouret again, everything was in order. One evening she was just going to go up to her room again when Deloche, who was standing under an archway on the lookout for her, stopped her as she passed. He was in very good mood, he had just heard the great news, the whole shop was talking about it, he said. And he gaily recounted to her the gossip of the counters.

"You know, the ladies in the ready-made department look pretty silly!"

Then, breaking off:

"By the way, you remember Clara Prunaire... Well! It seems that she and the boss... D'you get me?"

He had become very red. She, quite pale, exclaimed:

"Monsieur Mouret!"

"It's an odd taste, isn't it?" he went on. "A woman who looks like a horse... That little thing from the lingerie department that he had twice, last year, was at least nice. Anyway, it's his affair."

Once back in her room, Denise felt faint. It was because she had gone upstairs too quickly, of course. Leaning her elbows on the window sill, she had a sudden vision of Valognes, of the empty street, with its mossy paving stones, which she used to see from her room as a child, and she was seized with a desire to live there again, to take refuge in the oblivion and peace of the country. Paris got on her nerves, she hated the Bonheur des Dames, she couldn't think why she had agreed to go back there. She was sure to suffer there again; since hearing Deloche's stories she was already suffering from some nameless distress. And then, for no reason, a flood of tears forced her to leave the window. She cried for a long time, and then recovered a little courage with which to go on living.

The next day, at lunchtime, Robineau sent her on an errand, and as she was passing by the Vieil Elbeuf and saw that Colomban was alone in the shop, she pushed open the door. The Baudus were having lunch, the sound of forks could be heard at the far end of the little hall.

"You can come in," said the shop assistant, "they're at lunch."

But she signalled to him to be silent and led him into a corner. Lowering her voice, she said:

"It's you I want to talk to... Haven't you any heart? Can't you see that Geneviève loves you, and that it'll be the death of her?"

She was shaking all over, she was once more in the throes of the fever she had been in the day before. Startled, taken aback by this sudden attack, he could not think of anything to say.

"Can't you understand?" she went on. "Geneviève knows that you love someone else. She told me so, she sobbed like a child... Oh! the poor little thing! She doesn't weigh much, believe me! You should see her little arms! It's enough to make one weep... Really, you can't leave her to die like that!"

Finally, completely overwhelmed, he spoke.

"But she isn't ill, you're exaggerating... I can't see it myself... And then, it's her father who's putting off the wedding."

Denise harshly pointed out that this was a lie. She had sensed that the slightest insistence from the young man would have persuaded her uncle. As to Colomban's surprise, that was not pretence: he had really never noticed that Geneviève was slowly dying. It came as a very disagreeable eye-opener to him. So long as he had been unaware of it, he had not had very much with which to reproach himself.

"And who for?" Denise went on. "For a nobody! Why, don't you know what sort of a person you love? I didn't want to make you unhappy before, I've often avoided answering your endless questions... Well, she carries on with everyone, she doesn't care a straw for you, you'll never have her, or else you'll have her as others have, once in a while in passing."

Very pale, he was listening to her and, at each phrase that she flung in his face through clenched teeth, his lips trembled slightly. She was giving way to a rage of which she had not been conscious, and had suddenly become cruel.

"Anyway," she gave a final shriek, "she's living with Monsieur Mouret, if you want to know!"

Her voice was choking, she had become even paler than he was. They looked at each other.

Then he stammered:

"I love her."

At that Denise felt ashamed. Why was she talking to the lad like that, and what had made her lose her temper? She remained mute, the simple words which he had just replied were reverberating in her heart with a distant sound of bells which deafened her. "I love her, I love her," the words echoed. He was right, he couldn't marry anyone else.

As she was turning round she caught sight of Geneviève on the dining-room threshold.

"Be quiet!" she said rapidly.

But it was too late, Geneviève must have heard. All the blood had left her face. Just at that moment a customer opened the door; it was Madame Bourdelais, one of the few remaining faithful of the Vieil Elbeuf, where she found hard-wearing articles; Madame de Boves had followed the fashion and gone over to the Bonheur long ago; even Madame Marty, completely conquered by the enticing displays opposite, did not come any more. Geneviève was forced to step forwards in order to say in her toneless voice:

"What does Madame require?"

Madame Bourdelais wanted to see some flannel. Colomban took down a length from the shelf. Geneviève showed her the material – and there they both were, their hands cold, close together behind the counter. Meanwhile Baudu was coming out last of all from the little dining room, following his wife, who had gone to sit down at the cash desk. But he did not at first interfere in the sale; he had smiled at Denise and remained standing, looking at Madame Bourdelais.

"That's not pretty enough," she was saying. "Show me what you have that is stronger."

Colomban took down another length. There was a silence. Madame Bourdelais was examining the material.

"And how much is it?"

"Six francs, Madame," Geneviève replied.

The customer made a gesture of annoyance. "Six francs! But they've got the same thing opposite at five francs!"

Baudu winced slightly. He could not help intervening, very politely. No doubt Madame had made a mistake: those goods should have been sold at six francs fifty, it was impossible for anyone to sell them at five francs. She must certainly be thinking of some other material.'

"No, no," she was repeating, with the obstinacy of a middle-class woman who prided herself on being an expert.

"It's the same material. Perhaps it's even slightly thicker."

In the end the argument became acrimonious. Baudu, with a furious face, was making an effort to remain smiling. His resentment against the Bonheur des Dames was bursting in his breast.

"Really," said Madame Bourdelais in the end. "You'll have to treat me more civilly, or else I shall go across the road, like the others."

Then he lost his head and, shaken with pent-up rage, shouted:

"Very well! Go across the road then!"

At that she stood up, deeply offended, and left without looking back, replying as she did so:

"That's just what I'm going to do, Monsieur."

They were dumbfounded. The master's violence had startled them all. He himself was still frightened and trembling at what he had just said. The phrase had slipped out against his will, in an outburst of long-suppressed resentment. And now the Baudus, motionless, their arms sagging, were watching Madame Bourdelais as she was crossing the street. She seemed to them to be carrying away their fortune with her. When she went through the high doorway of the Bonheur, at her leisurely pace, when they saw her back lost in the crowd, they felt as if something had been torn away from them.

"There goes another they're taking away from us!" murmured the draper.

Then, turning towards Denise, of whose new appointment he was aware, he said:

"You too, they've taken you back... There now, I don't hold it against you. Since they've got the money, they've got the power."

Just at that moment Denise, still hoping that Geneviève had not been able to overhear Colomban, was whispering in her ear:

"Cheer up, do, he loves you."

But, in a very low voice the girl replied:

"Why do you lie? Just watch! He can't help it, he's looking over there... I know very well that they've stolen him from me, like they steal everything from us."

She sat down in the seat at the cashier's desk, beside her mother. The latter had no doubt guessed the fresh blow the girl had received, for her eyes, full of anguish, went from her to Colomban and then travelled back to the Bonheur again. It was true, it was stealing everything from them: from the father, his money; from the mother, her dying child; from the daughter, a husband for whom she had waited ten years. Faced with this condemned family Denise, whose heart was flooded with compassion, was afraid for a moment that she was wicked to go back. Was she not once more going to lend a hand to the machine which was crushing the poor? But it was as if she was being swept along by some kind of force, she felt that she was not doing wrong.

"Pooh!" Baudu resumed, in order to bolster up his courage. "We shan't die of it! If we lose one customer, we'll find a couple more... Listen, Denise: I've got here seventy thousand francs which are going to make that Mouret of yours have sleepless nights... Come along, the rest of you! Don't look as if you were at a funeral!"

But he could not cheer them up, and he himself relapsed once more into bleak despair – and there they all stood, looking at the monster, drawn by it, obsessed by it, gorging themselves on their misfortune. The work was almost finished, the scaffolding had been taken away from the front of the building, one whole section of the colossal edifice was visible, its walls white, with spacious, light shop windows in them. Just then, all along the pavement which was at last open to traffic again, eight vans were lined up and were being loaded one after the other by porters outside the dispatch office. A ray of sunlight was cutting through the street, and in it the green door panels picked out in yellow and red were sparkling like mirrors, sending blinding reflections right into the depths of the Vieil Elbeuf. The coachmen, dressed in black and with a dignified bearing, were holding the horses, superb teams, tossing their silver-plated bridles on short rein. Each time a van was full there was a resounding rumble on the paving stones which made the small neighbouring shops shake.

And then, faced with this triumphal procession which they had to suffer twice a day, the Baudus felt their hearts breaking. The father's courage left him as he wondered where that continual stream of goods could be going; whereas the mother, made ill by her daughter's anguish, went on looking without seeing anything, her eyes drowned with great tears.

9

O N MONDAY, 14th March, the Bonheur des Dames was inaugurating its new building by a grand display of summer fashions, which was to last for three days. Outside, a bitter north wind was blowing, and passers-by, surprised by this return of winter, were hurrying along, buttoning up their overcoats. Meanwhile, the small shops in the neighbourhood were in a ferment of excitement, and the pale faces of the small tradesmen could be seen pressed against their windows, busy counting the first carriages which were drawing up outside the new main entrance in the Rue Neuve-Saint-Augustin. This entrance, as towering and vast as the porch of a church, surmounted by a group portraying Industry and Commerce shaking hands in the midst of a wealth of symbolic emblems, was sheltered by a vast awning which, freshly gilded, seemed to light up the pavements with a flash of sunlight. To the right and left the shopfronts stretched out, their whiteness still looking garish, going round the corners into the Rue Monsigny and the Rue de la Michodière, occupying the whole block except on the side of the Rue du Dix-Décembre, where the Crédit Immobilier was going to build. When the small tradespeople raised their heads they saw along the whole length of this barrack-like extension, pile upon pile of goods visible through the plate-glass windows which from the ground floor to the second floor made the shop open to the public gaze. This enormous block, this colossal bazaar blotted out their sky, and seemed to them to have something to do with the cold with which they were shivering, behind their icy counters.

Meanwhile, from six o'clock onwards, Mouret was there, giving his final orders. In the centre, on a straight line from the main entrance, a broad gallery ran from one end of the shop to the other, flanked on the right and left by two narrower galleries, the Monsigny Gallery and the Michodière Gallery. The courtyards had been glazed in and transformed into halls, and iron staircases ran from the ground floor, iron bridges had been thrown across from one end to the other on both floors. It so happened that the architect was intelligent, a young man in love with modernity, and he had made use of stone only for the basements and the corner pillars, and then had made the whole of the rest of the framework out of iron, with columns holding up the assembly of girders and beams. The counter-arches of the flooring and the internal partitions were of brick. Everywhere space and light had been gained, air was freely let in, the public had plenty of room to move about beneath the audacious curves of the wide-spaced trusses. It was the cathedral of modern business, strong and yet light, built for a multitude of customers. After the bargains by the door in the central gallery on the ground floor, there came the tie, glove and silk departments; the Monsigny Gallery was occupied by household linen and printed cotton goods, the Michodière Gallery by the haberdashery, hosiery, cloth and woollen departments. Then, on the first floor, there were the ready-made clothes, lingerie, shawls, lace and other new departments, while the bedding, carpet and furnishing materials, all the bulky goods and those which were difficult to handle, were relegated to the second floor. By this time there were altogether thirty-nine departments and eighteen hundred employees, of which two hundred were women. A whole world was springing up there, amidst the life echoing beneath the high metal naves.

Mouret's sole passion was the conquest of Woman. He wanted her to be queen in his shop, he had built this temple for her in order to hold her at his mercy there. His main tactics consisted in intoxicating her with flattering attentions, trading on her desires and exploiting her effervescence. Therefore he racked his brains night and day in search of new, bright ideas. Already wishing to eliminate the fatigue of stairs for delicate ladies, he had had two lifts, upholstered in velvet, installed. Next, he had just opened a buffet, where fruit juices and biscuits were served free of charge, and a reading room, a colossal gallery excessively richly decorated, in which he even ventured to hold picture exhibitions. But his subtlest idea was, when dealing with women devoid of coquetry, that of conquering the mother through the child; he let no force go untapped, speculated upon every kind of feeling, created departments for little boys and girls, stopped the mothers on their way past by offering pictures and balloons to their babies. This free gift of a balloon to each customer who bought something was a stroke of genius; they were red balloons, made of fine India rubber and with the name of the shop written on them in big letters; when held on the end of a string they travelled through the air, parading a living advertisement through the streets!

Publicity was, above all, a tremendous force. Mouret spent as much as three hundred thousand francs a year on catalogues, advertisements and posters. For his sale of summer fashions he had sent out two hundred thousand catalogues, of which fifty thousand, translated into all languages, were sent abroad. Now he had them illustrated with drawings, and even enclosed samples with them, glued onto the pages. His displays were bursting out everywhere, the Bonheur des Dames was staring the whole world in the face, invading walls, newspapers and even the curtains of theatres. He professed that Woman was helpless against advertisements, that in the end she inevitably went to see what the noise was about. Thus analysing her like a great moralist, he would set even more cunning snares for her. For example, he had discovered that she was unable to resist cheapness, that she bought things without needing them if she thought she was getting a bargain, and it was on this observation that he based his system of price reductions: he gradually reduced the prices of goods which were not sold, preferring to sell them at a loss, faithful to the principle of a rapid turnover of stocks. Then, penetrating even further into Woman's heart, he had recently devised "returns", a masterpiece of seduction worthy of the Jesuits. "Take it all the same, Madame: you can return the article to us if you find you don't like it." And a woman who was resisting would find in that a final excuse, a possibility of going back on an act of folly: her conscience satisfied, she would buy it. By now returns and price reductions were already part of the standard methods of the new business.

But it was in the interior decoration of shops that Mouret revealed himself as a master without rival. He laid it down as a law that not a corner of the Bonheur des Dames was to remain unfrequented; everywhere he insisted upon noise, crowds, life – for life, he would say, attracts life, gives birth and multiplies. He put this law into practice in a variety of different ways. First of all there should be a crush at the entrance, it should seem to people in the street as if there was a riot in the shop, and he produced this crush by putting remnants in the entrance, shelves and baskets overflowing with articles at very low prices, so that working-class people accumulated, barring the threshold, and gave the impression that the shop was bursting with customers, when often it was only half full. Then, all through the galleries, he had the art of hiding the departments which were standing idle – the shawl department in summer and the cotton materials in winter, for example; he would surround them with active departments, drowning them in a hubbub. He was the only one so far to think of putting the carpet and furniture departments on the second floor, for in those departments customers were more rare, and the presence of them on the ground floor would have created cold, empty gaps. If he could have found a way of making the street run right through his shop, he would have done so.

Just then Mouret was in the throes of a fit of inspiration. On Saturday evening, as he was giving a last glance at the preparations for Monday's big sale which they had been busy with for a month, he had suddenly realized that the arrangement of departments which he had adopted was silly. It was, all the same, an absolutely logical arrangement – materials on one side, manufactured goods on the other – an intelligent system, which should make it easy for customers to find their own way about. In the past, in the muddle of Madame Hédouin's little shop, he had dreamt of this system, and now, on the day when he was putting it into effect, he felt his faith in it shaken. Suddenly he had shouted out that he wanted all that "broken up". It was a question of moving half the shop; they had forty-eight hours in which to do it. The staff, startled and jostled, had had to spend two nights and the whole of Sunday in the midst of an appalling mess. Even on Monday morning, an hour before the opening, the goods were not yet in place. Undoubtedly the director was going out of his mind, no one could understand it at all; the consternation was general.

"Come along! Let's hurry!" Mouret was shouting, with the calm assurance born of his genius. "Here are some more suits that I want taken upstairs… And are the Japanese things installed on the central landing? Come on, my lads, one last effort, you'll see what a sale we'll have in a minute!"

Bourdoncle too had been there since dawn. He understood no better than the others, and was watching the director with an air of anxiety. He had not dared question him, knowing how he was wont to greet people in such moments of crisis. All the same, he decided to risk it, and asked gently:

"Was it really necessary to turn everything upside down like that, on the eve of our opening?"

At first Mouret shrugged his shoulders without replying. Then, since Bourdoncle ventured to insist, he burst out:

"So that the customers should all huddle together in the same corner, I suppose? A fine geometrical idea I had when I thought of that! I should never have forgiven myself... Can't you understand that I was localizing the crowd? A woman would come in, go straight where she wanted, pass from the petticoat to the dress, from the dress to the coat and then leave, without even having got a bit lost! Not one of them would so much as have seen our shop!"

"But," Bourdoncle pointed out, "now that you've muddled it all up and thrown everything all over the place, the staff will wear out their legs taking customers from department to department."

Mouret made a superb gesture.

"I don't give a damn! They're young, it'll make them grow. And if they walk about, so much the better! They'll look more numerous, they'll swell the crowd. So long as there's a crush, all will be well!"

He was laughing, and deigned to explain his idea, lowering his voice as he did so:

"Here, Bourdoncle, listen to what'll happen... Firstly, this continual coming and going of customers scatters them all over the place, multiplies them and makes them lose their heads; secondly, as they have to be conducted from one end of the shop to the other – for example if they want a lining after having bought a dress – these journeys in every direction triple, for them, the size of the shop; thirdly, they are forced to go through departments where they wouldn't have set foot, temptations there catch them as they pass and they succumb; fourthly..."

Bourdoncle was laughing with him. Then Mouret, delighted, stopped in order to shout to the porters:

"That's fine, my lads! Now, a spot of sweeping, and it'll look splendid!"

But, turning round, he caught sight of Denise. He and Bourdoncle were by the ready-made clothes department, which he had just split into two by having the dresses and suits taken up to the second floor, at the other end of the shop. Denise, the first to come down, was wide-eyed, bewildered by the new arrangements.

"What's this," she murmured, "We're moving?"

This surprise appeared to amuse Mouret, who adored theatrical effects of that sort. Denise had been back at the Bonheur since the beginning of February, and she had been agreeably surprised to find, on meeting the staff again, that it was polite and almost respectful. Madame Aurélie, above all, was kindly disposed to her; Marguerite and Clara seemed resigned; even old Jouve was obsequious in a rather embarrassed way, as if he wanted to wipe out the unpleasant memory of the past. The fact that Mouret had said a word sufficed, everyone was whispering, watching her as they did so. In the midst of this universal friendliness, the only things which rather hurt her were Deloche's curious sadness and Pauline's inexplicable smiles.

Meanwhile, Mouret was still looking at her with delight:

"Well, Mademoiselle, what are you looking for?" he asked at last.

Denise had not seen him. She blushed slightly. Since her return he had taken an interest in her, and this touched her very much. Without her knowing why, Pauline had described the director's love affairs with Clara to her in detail – where he saw her, what he paid her – and she often brought the subject up again, even adding that he had another mistress, that same Madame Desforges who was well known to the whole shop. Such stories upset Denise, and in his presence she was again seized with the fears she had had in the past, with an uneasiness in which her gratitude struggled against her anger.

"It's all this moving house," she murmured.

Then Mouret came closer in order to say to her in a lower voice:

"This evening, after the sale, will you come and see me in my office? I want to speak to you."

She nodded in confusion without uttering a word, and went into the department, where the other salesgirls were arriving. But Bourdoncle had overheard Mouret, and was watching him with a smile. He even ventured to say, when they were alone:

"That girl again! Look out, it'll end up being serious!"

Mouret sharply defended himself, hiding his emotion beneath an air of casual superiority.

"Don't be silly! The woman who can catch me is not yet born, old chap!"

As the shop was opening at last, he rushed to give a final glance at the various departments. Bourdoncle shook his head. That girl Denise, who was so simple and gentle, was beginning to worry him. He had defeated her once already by dismissing her ruthlessly. But here she was, reappearing again, and he was treating her as a serious enemy, saying nothing but once more biding his time.

He caught up Mouret, who was downstairs in the Saint-Augustin Hall opposite the entrance, shouting:

"Who the devil d'you think I am? I said that the blue parasols were to be round the edge... I want all that broken up, and look sharp about it!"

He was deaf to all arguments, a team of porters had to rearrange the display of parasols. Seeing some customers approaching, he even had the doors closed for an instant; he was saying over and over again that he would rather not open at all than leave the blue parasols in the centre. It ruined his composition. Those who had a reputation as window-dressers – Hutin, Mignot and one or two others – were coming to have a look, craning their necks, but they were pretending not to understand what he meant, for they belonged to a different school.

Finally the doors were opened again, and people streamed in. From the very beginning, even before the shop was full, there was such a crush in the entrance hall that the police had to be called in to keep the crowd moving on the pavement. Mouret's calculations had been right, all the housewives, a serried throng of shopkeepers' wives and women in bonnets, were taking by storm the bargains, the remnants and oddments, which were displayed right into the street. Outstretched hands were continually feeling the materials hanging by the entrance, a calico at thirty-five centimes, a salt-and-pepper cloth in a wool-and-cotton mixture at forty-five centimes – above all an Orleans cloth at thirty-eight centimes which was playing havoc with poor purses. There was much elbowing, a feverish scrimmage round the cash desks and the baskets in which goods at reduced prices

– laces at ten centimes, ribbons at twenty-five centimes, garters at fifteen, gloves, petticoats, ties, cotton socks and stockings – were overflowing and disappearing, as if devoured by the voracious crowd. In spite of the cold weather, the salesmen who were selling right outside on the pavement were insufficient. A fat woman screamed. Two little girls were almost suffocated.

All the morning the crush increased. Towards one o'clock queues were being formed, the street was barricaded as if during riots. Just as Madame de Boves and her daughter Blanche were standing hesitantly on the opposite pavement, they were approached by Madame Marty, who was likewise accompanied by her daughter Valentine.

"What a crowd, eh?" said the former. "They're killing each other inside. I shouldn't have come, I was in bed, then I got up because I wanted a breath of fresh air."

"It's the same with me," the other declared, "I promised my husband to go and see his sister in Montmartre. Then, as I was passing I remembered that I needed some shoelaces. One might as well buy them here as anywhere else, mightn't one? Oh! I shan't spend a penny! I don't need anything anyway."

They had not, however, taken their eyes off the door, and they were caught up and carried away by the current of the crowd.

"No, no, I'm not going in, I'm frightened," murmured Madame de Boves. "Let's go away, Blanche, we shall be pulverized."

But her voice was growing weaker, and she was gradually giving way to the desire to enter where everyone else was entering; her fear was melting away in the irresistible lure of the crush. Madame Marty had also given way. She was repeating:

"Hold my dress, Valentine... My goodness! I've never seen anything like this. You're carried along. What is it going to be like inside!"

Seized by the current, the ladies were no longer able to turn back. As rivers draw the stray waters of a valley together, so it seemed that the stream of customers, flowing right through the entrance hall, was drinking in the passers-by from the street, sucking in the population from the four corners of Paris. They were only advancing very slowly, jammed so tight that they were out of breath, held upright by shoulders and stomachs, of which they could feel the flabby warmth, and their gratified desire was revelling in this arduous approach, which whipped up their curiosity even more. There was a medley of ladies dressed in silk, of tradesmen's wives in shabby dresses, of hatless girls, all of them out of breath, all of them stirred, fired by the same passion. A few men, swamped by all those ample bosoms, were casting anxious glances around them. In the very thick of the crowd a nurse was holding up her baby high in the air, and it was laughing with pleasure. And only one thin woman was losing her temper, bursting out into ill-natured phrases, and accusing a woman near her of winding her.

"I really think my petticoat will get left behind here," Madame de Boves was repeating.

Silent, her face still fresh from the air outside, Madame Marty was craning her neck above the heads to see, before the others did, the depths of the shop stretching away. The pupils of her grey eyes were as small as those of a cat coming in from the daylight, and she had the fresh complexion and clear gaze of someone awakening.

"Ah! At last!" she said, letting out a sigh.

The ladies had just managed to extricate themselves. They were in the Saint-Augustin Hall, and were extremely surprised to find it almost empty. But a sensation of well-being was creeping over them, they felt they were entering spring, after leaving the winter of the street. Whereas outside the icy wind of sleet storms was blowing, in the galleries of the Bonheur the warm summer months were already there, with light materials, the flowery brilliance of soft shades and the rustic gaiety of summer dresses and parasols.

"Just look!" cried Madame de Boves, brought to a standstill and gazing upwards.

It was the display of parasols. All open and rounded like shields, they covered the hall from the window in the ceiling to the varnished-oak dado. They formed festoons around the arcades of the upper storeys; they hung down in garlands all along the pillars; along the balustrades of the galleries, and even on the banisters of the staircases, they ran in serried ranks, symmetrically arranged everywhere, splashing the walls with red, green and yellow, they seemed like great Venetian lanterns, lit for some colossal festivity. In the corners there were complicated patterns, stars made of parasols at ninety-five centimes, and their light shades – pale blue, creamy white, soft pink – were burning with the gentleness of a night light, while above huge Japanese sunshades covered with golden coloured cranes flying across a purple sky were blazing with glints of fire.

Madame Marty was trying to think of a phrase to express her delight and could only exclaim:

"It's enchanting!"

Then, trying to remember her way, she said:

"Now let's see, shoelaces are in the haberdashery... I'll just buy my shoelaces and then I'm off."

"I'll go with you," said Madame de Boves. "We'll just walk through the shop, and nothing more, won't we, Blanche?"

But at the very door the ladies were lost. They turned to the left and, as the haberdashery had been moved, they found themselves in the midst of ruching, then surrounded by head-dresses. It was hot under the covered galleries; the heat was that of a greenhouse, moist and shut in, laden with the insipid smell of material, and in it the trampling of the crowd was smothered. Then they came back to the entrance, where a stream of people leaving was forming, a whole interminable procession of women and children, above which there floated a cloud of red balloons. Forty thousand balloons had been prepared, there were boys specially detailed to distribute them. Looking at the departing buyers, it seemed as if there was in the air above them a flight of enormous soap bubbles, on the end of invisible strings, reflecting the fire of the sunshades. The shop was all lit up by them.

"What a crowd," Madame de Boves was declaring. "One doesn't know where one is any more."

However, the ladies could not stay in the eddy by the doorway, right in the scrimmage of the entrance and exit. Fortunately, Inspector Jouve came to their assistance. He was standing in the entrance hall, solemn-looking and on the alert, staring at every woman who passed. Being specially in charge of the internal security service, he was nosing out thieves, and in particular would follow pregnant women, when the feverish look in their eyes aroused his suspicions.

"The haberdashery, Mesdames?" he said obligingly. "Turn to the left, look, over there, behind the hosiery."

Madame de Boves thanked him. But Madame Marty, on turning round, had found that her daughter Valentine was no longer with her. She was just beginning to be alarmed when she caught sight of her, already in the distance at the end of the Saint-Augustin Hall, deeply absorbed in front of an auction table, on which women's scarves at ninety-five centimes were piled up. Mouret employed auctioneering, the method of selling goods by word of mouth, by which customers were caught and robbed of their money, for he made use of any kind of advertisement, he jeered at the discretion of some of his colleagues, who held the opinion that the goods alone should speak for themselves. Special salesmen, loafing Parisians with the gift of the gab, got rid of considerable quantities of small, trashy articles in this way.

"Oh! Mamma!" murmured Valentine. "Just look at these scarves. They've got an embroidered bird on the corner."

The salesman was putting the article across to the public, swearing that it was all silk, that the manufacturer had gone bankrupt, and that a bargain like that would never occur again.

"Ninety-five centimes, can it be true?" Madame Marty, captivated like her daughter, was saying. "Why, I might as well take two of them, that won't ruin us!"

Madame de Boves remained disdainful. She detested word-of-mouth selling, a salesman who called out to her put her to flight. Madame Marty was surprised; she did not understand this showman's nervous, horrid patter, for her character was quite different, she was one of those women who are happy to be taken by force, to steep themselves in the blandishment of a public solicitation and have the pleasure of feeling everything with their hands, wasting their time in useless words.

"Now," she resumed, "let's go quickly for my shoelaces... I don't even want to see anything more."

However, as they were going through the silk scarves and the glove department, her will once again weakened. There, in the diffused light, stood a bright and gaily coloured display making a delightful effect. The counters, symmetrically placed, looked like flower beds, transforming the hall into a formal garden, beaming with a range of soft flower tones. Exposed on the wooden counters, falling from overcrowded shelves and in boxes which had been ripped open, there was a harvest of silk scarves, in the brilliant red of geraniums, the milky white of petunias, the golden yellow of chrysanthemums, the sky blue of verbena, and higher up there was another mass of blossom entwined on brass stems – fichus strewn about, ribbons unrolled, a dazzling strand extending and twisting up round the pillars and multiplying in the looking glasses. But the crowd was being drawn above all by a Swiss chalet in the glove department, made entirely of gloves: it was Mignot's masterpiece, and had taken two days to make. First of all, black gloves formed the ground floor; then came straw-coloured gloves, gloves in greyish green and burgundy, forming part of the decorations, outlining the windows, sketching in the balconies, replacing tiles.

"What does Madame require?" asked Mignot, seeing Madame Marty rooted in front of the chalet. "Here are some suede gloves at one franc seventy-five, the finest quality…"

He was an inveterate word-of-mouth salesman, calling out to passing women from the far end of his counter, pestering them with his politeness. As she shook her head in refusal, he went on:

"Tyrolean gloves at one franc twenty-five… children's gloves from Turin, embroidered gloves in all colours…"

"No, thank you, I don't want anything," Madame Marty declared.

But he could feel that her voice was softening, he attacked her more roughly by holding the embroidered gloves in front of her; she was helpless to resist and bought a pair. Then, as Madame de Boves was watching her with a smile, she blushed.

"I am a child, aren't I? If I don't hurry up and get my shoelaces and make my escape, I'm lost!"

Unfortunately, there was such a congestion in the haberdashery department that she could not get served there. They had both been waiting for ten minutes and were beginning to get annoyed, when an encounter with Madame Bourdelais and her three children took up their attention. Madame Bourdelais was explaining, with the calm manner of a pretty yet practical woman, that she had wanted to show it all to the children. Madeleine was ten years old, Edmond was eight and Lucien four; they were laughing with delight, it was a cheap outing that had been promised them for a long time.

"I'm going to buy a red sunshade, they're so amusing," said Madame Marty suddenly; she was walking up and down, growing impatient at waiting there doing nothing.

She had chosen one at fourteen francs fifty. Madame Bourdelais, who had watched the purchase with a look of disapproval, said to her in a friendly way:

"You shouldn't be in such a hurry. In a month's time you'd have got it for ten francs... They won't catch me like that!"

And she explained the theory which, being a good housewife, she had evolved. Since the shops were lowering prices, one only had to wait. She did not want to be exploited by them, it was she who took advantage of their real bargains. There was even a spark of malice in her battle with the shops, she boasted that she had never let them make a half-penny's profit.

"Well," she ended by saying, "I've promised to show my little brood some pictures, upstairs in the lounge... Why don't you come with me, you've plenty of time?"

At that the shoelaces were forgotten, Madame Marty gave in at once, whereas Madame de Boves refused, preferring to go all round the ground floor first. In any case, the ladies sincerely hoped that they would meet again upstairs. Madame Bourdelais was looking for a staircase when she caught sight of one of the lifts, and she pushed the children into it, to make the outing complete. Madame Marty and Valentine also entered the narrow cage, in which people were squeezed together tightly, but the looking glass, the velvet seats and the decorated brass door took up their attention to such an extent that they arrived on the first floor without even having felt the gentle gliding of the machine. In any case, another treat was awaiting them, as soon as they went into the lace gallery. As they were passing by the buffet, Madame Bourdelais did not neglect to gorge her little family on fruit juice. The room was square, with a large marble counter; at either end silver-plated fountains flowed with a thin trickle of water; behind, on shelves, bottles were lined up. Three waiters were continually wiping and filling glasses. In order to control the thirsty customers it had been necessary, with the assistance of a velvet-covered barrier, to form a queue, similar to those at theatre doors. There was a terrible crush there. Some people, losing all scruples when faced with the free dainties, were making themselves ill.

"Well! Where on earth are they?" exclaimed Madame Bourdelais when she had extricated herself from the mob, and after having wiped the children's faces with her handkerchief.

Then she caught sight of Madame Marty and Valentine at the end of another gallery, far away. They were both still buying, drowned beneath an overflow of petticoats. It was hopeless, mother and daughter disappeared, being swept along by a fever of spending.

When she finally arrived in the reading-and-writing room, Madame Bourdelais installed Madeleine, Edmond and Lucien at the large table; then she helped herself to some albums of photographs from a bookcase and took them over to them. The dome of the long room was laden with gilding; at either end monumental fireplaces faced each other; mediocre pictures, very ornately framed, covered the walls; and between the pillars, in front of each of the arched bays opening on to the shop, there were tall green plants in majolica pots. A whole crowd of silent people surrounded the table, which was littered with magazines and newspapers, and furnished with stationery and ink-pots. Ladies were removing their gloves, writing letters on paper bearing the stamp of the shop, and crossing out the heading with a stroke of the pen. A few men, lolling back in the depths of easy chairs, were reading newspapers. But many people remained there without doing anything; there were husbands waiting for wives left behind in the departments, young ladies discreetly on the lookout for the arrival of a lover, elderly parents deposited there as if in a cloakroom, to be picked up again on leaving. This crowd, comfortably seated, was resting, glancing through the open bays into the depths of the galleries and halls, a distant voice from which could be heard above the slight scratching of pens and the rustling of newspapers.

"What! You here!" said Madame Bourdelais. "I didn't recognize you."

Near the children, a lady was disappearing behind the pages of a magazine. It was Madame Guibal. She seemed put out by the encounter. But she recovered immediately, and said that she had come upstairs to sit down a little, in order to escape the crush of the crowd. And when Madame Bourdelais asked her if she had come to make some purchases, she replied in her languid way, veiling the ruthless egoism of her gaze behind her eyelids as she did so:

"Oh no! On the contrary, I've come to bring something back. Yes, some curtains that I'm not satisfied with... only, there are so many people that I'm waiting until I can get near the department."

She chatted, said that the "returns" system was very useful; previously, she never used to buy anything, whereas now she occasionally yielded to temptation. To tell the truth, she returned four out of five articles, she was beginning to be known in all the departments for the odd dealings which were suspected to be behind the everlasting dissatisfaction which made her bring articles back one by one, after having kept them for several days. While she was speaking, she did not take her eyes off the door of the room, and she seemed relieved when Madame Bourdelais turned round to her children so as to explain the photographs to them. Almost at the same moment Monsieur de Boves and Paul de Vallagnosc came in. The Count, who was pretending to show the young man round the new shop, exchanged a quick look with her; then she buried herself in her reading again, as if she had not noticed him.

"Why, Paul!" a voice came from behind the gentlemen.

It was Mouret, who was engaged in keeping his eye on the various departments. There were handshakes, and he asked at once:

"Has Madame de Boves done us the honour of coming?"

"I'm afraid not," the Count replied, "and to her great regret. She's not well... Oh, it's nothing serious."

But suddenly he pretended to catch sight of Madame Guibal. He made his escape and went up to her, hat in hand; the other two were content to greet her from a distance. She too was pretending to be surprised. Paul had given a smile; he understood, at last, and he told Mouret in a low voice how he had met the Count in the Rue Richelieu and how the latter, having done his best to avoid him, had in the end dragged him off to the Bonheur under the pretext that one simply had to see it. For a year the lady had been extracting what money and pleasure she could from the Count, never writing to him, but always arranging to meet him in public places, in churches, museums or shops, where they could conspire together.

"I believe each time they meet they go to a different hotel room," the young man was murmuring. "Last month, when he was on a tour of inspection, he wrote to his wife every other day from Blois, from Libourne, from Tarbes, and yet I'm convinced that I saw him going into a family boarding house near the Batignolles... Just look at him, do! Isn't he handsome, standing there in front of her, with all the decorum of an official! That's the old France for you, my friend, the old France!"

"What about your marriage?" asked Mouret.

Without taking his eyes off the Count, Paul replied that they were still waiting for his aunt to die. Then, with a triumphant air, he said:

"There, did you see? He bent down and slipped her an address. There, she's taking it, with her most virtuous expression: she's a real terror, that dainty redhead is, with her unconcerned air... Well, there are fine goings-on in your shop!"

"Oh!" said Mouret smiling. "It's not my shop, the ladies are at home here!"

He went on to joke about it. Love, like swallows, brought luck to houses. Of course he knew all about them, the tarts who had their beat along the counters, the ladies who, by chance, met a friend there, but if they did not buy anything, they at least swelled the numbers, they warmed up the shop. While he was speaking, he led his old schoolfellow along and made him stand on the threshold of the room, facing the great central gallery, the succeeding halls of which were stretching out below them. Behind them, the writing room was still plunged in meditation, with its little sounds of fidgety pens and rustling newspapers. An old gentleman had fallen asleep over the *Moniteur*.* Monsieur de Boves was studying the pictures, with the obvious intention of losing his future son-in-law in the crowd. And, alone in the midst of the calm, Madame Bourdelais was amusing her children at the top of her voice, as if in conquered territory.

"You can see, they're at home here," repeated Mouret with a grand gesture, indicating the congestion of women with which the departments were bursting.

Just then Madame Desforges, who had almost had her coat torn off by the crowd, was at last entering and going through the first hall. Then, when she reached the main gallery, she looked up. It was like the nave of a station, surrounded by the balustrades of the two upper storeys, intersected by hanging staircases, and with suspension bridges crossing it. The iron staircases, with double spirals, opened out in bold curves, multiplying the landings; the iron bridges, thrown across the void, were running straight through it, very high up – and beneath the pale light from the windows all this metal formed a delicate piece of architecture, a complicated lacework through which the daylight passed, in which storeys were piled one on top of the other and halls were opening out, through which other storeys and other halls could be glimpsed ad infinitum. Metal held sway everywhere; what is more, the young architect had had the honesty and courage not to disguise it under a layer of whitewash imitating stone or wood. Downstairs, so as not to overshadow the merchandise, the decorations were sober, large plains of one colour, in a neutral tint; then, as the metal framework rose, so the capitals of the columns became richer, the rivets formed rosettes, the corbels and brackets were loaded with sculpture; finally, at the top, there was a brilliant burst of green and red paint, in the midst of a wealth of gold, cascades of gold, a whole crop of gold, right up to the very windows, the panes of which were enamelled and inlaid in gold. Beneath the covered galleries, those bricks of the counter-arches which were visible were also enamelled in bright colours. Mosaics and ceramics were introduced into the decorations, brightening up the friezes, lighting up the austerity of the general effect with their fresh tones, while the staircases, with banisters covered with red velvet, were decorated with a strip of reticulated, polished ironwork, shining like the steel of armour.

Although she was already familiar with the new building, Madame Desforges had stopped, struck by the turbulent life which that day was animating the immense nave. Downstairs, the eddy of the crowd was going on all round her, its dual stream of entry and exit making itself felt as far as the silk department; the crowd was still very mixed, although with the advent of the afternoon more ladies were to be seen among the tradespeople and housewives; there were many women in mourning, wearing long veils; there was still a number of errant nurses, shielding their babies with their stretched-out elbows. This sea of multicoloured hats, of bare heads, fair or dark, was flowing from one end of the gallery to the other, looking blurred and faded beside the startling brilliance of the materials. Wherever she looked Madame Desforges could see nothing but enormous placards with huge figures on them, garish spots standing out against the bright prints, the glossy silks, the sombre woollens. Heads were half cut off from sight by piles of ribbons, a wall of flannel stood out like a headland, everywhere mirrors were making the shop recede further into the distance, reflecting displays together with patches of the public – inverted faces, bits of shoulders and arms – while to the left and right glimpses could be caught of side galleries, the snowy drifts of household linen, the dappled depths of the hosiery – lost in the distance, illuminated by a ray of light from some bay window – where the crowd had become nothing but a dusting of humanity. Then when Madame Desforges looked up she saw all up the staircases, along the suspension bridges, round the balustrades of each storey, an unbroken, murmuring stream of people ascending, a whole multitude of people in the air, travelling through the fretwork of the enormous metal frame, silhouetted in black against the diffused light of the enamelled panes. Great gilded chandeliers were hanging from the ceiling; an awning of carpets, of brocades, of materials worked with gold, was hanging down, draping the balustrades with brilliant banners, and from one end to the other there were flights of lace, flutterings of muslin, triumphal wreaths of silk, apotheoses of half-clad lay figures – and finally, above all this confusion, right at the very top, the bedding department was displaying little iron bedsteads together with their mattresses and draped with white curtains, seemingly suspended and looking like a dormitory of schoolgirls sleeping in the midst of the trampling of the customers, who became rarer as the departments rose higher.

"Does Madame require some cheap garters?" said a salesman to Madame Desforges, seeing her motionless. "All silk, one franc forty-five."

She did not deign to reply. Around her the auctioneers were yelping, growing ever more excited. All the same, she did want to know where she was. Albert Lhomme's cash desk was on her left; he knew her by sight and, completely unhurried in the midst of the stream of invoices with which he was being besieged, he took the liberty of giving her a pleasant smile; behind him, Joseph was struggling with the string box, unable to cope with doing up the parcels. Then she realized where she was; the silk department must be ahead of her. But the crowd was growing to such an extent that it took her ten minutes to get there. The red balloons at the end of their invisible strings had multiplied in the air; they were piling up into crimson clouds, streaming gently towards the doors, continuing to pour out into Paris – and when they were held by very small children with the strings tightly wound round their little hands, Madame Desforges had to bend her head down beneath the flight of balloons.

"What, Madame, you've ventured in here?" exclaimed Bouthemont gaily, as soon as he caught sight of Madame Desforges.

Nowadays the section manager, who had been taken to her house by Mouret himself, occasionally went there for tea. She considered him common but extremely pleasant, with a fine full-blooded temperament which she found surprising and amusing. What is more, two days earlier, without thinking, he had told her straight out about Mouret's love affair with Clara, with the stupidity of a coarse lad who enjoyed a good laugh – and, eaten up with jealousy, hiding her wound under an air of disdain, she had come in order to discover who the girl was, for he had simply said it was a young lady from the ready-made department, refusing to name her.

"Is there something we can do for you?" he resumed.

"Certainly, otherwise I shouldn't have come... Have you some silk suitable for a matinée jacket?"

She hoped to extract the name of the girl from him, for she had been seized with an urge to see her. He had immediately summoned Favier, and he started to chat with her again while waiting for the salesman, who was just finishing serving a customer, the "pretty lady" it so happened, that beautiful fair woman of whom all the department was wont to talk, without knowing anything about her life or even her name. This time the pretty lady was in deep mourning. Fancy that! Whom had she lost, her husband or her father? Certainly not her father or she would have looked sadder. Well, so there, she was not a tart, she had a real husband – unless of course she was in mourning for her mother? In spite of the amount of work, the department exchanged conjectures for a few minutes.

"Hurry up, it's intolerable!" shouted Hutin to Favier, who was coming back from escorting his customer to the cash desk. "When that lady's there you take an endless time... As if she cares about you!"

"Not half as little as I care about her," replied the irritated salesman.

But Hutin threatened to report him to the management if he did not have more regard for the customers. Ever since the department had banded together to get him Robineau's place he had become a real terror, peevishly severe. In fact, he was so unbearable, after all the promises of good comradeship with which he had previously buttered up his colleagues, that they, from then on, secretly supported Favier against him.

"Come on now, don't answer back," Hutin went on severely. "Monsieur Bouthemont is asking you for some foulard, the palest designs."

In the middle of the department an exhibition of summer silks was illuminating the hall with the brilliancy of dawn, like the rising of a star amidst the most delicate shades of daylight – pale pink, soft yellow, clear blue, a shimmering scarf of all the colours of the rainbow. There were foulards as fine as a cloud, surahs lighter than the down blown from trees, satiny Pekin fabrics with the supple skin of a Chinese virgin. And there were also pongees from Japan, tussores and corahs from India, not to mention French light silks – fine stripes, tiny checks, floral patterns, every design imaginable – which conjured up visions of ladies in furbelows walking on May mornings beneath great trees in a park.

"I'll take this one, the Louis XIV design with nosegays of roses on it," said Madame Desforges in the end.

While Favier was measuring it, she made one last attempt to pump Bouthemont, who had remained near her.

"I'm going up to the ready-made department to look at some travel coats... Is she fair, the girl you were telling me about?"

The section manager, who was beginning to be alarmed by her insistence, merely smiled. But, just then, Denise happened to pass by. She had just handed over Madame Boutarel – the provincial lady who came to Paris twice a year in order to squander at the Bonheur the money which she skimped from her housekeeping – to Liénard, in the merinos. And, as Favier was already taking Madame Desforges's foulard, Hutin, thinking to annoy him, stopped the girl as she went by.

"Don't trouble, Mademoiselle will be so good as to accompany Madame."

Denise, confused, of course consented to take charge of the parcel and the invoice. She could not meet the young man face to face without feeling ashamed, as if he reminded her of some past indiscretion. Yet the sin had only been in her dreams.

"Tell me," Madame Desforges asked Bouthemont in a very low voice, "isn't this the girl who was so clumsy? So he's taken her on again then? Why, she must be the heroine of the adventure!"

"Perhaps," replied the section manager, still smiling and determined not to tell the truth.

Then, preceded by Denise, Madame Desforges slowly ascended the staircase. She was forced to stop every other second so as not to be carried away by the stream of people coming down. In the living vibration which was shaking the whole shop, the iron stringers of the staircase had a perceptible motion beneath the feet, as if trembling at the breath of the crowd. A dummy was firmly fixed on each step, displaying a motionless garment, a suit or an overcoat or a dressing gown; they looked like a double row of soldiers lined up for some triumphal procession, and each one had a little wooden handle, like the handle of a dagger plunged into the red flannel, bleeding where the neck had been severed.

Madame Desforges was at last reaching the first floor when a thrust even rougher than the others immobilized her for a moment. The ground-floor departments, the scattered crowd of customers which she had just gone through, were now below her. A fresh spectacle greeted her, an ocean of heads seen foreshortened, hiding the bodices beneath them, swarming with ant-like activity. The white placards had become nothing but thin lines, the piles of ribbon were crushed, the headland of flannel was a narrow wall cutting across the gallery; whilst the carpets and embroidered silks which decked the balustrades were hanging at her feet, like processional banners attached to the rood screen of a church. In the distance she could pick out the corners of the side galleries, just as, from the height of the eaves of a steeple, one can pick out the corners of neighbouring streets where the black spots of passers-by are moving. But she was above all surprised when, exhausted as she was and her eyes blinded by the brilliant medley of colours, she closed her eyelids and found herself even more conscious of the crowd because of the muffled sound of a rising tide it was making and the human warmth being given off by it. A fine dust was rising from the floor, laden with the odour of Woman, the odour of her underlinen and the nape of her neck, of her skirts and of her hair, a penetrating, all-pervading odour which seemed to be the incense of this temple dedicated to the worship of her body.

Mouret, still standing outside the reading room with Vallagnosc, was breathing in this odour, intoxicating himself with it, repeating as he did so:

"They're at home, I know some women who pass the day here, eating cakes and writing their letters. It only remains for me to put them to bed."

This joke drew a smile from Paul, who with the boredom born of his pessimism still considered the turbulence aroused in this section of humanity by such frippery to be idiotic. When he came to see his old school friend, he would go away almost annoyed at seeing him so vibrating with life in the midst of his multitude of coquettes. Would not one of them, empty-headed and empty-hearted as they were, teach him the stupidity and uselessness of existence? Precisely on that day, Octave seemed to be losing his splendid poise; he who usually breathed fire into his customers with the calm grace of someone operating a machine seemed to have been caught up in the wave of passion which was gradually consuming the shop. Since he had seen Denise and Madame Desforges coming up the main staircase he was talking more loudly, gesticulating in spite of himself, and although he pretended not to turn his head round towards them, he was nevertheless becoming more and more animated as he felt them approaching. He was getting red in the face, his eyes held something of the bewildered rapture which progressively flickered in the eyes of the customers.

"You must be robbed like anything," murmured Vallagnosc, who thought the crowd had a criminal look about it.

"Yes, you can't imagine how much, old chap."

And excitedly, delighted to have something to talk about, he gave a wealth of detail and told him the facts, dividing thieves into categories. First of all there were the women who were professional thieves, those who did the least harm, for the police knew almost all of them. Then came women with a mania for stealing, with a perverted desire, a new kind of neurosis which had been scientifically classified by a mental specialist who had observed the acute temptation exercised on them by big shops. Finally, there were pregnant women, who usually specialized in stealing one type of goods: thus, for example, the police superintendent had discovered in the home of one of them two hundred and forty-eight pairs of pink gloves stolen from every counter in Paris.

"So that's why the women here have such an odd look in their eye!" Vallagnosc murmured. "I was watching them, with their greedy, guilty looks of mad creatures... A fine school of honesty, upon my word!"

"Why!" Mouret replied. "In spite of making them at home here, one can't really let them take away the merchandise under their coats... And very well-bred people do it too. Last week we had a chemist's sister and an appeal court judge's wife. We're trying to hush it up."

He broke off in order to point out Inspector Jouve, who at that precise moment was shadowing a pregnant woman downstairs in the ribbon department. This woman, whose enormous belly was suffering a great deal from the pushes the public was giving it, was accompanied by a woman friend whose business it was, no doubt, to defend her against the rougher buffets; each time she stopped in a department Jouve did not take his eyes off her, while her friend near her was rummaging coolly in the depths of the display boxes.

"Oh! He'll nab her," Mouret went on. "He knows all their tricks."

But his voice trembled, the laugh he gave was forced. Denise and Henriette, for whom he had been on the lookout all the time, were at last pressing behind him, after having had great difficulty in freeing themselves from the crowd. He turned round and greeted his customer with the discreet greeting of a friend who does not want to compromise a woman by stopping her in the middle of a crowd. But she, on the alert, had quite taken in the glance with which he had first enveloped Denise. This girl must definitely be the rival whom she had had the curiosity to come and see.

In the ready-made department the salesgirls were losing their heads. Two girls were ill, and Madame Frédéric, the assistant buyer, had calmly given notice the day before, had gone to the pay desk to have her account made up, and had dropped the Bonheur from one minute to the next, just as the Bonheur was wont to drop its employees. Since the morning, in the heat of the sale, they had talked of nothing but this incident. Clara, kept on in the department because of Mouret's whim, considered it "a jolly good thing"; Marguerite was describing Bourdoncle's exasperation; while Madame Aurélie, harassed, was declaring that Madame Frédéric might at least have warned her, for no one could have imagined such deceit. Although Madame Frédéric had never confided in anyone, she was nevertheless suspected of having left the drapery business in order to marry the owner of the public baths not far from the Halles.

"Madame requires a travel coat?" Denise asked Madame Desforges, after having offered her a chair.

"Yes," the latter replied curtly, determined to be uncivil.

The department's new decorations were of an austere richness, tall cupboards of carved oak mirrors taking up the whole width of the wall panels, a red carpet which deadened the continual tread of the customers. While Denise was fetching the travel coat, Madame Desforges, looking around her, caught sight of herself in a mirror, and she sat there contemplating herself. Was she growing old then, if he was unfaithful to her with the first girl who turned up? The mirror reflected the whole department, with all its boisterousness, but she saw nothing but her own pale face, she did not hear Clara behind her telling Marguerite about one of Madame Frédéric's mystifications, how she used to take a roundabout way, morning and evening, going along the Choiseul arcade, so as to create the impression that she lived, perhaps, on the left bank.

"Here are our latest models," said Denise. "We have them in several colours."

She was displaying four or five coats. Madame Desforges considered them with an air of disdain and, as each one was shown her, became more difficult. Why all those gathers, which made the garment look skimpy? And this one, with square shoulders, looked as if it was cut out with an axe! It's all very well to travel, but one didn't want to look like a sentry box.

"Show me something else, Mademoiselle."

Denise was unfolding the garments and folding them up again without allowing herself to make a gesture of irritation. And it was precisely her serene patience which was making Madame Desforges even more exasperated. Her glance kept on returning to the mirror opposite her. Now she was looking at herself in it beside Denise, she was making comparisons. Was it really possible for someone to prefer that insignificant creature to her? She remembered now, this creature was certainly the one she had seen before who, when she had first started work, had had such an idiotic expression and had been as awkward as a goose girl fresh from her village. Of course nowadays she did hold herself better, looking prim and proper in her silk dress. Only how insignificant she was, how commonplace!

"I will go and get some other models to show Madame," Denise was saying calmly.

When she came back the scene started all over again. This time it was the materials which were too heavy and were no good at all. Madame Desforges was turning round, raising her voice, trying to attract Madame Aurélie's attention in the hope that she would get the girl into trouble. But the latter, since she had rejoined the shop, had little by little conquered the department; she was at home there now, and the buyer even acknowledged that she had qualities rare in a salesgirl – stubborn gentleness and smiling conviction. And so Madame Aurélie gave a slight shrug of her shoulders, taking care not to interfere.

"If Madame would be so good as to point out the type of thing?..." Denise was asking once more with a polite insistence which nothing could discourage.

"But you haven't got a thing!" cried Madame Desforges.

She broke off, surprised to feel a hand placed on her shoulder. It was Madame Marty, who was being swept through the shop by her attack of spending. Since buying the scarves, the embroidered gloves and the red sunshade, her purchases had swelled to such an extent that the last salesman had just made up his mind to put the parcels which were making his arms break down on a chair, and he was walking ahead of her, pulling behind him the chair, on which petticoats, table napkins, curtains, a lamp and three doormats were piled up.

"Hello!" she said. "Are you buying a travel coat?"

"Oh! Goodness, no," replied Madame Desforges. "They're awful!"

But Madame Marty had found a striped coat which she thought was not too bad all the same. Her daughter Valentine was already examining it. So Denise, in order to rid the department of the article, a model from the preceding year, called Marguerite; she, after a glance from her companion, described it as an exceptional bargain. When she had sworn that it had twice been reduced in price, that from a hundred and fifty francs it had been reduced to a hundred and thirty, and that it was now priced at a hundred and ten, Madame Marty was powerless to resist the temptation of such cheapness. She bought it, and the salesman who was accompanying her abandoned the chair, together with a whole wad of invoices attached to the goods.

Meanwhile, behind the ladies' backs, in the midst of the hustle of the sales, the gossip of the department about Madame Frédéric was continuing.

"Honestly, was she going with someone?" a little salesgirl, new to the department, was asking.

"The man from the baths, to be sure!" Clara replied. "You've got to watch those widows who look so steady."

Then, while Marguerite was making out the bill for the coat, Madame Marty looked round, and indicating Clara with a slight flutter of her eyelids, she said in a very low voice to Madame Desforges:

"She's Monsieur Mouret's whim of the moment."

The other, surprised, looked at Clara, then her eyes travelled back to Denise again as she replied:

"Oh no, not the large girl, the little one!"

And, as Madame Marty was not daring to insist, Madame Desforges added in a louder voice, full of a lady's contempt for housemaids:

"The small girl and the large one too, perhaps, anyone who's willing!"

Denise had heard. She looked up with her large, innocent eyes at the lady who was thus wounding her and whom she did not know. Doubtless it was the person she had been told about, the woman whom her employer used to visit outside. In the look which they exchanged Denise had such sad dignity, such candid innocence, that Henriette felt embarrassed.

"As you haven't got anything to show me," she said curtly, "kindly conduct me to the dresses and suits."

"Why," said Madame Marty, "I'll go there with you... I wanted to look at a suit for Valentine."

Marguerite took the chair by its back and pulled it the wrong way round on its back legs, which were gradually getting worn out by such carting about. Denise was only carrying the length of foulard which Madame Desforges had bought. It was quite a journey, now that the suits and dresses were on the second floor, at the other end of the shop.

The great trek all through the overcrowded galleries began. At the head of the procession went Marguerite pulling the chair like a little cart, slowly opening up a path. From the lingerie department onwards, Madame Desforges complained: how ridiculous they were, these bazaars where you had to go two miles to lay your hands on the slightest thing! Madame Marty too was saying that she was dead with tiredness, but nevertheless she was intensely enjoying her tiredness, the lingering death of her energies, in the midst of the inexhaustible spread of merchandise. Mouret's streak of genius held her completely in its grip. As she passed through each department she was stopped in her tracks by it. She made a first halt at the trousseaux, tempted by chemises which Pauline sold to her, and Marguerite then got rid of the chair, which Pauline had to take over. Madame Desforges could have continued her walk in order to liberate Denise more quickly, but she seemed happy to feel the girl standing behind her, motionless and patient, while she too lingered, giving her friend advice. At the baby linen the ladies went into ecstasies, without buying anything. Then Madame Marty began weakening again; she succumbed successively to a black satin corset, some fur cuffs being sold at a reduced price because of the season and some Russian lace with which, at that time, table linen was trimmed. All that was piling up on the chair, the parcels were mounting, making the wood creak, and the salesmen who were succeeding each other harnessed themselves to it with increasing difficulty as the load became heavier.

"This way, Madame," Denise said without complaint after each halt.

"But it's idiotic!" Madame Desforges was exclaiming. "We'll never get there. Why didn't they put the dresses and suits near the ready-made department? What a mess it is!"

Madame Marty, whose eyes were dilating, intoxicated as she was by this parade of handsome things dancing before her eyes, was repeating in an undertone:

"My goodness! What will my husband say? You're right, there's no system in this shop. One loses one's way, one does silly things."

On the great central landing the chair had difficulty in getting through. Precisely just there Mouret had cluttered up the landing by spreading out a display of fancy goods – cups with gilded zinc mounts, work baskets and trashy liqueur cabinets – because he considered that most people were able to move about there too easily, that there was no crush there. He had also authorized one of his salesmen to display there, on a small table, Chinese and Japanese curiosities, a few trinkets at low prices, which the customers were snatching up. It was an unexpected success, he was already thinking of enlarging this type of trade. While two porters were taking the chair up to the second floor, Madame Marty bought six ivory buttons, some mice made of silk and an enamelled match case.

On the second floor the expedition started again. Denise, who had been taking customers round like that since the morning, was ready to drop with exhaustion, but she was still dutiful, gentle and polite. She had to wait for the ladies once again at the furnishing fabrics, where an enchanting cretonne had caught Madame Marty's eye. Then, in the furniture department, the latter hankered for a work table. Her hands were trembling, she laughingly begged Madame Desforges to prevent her from spending any more, when a meeting with Madame Guibal gave her an excuse. It was in the carpet department, Madame Guibal had at last come upstairs to return a whole purchase of oriental door curtains which she had made five days earlier; she was chatting, standing facing the salesman, a great strapping young man who, from morning to night with the arms of a wrestler, was moving loads which were enough to kill an ox. Naturally, he was in consternation at this "return", which robbed him of his percentage. Therefore he was trying to make the customer feel confused; he scented some shady goings-on, she had probably given a ball, and the door curtains had been taken from the Bonheur so as to avoid hiring them from a carpet dealer: he knew that that sort of thing was sometimes done by the thrifty middle classes. Madame must have some reason for returning them; if it was the designs or the colours which did not suit Madame, he would show her something else, there was a very wide assortment. To all these insinuations Madame Guibal was replying calmly, with the confident air of a woman of regal bearing, that she did not like the door curtains any more, without condescending to add an explanation. She refused to see any others, and he had to give in, for the salesmen had orders to take back goods, even when they noticed that they had been used.

As the three ladies were walking away together, and Madame Marty, conscience-stricken, was once more coming back to the question of the work table which she did not need at all, Madame Guibal said to her in her calm voice:

"Well! You can return it… Didn't you see? It's no more difficult than that… Anyhow, have it sent to your house. One puts it in one's drawing room, one looks at it; then, when you're sick of it, you return it."

"That's an idea!" exclaimed Madame Marty. "If my husband gets too angry, I'll return the whole lot to them."

This was her supreme excuse, she no longer counted the cost but went on buying with the secret desire of keeping it all, for she was not the kind of woman who returns things.

At last they arrived at the dresses and suits. But as Denise was about to hand over to one of the salesgirls the foulard purchased by Madame Desforges, the latter appeared to change her mind, and declared that she would definitely take one of the travel coats, the light grey one, and Denise had to wait obligingly in order to reconduct her back to the ready-made department. The girl was quite aware that at the back of the capricious behaviour of this imperious customer there was the wish to treat her as a servant, but she had sworn to herself that she would stick to her job, she kept up her calm manner in spite of her pounding heart and her rebellious pride. Madame Desforges did not buy anything in the dress-and-suit department.

"Oh, Mamma!" Valentine was saying. "That little suit there, if it fits me…"

In a low voice Madame Guibal was explaining her tactics to Madame Marty. When she liked a dress in a shop she would have it sent to her, she would copy the pattern, and then return it. And Madame Marty bought the suit for her daughter, murmuring as she did so:

"It's a good idea! How practical you are, my dear!"

They had had to abandon the chair. It had remained marooned in the furniture department, beside the work table. The weight was becoming too much for it, the back legs were threatening to break, and it was decided that all the purchases should be centralized at one cash desk in order to be sent down subsequently to the dispatch service.

Then the ladies, still conducted by Denise, wandered around. They put in an appearance once again in all the departments. It seemed as if there was no one but them on the steps of the staircases and all along the galleries. Every other moment encounters held them up. Thus they ran into Madame Bourdelais and her three children again, near the reading room. The children were loaded with parcels; Madeleine had a dress for herself over her arm, Edmond was carrying a collection of small shoes, while the youngest, Lucien, was wearing a new peaked cap.

"You too!" said Madame Desforges laughingly to her old school friend.

"Don't talk to me about it!" exclaimed Madame Bourdelais. "I'm furious. They get at you through these little fellows now! You know, it isn't as if I'm extravagant for myself! But how can one resist these little things who want everything? I brought them here for a walk, and now I'm rifling the shop!"

It so happened that Mouret, who was still with Vallagnosc and Monsieur de Boves, was listening to her with a smile. She caught sight of him and complained to him gaily, but with a basis of real irritation, about the snares laid for motherly love; the idea that she had just succumbed to the fevers aroused by advertisement made her indignant – and he, still smiling, bowed, enjoying his triumph. Monsieur de Boves had manoeuvred so as to get nearer to Madame Guibal, whom he finally followed out, trying for a second time to lose Vallagnosc as he did so – but the latter, tired by the mob, hastened to rejoin the Count. Once more, Denise had stopped to wait for the ladies. She was standing with her back to them, Mouret himself was pretending not to see her. From that moment on Madame Desforges, with the delicate flair of a jealous woman, no longer had any doubts. While he, as the courtly owner of the shop, was paying her compliments and walking a few steps at her side, she was reflecting, she was wondering how to convict him of his treachery.

Meanwhile, Monsieur de Boves and Vallagnosc, who were walking ahead with Madame Guibal, were arriving at the lace department. It was a luxurious salon near the ready-made department, lined with showcases, the carved-oak drawers of which had folding flaps. Spirals of white lace twined around the pillars, which were covered with red velvet; from one end of the room to the other there were threaded stretches of guipure lace; while on the counters there were avalanches of big cards around which were wound Valenciennes, Mechlin, needlepoint lace. At the end of the room two ladies were sitting before a transparency of mauve silk onto which Deloche was throwing some Chantilly – and they, silent, were looking without making up their minds.

"Why!" said Vallagnosc, very surprised. "You said Madame de Boves was not well... But there she is, standing over there with Mademoiselle Blanche."

The Count could not help giving a start, throwing a sideways glance at Madame Guibal as he did so.

"So she is, upon my word!" he said.

It was very hot in the salon. The customers, who were suffocating there, were pale-faced and shiny-eyed. It seemed as if all the seductions of the shop had been leading up to this supreme temptation, that it was there that the hidden alcove of downfall was situated, the place of perdition where even the strongest succumbed. Hands were being plunged into the overflowing pieces of lace, quivering with intoxication from touching them.

"It looks as if these ladies are ruining you," resumed Vallagnosc, amused by the encounter.

Monsieur de Boves made the gesture of a husband all the more sure of his wife's common sense because he did not give her a penny. She, having tramped all the departments with her daughter without buying anything, had just ended up in the lace department in a passion of unsatisfied desire. Tired out, she was nevertheless standing at a counter. She was rummaging in the heap of lace, her hands were growing limp, waves of fever were mounting all up her body. Then suddenly, as her daughter was turning her head away and the salesman was walking off, she tried to slip a piece of Alençon under her coat. But she gave a start and dropped the piece, on hearing Vallagnosc's voice saying gaily:

"We've caught you out, Madame!"

For a few seconds she remained mute, dead white. Then she explained that, as she had felt much better, she had wanted to get a breath of air. When she at last noticed that her husband was with Madame Guibal, she completely recovered herself, and looked at them in such a dignified way that Madame Guibal felt obliged to say:

"I was with Madame Desforges – these gentlemen ran into us."

Just then the other ladies arrived. Mouret had accompanied them, and he detained them a moment longer in order to point out to them Inspector Jouve, who was still shadowing the pregnant woman and her friend. It was very odd, one couldn't imagine what a lot of thieves were arrested in the lace department. Madame de Boves, listening to him, was visualizing herself – forty-five years old, well-off, her husband in an important position – with a policeman on either side of her; she was not at all conscience-stricken, she was only thinking that she should have slipped the length of lace up her sleeve. Jouve, meanwhile, had just made up his mind to nab the pregnant woman, having given up hope of catching her red-handed, and suspecting her in any case of having filled her pockets up by such nimble sleight of hand that it had escaped him. But when he had taken her aside and searched her, to his confusion he found nothing, not even a scarf or a button. The friend had disappeared. Suddenly he understood: the pregnant woman was only there to keep him occupied, it was the friend who was stealing.

The story amused the ladies. Mouret, a little annoyed, merely said:

"Old Jouve's been done this time... He'll have his revenge."

"Oh!" concluded Vallagnosc, "I don't think he's up to it... In any case, why do you display so much merchandise? You deserve to be robbed. You shouldn't tempt poor defenceless women to that extent."

It was the last word, and in the mounting fever of the shop it struck the jarring note of the day. The ladies were separating, going through the congested departments for the last time. It was four o'clock, the rays of the setting sun were entering obliquely through the wide bays on the front of the shop, obligingly lighting up the windows of the halls, and in this red, firelike brightness, the thick dust, raised from the morning onwards by the continual trampling of the crowd, was floating upwards like a golden steam. A sheet of fire was running through the big central gallery, making the staircases, the suspension bridges and all the hanging iron lacework stand out against a background of flames. The mosaics and the ceramics of the friezes were sparkling, the reds and greens of the paintwork were being lit up by the fires from the gold so lavishly applied. It was as if the displays, the palace of gloves and ties, the clusters of ribbons and laces, the tall piles of woollens and calicoes, the variegated flower beds blossoming with light silks and foulards were now burning in live embers. The mirrors were glittering, resplendent.

The display of sunshades curved like shields was throwing off metallic glints. In the distance, beyond streaks of shadow, there were faraway, dazzling departments, teeming with a mob made fair by the sunshine.

In this final hour, in the thick of the overheated air, women were reigning supreme. They had taken the shop by storm, they were camping in it as in conquered territory, like an invading horde which had settled among the wreckage of goods. The salesmen, deafened, aching all over, had become nothing but their tools, which they used with sovereign tyranny. Fat women were pushing their way through the crowd. Thinner ones were standing their ground, becoming overbearing. All of them, their heads held high and their gestures off-handed, were at home there, they showed no civility to each other, but were making use of the shop to such an extent that they were even rubbing off the paint from the walls. Madame Bourdelais, wanting to get back some of the money she had spent, had once more conducted her three children to the buffet; by now the customers were hurling themselves at it in a paroxysm of greed, even the mothers were gorging themselves on Malaga; since the opening eighty litres of fruit juice and seventy bottles of wine had been drunk. After having bought her travelling coat Madame Desforges had been presented with some pictures at the cash desk, and she was wondering, as she went away, how she could get hold of Denise in her house and humiliate her there in the presence of Mouret himself, in order to watch their faces and gain a certainty from them. Finally, just as Monsieur de Boves was successfully losing himself in the crowd and disappearing with Madame Guibal, Madame de Boves, followed by Blanche and Vallagnosc, had had the whim to ask for a red balloon, although she had not bought anything. It was always like that, she would not go home empty-handed, she would win the friendship of her caretaker's little girl with it. At the distribution counter they were starting on their fortieth thousand: forty thousand red balloons had taken flight in the hot air of the shop, a whole cloud of red balloons which by then was floating from one end of Paris to the other, carrying the name of the Bonheur des Dames up to heaven!

It was striking five o'clock. Of all the ladies, only Madame Marty remained alone with her daughter through the final paroxysms of the sale. She could not tear herself away, dead tired though she was; she was held there by such strong ties that she kept on retracing her footsteps needlessly, scouring the departments with insatiable curiosity. It was the hour during which the mob, spurred on by advertisements, finally got completely out of hand; the sixty thousand francs spent on announcements in the newspapers, the ten thousand posters on walls and the two hundred thousand catalogues which had been circulated had emptied the women's pockets and left their nerves suffering from the shock of such intoxication; women were still shaken by all Mouret's devices, lowered prices, "returns", all his constantly renewed attentions. Madame Marty was lingering by the auction tables, amid the hoarse calls of the salesmen, the sound of gold from the cash desks and the rumble of parcels falling into the basements; yet once more she walked across the ground floor, through the household linen, the silk, the gloves, the woollens; then she went upstairs, again surrendering herself to the metallic vibration of the hanging staircases and suspension bridges, returning to the coats, to the underwear, to the laces, penetrating as far as the second floor, to the heights of the bedding and furniture – and everywhere the salesmen, Hutin and Favier, Mignot and Liénard, Deloche, Pauline and Denise, their legs dead tired, were making an effort, snatching victory out of the customers' final fever. Since the morning this fever had been gradually growing, like the very intoxication which was exuded by the materials which were being handled. The crowd was blazing under the fire of the five-o'clock sun. By now Madame Marty had the animated and hysterical face of a child that has drunk undiluted wine. She had come into the shop, her eyes clear and her skin fresh from the cold of the street, and her eyes and skin had gradually become scorched by the sight of all that luxury of those violent colours, the continual succession of which inflamed her passion. When she finally left, after having said that she would pay at home, terrified by the figures on her bill, her features were drawn and she had the dilated eyes of a sick woman. She had to fight her way out of the stubborn crush by the door; people were killing each other in the massacre of the remnants there. Then, outside on the pavement, when she had again found her daughter whom she had lost, the keen air made her shiver, and she was still frightened, unhinged by the neurosis caused by big shops.

That evening, as Denise was returning from dinner, a porter summoned her.

"Mademoiselle, you're wanted by the management."

She had forgotten the order that Mouret had given her in the morning to go to his office after the sale. He was standing waiting for her. As she went in she did not push the door to, and it remained open.

"We are very pleased with you, Mademoiselle," he said, "and we have decided to give you proof of our satisfaction... You know about the shameful way Madame Frédéric left us. From tomorrow you will take her place as assistant buyer."

Motionless from surprise, Denise was listening to him. She murmured in a shaking voice:

"But, Monsieur, there are salesgirls who've been in the department much longer than I have."

"Well and what of it?" he went on. "You are the most capable one, the most responsible. It's very natural that I should choose you... Aren't you pleased?"

At that she blushed. She felt a delicious sensation of happiness and embarrassment in which her initial fear was dissolving. Why had she thought first and foremost of the assumptions with which this unlooked-for favour would be greeted? And she remained confused, in spite of her surge of gratitude. He was smiling and looking at her, standing there in her simple silk dress with no jewellery, with no other extravagance than her regal head of fair hair. She had slimmed down, her skin was fair and there was an air of delicacy and seriousness about her. The skinny insignificance she had had in the past was developing into a charm which was discreet yet penetrating.

"It's very kind of you, Monsieur," she stammered. "I don't know how to express—"

But her words were cut short. Framed in the doorway stood Lhomme. With his sound hand he was holding a big leather wallet, and his mutilated arm was pressing an enormous portfolio to his chest; behind him, his son Albert was carrying a load of bags which was making his arms break.

"Five hundred and eighty-seven thousand, two hundred and ten francs thirty centimes!" exclaimed the cashier, whose flabby, worn face was seemingly illuminated with a ray of sunshine by the reflection of such a sum.

That was the takings for the day, the largest which the Bonheur had ever had. Far away – in the depths of the shop through which Lhomme had just slowly walked with the heavy step of an overloaded ox – could be heard the hum, the stir of surprise and joy which these giant takings left in their wake.

"Why, it's magnificent!" said Mouret, delighted. "My dear Lhomme, put it down there, have a rest, for you're at the end of your tether. I'll have all this money taken to the counting house… Yes, yes, put it all on my desk. I want to see it piled up."

He was as gay as a child. The cashier and his son unloaded themselves. The wallet gave the clear tinkle of gold, streams of silver and copper came from two of the bursting sacks, while the corners of banknotes were sticking out from the portfolio. The whole of one end of the large desk was covered, it was like the crumbling of a fortune which had taken ten hours to collect.

When Lhomme and Albert had retired, mopping their brows, Mouret remained motionless for a moment, lost in thought, his eyes on the money. Then he looked up and caught sight of Denise, who had moved to one side. At the sight of her he began to smile once more, he made her come forwards, and ended by saying that he would give her as much as she could take in one handful – and beneath his joke there was a pact of love.

"There, in the wallet! I bet there'll be less than a thousand francs, your hand is so small!"

But she drew back again. So he was in love with her, was he? Suddenly she understood, she felt the growing passion of the wave of desire with which he had been surrounding her ever since her return to the ready-made department. What overwhelmed her even more was feeling her own heart beating as if it would burst. Why did he offend her with all that money, when she was brimming over with gratitude and he could have taken away all her resistance with one friendly word? He was coming closer to her, still joking, when, to his great annoyance, Bourdoncle appeared under the pretext of telling him the attendance figures, the enormous figure of seventy thousand customers who had visited the Bonheur that day. She hastened to leave, after having thanked him once again.

10

STOCK-TAKING TOOK PLACE on the first Sunday in August, and it had to be finished by the same evening. All the employees were at their posts the first thing in the morning as if it was a weekday, and behind closed doors the task had begun in the shop now empty of customers.

Denise had not gone down at eight o'clock with the other salesgirls. She had been confined to her room since the preceding Thursday with a sprained ankle, acquired when going up to the workrooms, and was really by then much better, but Madame Aurélie was pampering her, so she was not hurrying, but was finishing putting her shoe on with difficulty, resolved to put in an appearance in the department all the same. Nowadays the girls' rooms were on the fifth floor of the new buildings, all along the Rue de Monsigny; there were sixty of them on either side of a corridor, and they were more comfortable, although they still were furnished with an iron bedstead, a large cupboard and a little walnut dressing table. As their lot there was improving, so the salesgirls' personal habits were becoming cleaner and more refined; they began to affect expensive soap and dainty underclothes, there was a natural upwards movement towards the middle class, but coarse words could still be heard being bandied about, and doors were slammed as the girls dashed in and out morning and evening, as if in a third-rate hotel. In any case Denise, being assistant buyer, had one of the biggest rooms, with two dormer windows facing the street. Now that she was well off she allowed herself some luxury – a red eiderdown covered with lace, a small carpet in front of the cupboard, two blue glass vases on the dressing table in which some roses were wilting.

When she had put on her shoes she tried to walk about in the room. She had to hold on to the furniture, for she was still lame. But she would get better with practice. All the same, she had been right to refuse an invitation to dine with her Uncle Baudu that evening, and to ask her aunt to take out Pépé, whom she had once more put to lodge with Madame Gras. Jean, who had come to see her the day before, was also dining with his uncle. She was still gingerly trying to walk, making up her mind that she would go to bed early so as to rest her leg, when Madame

Cabin, the supervisor, knocked on the door and, with an air of mystery, gave her a letter.

When the door was closed again Denise, astonished by the woman's discreet smile, opened the letter. She let herself sink into a chair; the letter was from Mouret, and in it he said he was happy to hear that she was better, and invited her to come down that evening to dine with him, as she could not go out. The tone of the note, at the same time familiar and paternal, had nothing offensive about it, but it was impossible for her to misconstrue it, the Bonheur was well aware of the true significance of such invitations, they had become legendary. Clara had dined with him, and others had too – all the girls who had caught their employer's eye. After the dinner, so wags among the salesmen used to say, came the dessert. And the girl's pale cheeks were gradually flooded with colour.

The letter slid into her lap and, her heart pounding, Denise remained with her eyes fixed on the blinding light from one of the windows. In this very room, during hours of insomnia, she had been forced to make a confession to herself: if she still trembled when he was passing, she knew now that it was not from fear, and her uneasiness in the past, her former dread could have been nothing but her scared ignorance of love, the ferment caused by passions which were then beginning to dawn in her childish shyness. She did not reason about it, she only felt that she had always loved him, ever since the first moment when she had stood trembling and stammering in front of him. She had loved him when she had been in awe of him as a pitiless master, she had loved him when her bewildered heart, giving way to a need for affection, had unconsciously dreamt of Hutin. She might perhaps have given herself to another, but never had she loved anyone but him, from whom a mere glance terrified her. She was reliving all the past, it was unfolding before her in the light from the window – the harsh treatment she had suffered at the beginning, the walk which had been so pleasant beneath the dark shade of the trees in the Tuileries, and lastly his desire, which had been brushing against her ever since her return to the shop. The letter slipped right onto the floor, Denise was still looking at the window, the direct sunlight of which was dazzling her.

Suddenly there was a knock on the door, and she hastened to retrieve the letter and hide it in her pocket. It was Pauline who, having found a pretext to escape from her department, had come to have a chat with her.

"Are you better, my dear? We never see each other nowadays."

But as it was forbidden to go upstairs to their rooms and, above all, for two girls to shut themselves up there together, Denise led her to the end of the corridor where there was a common room – an attentive gesture on the part of the director to the girls, who could chat or work there until eleven o'clock. The room, decorated in white and gold, had the commonplace bareness of a hotel room, and was furnished with a piano, a pedestal table in the centre and armchairs and sofas covered with white loose covers. In any case, after spending a few evenings together there in the first flush of its novelty, the salesgirls could no longer meet there without immediately starting to quarrel with each other. They had yet to be educated to this, the little phalansterian city lacked harmony. In the meantime there was never anyone there in the evening but the assistant buyer from the corset department, Miss Powell, who used to strum Chopin jarringly on the piano and whose envied talent succeeded in putting the others to flight.

"You see, my foot is better," said Denise. "I was coming down."

"My goodness!" exclaimed Pauline. "There's enthusiasm for you! I'd stay and have a snooze if I had an excuse!"

They were both sitting on a sofa. Pauline's attitude had changed since her friend had become assistant buyer in the ready-made department. There had crept into her good-natured heartiness a shade of respect, of surprise that the salesgirl who had been such a skinny little thing in the past was now on the road to success. However, Denise was very fond of her and, out of the two hundred women now employed in the shop who were always rushing about in it, she confided only in her.

"What's the matter?" Pauline asked sharply, when she noticed the girl's agitation.

"Oh, nothing," she assured her with an embarrassed smile.

"Oh no, there is something the matter... Don't you trust me then, if you won't tell me your troubles any more?"

At that Denise, her breast swelling with emotion and unable to recover her composure, gave way. She held out the letter to her friend, stammering as she did so:

"Look! He's just written to me!"

When they were together they had never so far mentioned Mouret openly. But their very silence was like a confession of what was secretly preoccupying them. Pauline knew everything. After having read the letter she clasped Denise to her and, putting her arm round her waist, murmured gently:

"My dear, if you want me to be frank, I thought it had happened already... No, you really mustn't be shocked about it, I assure you the whole shop must think the same as me. Why, he promoted you to assistant buyer so quickly, and then he's always after you, it's plain as a pikestaff!"

And she gave her a resounding kiss on the cheek. Then she questioned her:

"You'll go tonight, of course?"

Denise looked at her without replying. Then suddenly she burst into sobs, her head resting on her friend's shoulder. The latter was extremely surprised.

"Come now, calm down. There's nothing in it to upset you like that."

"No, no, leave me alone," stammered Denise. "If only you knew how grieved I am! Since getting that letter I've ceased living... Let me cry, it makes me feel better."

Feeling sorry for her without, however, understanding, Pauline tried to console her. First of all, he was no longer seeing Clara. They did say that he visited a lady outside the shop, but that was not proved. Then she explained that one couldn't be jealous of a man of his position. He had too much money; after all, he was the master.

Denise was listening to her, and if she had not been aware of her love before, she could no longer have any doubts about it after the pain with which Clara's name and the allusion to Madame Desforges wrung her heart. She could hear Clara's disagreeable voice, she could see Madame Desforges once more as, with the contempt of a rich woman, she had made her follow her round the shop.

"So you'd go, would you?" she asked.

Without a moment's thought, Pauline burst out:

"Of course, how could one do anything else?"

Then she reflected and added:

"Not now, I wouldn't, but in the past, because now I'm going to marry Baugé, and it wouldn't really be right."

Indeed Baugé, who had recently left the Bon Marché for the Bonheur, was going to marry her towards the middle of the month. Bourdoncle did not care very much for married couples; however they had obtained permission, and they even hoped to have a fortnight's leave.

"You can see for yourself," declared Denise, "when a man loves you, he marries you... Baugé is marrying you."

Pauline laughed heartily.

"But, my dear, it's not the same thing. Baugé is marrying because he's Baugé. He's my equal, it's plain sailing... Whereas Monsieur Mouret's quite different! D'you think Monsieur Mouret could marry one of his salesgirls?"

"Oh no! Oh no!" cried the girl, shocked by the absurdity of the question. "And that's why he shouldn't have written to me."

This reasoning completed Pauline's astonishment. Her broad face with small, gentle eyes was assuming a look of motherly commiseration. Then she stood up, opened the piano, and gently played 'Le Roi Dagobert' with one finger, no doubt in order to brighten up the situation. Sounds from the streets, the distant chant of a man selling green peas, were wafting up to the bare drawing room, which the white loose covers seemed to make even more empty-looking. Denise was leaning back on a couch, her head against the woodwork, shaken by a fresh bout of sobs, which she was muffling in her handkerchief.

"What again!" Pauline went on, turning round as she did so. "You really aren't being sensible... Why did you bring me in here? We'd have done better to stay in your room."

She knelt down in front of her, and began preaching to her again. How many girls would have liked to be in her place! And what's more, if the idea did not appeal to her, it was very simple: she had only to say no, without taking it to heart so much. But she ought to think it over before jeopardizing her job with a refusal which would be quite inexplicable, as she had no other commitments. Was it really so awful? And the lecture was ending with some gaily whispered jokes, when a sound of footsteps came from the corridor.

Pauline ran to the door and peeped out.

"Sh! It's Madame Aurélie!" she murmured. "I'm off... And you, you wipe your eyes. You don't want everyone to know."

When Denise was alone she stood up and choked back her tears and, her hands still trembling for fear that she might be caught like that, she closed the piano, which her friend had left open. She heard Madame Aurélie knocking at the door of her room, so she left the drawing room.

"What's this? You're up!" exclaimed the buyer. "It's very rash of you, my dear child, I was just coming up to see how you are, and to tell you that we don't need you downstairs."

Denise assured her that she was better, and that it would do her good to work, to take her mind off it.

"It won't tire me, Madame. You give me a chair to sit on, and I'll do the accounts."

They both went downstairs. Madame Aurélie, full of attentions, insisted that she should lean on her shoulder. She must have noticed that the girl's eyes were red, for she was scrutinizing her on the sly. No doubt there was little that she did not know.

Denise had at last conquered the department; it was an unexpected victory. After having struggled in the past for almost ten months, suffering the tortures of a drudge without exhausting the ill will of her fellow workers, she had now succeeded in dominating them in a few weeks, and found them docile and respectful towards her. Madame Aurélie's sudden affection had been of great assistance to her in the ungrateful task of winning people over; it was whispered that the buyer was wont to oblige Mouret by rendering him certain services of a delicate nature, and she had taken the girl under her wing with such enthusiasm that Denise must indeed have been specially commended to her. But Denise too had made use of all the charm she had in order to disarm her enemies. The task was made more difficult by the fact that she had to live down her appointment to the post of assistant buyer. The girls railed at the injustice, accusing her of having won the job over dessert with the director; they even added salacious details. Yet in spite of their rebelliousness, the title of assistant buyer had an effect on them, and Denise had acquired an authority which astonished and quelled into submission even those who were most hostile to her. Soon she found flatterers among the newcomers, and her gentleness and modesty completed the conquest. Marguerite came over to her side. Only Clara went on being unkind, and would still venture to use the old insult "Touslehead", which no longer amused anyone. As she was lazy in a garrulous and conceited way, she had taken advantage of Mouret's brief craze for her in order to shirk work, and when he had tired of her immediately, she had not even made any recriminations, for she lived in such a whirl of amorous confusion that she was incapable of jealousy, and was content merely to obtain the advantage of her idleness being tolerated. However, she considered that Denise had robbed her of Madame Frédéric's job. She would never, in fact, have accepted it because of the worry it involved, but she was annoyed by this lack of courtesy, for she had the same claim to it as Denise had, and a prior claim, what is more.

"Why! Here comes the maternity case!" she murmured when she caught sight of Madame Aurélie leading Denise in on her arm.

Marguerite shrugged her shoulders, saying:

"If you think that's funny..."

Nine o'clock was striking. Outside, a blazing blue sky was warming the streets, cabs were bowling along towards the stations, the whole population, in long queues and dressed in its Sunday best, was escaping to the woods and suburbs. Inside the shop, which was flooded with sunshine from the big open bay windows, the imprisoned staff had just begun the stock-taking. The doorknobs had been removed, people on the pavement were stopping to look through the windows, amazed to see the shop closed when they could perceive such extraordinary activity inside. From one end to the other of the galleries, from the top floor to the basement, there was a stampede of employees, their arms raised in the air, parcels flying above their heads – and all this was taking place in a storm of shouting, figures being called out, confusion growing and bursting out into a deafening din. Each of the thirty-nine departments was carrying out its task on its own, without taking any notice of the adjoining departments. In any case, they had hardly started to tackle the shelves, there were so far only a few lengths of material on the ground. The machine would have to get going if they wanted to finish the same evening.

"Why did you come down?" Marguerite went on kindly, speaking to Denise. "You'll only hurt your foot, and we have enough people."

"That's what I told her," declared Madame Aurélie. "But she wanted to come down and help us all the same."

Work was interrupted, all the girls were dancing attendance on Denise. They were complimenting her, and listening with exclamations to the history of her sprained ankle. In the end Madame Aurélie made her sit down at a table; it was agreed that she would merely enter the goods as they were called out. In any case, on the stock-taking Sunday, every member of the staff who was capable of holding a pen was commandeered: the shopwalkers, the cashiers, the bookkeepers, down to the porters; the various departments shared these one-day assistants between them, in order to get through the job as quickly as possible. Thus, Denise found herself installed near Lhomme the cashier and Joseph the porter, who were both bent over large sheets of paper.

"Five coats, cloth, trimmed fur, size three, at two hundred and forty!" Marguerite was shouting. "Four ditto, size one, at two hundred and twenty!"

The work began again. Behind Marguerite three salesgirls were emptying cupboards, sorting the goods, giving them to her in bundles, and, when she had called them out, she would throw them onto the tables, where they were gradually piling up in enormous heaps. Lhomme was entering them, and Joseph was compiling another list as a cross-check. Meanwhile Madame Aurélie herself, assisted by three other salesgirls, was for her part enumerating silk garments, which Denise was entering on a sheet of paper. Clara had orders to watch the heaps, to arrange them and pile them up so that they took up as little room as possible, but her mind was not on her job, and some piles were falling down already.

"I say," she asked a little salesgirl who had joined the shop that winter, "have you had a rise? D'you know that they're going to give the assistant buyer two thousand francs which means that with the interest she gets she'll be earning almost seven thousand."

The little salesgirl replied, without ceasing to handle the cloaks, that if they did not put her salary up to eight hundred francs she would leave the place. Increases in salaries were made on the day after the stock-taking; at this time of the year, too, when the turnover for the year was known, the heads of departments received their interest on the increase in this figure compared with the preceding year. Therefore, in spite of the uproar and hurly-burly of the job in hand, avid gossip was going on. Between calling out two articles the talk was of nothing but money. There was a rumour that Madame Aurélie would get over twenty-five thousand francs; such a sum made the girls very excited. Marguerite, the best salesgirl after Denise, had made four thousand five hundred francs, of which fifteen hundred was her fixed salary, and about three thousand her percentage – whereas Clara had not reached two thousand five hundred altogether.

"A lot I care about those rises of theirs!" the latter was continuing, addressing the little salesgirl. "If Papa was dead – gosh! – how I'd leave them in the lurch! But what does exasperate me is that little slip of a woman's seven thousand francs. Doesn't it you, eh?"

Madame Aurélie broke into the conversation violently. Turning round majestically, she said:

"Do be quiet, Mesdemoiselles! Upon my word, one can't hear oneself speak!"

Then she started shouting out again:

"Seven mantles, Sicilian silk, size one, at a hundred and twenty! Three pelisses, surah, size two, at a hundred and fifty! Have you caught up, Mademoiselle Baudu?"

"Yes, Madame."

Clara was obliged to turn her attention to the armfuls of clothes piled up on the tables. She pushed them together to make more room. But soon she left them again in order to reply to a salesman who was looking for her. It was Mignot, playing truant from the glove department. He whispered a request for twenty francs; he already owed her thirty which he had borrowed from her on the day after the races, after having lost his week's salary on a horse; this time he had squandered in advance the commission which he had been paid the day before, and had not got fifty centimes left for his Sunday. Clara had only ten francs on her, which she lent him with fairly good grace. Then they chatted, they talked of how a party of six of them had gone to a restaurant in Bougival, and how the women had paid their share; it was better like that, everyone felt at ease. Then Mignot, wanting his twenty francs, went and bent down to Lhomme's ear. The latter, his writing brought to a standstill, seemed to be overwhelmed with confusion. However, he did not dare refuse, and was looking for a ten-franc piece in his purse when Madame Aurélie, surprised at no longer hearing the voice of Marguerite, who had had to break off, caught sight of Mignot and took in the whole situation. She harshly sent him away from the department, for she did not want people coming to distract the girls! The truth of the matter was that the young man made her apprehensive, for he was a great friend of her son Albert, and his accomplice in the shady pranks which she was terrified would end badly one day. Therefore, when Mignot had taken the ten francs and made off, she could not help saying to her husband:

"Well, really! Fancy letting yourself be taken in like that!"

"But, my dear, I really couldn't refuse the lad—"

She shut him up with a shrug of her broad shoulders. Then, as the salesgirls were slyly making fun of this family argument, she went on severely:

"Come along now, Mademoiselle Vadon; let's not fall asleep!"

"Twenty overcoats, double cashmere, size four, at eighteen francs fifty!" Marguerite rapped out in her sing-song voice.

Lhomme, his head bowed, was once more writing. Little by little his salary had been raised to nine thousand francs, but he still remained humble towards Madame Aurélie, who earned almost three times as much as that for the family.

For a time the work went ahead. Figures were ringing out, parcels of clothes were raining thick and fast on to the tables. But Clara had thought of another amusement: she was teasing Joseph the porter about the crush he was supposed to have on a young lady employed in the sample department. This girl, already twenty-eight years old, thin and pale, was the protégée of Madame Desforges, who had tried to make Mouret take her on as a salesgirl by telling him a touching story: how she was an orphan, the last of the Fontenailles, a very old and aristocratic family from Poitou; how she had turned up in Paris with a drunken father; how she had remained virtuous in spite of her misfortune; and how her education had unfortunately, been too rudimentary for her to become a teacher or to give piano lessons. Usually Mouret lost his temper when people recommended poor society girls to him; there was no one so inefficient, he was wont to say, so unbearable, so insincere – and in any case one could not just become a salesgirl on the spur of the moment, one had to serve an apprenticeship, it was a complex and difficult profession. However, he took Madame Desforges's protégée, but put her in the sample department; in order to oblige his friends, he had already found jobs for two countesses and a baroness in the publicity department, where they were doing up envelopes and wrappers. Mademoiselle de Fontenailles earned three francs a day, on which she could just manage to live in a little room in the Rue d'Argenteuil. Joseph, beneath the silent starchiness of an old soldier had a soft heart, which had in the end been touched by the sight of her going about so sad-looking and poorly dressed. He did not own up to it, but he would blush when the girls from the ready-made department teased him; the sample department was in an adjacent room, and the girls had noticed him endlessly hanging about there outside the door.

"Joseph has fits of absent-mindedness," Clara was murmuring. "His head keeps on turning towards the lingerie."

Mademoiselle de Fontenailles had been conscripted to help with the stock-taking at the trousseau counter. As the lad was, in fact, continually casting glances at the counter, the salesgirls began to laugh. He became confused and buried his nose in his papers, while Marguerite, in order to smother the burst of mirth which was tickling her throat, was shouting more loudly:

"Fourteen jackets, English cloth, size two, at fifteen francs."

This time the voice of Madame Aurélie, who was in the process of calling out the cloaks, was drowned. With an offended air and majestic deliberation she said:

"A little quieter, Mademoiselle. We are not in the market... And you're all of you very silly to amuse yourselves in that childish way when time is so precious."

Just then, as Clara was no longer watching the piles of clothes, a catastrophe occurred. Some coats slipped off the table and all the other piles there were pulled after them and fell down one after another. The carpet was littered with them.

"There, what was I saying?" cried the buyer, beside herself. "Do take a little care, Mademoiselle Prunaire, it's really becoming intolerable!"

But a perceptible tremor had run round the room; Mouret and Bourdoncle were just appearing, making their tour of inspection. Voices started calling out again, pens scratched, while Clara hastened to pick up the clothes. The director did not interrupt the work. He remained there for a few minutes, silent and smiling; his face was gay and victorious, as it generally was on stock-taking days, and his lips alone betrayed a nervous quiver. When he caught sight of Denise he almost let a gesture of astonishment escape him. So she had come down, had she? His eyes met those of Madame Aurélie. Then, after a short hesitation, he moved away and went into the trousseau department.

Meanwhile Denise, her attention aroused by the slight murmur, had raised her head. Having recognized Mouret, she had once more quite simply bent over her papers. A feeling of calmness had been stealing over her ever since she had begun writing mechanically to the rhythmic tune of the articles being called out. She always gave way to her sensitive nature's initial overflow of feeling like that: tears would choke her, intense emotion doubled her suffering; then she would come to her senses again, she would regain her splendid, cool courage and a gentle yet inexorable strength of will. Now, with clear eyes and pale face, she was without a tremor, absorbed in her task, resolved to subdue her heart and follow only her head.

Ten o'clock was striking, and in the commotion from all the departments the din of the stock-taking was growing. And beneath all the shouts being uttered without respite and mingling from all sides, the same news was circulating with amazing rapidity: every salesman knew already that Mouret had that morning written to invite Denise to dinner. It was Pauline who had let the cat out of the bag. As she had gone downstairs again, still shaken, she had met Deloche in the lace department and, without noticing that Liénard was talking to the young man, had got the news off her chest.

"It's happened, you know... She's just got the letter. He's invited her for this evening."

Deloche had turned quite pale. He had understood, for he often questioned Pauline, and they both talked every day about their mutual friend, about Mouret's soft spot for her, about the famous invitation which would, in the end, wind up the adventure. Moreover, she used to scold him for secretly loving Denise, who would never grant him anything, and she would shrug her shoulders when he approved of the girl resisting the director.

"Her foot is better, she's coming down," she continued. "Don't make such a long face... What's happened is a bit of luck for her."

And she hurried back to her department.

"Ah! I see!" murmured Liénard, who had overheard. "It's about the young lady with the sprained ankle... Well! You who were defending her in the café last night, you had good reason to be in a hurry about it, didn't you?"

And he too, made his escape, but by the time he got back to the woollens he had already told the story of the letter to four or five salesmen. And after that in less than five minutes it was all round the shop.

Liénard's last sentence referred to a scene which had taken place the day before in the Café Saint-Roch. Nowadays he and Deloche were never apart. The first salesman had taken Hutin's room at the Hôtel de Smyrne when the latter, promoted to assistant buyer, had taken a little three-roomed flat for himself; and the two shop assistants came to the Bonheur together in the morning and waited for each other in the evening so as to go home together. Their rooms, which were adjacent, looked out over the same dark courtyard – a narrow hole, the smells from which poisoned the hotel. They got on well together, in spite of their disparity, one squandering without a thought the money which he drew from his father, and the other penniless, obsessed by ideas of economy; they did, all the same, have one thing in common – their clumsiness as salesmen, which left them both vegetating in their departments, without increases in salary. After they had finished work they spent most of their time at the Café Saint-Roch. Devoid of customers during the daytime, at about half-past eight this café would fill up with an overflowing stream of shop assistants, the stream which had been let into the street through the big doorway in the Place Gaillon. From then on, bursting out in the midst of the thick pipe smoke, there was a deafening noise of dominoes, of laughter and of shrill voices. Beer and coffee flowed. In the left-hand corner Liénard would ask for expensive things, while Deloche made do with a glass of beer which he took four hours to drink. It was here that he had heard Favier, at a neighbouring table, saying abominable things about Denise, how she had "caught" the director by pulling up her skirts when she was going up a staircase in front of him. Deloche had had to control himself in order not to hit him. Then, as Favier had continued, saying that the girl went downstairs every night to meet her lover, Deloche, mad with fury, had called him a liar.

"What a rotter he is! He's lying, he's lying, d'you hear?"

In the emotion which was rending him he let out confessions in a stammering voice, pouring out his heart.

"I know her, I know all about it... She's never been fond of any man except one: yes, Monsieur Hutin, and as he didn't notice it he can't even boast of having touched her with his little finger."

An account of this quarrel, exaggerated and distorted, had already been amusing the shop, when the story of Mouret's letter went the rounds. It so happened that Liénard confided the news first of all to a silk salesman. In the silk department stock-taking was going with a swing. On stools, Favier and two assistants were emptying the shelves, passing the lengths of material as fast as they could to Hutin who, standing in the middle of a table, was calling out the figures after having consulted the labels; then he would throw the lengths of material on to the ground, they were gradually littering the floor, rising like a spring tide. Other employees were writing, Albert Lhomme was helping them, his complexion blotchy from having been up all night in a low dance hall. A flood of sunshine was falling from the hall windows, through which could be seen the blazing blue of the sky.

"Do draw the blinds," shouted Bouthemont, who was very busy supervising the job. "That sun's unbearable!"

Favier, who was stretching up to reach a piece of material, grumbled under his breath:

"How can they shut people up in this gorgeous weather! There's no danger of it raining on a stock-taking day! And they keep us under lock and key like galley slaves while the whole of Paris is out walking!"

He passed the material to Hutin. The yardage was written on the label, and each time some material was sold the quantity sold was deducted from it, which made the work much simpler. The assistant buyer shouted:

"Fancy silk, small checks, twenty-one yards at six francs fifty!"

And the silk went to swell the pile on the ground. Then he went on with a conversation which he had already begun by saying to Favier:

"So he wanted to fight you?"

"Why, yes! I was quietly drinking my beer... As if it was worth his while to say I was lying! She's just had a letter from the boss inviting her to dinner... The whole place is talking about it."

"What! I thought it had happened long ago!"

Favier was holding out another piece of material to him.

"I know, I could have sworn it had. It looked as if they'd been together for ages."

"Ditto, twenty-five yards!" rapped out Hutin.

The muffled thud of the material could be heard as he added in a lower voice:

"You know she led a pretty fast life in that old madman Bourras's house."

Now the whole department was making fun about it, without however interrupting the work. They were murmuring the girl's name to themselves, backs were heaving with laughter, there was a licking of lips at this tasty bit of gossip. Even Bouthemont, who became expansive when dubious stories were being told, could not refrain from letting out a joke, the bad taste of which made him burst with pleasure. Albert, who had woken up, swore that he had seen the assistant buyer from the ready-made department between two soldiers at the Gros-Caillou. At that moment Mignot was coming downstairs with the twenty francs he had just borrowed; he had stopped, and was slipping ten francs into Albert's hand, arranging as he did so where he would meet him that evening: the spree they had been planning, which had been held up by lack of money, was possible after all, in spite of the insignificance of the sum. Handsome Mignot made such a coarse remark when he learnt of the sending of the letter that Bouthemont felt obliged to intervene:

"That's enough now, gentlemen. It's not our business... Come along, come along now, Monsieur Hutin."

"Fancy silk, small checks, thirty-two yards, at six francs fifty!" the latter shouted.

Pens were moving once more, bundles of goods were falling regularly, the tide of materials was still rising, as if the waters of a river had been poured into it. The roll call of fancy silks went on ceaselessly. Then Favier remarked under his breath that there was going to be a pretty stock: mighty pleased the management would be – that great idiot Bouthemont might be the best buyer in Paris, but as a salesman there had never been such a dud! Hutin was smiling, delighted, approving with a friendly glance, for after having himself introduced

Bouthemont into the Bonheur des Dames in the past in order to get Robineau out, he was undermining him in his turn with the dogged aim of taking his place. It was the same type of warfare as before – treacherous insinuations were slipped into the ears of the directors, he was overzealous in order to push himself forward, a whole campaign was being waged with suave cunning. Meanwhile Favier, to whom Hutin was now being condescending, was furtively watching him with a cold and jaundiced eye, as if he had worked out how many mouthfuls the stocky little man would be, and it looked as if he was waiting until his comrade had devoured Bouthemont in order to devour him in his turn afterwards. He hoped to have the job of assistant buyer if Hutin were to become head of the department. Then they would see. Both of them, seized with the fever which was raging from one end of the shop to the other, were talking of probable increases in salary, without ceasing to call out the stock of fancy silks as they did so: Bouthemont was expected to get his thirty thousand francs that year; Favier was estimating his salary and percentage at five thousand five hundred. Each season the turnover of the department was increasing, the salesmen in it were rising in rank and doubling their pay, like officers during a campaign.

"Now then, haven't you finished these light silks yet?" said Bouthemont suddenly, with an irritated air. "What a washout this spring has been, nothing but rain! People haven't bought anything but black silks!"

His fat, laughing face darkened, he was watching the pile on the ground spreading, while Hutin was repeating more loudly, in a ringing voice tinged with triumph:

"Fancy silk, small checks, twenty-eight yards, at six francs fifty!"

There was still another whole shelf. Favier, his arms worn out, was being slow. As he finally gave the last lengths of material to Hutin he resumed in a low voice:

"I say, I was forgetting... Have you been told that the assistant buyer from the mantles used to be gone on you?"

The young man appeared to be very surprised.

"Really? How so?"

"Yes, that great idiot Deloche told us the secret... I remember how she used to make eyes at you in the past."

Since he had become assistant buyer Hutin had dropped music hall singers and now affected schoolteachers. Very flattered in his heart of hearts, he replied with an air of scorn:

"I like them better upholstered, my dear fellow, and then one doesn't go about with just anyone, like the director does."

He broke off and shouted:

"White poult, thirty-five yards, at eight francs seventy-five!"

"Ah! At last!" murmured Bouthemont, relieved.

But a bell was ringing, it was for the second meal service to which Favier usually went. He got down from the stool and another salesman took his place; he had to step over the surge of lengths of material which had risen still further on the floor. Now similar avalanches were littering the ground in all the departments; the shelves, boxes, cupboards were gradually emptying, while the merchandise was overflowing everywhere, underfoot, between the tables, in a continual spate. In the household linen the dull sound of piles of calico falling could be heard, in the haberdashery there was a faint rattling of boxes, and distant rumblings were coming from the furniture department. All the voices were sounding at the same time, shrill voices and thick voices, figures were whistling through the air, the immense nave was resounding with a rattling roar, the roar of forests in January, when the wind whistles in the branches.

Favier got clear at last and went upstairs to the dining room. Since the extensions had been made to the Bonheur des Dames, these were situated on the fourth floor, in the new buildings. As he was hurrying along he caught up with Deloche and Liénard, who had gone up ahead of him; he fell back to walk with Mignot, who was following him.

"Damn it!" he said in the kitchen corridor, looking at the blackboard on which the menu was inscribed. "You can certainly see it's stock-taking. There's a real treat for you! Chicken or rehashed mutton, and artichokes with salad oil! That mutton of theirs will get a pretty cold shoulder!"

Mignot was sniggering, murmuring as he did so:

"Is there fowl pest about, then?"

Meanwhile Deloche and Liénard had taken their helpings and had moved on. Then Favier, leaning through the hatch, said in a loud voice:

"Chicken."

But he had to wait; one of the waiters who was carving had just cut his finger, and this was causing confusion. Favier remained facing the hatch, looking into the kitchen. It was a giant installation, with its central range on which two rails fixed to the ceiling carried, by means of a system of pulleys and chains, the colossal cooking pots, which four men could not have lifted. Chefs, silhouetted in their white clothes against the dark red of the cast iron, mounted on iron ladders and armed with skimmers on the end of long sticks, were supervising the hot-pot for the evening. Then, against the wall, there were gridirons big enough for burning martyrs, saucepans in which a whole sheep could be fricasséed, a monumental plate-warmer, a marble basin filled with a continual trickle of water. One could also glimpse a scullery to the left, with sinks in it like swimming pools, whereas on the other side there was a larder where red meat could be seen hanging on steel hooks. A potato-peeling machine was running with the tick-tock of a mill. Two little carts, full of picked salad, were passing, pulled along by assistants who were going to put them in the cool, under a fountain.

"Chicken," repeated Favier, seized with impatience.

Then, turning round, he added in a lower voice:

"One of them has cut himself… it's disgusting, it's dripping into the food!"

Mignot wanted to see. A whole queue of shop assistants was growing, there was laughter and pushing. The two young men, their heads in the hatch, were communicating their thoughts to each other at the sight of the phalansterian kitchen, in which even the small utensils, down to the very skewers and larding needles, seemed gigantic. Two thousand lunches and two thousand dinners had to be served there, not to mention the fact that the number of employees was increasing from week to week. It was a yawning chasm, in one day it swallowed up sixteen hectolitres of potatoes, a hundred and twenty pounds of butter and six hundred kilograms of meat, and at each meal three casks had to be tapped, almost seven hundred litres of wine flowed over the counter of the bar.

"Ah! At last!" muttered Favier, when the chef on duty reappeared with a pan from which he speared a drumstick for him.

"Chicken," said Mignot, behind him.

Holding their plates, both of them went into the dining room, after having taken their portions of wine at the bar, while behind their backs the word "chicken" was sounding regularly without respite, and the chef's fork could be heard spearing the pieces, with a little rapid, rhythmic sound.

Nowadays the shop assistants' dining room was an immense hall in which the five hundred people could be accommodated with ease for each of the three meal services. The places were laid on long mahogany tables placed parallel across the room; at either end of the hall similar tables were set apart for shopwalkers and heads of departments, and there was in the middle a counter where supplementary dishes could be obtained. Large windows on the right and left illuminated the long rooms with a white brightness; the ceiling, in spite of being almost fourteen feet high, seemed low, crushed down by the inordinate development of the other dimensions. On the walls, which were painted a shade of pale yellow oil paint, shelves for table napkins were the only ornaments. Beyond this first dining room came that of the porters and coachmen, where meals were served irregularly, as their work permitted.

"What! Mignot, you've got a drumstick too!" said Favier, when he was seated at one of the tables, opposite his companion.

Other shop assistants installed themselves around them. There was no tablecloth, and the plates made cracked sounds on the mahogany; in this corner of the room everyone was exclaiming, for the number of drumsticks were truly prodigious.

"Some more birds with nothing but feet!" pointed out Mignot.

Those who had bits of carcass were annoyed. And yet the food had greatly improved since the new alterations. Mouret no longer dealt with a contractor for a fixed sum; he now ran the kitchen himself and had made it an organized service like one of his departments, with a cook, under-cooks and an inspector, and if he spent more as a result, he obtained more work from his better-fed staff – a calculation based on practical humanitarianism, which had for a long time dismayed Bourdoncle.

"Never mind, mine's tender all the same," Mignot resumed. "Do pass the bread!"

The big loaf was going round; having cut himself a slice, as he was the last to have it he replunged the knife into the crust. Some latecomers were rushing up one after another, ferocious appetites redoubled by the morning's work were raging all down the long tables, from one end of the dining room to the other. There was a growing clatter of forks, the glug-glug of bottles being emptied, the clink of glasses being put down again too hard, the grinding sound of five hundred solid jaws energetically munching. Words, which were rare so far, were smothered in full mouths.

Meanwhile Deloche, seated between Baugé and Liénard, was almost opposite Favier, only a few places away. Each had cast a glance of spite at the other. Their neighbours, acquainted with their quarrel of the day before, were whispering. There had been laughter over the bad luck of Deloche, who was always starving and who always, as if by some malign destiny, chanced on the worst bits at the table. This time he had just arrived with a chicken gizzard and the remains of a carcass. Silently, he let them go on joking, he was devouring great mouthfuls of bread and peeling the gizzard with the infinite skill of a lad who held meat in respect.

"Why don't you complain?" Baugé said to him.

But he shrugged his shoulders. What was the good? It was never a success. When he did not resign himself, things always went worse.

"You know, the cotton-reelers have a club of their own now," related Mignot suddenly. "Yes, really, the Reel Club... They have it in the house of a wine merchant in the Rue Saint-Honoré, who lets them a room on Saturdays."

He was talking of the haberdashery salesmen. At that the whole table brightened up. Between two mouthfuls, their voices clogged with food, each one of them put in a word, added a detail; it was only the persistent readers who remained silent and lost to the world, their noses buried in a newspaper. Everyone was agreed; each year shop assistants were bettering themselves. About half of them nowadays could speak German or English. It was no longer smart to go and kick up a shindy at Bullier's, to make the rounds of the cafés in order to whistle at the ugly girls singing in them. No, about twenty of them would get together now and found a club.

"Have they got a piano like the linen dealers?" asked Liénard.

"Has the Reel Club a piano? I should jolly well think so!" exclaimed Mignot. "And they play on it, they sing! There's even one of them, that little fellow Bavoux, who reads poetry."

The mirth was redoubled, they made fun of Bavoux; however there was great respect beneath their laughter. Then they talked about the play at the Vaudeville, in which a draper's assistant played an unpleasant part; several of them were getting annoyed about it, while others were worrying about when they would be able to get away that evening, for they were going to parties given by bourgeois families. From every corner of the immense hall similar conversations were proceeding, in the midst of the growing din of crockery. In order to get rid of the smell of food and the hot steam which was rising from five hundred uncovered plates, they had opened the windows, the lowered blinds of which were burning hot from the oppressive August sun. Scorching blasts of hot air were coming from the streets, glints of gold were making the ceiling yellow, bathing the sweating men at lunch in an auburn light.

"How can they shut one up like this on a Sunday, in such weather!" Favier repeated.

This remark brought the gentlemen back to the subject of the stock-taking. It was a superb year. And they went on to talk about salaries, rises, the eternal subject, the thrilling question which always stirred them. It was always the same thing on the days when they had chicken, excitement would break out, in the end the noise was unbearable. When the waiters brought the artichokes they could no longer hear themselves speak. The inspector on duty had orders to be tolerant.

"By the way," Favier exclaimed. "You know what's happened?"

But his voice was drowned. Mignot was asking:

"Who doesn't like artichokes? I'll swap my dessert for an artichoke."

No one replied. Everyone liked artichokes. This lunch would go down as a good one, for they had seen that there were peaches for dessert.

"He's invited her to dinner, old man," Favier was saying to his right-hand neighbour, concluding the story. "What! You didn't know?"

The whole table knew, and they were tired of talking about it all morning. Jokes, always the same ones, passed from mouth to mouth. Deloche was quivering, in the end he fixed his eye on Favier, who was insistently repeating:

"If he hasn't had her, he'll get her... and he won't be the first to have her. Oh no, he won't be the first!"

He too was looking at Deloche. He added provocatively:

"Those who like them bony can treat themselves to her for five francs."

Suddenly, he lowered his head. Deloche, yielding to an irresistible urge, had just thrown his last glass of wine into Favier's face, blurting out as he did so:

"There! You dirty liar, I should have done it yesterday!"

This caused a scene. Favier's neighbours had been spattered with a few drops, but his hair was only slightly damp; the wine, thrown too hard, had fallen on the other side of the table. But people were annoyed. So he must be sleeping with her then, if he defended her like that! What a ruffian! He deserved a box on the ears to teach him how to behave. Voices were lowered, however, someone warned them that the inspector was approaching, and there was no point involving the management in the quarrel. Favier was content to say:

"If he'd got me you'd have seen what a shindy I'd have made!"

It all finished up with jeers. When Deloche, still trembling, wanted to take a drink in order to hide his embarrassment and mechanically seized his empty glass, there was laughter. He put his glass down again awkwardly and set about sucking the artichoke leaves which he had already eaten.

"Pass the bottle to Deloche, do," said Mignot calmly, "he's thirsty."

The laughter was redoubled. The young gentlemen were taking clean plates from the piles which were standing at intervals on the table: the waiters were taking round the dessert, baskets full of peaches. And they all held their sides with laughter when Mignot added:

"Everyone to their own taste, Deloche eats his peaches with wine."

The latter remained motionless. His head bowed, seemingly deaf, he appeared not to hear the jokes, he was feeling hopeless regret for what he had just done. They were right, what claim had he to defend her? Now people would say all sorts of dreadful things, he could have hit himself for having compromised her like that when wanting to prove her innocent. It was his usual luck, it would have been better if he had died on the spot, for he could not even give way to the instincts of his heart without doing something silly. Tears were coming into his eyes. Was it not his fault too that the shop was talking about the letter the director had written? He could hear them all sneering with crude words about the invitation, the secret of which had been confided only to Liénard, and he blamed himself, he should not have allowed Pauline to speak about it in front of a third person, he held himself responsible for the indiscretion which had been committed.

"Why did you tell everyone about it?" he murmured finally, in a pained voice. "It's very wrong."

"Me!" replied Liénard. "But I only told one or two people, insisting on secrecy... How can one tell how things get around?"

When Deloche finally brought himself to drink a glass of water, the whole table burst out laughing again. The meal was finishing, the employees, lolling back in their chairs, were awaiting the sound of the bell, shouting to each other from afar with a lack of restraint brought on by the meal. Few supplementary dishes had been asked for at the big central counter, especially as, that day, it was the shop which was paying for the coffee. Cups were steaming, sweaty faces were shining under the hazy fumes floating like clouds of blue cigarette smoke. In the windows the blinds were hanging down motionless, without flapping at all. One of them rolled up again, and a stream of sunshine crossed the hall, lighting up the ceiling. The hubbub of voices was beating against the walls with such a noise that the sound of the bell was at first heard only by the tables near the door. They got up, and the stampede as they left filled the corridors for a long time.

Meanwhile, Deloche had lagged behind in order to escape the witticisms which were still going on. Even Baugé went out ahead of him – and Baugé was usually the last to leave the dining room, as he would then go a roundabout way and meet Pauline as she was going into the women's dining hall: they had agreed on this scheme as the only way they could see each other for a minute during working hours. But that day, just as they were kissing each other full on the lips in a corner of the corridor, Denise, who was also going up to lunch, came on them unawares. She was walking with difficulty, because of her foot.

"Oh, my dear!" stammered Pauline, very red, "you won't say anything, will you?"

Baugé, with his huge limbs and build of a giant, was trembling like a little boy. He murmured:

"You know, they'd very likely throw us out... Our marriage may have been announced, but those dirty dogs don't understand that people kiss!"

Denise, quite upset, pretended that she had not seen them. And Baugé was making his escape when Deloche, who was going the longest way round, appeared in his turn. He wanted to apologize, he stammered phrases which Denise did not at first understand. Then, as he was reproaching Pauline for having spoken in front of Liénard, and as Pauline became embarrassed, the girl at last understood the words people had been whispering behind her back all morning. So it was the story of the letter which was going round! Once more the shiver which this letter had given her ran down her spine, she felt as if she was being undressed by all those men.

"I didn't know," Pauline was repeating. "In any case, there's nothing bad about it... Let them talk, they're all wild about it, you bet!"

"My dear," said Denise in the end, in her sensible way, "I'm not cross with you at all... You've only said what's true. I've received a letter, and it's up to me to reply to it."

Deloche went away cut to the heart, for he had understood that the girl was taking the situation for granted and would keep the appointment that evening. When the two salesgirls had lunched, in a small dining room next to the big one, where the women were served more comfortably, Pauline had to help Denise downstairs, as her foot was getting tired.

Downstairs, in the overexcitement of the afternoon, the stock-taking was proceeding with even more bustle. The time had come when they had to put their backs into it, when, faced with the little work that had been done in the morning, all efforts were straining in order to finish by the evening. Voices were being raised even more; nothing could be seen but waving arms, still emptying shelves, throwing down the merchandise, and it was no longer possible to walk about, the rising spate of piles and bales on the floor now reached the level of the counters. A surge of heads, brandished fists, and flying limbs seemed to be losing itself in the depths of the departments, in a distant confused riot. It was the final fever of bustle, the machine at breaking point, while outside the plate-glass windows all around the closed shop there still went occasional passers-by, wan with the stifling boredom of Sunday. On the pavement in the Rue Neuve-Saint-Augustin, three big hatless girls with a sluttish air about them had taken their stand, their faces brazenly pressed to the windows, trying to see the strange sort of mess being cooked up inside.

When Denise went back into the ready-made department Madame Aurélie left Marguerite to finish calling out the garments. The checking remained to be done and, requiring quiet in which to do it, she retired into the pattern room, taking the girl with her.

"Come with me, we'll compare the two lists… Then you can add it up."

But, as she wanted to leave the door open in order to keep an eye on the girls, the din came in and they could no longer hear a thing, even at the far end of the room. It was a vast, square room, furnished only with chairs and three long tables; in one corner stood great mechanical cutters for making the patterns. Whole lengths of material went through them, in one year more than sixty thousand francs' worth of material was sent out, thus cut up into strips. From morning to night the cutters were chopping up silk, wool and linen with the sound of a scythe. Afterwards the pattern books had to be put together, either glued or sewn. And there was also, between the two windows, a small printing press for the labels.

"Quieter, please!" Madame Aurélie, who could not hear Denise reading out the articles, would shout from time to time.

When the checking of the first lists had been completed, she left the girl seated at one of the tables, deep in adding up. Then she reappeared almost immediately and installed Mademoiselle de Fontenailles there, as she was no longer needed by the trousseau department which had handed her over. It would save time if Mademoiselle de Fontenailles were also to add up. But the apparition of the Marchioness, as Clara called her, had stirred up the department. They were laughing, they were teasing Joseph, ferocious words were coming through the door.

"Don't move, you're not in my way at all," said Denise, seized with deep pity. "Here, my inkstand will do, you can share it with me."

Mademoiselle de Fontenailles, stupefied by her downfall, could not even find a word of gratitude. She looked as if she drank, her emaciated body had a livid hue, and only her hands, white and slender, still bore witness to her distinguished ancestry.

However, the laughter suddenly stopped, and they could hear the work resuming its regular hum. It was Mouret once again making a tour of the departments. He stopped to look for Denise, surprised at not seeing her. With a sign he beckoned to Madame Aurélie, and they both moved to one side and talked in low voices for a moment. He must have been questioning her. With a glance she indicated the pattern room, then appeared to be giving him a report. Doubtless she was relating that the girl had cried that morning.

"Splendid!" said Mouret out loud, drawing nearer. "Show me the lists."

"This way, Monsieur," the buyer replied, "we've escaped from the din."

He followed her into the neighbouring room. Clara was not taken in by this manoeuvre: she murmured that they might as well go and fetch a bed straight away. But Marguerite was throwing the garments to her more quickly in order to keep her busy and stop her talking. Wasn't the assistant buyer a good sort? Her affairs did not concern anyone else. The department was aiding and abetting, the salesgirls were making more noise and fuss, the backs of Lhomme and of Joseph were swelling out, as if becoming soundproof. And Inspector Jouve, having noticed Madame Aurélie's tactics from afar, came to walk up and down outside the door of the sample room, with the regular step of a sentry on guard awaiting his superior's convenience.

"Give Monsieur the lists," said the buyer as she went in.

Denise gave them to him, then remained looking up at him. She had given a slight start, but had controlled herself, and she remained splendidly composed, her cheeks pale. For a moment Mouret appeared to be absorbed in the list of articles, without glancing at the girl. Silence reigned. Then Madame Aurélie went up to Mademoiselle de Fontenailles, who had not even looked round, and, seemingly finding fault with her addition, she said to her in a low voice:

"Go along and help with the parcels, do... You're not used to doing figures."

Mademoiselle de Fontenailles rose, and went back to the department, where whisperings greeted her. Joseph, under the mocking eyes of the girls, was writing all crooked. Clara, delighted to receive an assistant, was jostling her all the same because of the hatred she felt for all women in the shop. How idiotic it was, when one was a marchioness, to have an odd-job man falling in love with one! And she envied her that love.

"Very good, very good!" Mouret was repeating, still pretending to read.

Madame Aurélie, meanwhile did not know how to withdraw decently in her turn. She was marking time, going to look at the mechanical cutters, furious that her husband had not invented a pretext for calling her, but he never thought of serious things, he would have died of thirst beside a pond. In the end it was Marguerite who had the wit to come and ask her about something.

"I'll go and see," replied the buyer.

And, her dignity safeguarded from then on, as she had an excuse in the eyes of the girls who were watching her, she left Mouret and Denise, whom she had just brought together, alone, and went out of the room with a majestic gait, her profile so lofty that the salesgirls did not dare even to indulge in a smile.

Mouret had slowly replaced the lists on the table. He was looking at the girl, who remained seated, pen in hand. She did not look away, she had only become paler.

"You're coming tonight?" he asked in a low voice.

"No, Monsieur," she replied. "I can't. My brothers are going to be at my uncle's, and I've promised to dine with them."

"But what about your foot? You walk with too much difficulty."

"Oh, I'm quite able to get as far as that, I've been feeling much better since this morning!"

Faced with this calm refusal, he had become pale in his turn. His sensitive pride was making his lips quiver. Nevertheless, he controlled himself, and with the air of a kindly employer merely taking an interest in one of his shopgirls, he resumed:

"Come now, if I invite you... You know what regard I have for you."

Denise maintained her respectful attitude.

"I am very touched, Monsieur, by your kindness to me, and I thank you for the invitation. But I must repeat that it's impossible, my brothers are expecting me this evening."

She was obstinately refusing to understand. Meanwhile the door had remained open, and she could very well feel the whole shop urging her on. In a friendly way Pauline had called her a silly ass, and the others would laugh at her if she refused the invitation. Madame Aurélie, who had left the room; Marguerite, whose raised voice she could hear; Lhomme, whose motionless and discreet back she could see – they all desired her fall, they were all throwing her at their employer. And the distant hum of the stock-taking, the millions of goods being called out in ringing tones, being turned over in armfuls, was like a hot wind fanning passion towards her.

There was a silence. At times the noise drowned the words of Mouret, accompanying them with the formidable din of a king's fortune won in battle.

"Well, when will you come?" he asked again. "Tomorrow?"

This simple question upset Denise. For a moment she lost her composure and blurted out:

"I don't know... I can't..."

He smiled, he tried to take her hand, which she drew back.

"What are you afraid of then?"

But she was already holding her head up again, she was looking him straight in the face, and she said, smiling in her gentle, gallant way as she did so:

"I'm not afraid of anything, Monsieur... One only does what one wants to do, doesn't one? I just don't want to, that's all!"

As she stopped speaking she was surprised to hear a creak. She turned round and saw the door slowly closing by itself. Inspector Jouve had taken it upon himself to close it. Doors formed part of his duties, none of them were supposed to remain open. Then he went gravely back to his sentry post again. No one appeared to notice the door being closed in this simple way. Only Clara let out a crude word in the ear of Mademoiselle de Fontenailles, who went deathly pale.

Meanwhile, Denise had stood up. Mouret was saying to her in a low and trembling voice:

"Listen, I love you... You've known it for a long time, don't play the cruel game with me of pretending not to know... And don't be afraid of anything. I've wanted to call you into my office hundreds of times. We would have been alone, I would only have had to bolt the door. But I didn't want to, you can see yourself that I'm talking to you, where anyone can come in... I love you, Denise."

She was standing there, her face white, still looking him straight in the face.

"Tell me, why do you refuse? Haven't you any needs? Your brothers are a heavy responsibility. Anything you ask me for, everything you require from me—"

With a word, she cut him short:

"Thank you, I'm earning more than I need now."

"But it's freedom I'm offering you, it's a life of pleasure and luxury... I'll set you up with a home of your own, I'll insure that you'll be well off."

"No thank you, I'd be bored doing nothing... I wasn't ten years old when I started to earn my living."

He made a frantic gesture. She was the first woman not to yield. He had only to stoop to get the others, they all waited on his whim like obedient servants, but she was saying no, without even giving a reasonable pretext. His desire, controlled for so long, whipped up by her resistance, was becoming exacerbated. Perhaps he was not offering her enough? He redoubled his efforts, urging her even more strongly.

"No, no, thank you," she replied each time, without weakening.

Then a cry from the heart escaped him:

"Can't you see how I'm suffering? Yes, it's idiotic, I'm suffering like a child!"

Tears had moistened his eyes. A fresh silence reigned. Behind the closed doors the muffled hum of the stock-taking could still be heard. It was like a dying sound of triumph, the accompaniment to the master's defeat was discreet.

"But if I wish it..." he said in a passionate voice, seizing her hands as he did so.

She let him hold them, her eyes grew dim, all her strength was ebbing away. She felt a warmth coming to her from the man's hot hands, filling her with delicious indolence. My goodness! How she loved him, and what sweetness she would have tasted if she had flung her arms round his neck and leant on his breast!

"I wish it, I wish it," he was repeating, beside himself. "I'll expect you this evening, or I'll take steps..."

He was becoming brutal. She uttered a faint cry; the pain which she felt at her wrists gave her back her courage. With a jerk, she freed herself. Then, standing erect and seemingly made bigger by her defencelessness, she said:

"No, leave me... I'm not a Clara, to be dropped the next day. And then, Monsieur, there's someone else you love, yes, that lady who comes here... Stay with her. I'm not the sort of person who shares."

Surprise held him motionless. What was she saying and what did she want then? Never did the girls he picked up in the departments worry themselves about being loved. He should have laughed about it, yet this attitude of gentle pride completed the confusion in his heart.

"Monsieur," she went on, "open the door again. It is not fitting for us to be together like this."

Mouret obeyed and, his temples buzzing, not knowing how to hide his anguish, he resummoned Madame Aurélie, lost his temper about the stock of cloaks, said that the prices would have to be lowered, and continue to be lowered so long as a single one remained. It was the rule of the shop, they got rid of everything each year, they sold goods at a sixty per cent loss rather than keep an out-of-date model or a shop-soiled material. As it happened Bourdoncle, looking for the director, had been waiting for him for a minute or two; he had been stopped outside the closed door by Jouve, who had whispered a word or two in his ear with a serious air. He was growing impatient, without however having the courage to interrupt the tête-à-tête. Was it really possible? On such a day too, and with that puny creature! When at last the door opened, Bourdoncle spoke of the fancy silks, the stock of which was going to be enormous. It was a relief for Mouret to be able to shout as much as he liked. What was Bouthemont thinking of? He moved off, declaring as he did so that he would not tolerate a buyer so much lacking in flair that he committed the folly of laying in more goods than sales justified.

"What's the matter?" murmured Madame Aurélie, quite over-whelmed by these reproaches.

The girls looked at each other in surprise. At six o'clock the stock-taking was finished. The sun was still shining, a pale summer sun, the golden reflection of which was coming through the hall windows. In the torrid air of the streets tired families were already coming back from the suburbs, loaded with bunches of flowers and dragging their children along. One by one, the departments had grown silent. Nothing could be heard in the galleries but the belated shouts of a few salesmen emptying a last shelf. Then these voices too became silent, nothing remained of the day's hubbub but a mighty chill hanging over the fearsome avalanche of merchandise. Now the shelves, the cupboards, the boxes and cases were empty: not a yard of material, not a single object had remained in its place. The huge shop had nothing to show but its framework, its woodwork completely devoid of goods, as on the day it had been installed. This bareness was the visible proof of the complete and accurate returns of the stock-taking. And, on the ground, sixteen millions' worth of goods was piled up, it was a rising sea which had, in the end, submerged the tables and counters. The salesmen, plunged in it up to their shoulders, were beginning to put each article back. It was hoped that they would have finished by ten o'clock.

As Madame Aurélie, who belonged to the first dinner service, was coming back from the dining room, she brought news of the turnover for the year, a figure which had just been worked out by adding up those of the various departments. The total was eighty million, ten million more than the preceding year. There had been an actual loss only on the fancy silks.

"If Monsieur Mouret isn't satisfied, I don't know what he wants," added the buyer. "Why! He's over there, at the top of the main staircase, looking furious."

The girls went to have a look at him. He was standing alone, his face saturnine, looking down at the millions scattered at his feet.

"Madame," Denise came to inquire at that moment, "would you be good enough to let me go to my room? I'm no longer any use because of my leg, and as I've got to dine at my uncle's with my brothers..."

There was astonishment. So she had not succumbed? Madame Aurélie hesitated, appeared to be on the verge of forbidding her to go out, her voice curt and displeased; while Clara, full of disbelief, was shrugging her shoulders: don't worry, it was quite simple, he didn't want her any more! When Pauline learnt of this ending to the story, she was standing with Deloche by the layettes. The young man's sudden joy made her furious: a fine lot of good it did him, didn't it? It made him happy, did it, that his friend was silly enough to miss making her fortune? Bourdoncle, who did not dare go and disturb Mouret in his lonely isolation, was walking about amid the noise, disconsolate himself and full of misgivings.

Meanwhile, Denise went downstairs. As she was slowly reaching the bottom of the small left-hand staircase, leaning on the banisters, she came upon a group of sniggering salesmen. Her name was pronounced; she felt that they were still talking about her affair. They had not seen her.

"Nonsense; it's all put on!" Favier was saying. "She's riddled with vice... Yes, I know someone she wanted to take by force."

He was looking at Hutin who, in order to preserve his dignity as assistant buyer, was standing a few paces away, without taking part in the jokes. But he was so flattered by the look of envy with which the others were gazing at him that he deigned to murmur:

"My goodness, what a bore she was, that girl!"

Denise, cut to the heart, caught hold of the banisters. They must have seen her, for they all scattered amid laughter. He was right; she blamed herself for her ignorance in the past, when she used to dream about him. But how despicable he was, and how she despised him now! She felt deeply disturbed: it was strange that a moment ago she had found strength to repulse a man whom she adored, whereas in the past she had felt such weakness in the presence of that wretched boy, whose love she had only dreamt about! Her reason and her courage were foundering in these contradictions of her nature, which she could no longer clearly interpret. She hastened to go through the hall.

Then, while a shopwalker was opening the door which had been closed since the morning, an instinct made her raise her head, and she caught sight of Mouret. He was still at the top of the staircase, on the big central landing overlooking the gallery. But he had forgotten the stock-taking, he did not see his empire, the shop bursting with riches. Everything had disappeared – the resounding victories of yesterday, the colossal fortune of tomorrow. With a look of despair he was watching Denise, and when she had gone through the door, there was nothing left for him any more; the shop became dark.

11

O N THAT DAY BOUTHEMONT was the first to arrive at Madame Desforges's house at four o'clock for tea. She was alone, so far, in her large Louis XVI drawing room, the bronzes and brocades of which had a bright gayness; when she saw him she stood up with an air of impatience, saying as she did so:

"Well?"

"Well!" replied the young man, "when I told him that I would be sure to come and call on you, he definitely promised me he would come."

"You gave him to understand that I'm expecting the Baron today?"

"Of course... That's what seemed to make him make up his mind."

They were talking of Mouret. He had, the year before, taken a sudden liking to Bouthemont, to the extent of admitting him to his private life, and he had even introduced him into Henriette's house, being happy to have an obliging person on the spot there who slightly enlivened a liaison of which he was beginning to tire. Thus, the buyer from the silk department had finally become the confidant of his employer and of the pretty widow: he ran small errands for them, talked about one of them to the other, sometimes patched up their quarrels. Henriette, in her fits of jealousy, allowed herself a degree of intimacy with him that he had found surprising and embarrassing, for she would lose all the discretion which, as a woman of the world using all her skill to keep up appearances, she possessed.

She exclaimed violently:

"You should have brought him with you. Then I'd have been sure."

"How could I?" he said with a good-natured laugh. "It's not my fault if he escapes all the time nowadays... Oh but he's very fond of me all the same. Without him, I should be in difficulties in the shop."

Indeed, since the last stock-taking, his position at the Bonheur des Dames was precarious. In spite of his excuses that the wet weather was to blame, he was not forgiven his considerable stocks of fancy silks, and as Hutin was making the most of the affair by undermining his reputation with his superiors with redoubled crafty energy, he could very well feel the earth crumbling away beneath his feet. Mouret had condemned him, doubtless by now bored by having a witness who hindered him from breaking off his liaison and tired of profitless familiarity with him. But, following his usual technique, he was pushing Bourdoncle to the fore; it was Bourdoncle and the other directors who were demanding Bouthemont's dismissal at every meeting, whereas Mouret was holding out against them, at the risk of creating great difficulties for himself – so he said – and stoutly defending his friend.

"Well, I shall wait," Madame Desforges went on. "You know that girl should be here at five... I want to bring them face to face. I must discover their secret."

Once more she went over the plan she was contemplating; in her excitement, she repeated how she had begged Madame Aurélie to send Denise to her to look at a coat which was not right. Once she had the girl there in her room, she would easily find some way of calling Mouret – and after that she would take action.

Bouthemont, sitting facing her, was looking at her with his handsome laughing eyes, which he was trying to make look serious. The gay young fellow with his ink-black beard, a roisterer whose hot Gascon blood tinged his face with crimson, was thinking that society women had very little good in them, and that they certainly let loose a fine stream of things once they made up their minds to unbosom themselves. His friends' mistresses, who were shopgirls, certainly did not venture to make confidences in more detail.

"Come now," he ventured to say at last, "why should you worry about it? I swear to you that there's absolutely nothing between them."

"That's just it!" she exclaimed, "he loves that girl... I don't care about the others, they're just pickups, the chance encounter of a day!"

She spoke of Clara with contempt. She had in fact been told that Mouret, after Denise's refusal, had gone back once more to that big redhead with a face like a horse; probably it was a calculated move, for he kept her in the department, loading her with presents in order to draw attention to her. In any case, for almost three months now, he had been leading a terrific life of pleasure, scattering money with a lavishness which was causing comment: he had bought a house for a chorus girl of doubtful reputation, and he was being battened on by two or three other hussies at the same time, who seemed to be vying with each other in expensive and idiotic whims.

"It's that creature's fault," Henriette was repeating. "I feel he's ruining himself with the others because she's spurning him... In any case, what do I care about his money! I would have preferred him to have been poor. You who've become our friend, you know how much I love him."

She stopped, choking, on the verge of bursting into tears, and with a gesture of abandon she held out both her hands to him. It was true; she adored Mouret for his youth and his triumphs, never had a man possessed her completely like that, thrilling both her body and her pride, but with the thought of losing him she could also hear the knell of forty sounding, and she was wondering with terror how to fill the place of this great love.

"Oh! I'll have my revenge," she murmured, "I'll have my revenge if he behaves badly!"

Bouthemont found that her hands had remained in his. She was still beautiful, but she would be a nuisance as a mistress, and he did not care for that type at all. Yet it was something worth considering, it might perhaps be worthwhile risking complications.

"Why don't you set up on your own?" she said suddenly, withdrawing her hands.

He was taken aback. Then he replied:

"But one would have to have considerable capital... Last year an idea really did obsess me. I'm convinced that one could still find enough customers in Paris for one or two more big shops; only one would have to choose the district very carefully. The Bon Marché has got the Left Bank; the Louvre is in the middle; we at the Bonheur monopolize the rich districts of the west. There remains the north, where a rival to the Place Clichy could be created. And I'd discovered a superb site, near the Opéra..."

"Well?"

He began to laugh boisterously.

"Just imagine, I was silly enough to speak to my father about it. Yes, I was innocent enough to ask him to find shareholders in Toulouse."

He told her gaily about the old man's rage and how, in the depths of his little provincial shop, he was rabidly against the big Parisian stores. Bouthemont the elder, infuriated by the thirty thousand francs which his son earned, had replied that he'd rather give his money and that of his friends to charity than contribute a single penny to one of those shops, which were just the brothels of business.

"And what's more," the young man concluded, "one would need millions."

"And if they could be found?" said Madame Desforges artlessly.

He looked at her, suddenly serious. Were these just the words of a jealous woman? But without giving him time to question it, she added:

"Well, you know what an interest I take in you... We'll have to talk about it again."

The bell of the anteroom had sounded. She stood up and he, with an instinctive movement, drew his chair away, as if they might already be caught unawares. Silence reigned in the drawing room, with its gay, pleasant hangings and furnished with such a profusion of green plants that there was what looked like a miniature wood between the two windows. Standing, her ears strained towards the door, she was waiting.

"There he is," she murmured.

The servant announced:

"Monsieur Mouret, Monsieur de Vallagnosc."

She could not refrain from a gesture of anger. Why didn't he come alone? He must have gone to fetch his friend, fearing a possible tête-à-tête. Then she gave a smile and held out her hand to the two men.

"How rarely I see you nowadays! And that goes for you too, Monsieur de Vallagnosc."

Her figure was her despair, she squeezed herself into black silk dresses in order to conceal the fact that she was putting on weight. Yet her pretty head with her dark hair was still attractive and had not coarsened. Mouret was able to say to her familiarly, sweeping his eyes over her as he did so:

"There's no need to ask how you are. You're as fresh as a daisy."

"Oh! I'm too well," she replied. "In any case, I might have been dead, for all you know."

She was examining him in her turn, and thought he seemed very nervy and tired, with rings under his eyes and a livid complexion.

"Well!" she resumed in a tone which she tried to make agreeable. "I'm not going to return your flattery. You don't look at all well this evening."

"Work!" said Vallagnosc.

Mouret made a vague gesture, without replying. He had just caught sight of Bouthemont, and was nodding to him in a friendly way. During the time when they had been on very intimate terms he had been wont to carry off Bouthemont from the department himself, and take him to Henriette's in the middle of the afternoon rush hour. But times had changed, and he said to him in a low voice:

"You've sneaked out jolly early... You know, they noticed you going and they're furious in the shop."

He was talking of Bourdoncle and the other directors just as if he was not the master.

"Oh!" murmured Bouthemont uneasily.

"Yes, I want to talk to you... Wait for me, we'll leave together."

Meanwhile Henriette had sat down again, and all the time she was listening to Vallagnosc, who was telling her that Madame de Boves would probably be coming to see her, she did not take her eyes off Mouret. He was looking at the furniture and seemingly examining the ceiling, having relapsed into silence again. Then, as she was laughingly complaining that she no longer had anyone but men at her afternoon tea parties, he so far forgot himself as to let slip the phrase:

"I thought I should find Baron Hartmann here."

Henriette had grown pale. Doubtless she knew that he came to her house only in order to meet the Baron there, but he might have refrained from flinging his indifference in her face like that. Just then the door had opened, and the servant was standing before her. When she questioned him with a movement of her head, he leant down and said to her in a whisper:

"It's about that coat. Madame told me to inform her... The young lady is here."

Then she raised her voice so as to make herself heard and, working off all she had suffered from jealousy in words full of curt contempt, she said:

"Let her wait!"

"Shall I show her into Madame's dressing room?"

"No, no, let her stay in the anteroom!"

When the servant had gone out, she calmly resumed her conversation with Vallagnosc. Mouret, who had relapsed into lassitude again, had heard what she had said with half an ear, without taking it in. Bouthemont, preoccupied by the affair, was pondering. But almost immediately the door opened again, and two ladies were ushered in.

"Just fancy!" said Madame Marty, "I was getting out of the carriage when I saw Madame de Boves coming through the arcade."

"Yes," the latter explained, "the weather's good today, and as my doctor is always telling me I should walk..."

Then, after shaking hands all round, she asked Henriette:

"So you're engaging a new housemaid, are you?"

"No," she replied, astonished. "Why?"

"Well, I've just seen a girl in the anteroom who—"

Henriette laughingly interrupted her:

"Yes, isn't it funny? Shopgirls all look like housemaids... Yes, it's a girl who's come to alter a coat."

Mouret looked at her intently, with a shadow of suspicion. She went on talking with forced gaiety, describing how she had bought the coat ready-made at the Bonheur des Dames the week before.

"Why!" said Madame Marty. "So you no longer get your clothes from Sauveur?"

"Yes, my dear, I do, only I wanted to make an experiment. And then, I was quite pleased with the first thing I bought at the Bonheur, a travel coat... But this time it was not at all a success. No matter what you say, those shops of yours make one look frumpy. Oh! I don't make any bones about saying it in front of Monsieur Mouret. You'll never be able to dress a woman who's got any style about her."

Mouret was not defending his shop; his eyes were still on her, he was trying to reassure himself, telling himself that she would never dare to do such a thing. It was Bouthemont who had to defend the Bonheur.

"If all the society women who buy their clothes from us were to boast about it," he retorted gaily, "you'd be very surprised by the customers we have... Order a garment from us made to measure and it will be as good as one of Sauveur's, and it'll cost you half the price. But here you are – it's just because it's less expensive that it's less good."

"So the coat's not a success?" Madame de Boves went on. "Now I recognize the girl... It's rather dark in your anteroom."

"Yes," added Madame Marty, "I was trying to think where I'd seen that face... Well, go along my dear, do, don't stand on ceremony with us."

Henriette made a gesture of disdainful unconcern.

"Oh, later on, there's no hurry about it."

The ladies went on with their discussion about clothes from big department stores. Then Madame de Boves spoke of her husband who, she said, had just left on a tour of inspection to visit the stud farm at Saint-Lô, and Henriette just happened to be telling them how the day before Madame Guibal had had to go to the Franche-Comté because of an aunt's illness. She was not expecting Madame Bourdelais that day either, for at the end of each month she shut herself up with a seamstress so as to go through her children's clothes. Some secret anxiety, meanwhile, appeared to be worrying Madame Marty. Monsieur Marty's job at the Lycée Bonaparte was in jeopardy as a result of some lessons the poor man had been giving in some shady establishments which were doing quite a trade in baccalaureate diplomas; he frenziedly raised money where he could, in order to have enough to meet the orgies of spending which were ruining his home, and she, seeing him one evening weeping for fear of dismissal, had had the idea of using her friend Henriette's influence with a permanent undersecretary with whom she was acquainted at the Ministry of Education. Finally Henriette set her mind at rest with a few words. In any case, Monsieur Marty was going to come himself to discover his fate and to thank her.

"You look out of sorts, Monsieur Mouret," Madame de Boves observed.

"Work!" said Vallagnosc again, in his ironical, phlegmatic way.

Mouret, very sorry at having so far forgotten himself, got up briskly. He took his usual place in the midst of the ladies, regaining all his charm. Winter fashions were preoccupying him, he spoke of a large new consignment of lace. Madame de Boves questioned him about the price of Alençon point; she would perhaps buy some. She was now reduced to economizing the one franc fifty it cost for a cab, and would go home ill from having stopped to look at the shop windows. Wrapped in a coat which was already two years old, in her imagination she would drape all the expensive materials which she saw over her regal shoulders; it was just as if they had been torn off her back when she would wake to find herself dressed in her patched-up dresses, without hope of ever being able to satisfy her craving.

"Monsieur le Baron Hartmann," the servant announced.

Henriette noticed how joyfully Mouret took the newcomer's hand. The latter greeted the ladies and glanced at the young man with the shrewd look which at times lit up his coarse Alsatian face.

"Still among the frills and furbelows!" he murmured with a smile.

Then, being a friend of the family, he ventured to add:

"There's a most charming girl in the anteroom... Who is she?"

"Oh! No one," replied Madame Desforges in her unpleasant voice. "Just a shopgirl who's waiting."

As the servant was serving the tea the door remained ajar. He was going out and coming back again, putting the china cups, then plates of sandwiches and biscuits, on the pedestal table. Bright light, softened by the green plants, was illuminating the brass work in the vast drawing room, bathing the silk of the furniture in tender gaiety and, each time the door opened, a dim corner of the hall lit only by frosted glass windows could be seen. There, in the dark, a sombre form could be discerned, motionless and patient. Denise had remained standing: there was, indeed, a leather-covered seat, but pride kept her away from it. She was conscious of the insult. For half an hour she had been there, without a movement, without a word; those ladies and the Baron had stared at her in passing; bursts of conversation from the drawing room were now reaching her, she was outraged by the lack of concern of all that pleasant luxury – and still she did not move. Suddenly, through the opening of the door, she recognized Mouret. He too had guessed at her presence.

"Is it one of your salesgirls?" Baron Hartmann asked.

Mouret had succeeded in hiding his great agitation. His emotion only made his voice shake.

"Probably, but I don't know which."

"It's the little fair-haired one from the ready-made department," Madame Marty hastened to reply. "The one who is assistant buyer, I believe."

Henriette, in her turn, was looking at him.

"Ah!" he said, simply.

And he attempted to talk about the festivities in honour of the King of Prussia, who had arrived in Paris the day before. But the Baron slyly went back to the subject of girls working in large stores. He was feigning a desire for information, he was asking questions. What kind of girls were they usually? Were their morals really as bad as they were reputed to be? Quite a discussion started.

"Really," he was repeating, "you think they are decent girls?"

Mouret was defending their virtue with a conviction that was making Vallagnosc laugh. Then Bouthemont intervened, in order to save his master. My goodness! There was a bit of everything amongst them, hussies and decent girls as well. The level of their moral standard was rising, what is more. In the past in the drapery trade they had had nothing but the dregs of commerce, poor, empty-headed girls, girls who had come down in the commercial world; whereas nowadays families in the Rue de Sèvres, for example, were definitely bringing up their little girls for the Bon Marché. In short, when they wanted to behave themselves properly, they could, for unlike the working girls of the Paris streets they were not obliged to pay for their board and lodging: they were kept and fed, their existence was assured, though doubtless it was a very hard existence. What was worst of all was their neutral, ill-defined position, somewhere between shopgirls and ladies. Plunged into luxury as they were, often without initial education, they formed a nameless class apart. All their troubles and their vices were a result of that.

"As for me," said Madame de Boves, "I don't know anyone so disagreeable... One could slap them sometimes."

The ladies vented their malice. They devoured each other at the counters, woman ate woman there, in a bitter rivalry of money and beauty. The salesgirls felt disgruntled, jealous of well-dressed customers, ladies whose style they were trying to copy, and poorly-dressed customers, lower-middle-class women, felt even more sourly jealous of the salesgirls, those girls dressed all in silk from whom, when making a purchase costing a few pence, they wished to obtain the humbleness of a servant.

"No matter what you say," Henriette concluded, "all the poor wretches are for sale, like their goods!"

Mouret had the strength to smile. The Baron was studying him, touched by his efforts to master himself. Therefore he changed the conversation by once more mentioning the festivities in honour of the King of Prussia: they were superb, all Parisian business would profit from them. Henriette remained silent, and seemed to be thoughtful; she was divided between her desire to go on forgetting Denise in the hall and her fear that Mouret, now forewarned, might leave. In the end she got up from her chair.

"Will you excuse me?"

"Why of course, my dear!" said Madame Marty. "Look! I shall do the honours of your house!"

She stood up, took the teapot and filled the cups. Henriette had turned round towards Baron Hartmann.

"You'll be staying a few minutes longer, won't you?"

"Yes, I want to talk to Monsieur Mouret. We'll go and invade your small drawing room."

Then she went out, and her black silk dress rustled against the door like a snake making off through the undergrowth.

The Baron immediately manoeuvred so as to lead Mouret away, abandoning the ladies to Bouthemont and Vallagnosc. Standing by the window of the neighbouring drawing room, the Baron and Mouret chatted, lowering their voices, discussing a whole new scheme. For a long time Mouret had been cherishing the dream of realizing his old plan – the invasion of the entire block by the Bonheur des Dames, from the Rue Monsigny to the Rue de la Michodière, and from the Rue Neuve-Saint-Augustin to the Rue du Dix-Décembre. In this enormous block there was still a vast frontage on the Rue du Dix-Décembre which he did not own, and this was enough to spoil his triumph, he was tortured by the desire to complete his conquest by putting up a monumental façade there as an apotheosis. So long as the main entrance remained in the Rue Neuve-Saint-Augustin, in a dark street of ancient Paris, his work would remain shaky, would lack logic; he wanted to flaunt it before the new Paris – on one of those young avenues where, in full sunlight, there passed an ultra-modern throng; he could see it towering above everything, asserting itself as the giant palace of business, casting a bigger shadow over the town than the old Louvre did. But so far he had come up against the obstinacy of the Crédit Immobilier, which was still hanging on to its original idea of putting up a rival to the Grand Hotel all along the frontage site. The plans were ready, they were only waiting for the Rue du Dix-Décembre to be opened up in order to dig the foundations. Making a final effort, Mouret had at last almost succeeded in winning Baron Hartmann round.

"Well," the latter began, "we had a meeting yesterday, and I came here thinking I should see you, as I wanted to tell you what happened... They're still against it."

The young man allowed a gesture of irritation to escape him.

"It's unreasonable of them... What do they say?"

"My goodness! They say what I said to you myself, what I'm still inclined to think... Your façade is only a decoration, the new buildings will only increase the area of your shop by a tenth, and that means throwing away pretty considerable sums on a mere advertisement."

At that Mouret burst out:

"An advertisement! An advertisement! In any case, this one will be in stone, and it'll outlast us all. Can't you see that our business will increase tenfold! In two years we will get our money back. What does what you call a lost ground site matter, if that site brings in an enormous interest! You'll see what a crowd there'll be when our customers are no longer crammed into the Rue Neuve-Saint-Augustin, and can freely make an onslaught on us through a broad street in which six carriages will be able to travel abreast quite easily."

"Doubtless," resumed the Baron, laughing. "But you are, I repeat, a poet in your own way. These gentlemen consider that it would be dangerous to expand your business any more. They want to be prudent on your behalf."

"What! Prudence? I just don't understand... Don't the figures speak for themselves, don't they show the constant increase in our sales? First of all, with a capital of five hundred thousand francs, I had a turnover of two million. The capital was used four times over. Then it became four million, was used ten times over and produced forty million. Finally, after successive increases as a result of the last stock-taking, I've just ascertained that the turnover has now reached a total of eighty million – and the capital, which has not increased at all, for it is only six million, has therefore passed over our counters in the form of goods more than twelve times."

He was raising his voice, tapping the fingers of his right hand on his left palm, knocking off millions as if he was cracking nuts. The Baron interrupted him:

"I know, I know... But I presume you don't expect to go on increasing like that?"

"Why not?" said Mouret naively. "There's no reason why it should stop. The capital can be used fifteen times, I've been predicting it would for a long time. In certain departments it will even be used twenty-five and thirty times... and after that, well, after that we'll find a way to use it even more."

"Then you'll end by drinking the money of Paris as one drinks a glass of water?"

"Of course. Doesn't Paris belong to women, and don't the women belong to us?"

The Baron placed both his hands on his shoulders and looked at him in a fatherly way.

"Look! You're a nice lad, and I'm fond of you... One can't resist you. We're going to go into the idea seriously and I hope to be able to make them see reason. Up till now we have nothing but praise for you. The Bourse is dumbfounded by your dividends. You are probably right, it's better to put even more money into your business than to risk competition with the Grand Hotel, which would be hazardous."

Mouret's animation subsided, he thanked the Baron, but without putting his usual burst of enthusiasm into it, and the latter saw him turn his eyes towards the door of the neighbouring room, once more a prey to the secret anxiety which he was trying to hide. Meanwhile Vallagnosc, gathering that they were no longer talking business, had approached them. He was standing nearby, listening to the Baron, who was murmuring with the salacious manner of a one-time rake:

"I say, I believe they are having their revenge, aren't they?"

"Who d'you mean?" asked Mouret, embarrassed.

"Why, the women... They're tired of being in your clutches, now you're in theirs, my friend: fair exchange!"

He was joking, he knew about the young man's stormy love affairs. The mansion bought for the chorus girl and the enormous sums squandered on girls picked up in private rooms in restaurants diverted him, as if they were an excuse for the foolish things he had himself done in the past. His long experience was revelling in it.

"Really, I don't understand," Mouret was repeating.

"Ah! You understand very well. They always have the last word... That's why I used to think: it's impossible, he's just bragging, he's not as clever as that! And there you are – caught! Go on, take everything you can from Woman, exploit her like a coal mine, but in the end she'll exploit you and make you cough up! Take care, for she'll extract more blood and money from you than you'll have sucked from her."

He was laughing even more, and Vallagnosc, near him, was sniggering too, without saying anything.

"My goodness! One must try everything once, after all," Mouret confessed finally, pretending to be amused too. "Money's silly if one doesn't spend it."

"Now *that* I really approve of," the Baron went on. "Have your fun, my dear fellow. I'm not one to preach to you, nor to be anxious about the large investments we have entrusted to you... One must sow one's wild oats, one has a clearer head afterwards... And then, it's not so bad to ruin oneself when one is capable of rebuilding one's fortune again... But even if money means nothing, there are other ways of suffering, all the same..."

He stopped short, his laugh became sad, old sorrows were flitting through his ironical scepticism. He had followed the duel between Henriette and Mouret, for he was inquisitive and still fascinated by other people's amorous battles, and he fully sensed that the crisis had come, he guessed at the drama, for he knew about the story of that girl Denise, whom he had seen in the hall.

"Oh! As to suffering, that's not my line," said Mouret in a tone of bravado. "It's already quite enough to have to pay."

The Baron looked at him for a few seconds in silence. Without wishing to be too insistent, he added slowly:

"Don't try to make yourself out to be worse than you are... You'll lose something more than your money in that game... You'll lose some of your lifeblood, my friend."

He broke off, once more joking, in order to ask:

"Isn't that so? Doesn't it sometimes happen, Monsieur de Vallagnosc?"

"So they say, Monsieur le Baron," the latter declared simply.

Just at that moment, the door of the room opened. Mouret, who was about to reply, gave a slight start. The three men turned round. It was Madame Desforges, looking very gay; she merely put her head round the door, calling in a hurried voice:

"Monsieur Mouret! Monsieur Mouret!"

Then, when she caught sight of them, she said:

"Oh! Gentlemen, will you allow me to carry off Monsieur Mouret for a minute? The least he can do is to give me the benefit of his knowledge, for he's sold me an awful coat! The girl is an absolute idiot who doesn't know a thing... Come along now, I'm waiting for you."

He was hesitating, torn, recoiling from the scene which he could foresee. But he had to obey. The Baron was saying to him in his fatherly and at the same time mocking way:

"Go along, go along, do, my dear fellow. Madame wants you."

So Mouret followed her out. The door swung to again, and he thought he could hear Vallagnosc's derisive laughter, muffled by the hangings. In any case, his courage was exhausted. Ever since Henriette had left the drawing room and he had known Denise to be in jealous hands at the other end of the flat, he had been feeling a growing anxiety, nervous pangs which made him keep his ears open as if there was a distant sound of tears which made him wince with pain. What could the woman devise in order to torture her? All his love, that love which still astonished him, went out like a support and a consolation to the girl. Never had he loved anyone like that, never had he found such powerful charm in suffering. Being a man who had a busy life, the loves he had had – including Henriette herself, who was subtle and so pretty that the possession of her flattered his pride – had only been an agreeable pastime, sometimes a calculated one, in which he looked only for profitable pleasure. He would leave his mistresses' houses calm, and would go home to bed happy in his bachelor freedom, without a regret or a worry on his mind. Whereas now his heart was beating with anguish, his life had ceased to be his own, he could no longer enjoy the oblivion of sleep in his huge solitary bed. Denise possessed him all the time. Even at that moment, only she existed for him, and while he was following the other woman in fear of some distressing scene, he was thinking that he would, all the same, rather be there to protect her.

First of all they went through the bedroom, which was silent and empty. Then Madame Desforges, pushing open a door, went into the dressing room, into which Mouret followed her. It was a fairly spacious room, hung with red silk, furnished with a marble dressing table and a three-door cupboard with broad looking glasses on it. As the window looked over the courtyard, it was already dark there; and two gas jets had been lighted, their nickel-plated brackets extending on the right and left of the cupboard.

"Come now," said Henriette, "perhaps we shall get somewhere now."

On entering, Mouret had found Denise standing erect in the middle of the bright light. She was very pale, unpretentiously dressed in a cashmere jacket and with a black hat on her head, and she was holding over one arm the coat which had been bought at the Bonheur. When she saw the young man her hands shook slightly.

"I want Monsieur to give his opinion," Henriette resumed. "Help me, Mademoiselle."

Denise, drawing nearer, had to help her into the coat again. When she had tried it on the first time she had put pins in the shoulders, which did not sit properly. Henriette was turning round, studying herself in the looking glass.

"It's impossible, isn't it? Be frank."

"Indeed, you're right, it doesn't fit," said Mouret in order to cut the matter short. "It's quite simple, Mademoiselle will take your measurements and we will make you another one."

"No, I want this one, I need it immediately," she resumed hastily. "Only it's too tight across my chest – while it bags there, between the shoulders."

Then in a hard voice, she said:

"Looking at me won't make it fit any better, Mademoiselle! Come along now, think of something, find a way. It's your job."

Denise, without saying a word, began putting in pins once again. It took a long time: she had to go from one shoulder to the other; she even had to bend down, almost kneel for a moment in order to pull down the front of the coat. Madame Desforges, standing over her and passively accepting all the trouble she was taking, had the hard expression of a mistress difficult to please. Happy at having reduced the girl to this servant's task, she was giving her curt orders, watching Mouret's face for the slightest pucker of emotion as she did so.

"Put a pin here. No, no, not there, here, near the sleeve. Can't you understand? No, not like that, there – it's bagging again… And be careful, do, now you're pricking me!"

Twice more Mouret tried vainly to intervene in order to bring this scene to a close. His heart was pounding at his love's humiliation and, deeply moved by the way Denise was remaining silent, he loved her even more than he had before and was filled with tenderness for her. The girl's hand might still be trembling a little as a result of being treated like that in his presence, but she was accepting the exigencies of her calling with the proud resignation of a brave girl. When Madame Desforges had understood that they were not going to give themselves away, she tried other means, she had the idea of smiling at Mouret, of flaunting the fact that he was her lover. And so, as the pins had come to an end, she said:

"I say, darling, do look in the ivory box on the dressing table… Really, it's empty? Be a dear and go and look on the mantelpiece in the bedroom: you know, in the corner, by the looking glass."

She was showing that he was at home there, establishing him as a man who had slept there, who knew where the brushes and combs were kept. When he brought her a handful of pins he took them one by one and forced him to remain standing close to her, looking at her, talking to her in a low voice.

"I'm not hunchbacked, am I? Put your hand there, feel my shoulders, just for fun! Am I built like that?"

Slowly Denise had looked up, even paler than before, and in silence had gone on sticking the pins in again. Mouret could only see her thick fair hair twisted on the slender nape of her neck, but from the tremor which was stirring it he felt he could see the pain and mortification of her face. Now she would spurn him, she would send him back to that woman who did not even hide her liaison with him in front of strangers. And his hands itched to do something brutal, he could have beaten Henriette. How could he make her be quiet? How could he tell Denise that he adored her, that she alone existed for him at that moment, that he was sacrificing all his old loves of a day to her? A prostitute would not have taken the ambiguous liberties this lady was taking. He withdrew his hand and repeated:

"You are wrong to insist, Madame, since I myself consider that this garment is a misfit."

One of the gas jets was hissing, and in the stifling, moist air of the room nothing could be heard but this hot wheezing sound. The mirrors on the cupboard were reflecting broad patches of bright light on the red silk hangings, on which the shadows of the two women were dancing. A flask of verbena in which someone had forgotten to put back the stopper was giving off a vague, evasive smell of fading flowers.

"There, Madame, that's all I can do," said Denise at last, as she stood up.

She felt at the end of her tether. Twice, as if blinded, her eyes dim, she had dug a pin deep into her hand. Was he in the plot? Had he made her come in order to revenge himself for her refusal by showing that there were other women who loved him? This thought made her blood run cold, she could not even remember ever having had such need of courage, even during the terrible moments in her existence when she had been starving. It was really nothing to be humiliated like that, compared to seeing him practically in the arms of another woman as if she had not been there!

Henriette was inspecting herself in front of the looking glass. Once more, she broke into harsh phrases:

"It's beyond a joke, Mademoiselle. It's worse than it was before... Look how tight it is across the bosom. I look like a wet nurse."

At that Denise, her patience tried to breaking point, said something unfortunate:

"Madame is rather plump... We really can't make Madame any slimmer."

"Plump, plump," repeated Henriette who, in her turn, was growing pale. "Now you're becoming insolent, Mademoiselle... Really, I advise you not to pass personal remarks!"

Face to face, quivering, each was staring at the other. From that moment on both lady and shopgirl ceased to exist. They were no longer anything but women made equal by their rivalry. One of them had pulled the coat off violently and flung it on a chair, while the other was throwing the few pins which remained in her hand haphazard on to the dressing table.

"What surprises me," Henriette went on, "is that Monsieur Mouret tolerates such insolence... I thought, Monsieur, that you were more particular about your staff."

Denise had recovered her courageous composure. She replied gently:

"If Monsieur Mouret keeps me, it's because he has nothing to reproach me with... I am ready to apologize to you, if he insists on it."

Mouret was listening, startled by this quarrel, unable to think of a phrase to bring it to an end. He had a horror of such scenes between women, the asperity of which offended his eternal desire that everything should be graceful. Henriette wanted to drag a word from him which would condemn the girl, and as he remained silent, still hesitating, she egged him on with a final insult:

"It's a fine state of affairs, Monsieur, if I have to put up with insolence from your mistresses in my own home! A trollop picked up from the gutter!"

Two big tears welled from Denise's eyes. She had been holding them back for a long time, but the whole of her being was smarting from the insult. When he saw her weeping like that without answering back, in silent and despairing dignity, Mouret no longer hesitated; his heart went out to her with immense tenderness. He took her hands and blurted out:

"Go away quickly, my dear, forget all about this house."

Henriette, overwhelmed with amazement, choking with anger, was watching them.

"Wait," he continued, folding the coat up himself as he did so, "take back this garment. Madame will buy another one somewhere else... And don't cry any more, I beg of you. You know what a high opinion I have of you."

He accompanied her as far as the door, which he afterwards closed again. She had not said a word; only a pink flush had risen to her cheeks, while her eyes became moist with fresh tears, this time of delicious sweetness.

Henriette, choking, had taken out her handkerchief and was crushing it to her lips. All her plans had been reversed, she herself was caught in the trap she had laid. She was distraught at having gone too far, tortured by jealousy. To be left for a creature like that! Her pride was suffering more than her love.

"So that's the girl you love?" she said painfully when they were alone.

Mouret did not reply at once, he was walking up and down from the window to the door, trying to conquer his violent emotion. At last he stood still and, very politely, in a voice which he was trying to make cold, he said simply:

"Yes, Madame."

The gas jet was hissing in the stifling atmosphere of the dressing room. Dancing shadows were now no longer passing across the reflections in the looking glasses, the room seemed bare and had subsided into a sadness which was oppressive. Suddenly Henriette gave way to despair. She flung herself into a chair, twisting her handkerchief between her feverish fingers and repeating between her sobs:

"Oh God! How wretched I am!"

Motionless he looked at her for a few seconds. Then he calmly went away. Left alone, she wept amidst silence, with the pins strewn over the dressing table and floor in front of her.

When Mouret went back into the small drawing room, he found no one there but Vallagnosc, for the Baron had gone back to the ladies. As he was still feeling very shaken, he sat down at the end of the room on a sofa, and his friend, seeing how shattered he was, charitably came and planted himself in front of him so as to hide him from prying glances. At first they looked at each other without exchanging a word. Then Vallagnosc, who seemed inwardly amused by Mouret's agitation, finally asked in his bantering voice:

"Having a good time?"

Mouret did not seem to understand at first. But when he had remembered their conversations in the past about the empty stupidity and the pointless torture of life he replied:

"Certainly, I've never lived to such an extent... Ah! Don't make fun of it, old fellow, these moments when one is killed by suffering are the briefest ones of all!"

He lowered his voice and, with tears in his eyes which he had not properly wiped away, he went on gaily:

"Yes, you know all about it, don't you? They've just been mangling my heart, the two of them. But it's still all right, you know, the wounds they make are almost as good as caresses... I'm crushed, I'm at the end of my tether; it doesn't matter, you'd never believe how much I love life! Oh! I'll get her in the end, that little thing who'll have none of me..."

Vallagnosc said simply:

"And then?"

"Then? Why, I'll have her! Isn't that enough? If you think you're clever just because you refuse to be silly and to suffer! You're just gullible, that's all! You just try wanting a woman and getting her in the end; in one minute that makes up for all the unhappiness."

But Vallagnosc was making much of his pessimism. What was the good of working so hard, since money could not buy everything? If it had been him, on the day when he realized that when one had millions one could not even buy the woman one desired, he would have shut up shop and stretched himself out full length on his back without lifting a little finger any more. Listening to him, Mouret became serious. Then he retorted violently, for he believed in the omnipotence of his will.

"I want her, and I'll get her! And if she escapes me, you'll see what machinery I'll build up to cure myself. All the same, it'll be superb! You don't understand this language, old fellow: otherwise you'd know that action contains its own reward. Acting, creating, fighting against facts, overcoming them or being overcome by them – the whole of human health and happiness is made up of that!"

"It's an easy way of drowning one's sorrow," murmured the other.

"Well, I'd rather drown my sorrow… If one's got to die anyway, I'd rather die of passion than die of boredom!"

They both laughed, it reminded them of their old arguments at school. Then Vallagnosc, in a lifeless voice, went on to say how platitudinous everything was, taking a certain pleasure in doing so. The stagnancy and negativeness of his existence were almost a subject of boasting for him. Yes, the next day he would be bored at the ministry, as he had been bored the day before. In three years his salary had gone up by six hundred francs, he was now getting three thousand six hundred, not enough even to smoke decent cigarettes on; it was getting more and more idiotic, and if he didn't kill himself it was simply from laziness, to save himself the trouble. When Mouret mentioned his marriage with Mademoiselle de Boves, he replied that, in spite of his aunt's determination not to die, it was going to come off all the same – at any rate, so he thought, the parents were agreed to it, and he pretended not to have any will of his own. Why want something or not want it, as things never turned out as one desires? He quoted as an example his future father-in-law, who thought he had found in Madame Guibal an indolent blonde, the caprice of an hour, and who instead was driven along at the point of the whip by the lady, like an old horse on which one uses up the last remnants of strength. While people thought he was busy inspecting the stud farms at Saint-Lô, she was finishing devouring him in a little house which he had rented at Versailles.

"He's happier than you are," said Mouret, getting up.

"Oh! Certainly he is!" declared Vallagnosc. "Perhaps it's only doing wrong that's rather fun."

Mouret had recovered. He was longing to escape, but did not wish his departure to look like flight. Therefore, resolved to have a cup of tea, he and his friend went back into the large drawing room, both of them joking as they did so. Baron Hartmann asked him if the coat was all right now, and without turning a hair Mouret replied that so far as he was concerned, he had given it up as a bad job. At that, there were exclamations. While Madame Marty was hastening to pour out for him, Madame de Boves was accusing the shops of always having clothes that were too tight. In the end he was able to sit down beside Bouthemont, who was still there. They were soon forgotten by the ladies; in reply to the anxious questions of Bouthemont, who wanted to know his fate, he did not wait till they were outside in the street, but informed him at once that the gentlemen on the board had decided to dispense with his services. Between each sentence he took a sip of tea, protesting how sorry he was as he did so. Oh, there had been a quarrel from which he had scarcely recovered, for he had left the room beside himself with rage. Only what could he do? He couldn't break with those gentlemen just over a question of staff. Bouthemont, very pale, was even obliged to thank him.

"What a terrible coat it must be," pointed out Madame Marty. "Henriette is still at it."

Indeed, her prolonged absence was beginning to make everyone feel embarrassed. But at that very moment Madame Desforges reappeared.

"You're giving it up as a bad job too?" exclaimed Madame de Boves gaily.

"How so?"

Henriette displayed the greatest surprise.

"Yes, Monsieur Mouret told us that you couldn't do anything with it."

"Monsieur Mouret was joking. The coat will be perfectly all right."

She seemed very calm, all smiles. Doubtless she had bathed her eyelids, for they were quite fresh, without a trace of redness. Although the whole of her being was still quivering and bleeding, she found the strength to hide her torment beneath the mask of her society charm. When she offered some sandwiches to Vallagnosc, she did so with her customary laugh. Only the Baron, who knew her well, noticed the slight contraction of her lips and the melancholy fire which she had not been able to extinguish in the depths of her eyes. He could picture the whole scene.

"My goodness! Everyone to his own taste," Madame de Boves was saying, as she too accepted a sandwich. "I know women who wouldn't even buy a ribbon anywhere but at the Louvre. Others swear only by the Bon Marché... No doubt it's a question of temperament."

"The Bon Marché is frightfully provincial," murmured Madame Marty, "and one gets so jostled at the Louvre!"

The ladies had reverted to the subject of the big stores, Mouret had to give his opinion; he came back in their midst pretending to be impartial. What an excellent shop the Bon Marché was, reliable and respectable, but the Louvre was certainly frequented by smarter people.

"In fact, you prefer the Bonheur des Dames," said the Baron, smiling.

"Yes," Mouret replied calmly, "in our shop we like customers."

All the women present were of his opinion. That was what it really was, at the Bonheur it was as if they were at a gay, intimate party; when there, they felt they were ceaselessly courted with flattery and showered with adoration which captivated even the most virtuous. The shop's enormous success came from the seductive way it paid court to them.

"By the way," asked Henriette, wishing to appear very detached, "what about my protégée, what are you doing with her, Monsieur Mouret? You know, Mademoiselle de Fontenailles."

And turning towards Madame Marty she said:

"A marchioness, my dear, a poor girl who's found herself in reduced circumstances."

"Why," said Mouret, "she earns her three francs a day sewing pattern books together, and I think I'm going to marry her off to one of my porters."

"For shame! What a horrible idea!" exclaimed Madame de Boves.

He looked at her, then went on in his calm voice:

"What's so horrible about it, Madame? Isn't it better for her to marry a decent lad, a hard worker, rather than run the risk of being picked up by idlers in the street?"

Vallagnosc jokingly tried to interrupt.

"Don't encourage him, Madame. He'll tell you that all the old families of France should start selling calico."

"But," Mouret declared, "for many of them it would at least be an honourable end."

In the end they all laughed, the paradox seemed really too outrageous. He, however, went on extolling what he called the aristocracy of labour. A slight blush had tinged the cheeks of Madame de Boves, who was maddened by her straitened circumstances which reduced her to having to resort to expedient measures; whereas Madame Marty, on the contrary, seized with remorse at the thought of her poor husband, was full of approval. Just then the servant announced the teacher, who had come to fetch her. In his thin and shiny frock coat he looked gaunter than ever, even more dried up by his hard work. When he had thanked Madame Desforges for having mentioned him to the Minister, he cast at Mouret the apprehensive glance of a man faced with the disease of which he will die. He was surprised to hear the latter addressing him:

"Isn't it so, Monsieur, that work can achieve everything?"

His whole body gave a shudder as he replied:

"Work and economy – you must add economy, Monsieur."

Bouthemont, meanwhile had remained motionless in his chair. Mouret's words were still ringing in his ears. Finally he got up and went to tell Henriette in an undertone:

"You know he's given me notice – oh in a very nice way! – but I'll be damned if he won't regret it! I've just thought of a name for my shop: Aux Quatre Saisons,* and I'll take up my position near the Opéra!"

She looked at him and her eyes darkened.

"Count on me, I'm with you... Wait a moment."

She drew Baron Hartmann into a window recess. Without further ado she commended Bouthemont to him, presenting him as a bright young fellow who in his turn was going to revolutionize Paris by setting up in business on his own. When she spoke of an investment of capital for her new protégé, the Baron, although he was no longer surprised at anything, could not refrain from a gesture of dismay. This was the fourth young man of genius she was putting under his wing and he was beginning to feel ridiculous. He did not refuse outright, the idea of creating competition to the Bonheur des Dames quite appealed to him even, for he had already, in banking, had the idea of thus creating competition to himself in order to discourage other people from doing so. Besides, the affair amused him. He promised to look into it.

"We must talk about it this evening," Henriette came back to whisper in Bouthemont's ear. "At about nine o'clock, don't forget... The Baron is on our side."

At that moment the vast room was filled with voices. Mouret, still standing in the midst of ladies, had regained his composure: he was gaily defending himself for ruining them with frills and furbelows, offering to demonstrate with figures that he was making them save thirty per cent on all their purchases. Baron Hartmann was looking at him, once more overcome with the fraternal admiration of one who had himself frequented night haunts in the past. Well, so the duel was over, Henriette was overthrown, she would certainly not be the woman who must come to avenge the others. And he seemed to see once more the unostentatious profile of the girl he had glimpsed when passing through the hall. There she was, patiently waiting, and in her gentleness she was the only one who was formidable.

12

ON SEPTEMBER 25TH work was started on the new façade of the Bonheur des Dames. True to his promise, Baron Hartmann had carried the day at the last general meeting of the Crédit Immobilier. Mouret was at last within reach of realizing his dream: this frontage, which was going to spread all along the Rue du Dix-Décembre, seemed the very blossoming of his fortune.

Therefore he wanted to celebrate the laying of the foundation stone. He made a ceremony out of it, distributed bonuses to his salesmen and gave them game and champagne for dinner. People noticed his happy mood on the building site, and his victorious gesture as he cemented the stone with a stroke of the trowel. For weeks he had been worried, troubled by nervous anxiety which he did not always succeed in hiding; this triumph of his brought a respite to his unhappiness and took his mind off it. All that afternoon he seemed to have reverted to the gayness of a man in good fettle. But, from dinner onwards, when he went through the dining room in order to drink a glass of champagne with his staff, he once more looked feverish, he was smiling painfully and his features were drawn with the sickness which was gnawing at him and which he would not acknowledge. He had had a relapse.

Next day, in the ready-made department, Clara Prunaire did her best to be disagreeable to Denise. She had noticed Colomban's bashful love for her, and had taken it into her head to poke fun at the Baudus. She said in a loud voice to Marguerite, who was sharpening her pencil while waiting for customers:

"You know my sweetheart opposite... In the end I feel quite distressed about him, in that dark shop which no one ever goes into."

"He's not so badly off really," Marguerite replied. "He's supposed to marry his employer's daughter."

"Really?" Clara went on. "Then what fun it would be to steal him! I'll do it for a joke, honestly I will!"

She went on in that strain, delighted to feel that Denise was shocked. The latter forgave her immediately, but the thought of her dying cousin Geneviève being finished off by cruelty of that sort made her beside herself with rage. Just then a customer appeared, and as Madame Aurélie had gone down to the basement, Denise took charge of the department and summoned Clara.

"Mademoiselle Prunaire, you'd do better to see to this lady rather than chatting."

"I wasn't chatting."

"Please be quiet and see to Madame immediately."

Clara gave in, beaten. When Denise showed her strength like that, without raising her voice, no one could stand up to her. By her very gentleness she had won absolute authority for herself.

For a moment she walked in silence in the midst of the girls, who had become straight-faced. Marguerite had gone back to sharpening her pencil, the lead of which kept on breaking. She alone still approved of the assistant buyer not giving way to Mouret and, without owning up to the child she had had by mistake, she would nevertheless toss her head and declare that if people had any idea of the trouble caused by a piece of folly of that sort they would rather behave themselves.

"Are you losing your temper?" said a voice behind Denise.

It was Pauline, who was passing through the department. She had witnessed the scene, and was talking in a low voice, smiling as she did so.

"I really have to," Denise replied in the same way. "I can't manage my youngsters otherwise."

The girl from the lingerie department shrugged her shoulders.

"Go on with you, you'll be the queen of us all whenever you want to be."

She still could not understand her friend's refusal. At the end of August she had married Baugé, a really silly thing to do, as she herself was wont to say gaily. The terrifying Bourdoncle now treated her as if she was a dud, a woman lost to business. Her dread was that one fine day they would be sent away to love each other outside, for the gentlemen on the board decreed that love was deplorable and fatal to sales. Things had reached such a pitch that when she met Baugé in one of the galleries she would pretend not to know him. She had just had a close call; old Jouve had nearly caught her talking to her husband behind a pile of dusters.

"Look! He's followed me," she added, after having quickly described the incident to Denise. "Just look at him smelling me out with his big nose!"

Jouve, very spick and span in his white tie and his nose on the scent of some crime or other, was in fact just coming out of the lace department. But when he caught sight of Denise, he preened himself and went by with a kindly air.

"Saved!" murmured Pauline. "My dear, it's you who made him keep his mouth shut… I say, if I got into trouble, would you put a word in for me? Yes, yes, don't put on that astonished look, everyone knows that a word from you could revolutionize the shop."

She hurried back to her department. Denise had blushed, upset by these friendly insinuations. It was true, what was more. The flattery with which she was surrounded gave her some vague idea of her power. When Madame Aurélie came upstairs again and found the department peaceful and busy under the assistant buyer's supervision, she gave her a friendly smile. The buyer was even dropping Mouret himself, every day her friendliness was increasing towards the person who could, one fine day, aspire to her job of buyer. The reign of Denise was beginning.

Bourdoncle alone was not disarmed. The secret war which he was continuing to wage against the girl was based first and foremost on a natural antipathy. He detested her for her gentleness and charm. He also fought her as a baneful influence which would endanger the shop on the day when Mouret should succumb. It seemed to him that his master's business faculties must founder in the midst of such idiotic love; what had been won through women would be lost through that woman. All women left him cold, he treated them with the disdain of a frigid man whose profession it was to live on them and who, seeing them unmercifully stripped by his trade, had lost his last illusions. Instead of intoxicating him, the odour of seventy thousand female customers gave him unbearable sick headaches: as soon as he got home, he would beat his mistresses. And what worried him above all about this little salesgirl, who had little by little become so formidable, was the fact that he did not at all believe that she was disinterested, nor did he believe in the sincerity of her refusals. So far as he was concerned, she was playing a part, an extremely artful part, what is more, for if she had succumbed on the first day, Mouret would doubtless have forgotten her on the next; whereas by refusing she had whetted his desire, she was driving him mad, making him capable of all kinds of folly. A profligate, a prostitute steeped in vice would have acted no differently to this innocent girl. Therefore Bourdoncle had only to see her with her clear eyes, her gentle face and all her simple ways, to be seized now with real fear, as if faced by a vampire in disguise, the dark enigma of woman, death disguised as a virgin. How could he foil the tactics of this spurious ingénue? He no longer thought of anything except how to see through her stratagems, in the hope of unmasking them publicly; she was sure to make some mistake, he would catch her with one of her lovers and she would be turned out again, the shop would at last resume its smooth running of a well-made machine.

"Keep on the lookout, Monsieur Jouve," Bourdoncle would repeat to the inspector. "I'll reward you personally."

But Jouve went about it with a certain amount of indolence, for he knew something about women and was contemplating putting himself on the side of the child who might become the sovereign mistress of tomorrow. Even if he no longer dared touch her, he considered her infernally pretty. In the past a colonel of his had killed himself for a kid like that with a vacuous face, refined and modest, a single glance from whom could play havoc with hearts.

"I'm on the lookout, I'm on the lookout," he would reply. "But I can't discover a thing, word of honour!"

Yet there were stories going the rounds; beneath the flattery and respect which Denise could feel rising around her there was an undercurrent of foul gossip. By now the whole shop was recounting how in the past Hutin had been her lover; no one dared assert that the liaison still continued, but they were suspected of seeing each other from time to time. And Deloche was sleeping with her too: they were always meeting each other in dark corners, they used to chat together for hours. It was a real scandal!

"Well, you've got nothing on the buyer in the silk department, nothing on the young man in the lace department?" Bourdoncle would repeat.

"No, Monsieur, nothing so far," the inspector would aver.

It was above all with Deloche that Bourdoncle reckoned on catching out Denise. One morning he himself had caught sight of them laughing together in the basement. In the meantime, he treated the girl as one power treats another, for he no longer turned up his nose at her, he sensed that she was sufficiently powerful to overthrow him himself, in spite of his ten years' service, if he should lose the game.

"I commend the young man in the lace department to your attention," he would conclude each time. "They're always together. If you catch them, call me, and I'll deal with the rest."

Mouret, meanwhile, was living in agonies. How could that child torture him to such an extent? All the time he could picture her again, arriving at the Bonheur with her clumping shoes, her skimpy dress and her retiring air. She had fumbled for her words, everyone had laughed at her, he himself had thought her ugly at first. Ugly! And now with a glance she could have made him go down on his knees, he could only see her surrounded with radiance! Then she had been the lowest of the low in the shop, rebuffed, teased, treated by him like a strange animal. For months he had wanted to see how a girl would develop, he had amused himself with this experiment, without understanding that in so doing he was staking his heart. Little by little she had been growing, becoming formidable. Perhaps he had loved her from the very first minute, even at the time when he thought he felt only pity. Yet it had only been on the evening of their walk beneath the chestnut trees in the Tuileries that he had felt he belonged to her. His life had started from that moment; he could hear the laughter of a group of little girls, the distant trickle of a fountain, while she walked close beside him through the sultry shade in silence. From then on he had been at a complete loss, his fever had increased from hour to hour, his very lifeblood, the whole of his being was involved. A child like that – could it be true? Nowadays when she passed by the slight wind from her dress seemed to him so strong that it made him reel.

For a long time he had rebelled against it, and sometimes still it would make his blood boil, he wanted to break free from this idiotic obsession. What was there about her, after all, to enslave him like that? Had he not seen her in clogs? Had she not been taken on almost out of charity? If at least it had been a question of one of those superb creatures who draw the crowd! But that little girl, that little nobody! She had, in short, one of those sheeplike faces about which there was nothing to be said. She probably was not even very quick in the uptake, for he could remember what a bad start she had made as a salesgirl. Then after each bout of anger he would revert to his former passion, as if filled with holy terror at having insulted his idol. She supplied all the good to be found in women – courage, gaiety, simplicity – and her gentleness exuded a charm with the penetrating subtlety of perfume. One could ignore her, jostle her as if she was just anyone, but soon the charm would begin to take effect with a force which was slow but invincible; if she deigned to smile, one was hers for life. Then the whole of her pale face – her periwinkle eyes, her cheeks and her chin pitted with dimples – would smile, while her heavy fair hair seemed to light up too with a regal, all-conquering beauty. He would confess himself vanquished, she was as intelligent as she was beautiful, her intelligence came from all that was best in her. Whereas the other salesgirls in his shop had only a smattering of education, the peeling varnish of girls who have come down in the world, she without any false smartness retained the charm and savour of her origins. Behind her forehead, the pure lines of which gave proof of willpower and love of order, extremely liberal commercial ideas were being born of experience. He was ready to implore her on bended knee to forgive him for blaspheming in his moments of rebellion.

But why did she refuse with such obstinacy to yield? Twenty times had he implored her, increasing his offers, offering money, a great deal of money. Then he had told himself that she must be very ambitious, and had promised to make her buyer as soon as a department should be vacant. Yet she refused, she still refused! It was an amazement to him, a struggle which maddened his desire. The whole thing seemed impossible to him, the girl must capitulate in the end, for he had always considered a woman's virtue as a relative thing. He could no longer see any other objective, everything else disappeared in the sole desire to get her in his own house at last, to take her on his knee, kissing her on the lips – and at this vision the blood would throb in his veins and he would remain trembling, bowled over in his powerlessness.

From then on his days passed in the same painful obsession. The picture of Denise got up with him in the morning. He had dreamt of her during the night, she followed him to the big desk in his office where, from nine till ten, he signed bills and money orders – a task which he performed mechanically, without ceasing to feel that she was there, still saying no in her unruffled way. Then at ten o'clock there was the board meeting, a real cabinet meeting, at which the twelve people with a financial interest in the shop met and at which he had to preside: questions of internal organization were discussed, purchases were inspected, displays were decided on – and she was still there, he could hear her gentle voice amidst the figures, he could see her limpid smile through the most complicated financial discussions. After the board meeting she accompanied him, she made the daily inspection of the departments with him, and in the afternoon she came back with him to the manager's office and remained near his chair from two to four, when he saw a whole crowd of people – manufacturers from all over France, big businessmen, bankers, inventors; there was a continuous coming and going of money and brains, a crazy dance of millions of francs, rapid interviews at which the biggest deals on the Paris market were hatched. If he forgot her for a minute while deciding on the ruin or the prosperity of an industry, a twinge in his heart would remind him that she was still standing there, his voice would die away, he would ask himself what was the good of handling such a fortune if she would not yield. Finally, when five o'clock struck, he had to sign the mail, his hand once more began to work mechanically, while she would rise up more dominating than ever, taking him over completely in order that she alone might possess him during the solitary, passionate hours of the night. And the following day, the same programme would begin all over again, another of those days which were so busy, so full of immense labour, and which the mere slender shadow of a girl could sear with anguish.

But it was during his daily tour of inspection of the shop that he felt his misery most. To have built that gigantic machine, to reign over so many people and to be in agonies of suffering because a little girl would have none of him! He despised himself, he was dogged by the fever and shame of his malady. On some days a disgust for his power would seize him, going from one end of the galleries to the other he felt nothing but nausea. At other times he would have liked to extend his empire, to make it so huge that she might perhaps capitulate from admiration and fear.

First of all, downstairs in the basement, he would stop by the chute. It was still in the Rue Neuve-Saint-Augustin, but it had had to be enlarged; it was now a riverbed through which a continual flow of goods rolled with the loud voice of a flood tide; there were deliveries from every part of the world, queues of wagons from all the stations ceaselessly unloading a stream of packing cases and bales which, flowing underground, were being drunk up by the insatiable shop. He watched this torrent falling into his shop, he reflected that he was one of the masters of public wealth, that he held the future of the French textile industry in his hands, and yet he could not buy a kiss from one of his salesgirls.

Then he moved on to the receiving department, which now occupied that part of the basement which ran along the Rue Monsigny. In the pale light from the ventilators twenty tables were laid out; a whole tribe of assistants was hustling about there, emptying the packing cases, checking the goods, marking the prices on them, the roar of the nearby chute could be heard without respite, rising above the voices. Section managers would stop him, he had to clear up difficulties, confirm orders. The depths of the cellar were filling up with the delicate radiance of satins and the whiteness of linen, with a stupendous unpacking in which furs were mixed with lace, and fancy goods with oriental door curtains. Slowly he walked through these riches, strewn in disorder, piled up in their raw state. They would go upstairs and take fire from the displays, they would let a rush of money loose through the departments, no sooner were they taken upstairs than they were carried away in the mad flow of selling which swept through the shop. And he was thinking how he had offered the girl silks by the handful, velvets, whatever she wanted to take from those enormous heaps, and how she had refused with a little sign of her fair head.

Next he would go as usual to the other end of the basement in order to have a look at the dispatch department. Endless corridors stretched out, lit by gas; to the right and left the stockrooms, shut off by screens, were dozing in the darkness like subterranean shops, a whole commercial district of shops selling haberdashery, underwear, gloves and knick-knacks. Further on there was one of the three heating installations; further on still a firemen's post was guarding the central gasometer, enclosed in its metal cage. In the dispatch department he found the sorting tables already littered with loads of parcels, bandboxes and cardboard boxes, which were continually being brought down in baskets, and Campion, the head of the department, told him about the work in hand, while the twenty men under his command were distributing the parcels in compartments each bearing the name of one of the districts of Paris, from which porters subsequently took them up to the vehicles drawn up all along the pavement. People were calling out, names of streets were bandied about, instructions were shouted, there was all the din and excitement of a steamer about to weigh anchor. He remained there for a moment, motionless, watching the goods, on which he had just seen the shop gorging itself at the opposite end of the basement, being disgorged in front of him: the enormous stream came to an end there and went out from there into the street, after having lined the tills with gold. His eyes were becoming blurred; this colossal dispatch of goods no longer had any importance; he was left with nothing but the idea of travelling, the idea of going away to far countries, of abandoning everything, if she persisted in saying no.

Then he went upstairs again and continued his rounds, talking and getting more and more excited without being able to take his mind off his troubles. On the second floor he inspected the forwarding departments, picking quarrels and secretly getting exasperated by the perfect running of the machine which he had himself regulated. This was the department which from day to day was acquiring the greatest importance: by now it needed a staff of two hundred employees, of which some were opening, reading and sorting letters from the provinces and from abroad, while others were assembling in bins the goods required by the people who had sent the letters. The number of letters was increasing to such an extent that they were no longer counted; they were weighed, and up to a hundred pounds of them arrived a day. Mouret was going feverishly through the rooms occupied by the department, questioning Levasseur, who was in charge, about the weight of the mail: eighty pounds, ninety pounds, sometimes a hundred on Mondays. The figure was still rising, he should have been delighted. But he stood shuddering in the din which a nearby team of packers was making, nailing up packing cases. He was tramping the shop in vain: his obsession was still staring him in the face and, as his power was unfolded before him, as the mechanism of the department and the army of his staff processed past him, he felt the indignity of his powerlessness even more deeply. Orders from the whole of Europe were flowing in; a special mail van was necessary to bring all the letters – and she said no, she still said no.

He went downstairs again and inspected the main counting house, where four cashiers were guarding the two giant safes through which, in the preceding year, eighty-eight million francs had passed. He glanced at the office where the invoices were checked, which kept twenty-five specially picked, reliable employees busy. He went into the staff accounts office, a department consisting of thirty-five young men, beginners at accountancy, who had to check the debit notes and calculate the salesmen's percentages. He came back to the main counting house, grew irritated at the sight of the safes, as he walked amidst those millions, the uselessness of which was driving him mad. She still said no, always no.

Always no, in every department, in the sales galleries, throughout the shop! He would go from the silks to the drapery, from the household linens to the lace; he went upstairs, he would stop on the suspension bridges, prolonging his inspection with a maniacal and painful attention to minute detail. The shop had grown beyond measure, he had created department after department, he governed this new domain and was busy extending his empire to some fresh industries, the last to be conquered – and yet it was no, still no. Nowadays his staff would have peopled a small town: there were fifteen hundred salesmen, a thousand other employees of every kind, including forty shopwalkers and seventy cashiers; the kitchens alone kept thirty-six men busy. There were ten assistants for publicity, three hundred and fifty porters wearing livery, twenty-four resident firemen. And, in the stables, truly regal stables opposite the shop in the Rue Monsigny, there were a hundred and forty-five horses, magnificent teams which had already made a name. The four original vehicles which had so agitated the tradesmen of the district in the past, when the shop still only occupied one corner of the Place Gaillon, had gradually increased in number to sixty-two: there were small handcarts, one-horse cabs, heavy wagons drawn by two horses. They were ploughing through Paris continually, bearing the gold-and-purple emblem of the Bonheur des Dames on their sides, and decorously driven by coachmen dressed in black. They would even go outside the city walls, they visited the suburbs; they were met with in the empty byways of Bicêtre, all along the banks of the Marne, even beneath the shady trees of the forest of Saint-Germain; sometimes, from the depths of some sunny avenue miles from anywhere, in the midst of silence, one would suddenly see one of them loom into sight, passing by with its superb animals at the trot, flinging the violent advertisement of its varnished panels over the mysterious peace of noble nature. He dreamt of sending them even further afield into adjacent counties; he would have liked to hear them rattling over all the roads of France, from one frontier to the other. But he no longer even went to visit his horses, which he adored. What was the good of conquering the world like that, since it was no, still no?

Nowadays in the evening, when he reached Lhomme's cash desk he would still from habit look at the figure of the takings, written on a card which the cashier stuck on an iron spike at his side; rarely did the figure fall below a hundred thousand francs, sometimes it rose to eight or nine hundred thousand on days when there were special displays – but this figure no longer rang in his ears like a trumpet call, he would regret having looked at it, it left him with a feeling of bitterness, of hatred and contempt for money.

But Mouret's sufferings were to become even more acute. He became jealous. One morning, in the study before the board meeting, Bourdoncle ventured to hint to him that that slip of a girl in the ready-made department was making a fool of him.

"What d'you mean?" he asked, very pale.

"Why, yes! She has lovers right here in the shop."

Mouret had the strength to smile.

"I don't think about her any more, old chap. You can go ahead and talk about it... Who are they then, her lovers?"

"Hutin, so they assure me, and also a salesman in the lace department, Deloche, that big, stupid lad... I can't vouch for it, I haven't seen them. Only apparently it's as plain as a pikestaff!"

There was a silence. Mouret pretended to arrange the papers on his desk so as to hide the trembling of his hands. Finally, without looking up, he said:

"One must have proof, try and get me some proof... Oh, so far as I'm concerned, as I told you, I don't give a damn, in the end she got on my nerves. But we can't allow things like that in the shop."

Bourdoncle simply replied:

"Don't worry, you'll have proof one of these days. I'm on the lookout."

After that Mouret finally lost the remnants of his peace of mind. He no longer had the courage to bring this conversation up again, and he lived in continuous expectation of a catastrophe which would shatter his heart. And his anguish made him terrifying, the whole shop trembled. He now scorned to hide behind Bourdoncle and, having a febrile urge to be spiteful, he would carry out executions himself and relieve his feelings by abusing his power – that power which could do nothing to satisfy his only desire. Each time he made a tour of inspection it developed into a massacre; no sooner did he appear than a shudder of panic spread from counter to counter. It was just at the beginning of the winter slack season, and he made a clean sweep of the departments, piling up victims and pushing them all out into the street. His first thought had been to get rid of Hutin and Deloche; then he had reflected that if he did not keep them he would never discover anything, and so others suffered in their stead, the whole staff was threatened. In the evening, when he was alone again, his eyes would fill with tears.

One day, in particular, terror reigned. A shopwalker thought he had seen Mignot, the glover, stealing. There were always girls of dubious aspect prowling around his counter, and one of them had just been arrested, her hips festooned and her bosom stuffed with sixty pairs of gloves. From then on watch was kept, and the shopwalker caught Mignot red-handed, facilitating the sleight of hand of a tall blonde girl, a former salesgirl at the Louvre who had ended up on the street. The tactics were simple: he would pretend to be trying gloves on her, waiting until she had loaded herself up, and would then conduct her to a cash desk where she would pay for one pair of gloves. It so happened that Mouret was there when this happened. Usually he preferred not to become involved in incidents of this kind, which were frequent, for although it ran like a well-oiled machine, great disorder did reign in certain departments of the Bonheur des Dames, and not a week passed without an employee being dismissed for stealing. Even the management preferred to surround these thefts with the maximum possible silence, they considered it pointless to call in the police, for by so doing they would have been exposing one of the fatal weaknesses of big stores. Only on that particular day Mouret had an urge to lose his temper, and he dealt violently with handsome Mignot who, his face pale and drawn, was trembling with fright.

"I ought to call a policeman," Mouret was shouting, surrounded by the other salesmen. "Answer me! Who is this woman? I swear I'll send for the police if you don't tell me the truth."

The woman had been led away, two salesgirls were undressing her. Mignot stammered:

"Monsieur, I've never seen her apart from this... It's she who came—"

"Don't you dare lie to me!" Mouret interrupted with redoubled violence. "And there's no one here to warn us even! You're all just as bad, upon my word! We're in a regular den of thieves, robbed, pillaged, looted! It's enough to make one have everyone's pockets searched before they leave!"

There were audible murmurs. The three or four customers who were buying gloves were dismayed.

"Silence!" he went on furiously, "or I'll clear the shop!"

But Bourdoncle had rushed up, worried at the prospect of a scandal. He murmured a few words into Mouret's ear, the affair was taking an exceptionally serious turn, and he persuaded him to take Mignot into the shopwalker's office, a room situated on the ground floor near the Gaillon door. The woman was there, calmly putting her corset on again. She had just mentioned the name of Albert Lhomme. Mignot, questioned afresh, lost his head and sobbed: he was not to blame, it was Albert who sent his mistresses to him. At first he had just given them preferential treatment, he had let them benefit from bargains; then, when they had ended up stealing, he was already too deeply implicated to inform the management. Then the gentlemen learnt of a whole series of extraordinary thefts: how goods were carried off by prostitutes who went and attached them beneath their petticoats in the sumptuous lavatories which were installed near the buffet, surrounded by green plants; how a salesman would omit to call out a sale at a cash desk when he was conducting a customer there, and how he would share the price of it with the cashier; how there were even false "returns", goods which were given out to have been sent back to the shop, so that the money which had been fictitiously refunded could be pocketed; not to mention the oldest dodge of all, how parcels were taken out of the shop in the evening beneath an overcoat, twisted round a waist, or sometimes even hanging down someone's thighs. Thus, thanks to Mignot and doubtless to other salesmen whom he refused to name, Albert's cash desk had been a regular thieves' kitchen for fourteen months, a really shameless state of affairs, and the exact figure of the sums involved was never known.

Meanwhile, the news had spread through the departments. Uneasy consciences were all atremble, and even those who were quite sure of their own integrity stood in dread of the clean sweep which was being made. Albert had been seen disappearing into the shopwalkers' office. Then Lhomme had gone in, red in the face, already choking with apoplexy. Next, Madame Aurélie herself had been summoned; she was holding her head high in her shame and looking pale, with the flabby puffiness of a wax mask. The altercation lasted a long time, no one knew what happened exactly: it was said that the buyer from the ready-made department had slapped her son's face so hard that she'd made his head spin, and that his poor old father had wept; while the director, abandoning all his usual graciousness and swearing like a bargee, had been insisting on handing over the guilty parties to justice. However, the scandal was hushed up. Only Mignot was dismissed on the spot. Albert did not disappear until two days later; doubtless his mother had obtained a promise that the family should not be dishonoured by an immediate execution. But after the scene panic had reigned for several days more; Mouret had walked from one end of the shop to the other with a terrifying look in his eye, mowing down before him those who did so much as raise their eyes.

"What are you doing there, Monsieur, watching flies? Proceed to the pay desk!"

Finally, one day the storm burst over the head of Hutin himself. Favier, promoted to assistant buyer, was undermining the buyer so as to oust him from his place. His were the same old tactics – he sent underhand reports to the management, he took advantage of every opportunity for catching the head of the department in the wrong. Thus, one morning as Mouret was going through the silk department, he stopped, surprised to see Favier altering the price tags of a whole surplus stock of black velvet.

"Why are you lowering the prices?" he asked. "Who gave you the order to do so?"

The assistant buyer was making a great commotion over the job as if he had wanted to catch the director as he was passing. He replied with an air of innocent surprise:

"Why, it was Monsieur Hutin, Monsieur."

"Monsieur Hutin! Well, where is Monsieur Hutin?"

When the latter had returned from the reception desk, whither a salesman had been sent downstairs to fetch him, he was sharply called to account. What! He was now reducing prices on his own initiative! But he appeared to be very astonished in his turn, he had merely discussed the reduction with Favier, without giving a definite order. At that the latter put on the air of distress of an employee who feels obliged to contradict his superior. However, he would gladly take the blame, if by doing so he could get him out of a fix. From then on things began to go badly.

"You'd better get it into your head, Monsieur Hutin," Mouret was shouting, "that I've never tolerated such attempts at independence... We are the only people who decide on prices!"

He went on, in a rasping voice and with scathing intent, which surprised the salesmen, for this kind of argument usually took place out of sight, and anyway this case might really be the result of a misunderstanding. One could feel that he wanted to work off an unavowed grudge. So at last he had caught him out, this man Hutin, who was supposed to be Denise's lover! Now he could relieve his feelings a bit by making him severely aware that he was the master! And he was exaggerating the affair, he ended up by insinuating that the price reductions hid dishonest intentions.

"Monsieur," Hutin was repeating, "I intended to refer this reduction to you... It is really necessary, as you know, for these velvets have not sold well."

Mouret wanted to cut the matter short with a final scathing remark.

"Very well, Monsieur, we'll look into the matter... and don't do it again, if you value your job."

He turned his back. Hutin, stunned and furious, found only Favier to whom he could unburden his heart; he swore to him that he would go and fling his notice in that brute's face. Then he stopped talking about leaving, and merely raked up all the atrocious accusations which salesmen were wont to level against their employers. Favier, with shining eyes, was defending himself, making a great show of his sympathy. He had been obliged to reply, hadn't he? And then, how could one have expected such a fuss about nothing? What was the matter with the boss lately, he really was past praying for.

"Oh! As to what's the matter with him, everyone knows," Hutin went on. "It isn't as if it's my fault if that whore in the ready-made department is driving him crazy! You see, old chap, that's at the root of it. He knows that I've slept with her, and he doesn't like it – or else she wants to have me kicked out because I make things awkward for her... I swear to you I'll give her something to think about if ever she gets into my clutches."

Two days later, when Hutin had gone upstairs to the coat workroom which was right up in the attics in order to give some personal instructions to a seamstress, he gave a slight start on seeing, at the end of a corridor, Denise and Deloche leaning in front of an open window, and so deep in a heart-to-heart conversation that they did not look round. Then he noticed with surprise that Deloche was weeping, and the idea of having them caught unawares suddenly occurred to him. So he withdrew silently and, as he ran into Bourdoncle and Jouve on the staircase, he told them some story about one of the fire extinguishers which looked as if its door had been pulled off, so that they would go upstairs and run into the other two. Bourdoncle was the first to catch sight of them. He stopped short and told Jouve to go and fetch the director while he waited there. The shopwalker was forced to obey, very vexed at finding himself involved in an affair of that kind.

They were in an out-of-the-way corner of the vast world in which the multitudes in the Bonheur des Dames came and went. It was reached by a complicated network of stairs and corridors. The workrooms in the attics were a series of low rooms with sloping ceilings, lit by broad bay windows cut out of the zinc roof and furnished only with long tables and great cast-iron stoves; there were the lingerie-makers and lacemakers and beyond them the upholsterers and the dressmakers, who worked there winter and summer in stifling heat, surrounded by the smells peculiar to their trades, and in order to reach this unfrequented end of the corridor it was necessary to go right through that wing of the building, turn to the left after the dressmakers and go up five steps. The rare customers who were sometimes taken there by a salesman to see something they had ordered would recover their breath, exhausted and flustered, with the impression that they had been going round and round for hours and were a hundred miles away from the street.

Several times already Denise had found Deloche waiting for her. As assistant buyer, she was in charge of the department's dealings with the workrooms where, incidentally, only models were made and alterations carried out; she was always going upstairs to give instructions. He would lie in wait for her, inventing some pretext, slipping close behind her; then when he met her at the workroom door, he would pretend to be surprised. She had ended up by laughing about it, the meetings had become almost an accepted thing. The corridor ran along the side of the cistern, an enormous metal tank which contained sixty thousand litres of water, and there was on the roof a second one of equal size, which was reached by an iron ladder. Deloche would chat for a moment, leaning one shoulder against the cistern, for his huge body was always spent and bowed with fatigue. There were sounds of water gurgling, mysterious sounds which made the metal of the tank always have a musical vibration. In spite of the utter silence Denise would look round anxiously, thinking she saw a shadow flit across the bare walls which were painted bright yellow. But soon the window would attract them, they would lean their elbows on its sill, losing all count of time in merry chatter, in endless reminiscences of the country where they had spent their childhood. Beneath them extended the immense glazed roof of the central gallery, a lake of glass hemmed in by the distant roofs, as if by rocky coasts. And beyond they could see nothing but the sky, a sky which, with its flights of clouds and its delicate azure blue, was mirrored in the stagnant water of the window panes.

On that particular day, as it happened, Deloche was talking about Valognes.

"When I was six years old, my mother used to take me in a small cart to the market in the town. You know it's a good thirteen miles, we had to leave Bricquebec at five o'clock... It's very beautiful in our part of the world. Do you know it?"

"Yes, yes," Denise was slowly replying, looking into the distance, "I went there once, but I was very little... The roads have grass verges on either side, haven't they? And now and then there are sheep, let loose two by two, trailing their tethering ropes..."

She was silent for a little while, then resumed again with a vague smile:

"In our part of the world, the roads run straight for miles, between trees which make them shady... We have pastures surrounded by hedges which are taller than I am, where there are horses and cows... We've got a little river, and the water is very cold beneath the brushwood, in a place I can remember very well."

"It's just like our country, just like our country!" Deloche was exclaiming, delightedly. "There's nothing but grassland, and everyone surrounds his bit with hawthorns and elms and one feels at home, and it's all green – a green you don't see in Paris... My goodness! How I used to play at the bottom of the sunken path, going down from the mill!"

Their voices were dwindling away; there they remained, their eyes fixed on the sunny lake of the window panes and lost in it. From that blinding water a mirage was rising for them, they were seeing endless pastures, the Cotentin soaked with breezes from the ocean, bathed in a luminous haze which was melting away on the horizon in the delicate grey of a watercolour. Below them, beneath the colossal iron framework, there was the roar of selling in the silk department, the jarring sound of the machine at work, the whole shop was vibrating with the tramping of the crowd, the scurry of salesmen, the life of the thirty thousand people jammed together there – but they, carried away by their dream, felt this deep, muffled roar and thought they were listening to the wind from the sea going over the pastures, shaking the great trees as it went.

"My goodness, Mademoiselle Denise," stammered Deloche, "why aren't you kinder to me? And I love you so much too!"

Tears had come into his eyes, and when she tried to interrupt him with a gesture, he continued quickly:

"No, let me tell you this just once more... We get on so well together! One's always got something to talk about when one comes from the same part of the world."

He was choking with tears and at last she was able gently to say:

"You're not being sensible, you promised me not to talk about that any more... It's impossible. I'm very fond of you, because you're a splendid lad, but I want to stay free."

"Yes, yes, I know," he went on in a broken voice. "You don't love me. Oh! You may as well say it, I understand you, I've got nothing to make you love me... Why! There's only been one good hour in my life, that evening when I met you at Joinville, d'you remember? For a moment, underneath the trees where it

337

was so dark, I thought I felt your arm trembling. I was stupid enough to imagine—"

But she cut him short once more. Her sharp ears had just heard the footsteps of Bourdoncle and Jouve at the other end of the corridor.

"Listen, do, someone's coming."

"No," he said, preventing her from leaving the window. "It's in the cistern: extraordinary noises are always coming from it, you'd think there were people inside it."

He went on with his timid complaints. She, once more lulled into a daydream by his talk of love, was no longer listening to him, but was letting her glances stray over the roofs of the Bonheur des Dames. To the right and left of the glazed gallery, other galleries and other halls were shining in the sunshine, between gables pitted with windows and set out symmetrically like barrack wings. Metal framework was standing erect, there were ladders and bridges, the lacework of which stood out against the blue of the air, while the chimney from the kitchens, like a factory chimney, was belching out a great cloud of smoke, and the great square cistern, held high in the sky by iron pillars, had acquired the strange outline of some barbaric construction, raised up there by the arrogance of one man. In the distance the roar of Paris could be heard.

When Denise returned from space, from the far confines of the Bonheur, where her thoughts had been floating as if in some haven, she saw that Deloche had taken her hand. His face was so distressed that she did not take it back.

"Forgive me," he was murmuring, "it's finished now, it would make me too unhappy if you were to punish me by taking away your friendship... I swear to you that that's not what I intended to say to you. Yes, I'd promised myself to understand the situation, the..."

His tears were flowing once more, he was trying to steady his voice.

"For now I know what my lot in life is. It isn't as if my luck would change now. I was beaten back there at home, I'm beaten in Paris, beaten everywhere. I've been here four years now, and I'm still the lowest in the department... So I wanted to tell you that you shouldn't feel unhappy on my account. I won't bother you any more. Try to be happy, go and love someone else – yes, that would make me happy. If you're happy, I shall be happy… That'll be my joy."

He could not go on. As if to seal his promise, he had placed his lips on the girl's hand and was kissing it with the humble kiss of a slave. She was deeply touched, and with a sisterly compassion which toned down the pity in the words she said simply:

"You poor boy!"

But they gave a start and turned round. Mouret was facing them. For ten minutes Jouve had been looking for the director all over the shop. But the latter had been on the site for the new shopfront in the Rue du Dix-Décembre. Every day he spent hours there; he was attempting to take an interest in this work of which he had dreamt for so long. He found a refuge from his torments among the masons laying the corner piles in freestone and the metalworkers putting up great iron girders. Already the shopfront was rising up, outlining in skeleton the vast porch, the bays on the first floor, the growth of a palace. He would go up ladders, discuss the decorations – which were to be something quite new – with the architect, he would step over ironwork and bricks and even go down into the cellars, and the roar of the steam engine, the tick-tack of the windlasses, the banging of the hammers and the hubbub of the mass of workmen in that huge cage surrounded by echoing hoardings succeeded in numbing his feelings for an instant. He would leave there white with plaster, black with iron filings, his feet splashed by the taps of the hydrants, so little cured of his trouble that his anguish would come back and make his heart beat even more loudly as the din of the building site died away behind him. It so happened that on that particular day a diversion had restored his gaiety, he had been looking with great enthusiasm at an album of drawings of mosaics and glazed tiles with which the friezes were to be decorated, when Jouve, very out of breath and very annoyed at having to make his frock coat dirty among the building materials, had come to fetch him. At first he had shouted to him that they could very well wait for him; then, after the inspector had said a word to him in an undertone, he had followed him, shuddering with horror, entirely overwhelmed by his troubles again. Nothing else existed, the shopfront was crumbling before it had been set up: what was the good of this supreme triumph of his pride, if the mere name of a woman, murmured in an undertone, could torture him to that extent!

Upstairs Bourdoncle and Jouve thought it wise to disappear. Deloche had fled. Denise stood facing Mouret alone, paler than usual, but looking up at him frankly.

"Mademoiselle, kindly follow me," he said in a hard voice.

She followed him, they went down two floors and crossed the furniture and carpet departments without saying a word. When he was outside his study, he opened the door wide.

"Go in, please, Mademoiselle."

He closed the door again and went straight to his desk. The new director's study was more luxurious than the old one had been, green velvet hangings had replaced the rep, a bookcase inlaid with ivory took up the whole of one wall panel, but on the walls there was still nothing to be seen but the portrait of Madame Hédouin, a young woman with a beautiful, unruffled face, smiling in her golden frame.

"Mademoiselle," he said finally, trying to remain coldly severe, "there are some things which we cannot tolerate... Good behaviour is compulsory here..."

He was hesitating, picking his words in order not to give way to the rage which was mounting in his innermost being. What! It was that boy she loved, that wretched salesman, the laughing stock of his department! She preferred the humblest and gawkiest of them all to him, the master! For he had clearly seen them, she giving him her hand, and he covering that hand with kisses.

"I've been very good to you, Mademoiselle," he continued, making a fresh effort. "I never expected to be repaid in this way."

From the moment she entered, Denise's eyes had been drawn to the portrait of Madame Hédouin, and in spite of her great confusion she remained preoccupied by it. Every time she went into the director's study her glance crossed that of the painted lady. She was a little afraid of her, but felt nevertheless that she was very kind. This time, she felt as if, in her, she had a protector there.

"You're right, Monsieur," she replied gently, "I did wrong to stop and chat, and I'm sorry for my lapse... That young man comes from my part of the world."

"I'll kick him out!" shouted Mouret, putting all his suffering into this cry of fury.

And, shattered, abandoning his role of the director lecturing a salesgirl about infringing the rules, he launched forth into violent words. Wasn't she ashamed? A girl like her giving herself to a creature like that! And he even went so far as to make appalling accusations; he reproached her with Hutin, with others as well, using such a flood of words that she could not even defend herself. He was going to make a clean sweep, he would kick them all out. The stern dressing-down which, as he had followed Jouve, he had promised himself he would give her was degenerating into the coarse rudeness of a scene of jealousy.

"Yes, your lovers! People said you had them, and I was stupid enough not to believe them... There was no one but me! There was no one but me!"

Denise, stunned and flabbergasted, was listening to these hideous reproaches. She had not at first understood. Heavens! Did he take her for a loose woman then? A word even harsher than the rest made her go silently towards the door. To the gesture which he made to stop her, she said:

"That's enough, Monsieur, I'm going away... If you believe me to be what you say, I don't wish to remain another second in the shop."

He made a dash for the door.

"Defend yourself, at least! Say something!"

She stood very erect, in icy silence. For a long time in growing anxiety he pressed her with questions, and the virgin's silent dignity seemed once more to be the cunning ruse of a woman steeped in the tactics of passion. She could not have played a game more calculated to throw him at her feet, so torn with doubt was he, so anxious to be convinced.

"Come now, you say he comes from your part of the world... Perhaps you met each other there... Swear to me that nothing happened between you."

Then, as she maintained her silence, and was still trying to open the door and go away, he finally lost his head and gave vent to his suffering in a crowning outburst "My God! I love you, I love you... Why do you take pleasure in tormenting me like this? You can see very well that nothing else exists, that the people I've spoken about to you only affect me through you, that you're the only person who has any importance in the world... I thought you were jealous, and so I gave up my pleasures. People have told you that I had mistresses; well, I haven't any more, I hardly ever go out. When we were in that lady's house, didn't I show my preference for you? Didn't I break with her so as to belong to you alone? I'm still waiting for a word of thanks, a little gratitude... And if you're afraid of me going back to her you needn't worry: she's taking her revenge by helping one of our former assistants to found a rival shop... Tell me, must I go on my knees to move your heart?"

He had reached that point. He who would not tolerate his salesgirls making a slip, who threw them into the street at his slightest whim, found himself reduced to entreating one of them not to leave, not to abandon him to his misery. He was defending the door against her, he was ready to forgive her, to shut his eyes to everything if only she would condescend to lie about it. And he was speaking the truth; trollops picked up backstage in small theatres and nightclubs were becoming repugnant to him; he no longer saw Clara, he had not set foot again in Madame Desforges's house where Bouthemont was now reigning, pending the opening of the new shop, the Quatre Saisons, for which the newspapers were already full of advertisements.

"Tell me, must I go on my knees?" he repeated, choking with stifled tears.

She silenced him with a gesture, no longer able to hide her own confusion, deeply stirred by this tortured passion.

"You are wrong to make yourself unhappy, Monsieur," she replied at last. "I swear to you that those dreadful stories are all lies... That poor boy you saw just now is as little to blame as I am."

She was as splendidly frank as ever and her clear eyes were looking him straight in the face.

"Very well, I believe you," he murmured. "I won't send any of your friends away, since you've taken them all under your wing... But then why do you reject me, if you don't love anyone else?"

The girl was overcome with sudden embarrassment and diffident modesty.

"You do love someone, don't you?" he went on in a trembling voice. "Oh, you can say so, I don't hold any rights over your affections... You do love someone."

She was blushing deeply, it was on the tip of her tongue to say what was in her heart, and she felt that, with her emotion betraying her and her repugnance for falsehood allowing the truth to show on her face in spite of everything, it would be impossible to lie.

"Yes," she admitted weakly in the end. "Please don't say any more to me, Monsieur, you're distressing me."

In her turn she was suffering. Was it not already enough to have to defend herself against him? Would she also have to defend herself against herself, against the waves of tenderness which at times took away all her courage? When he talked to her like that, when she saw him so deeply moved, so overwhelmed, she did not know why she still resisted him, and it was only afterwards that she rediscovered at the very roots of her healthy-minded temperament, the self-respect and reason which kept her upright with virginal obstinacy. It was an instinctive longing for happiness that made her persist in refusing, in order to satisfy her need for a peaceful life, and not in order to conform to the idea of virtue. She would have fallen into his arms, her flesh conquered and her heart captivated, if she had not felt a resistance, almost a repulsion to the idea of the ultimate gift of herself cast into the unknown of the morrow. The thought of a lover frightened her – frightened her with that unreasoning fear which makes a woman blanch at the approach of the male.

Meanwhile Mouret had made a bleak gesture of discouragement. He did not understand. He turned round to his desk, where he shuffled some papers over and put them down again immediately, saying:

"I won't detain you any longer, Mademoiselle, I can't keep you against your will."

"But I'm not asking to leave," she replied with a smile. "If you think I'm respectable, I'll stay... You should always believe women to be respectable, Monsieur. There are many who are, I assure you."

Denise had, involuntarily, looked up at the portrait of Madame Hédouin, that lady who was so beautiful and wise, and whose blood, so they said, brought luck to the shop. Mouret followed the girl's glance with a start, for he seemed to have heard his dead wife uttering the phrase, one of her phrases, which he recognized. It was like a resurrection, in Denise he was rediscovering the good sense and sound balance, even down to her gentle voice, sparing of superfluous words, of her whom he had lost. He was deeply struck by this, and felt sadder than ever.

"You know that I belong to you," he murmured in conclusion. "Do what you will with me."

At that she went on gaily:

"All right, Monsieur. A woman's opinion, however humble she may be, is always worth listening to, if she's got a little sense… If you put yourself in my hands, I shall just make a decent man of you."

She was joking, with her simple manner which was so charming. In his turn he gave a feeble smile and conducted her to the door as if she was a lady.

The next day Denise was promoted to buyer. The management had split the suit-and-gown department into two, by creating a department for children's suits specially for her, which was set up near the ready-made department. Since her son's dismissal Madame Aurélie was on tenterhooks, for she could feel the management becoming cool towards her, and she saw the girl's power growing daily. Were they going to sacrifice her to Denise on some pretext or other? Her emperor-like mask, puffed up with fat, seemed to have grown thinner at the shame which now sullied the Lhomme dynasty, and she made much show of going away every evening on the arm of her husband, for they had been reconciled to each other by misfortune and understood that the trouble came from their home life being so helter-skelter; while her poor husband, who was even more affected than she was, and had a morbid fear lest he himself should be suspected of theft, would noisily count the takings twice over, performing real miracles with his bad arm as he did so. And so when she saw Denise promoted to buyer in the children's suits department, she felt such acute joy that she displayed feelings of the greatest affection towards her. It was really splendid of her not to have taken her job away from her! She overwhelmed her with tokens of friendship, from then on she treated her as an equal and often went with an air of ceremony to chat with her in the neighbouring department, like a queen mother visiting a young queen.

In any case, Denise was now at her zenith. Her appointment as buyer had broken down the last resistance around her. If, owing to that itch for gossip which always infects any assembly of men and women, people still talked, they nevertheless bowed very low to her, right down to the ground in fact. Marguerite, promoted to be assistant buyer in the ready-mades, was full of praise. Even Clara, filled with secret respect for such fortune which she herself was incapable of attaining, had bowed her head. But Denise's victory over the men – over Jouve, who only spoke to her now bent double, over Hutin, full of alarm at feeling his job precarious, over Bourdoncle, at last rendered powerless – was even more complete. When the latter had seen her coming out of Mouret's study, smiling, with her unruffled manner, and when the next day the director had insisted that the board should create the new department, he had given in, conquered by a holy terror of Woman. He had always given in like that to Mouret's charm, he recognized him as his master, in spite of the flaws in his genius and his idiotic impulsive actions. This time Woman had proved herself to be the stronger, and he was waiting to be swept away by the disaster.

For all that, Denise's triumph was peaceful and charming. She was touched by these marks of consideration, and tried to see in them sympathy for the misery she had gone through when she had joined the shop, and her final success after being courageous for so long. Therefore she welcomed the slightest signs of friendship with smiling joy, which made her really loved by some, for she was so gentle and affable and always ready to give of her heart. Only for Clara did she feel a repulsion which she could not control, for she had learnt that the girl had amused herself one evening by taking Colomban to her place as she had jokingly planned to do – and the assistant, carried away by his passion which had been satisfied at last, now slept out all the time, while the wretched Geneviève was dying. At the Bonheur people talked about it and thought it was an amusing intrigue.

But this sorrow, the only one which she had outside the shop, did not alter Denise's even temper. She was above all worth seeing in her department, surrounded by a crowd of children of all ages. A better job could not have been found for her, for she adored children. Sometimes there would be as many as fifty little girls and the same number of boys there, a regular boisterous boarding school let loose amid the desires of budding coquetry. The mothers would lose their heads completely. Soothing and smiling, she would get all the youngsters lined up on chairs, and when she saw some rosy-cheeked little girl in the crowd whose funny little face attracted her, she would feel like serving her herself and would bring the dress and try it on the chubby body with the tender care of a big sister. There would be peals of clear laughter, little cries of ecstasy would burst out in the midst of scolding voices. Sometimes a little girl of nine or ten years old, quite grown up already, when trying on a cloth coat would study it in front of a looking glass, turning round with an absorbed look and her eyes shining with the desire to please. The counters were littered with unfolded goods, dresses in pink or blue tussore for children from one to five, zephyr sailor suits, a pleated skirt and blouse decorated with appliquéd cambric, Louis XV-style costumes, coats, jackets, a jumble of small garments, stiff in their childish grace, rather like the wardrobe of a bevy of big dolls, taken out of cupboards and left to be ransacked. Denise always had some sweetmeats in the depths of her pocket, and would soothe the tears of some infant in despair at not being able to take a pair of red trousers away with him; she lived there among the little ones as if they were her own family, and she herself was made younger by all the innocence and freshness ceaselessly renewed around her.

Nowadays she often had long friendly conversations with Mouret. When she had to go to the director's office to get instructions or give information he would keep her there talking; he enjoyed listening to her. This was what she jokingly called "making a decent man of him". In her rational, far-seeing Norman mind all sorts of schemes were germinating, those ideas on modern business methods which she had already ventured to air at Robineau's, and some of which she had expressed on that fine evening when she and Mouret had walked together in the Tuileries gardens. Whenever she was doing something herself, whenever she saw a task being carried out, she was always obsessed with the need to put method into it, to improve the system. Thus, ever since she had joined the Bonheur des Dames, she had above all been shocked by the uncertain lot of the junior assistants; the sudden dismissals roused her indignation, she considered them clumsy and iniquitous – as harmful to the shop as they were to the staff. She was still seared by her sufferings in the early days, and her heart was wrung with pity each time she met a newcomer in one of the departments, with sore feet and eyes swollen with tears, dragging out her miserable existence in her silk dress, surrounded by the embittered persecution of the girls who had been there longer than she had. This dog's life made even the best girls go to the bad; their sad downward progress would begin: they were all worn out by their profession before they were forty, they would disappear, go off into the unknown, many would die in harness of consumption or anaemia, of fatigue and bad air, and some would end on the street. The more fortunate ones would marry and be buried at the back of some small provincial shop. Was the big shops' appalling consumption of flesh every year either humane or right? She would plead the cause of the cogs in the machinery, not from sentimental reasons, but from arguments based on the employer's own interests. When one wants a sound machine one uses good metal; if the metal breaks or is broken there is a halt in the work, repeated expense for getting it going again, a regular wastage of power. Sometimes she would grow excited, imagining a huge, ideal emporium, a phalanstery of trade, in which everyone would have his fair share of the profits according to his merits, and his future assured by a contract. At this Mouret would brighten up, in spite of his misery. He would accuse her of socialism, would nonplus her by pointing out the difficulties of putting all that into practice, for she spoke with the simplicity of her heart, and when she perceived a dangerous pitfall and had exhausted her own tender-hearted methods, she would bravely leave it all to the future. He was disturbed and fascinated by her young voice, still quivering from the ills she had suffered, and so full of conviction when pointing out reforms which would improve the shop; and although he laughed at her, he listened to her. The salesmen's lot was gradually improving, for the mass dismissals were replaced by a system of leave given during the off-season and, what is more, a friendly society was going to be created which would protect them against forced unemployment and would guarantee them a pension. This was the embryo of the vast workers' organizations to be created in the twentieth century.

What is more, Denise did not confine herself to staunching the open wounds with which she herself had bled; the subtle, feminine ideas which she whispered to Mouret delighted the customers. She had also made Lhomme a happy man by supporting the plan which he had been hatching for some time, of forming a band made up of members of the staff. Three months later Lhomme had a hundred and twenty musicians under his direction, his life's dream had come true. A big festival was arranged in the shop, a concert and a ball, in order to introduce the Bonheur's band to the customers and to the whole world. The newspapers took it up, and even Bourdoncle, who was in consternation at these innovations, had to acquiesce to such an enormous advertisement. Next an amusement room for the assistants was installed, with two billiard tables, as well as backgammon and chess boards. In the evenings, classes were held in the shop, there were English and German lessons, as well as lessons in grammar, arithmetic and geography; there were even lessons in riding and fencing. A library was created, ten thousand volumes were put at the disposal of the staff. In addition, there was a resident doctor who gave free consultations, there were baths, bars and a hairdressing saloon. Every need of life was provided for, everything was obtainable without leaving the building – study, refreshment, sleeping accommodation, clothing. The Bonheur des Dames was self-sufficient, both in pleasures and necessities. The whole centre of Paris was filled with the din, with this city of labour which was growing so freely out of the squalor of the streets, which had at last been opened up to the sunshine.

At that time there was a new wave of opinion in favour of Denise. Since Bourdoncle, now defeated, was wont to repeat in despair to his cronies that he would have given a great deal to put her in Mouret's bed himself, it had been established that she had not yielded, and that her all-powerfulness resulted from her refusals. And from then on she became popular. People realized that they were indebted to her for various comforts, and she was admired for her strength of will. There was one person, at any rate, who could keep the director under her thumb, who was avenging them all, and who knew how to get something more than promises out of him! At last someone had come who made people have some regard for the poor underdogs! When she went through the departments, with her delicate resolute expression and gentle yet invincible air, the salesmen would smile at her and felt proud of her, and would gladly have shown her off to the crowd. Denise was happy to allow herself to be swept along by this growing sympathy towards her. Heavens, could it really be true? She could see herself arriving in her shabby skirt, scared and lost among the gearwheels of the terrifying machine; for a long time she had had the sensation of being nothing, a grain of millet beneath the millstones crushing everyone beneath them –

and now she was the very soul of that world, only she mattered, with a word she could speed up or slow down the colossus lying vanquished at her feet. Yet none of this had been premeditated; she had simply turned up, with no ulterior motive and with nothing but her charming gentleness. Her supremacy sometimes caused her uneasy surprise: what on earth made them all obey her like that? It was not as if she was pretty or liable to harm them. Then, her heart soothed, she would smile, for there was nothing in her but goodness and sound sense, a love for truth and logic which was her sole strength.

Now that she was in favour, it was one of Denise's great joys to be able to help Pauline. The latter was pregnant, and was terrified about it, for two salesgirls in a fortnight had had to leave in the seventh month of their pregnancy. The management did not tolerate accidents of that kind, maternity was ruled out as being cumbersome and indecent; marriage was allowed at a pinch, but children were forbidden. Pauline, of course, did have a husband in the shop; but she was on her guard all the same, for that did not make her appearance any better in the department, and so as to delay her probable dismissal she laced herself in till she could hardly breathe, determined to hide her condition as long as she could. From having tortured her waist in this way one of the two salesgirls who had been dismissed had just had a stillborn child, and there was little hope of saving her either. Meanwhile Bourdoncle, thinking he saw a painful stiffness in her gait, was watching Pauline's complexion acquiring a leaden hue. One morning he was near her in the trousseau department when a porter who was taking away a parcel bumped into her so hard that she gave a cry and put both her hands on her stomach. He immediately led her away and made her confess, and then referred her dismissal to the board, under the pretext that she needed fresh air in the country; the story of the blow she had received would get around, if she had a miscarriage the effect on the public would be disastrous – one had occurred the year before in the baby-linen department. Mouret, who was not present at the board meeting, could only give his decision in the evening. But Denise had had time to intervene, and he silenced Bourdoncle in the name of the shop's own interests. Did he want to set all the mothers against them, offend all the young customers who had just had babies? It was grandiloquently decided that any married salesgirl who became pregnant would be put in the charge of a special midwife as soon as her presence in the department became an offence to morality.

The next day, when Denise went up to the sickroom to see Pauline, who had had to go to bed as a result of the blow she had received, the latter kissed her violently on both cheeks.

"How sweet you are! If it wasn't for you they'd have thrown me out... And don't worry, the doctor assures me everything will be quite all right."

Baugé, who had slipped away from his department, was also there on the other side of the bed. He too was stammering out his thanks, confused in the presence of Denise, whom he now treated as someone who had made good and was in a superior class. Ah, if he was to hear any more nasty remarks about her he'd see to it that people who were jealous had their mouths shut for them! But Pauline sent him away with a friendly shrug of her shoulders.

"My poor sweet, you're just talking nonsense... Off you go, and leave us to have a chat."

The sickroom was a long, light room, in which twelve beds with white curtains were lined up. The assistants who lived in the shop were nursed there when they were ill if they did not wish to go back to their families. But that day Pauline was the only person there, in a bed near one of the big windows which looked over the Rue Neuve-Saint-Augustin. Surrounded by all that innocent linen, in the sleepy air perfumed with a vague smell of lavender, confidences and fond whispered phrases began immediately.

"So he does what you want all the same? How unkind you are to make him unhappy! Come now, explain to me, since I've dared broach the subject. Can't you bear him?"

Pauline had kept her friend's hand in hers, for the girl was sitting by the bed and leaning her elbows on the bolster, and at this blunt and unexpected question Denise, overwhelmed with sudden emotion, had a momentary weakness. She let out her secret, hiding her face in the pillow and murmuring:

"I love him!"

Pauline was dumbfounded.

"What! You love him? But then it's very simple: say yes."

Denise, her face still hidden, was refusing with a vigorous shake of her head. And she was refusing precisely because she loved him, although she did not say so. Of course it was ridiculous, but that was the way she felt, she couldn't alter her nature. Her friend's surprise was increasing and she finally asked:

"So it's all so as to make him marry you?"

At that the girl sat up again. She was dumbfounded.

"He marry me! Oh no! Oh, I swear to you that I never wanted anything like that! No, a scheme like that never entered my head, and you know I've a horror of lying!"

"Well, my dear," Pauline went on gently, "if you had thought of making him marry you, you couldn't have set about it better… It'll have to finish somehow, after all, and there's nothing else except marriage, as you don't want the other business… Listen, I must warn you that everyone thinks the same thing: yes, they're all convinced that you're making him dance to your tune so as to get him to the registry office… My goodness! You are a funny woman!"

She was forced to console Denise, who had let her head fall on the bolster once again and was sobbing, repeating that she'd end up by going away, since people were always attributing ideas to her which had never even crossed her mind. She did not want anything, had no designs on anything, she only begged people to let her live in peace, with her sorrows and her joys, like everyone else. She would go away.

At the same moment, downstairs, Mouret was walking through the shop. He had wanted to numb his pain by visiting the building work once again. Months had passed, the new façade now rose up with monumental contours behind the vast hoarding of planks which hid it from the public. A whole army of decorators had set to work – marble masons and specialists in ceramics and mosaics – the central group of figures above the door was being gilded, while on the acroterium the pedestals which were to hold statues symbolizing the manufacturing towns of France were already being fixed in position. From morning to night, all along the Rue du Dix-Décembre which had recently been opened, an inquisitive crowd stood looking up, seeing nothing, but their heads full of the wonders which people were telling each other about this façade which was going to revolutionize Paris when it was opened. And it was precisely on that building site, where there was such a fever of activity, and among the artists who were completing the realization of his dream which had been started by the builders, that Mouret had just felt more bitterly than ever the vanity of his fortune. The thought of Denise had suddenly made his heart ache, that thought which would shoot through him without respite like a flame, like the twinge of an incurable disease. He had fled, unable to say a word of satisfaction, afraid of showing his tears, turning his back on his triumph, which was dust and ashes to him. The façade, built at last, seemed to him small, like a child's sandcastle, and even if it had extended from one end of the city to the other, or been as high as the stars, it would not have filled the emptiness of his heart, which only the "yes" of a mere child could fill.

When Mouret returned to his study he was choking with pent-up tears. What could it be she wanted? He no longer dared offer her money; the confused idea of marriage was beginning to dawn on him although, as a young widower, he rebelled against it. His powerlessness made him weep with nervous frustration. He was unhappy.

13

ONE NOVEMBER MORNING Denise was giving her initial instructions to her department, when the Baudus' maidservant came to tell her that Mademoiselle Geneviève had passed a very bad night, and that she wanted to see her cousin immediately.

"Say I'm coming at once," Denise replied, very worried. It was the sudden disappearance of Colomban which was proving fatal to Geneviève. First, because Clara had teased him, he had slept away from home; then, yielding to the madness of desire which sometimes strikes shifty, chaste young men, he had become that hussy's obedient slave, and one Monday had not returned, but had simply written a farewell letter to his employer full of the polished phrases of a man committing suicide. Perhaps at the bottom of this infatuation there was also the astute reckoning of a young man delighted to forgo a disastrous marriage; the drapery shop was just as sick as his future wife; it was the right moment to break it all off by doing something silly. Everyone quoted him as a fatal casualty of love.

When Denise arrived at the Vieil Elbeuf, Madame Baudu was there alone. She was motionless behind the cash desk, guarding the silence and emptiness of the shop, her little white face eaten up with anaemia. There was no shop assistant now, so the maid-servant would occasionally give the showcases a whisk with a feather duster, and there was even question of replacing her with a charwoman. Bitter cold was seeping down from the ceiling; hours passed without a customer coming to disturb her shadowy figure, and the goods, which were no longer shifted, were getting increasingly covered with the saltpetre rot from the walls.

"What is it?" asked Denise sharply. "Is Geneviève in danger?"

Madame Baudu did not reply immediately. Her eyes filled with tears. Then she stammered:

"I don't know anything, they don't tell me anything... Oh! It's the end, it's the end..."

Her eyes were drowning in tears. She was looking round the gloomy shop as if she felt her daughter and the shop departing together. The seventy thousand francs produced by the sale of the estate at Rambouillet had, in less than two years, melted away in the abyss of competition. In order to fight the Bonheur, which now stocked cloth for menswear, special types of velvet and liveries, the draper had made considerable sacrifices. He had just been finally crushed by his rival's duffels and flannels, an assortment such as had never before appeared on the market. Little by little the debt had grown; he had decided, as a last resort, to mortgage the ancient premises in the Rue de la Michodière where old Finet, their ancestor, had founded the shop, and now it was only a question of days, the process of disintegration was almost completed, the very ceilings seemed as if they would collapse and fly away as dust, like some barbarous, worm-eaten construction being carried away by the wind.

"Her father's upstairs," Madame Baudu went on in her broken voice. "We each spend two hours there; there has to be someone on duty. Oh, just as a precaution, for to tell the truth..."

Her gesture completed the sentence. They would have put up the shutters, but for their ancient business pride which made them still put a brave face on it in front of the neighbourhood.

"Then I'll go up, Auntie," said Denise whose heart was aching at the resigned despair which even the lengths of cloth were exuding.

"Yes, go up, go up quickly, my dear... She's waiting for you, she was asking for you all night. There's something she wants to say to you."

But just at that moment Baudu came downstairs. A bilious attack gave a greenish hue to his yellow face, and his eyes were bloodshot. Still walking very softly as he had done on leaving the sickroom, he murmured, as if he could have been heard upstairs:

"She's sleeping."

And, his legs worn out with tiredness, he sat down on a chair. With a mechanical gesture he wiped his forehead, puffing like a man who has just performed an arduous task. Silence reigned. Finally he said to Denise:

"You'll see her later... When she sleeps it's as if she's been cured to us."

The silence began again. The mother and father were gazing at each other face to face. Then, in undertones, they once more went over their troubles, neither naming anyone nor speaking to anyone in particular.

"Hand on my heart, I wouldn't have believed it! He was the last person to do it, I'd brought him up like my own son. If someone had come and told me, 'They'll take him away from you too, you'll see he'll go over to the other side,' I would have replied: 'Well, that'd mean there's no longer any God!' And he's done it, he has gone over to the other side. Oh, the wretch, he knew so much about real business, he had all the same ideas as me! And all for a monkey like that, for one of those mannequins who strut about in front of the windows of houses of ill fame! No, you know, it's against all reason!"

He was shaking his head, his vacant eyes were lowered and were looking at the damp tiles which had been worn away by generations of customers.

"D'you know what?" he went on in a lower voice. "Well, sometimes I feel that I'm the most to blame in our misfortune. Yes, it's my fault that our poor girl is upstairs, wasted with fever. Shouldn't I have married them off at once, without giving way to my idiotic pride, to my determination not to leave them the shop in a less prosperous state? She would have the man she loves now, and perhaps their youth would have been able to accomplish the miracle that I couldn't bring off... But I'm an old fool, I didn't understand anything about it, I didn't believe that people could fall ill for things like that... Really, that lad was extraordinary: he had a gift for selling, and such integrity, such simple manners, such order in all he did – in short, he was my pupil..."

He was holding his head high, still defending his own ideas via the assistant by whom he had been betrayed. Denise could not bear to hear him accusing himself and was so carried away by her emotion at seeing him who in the past had reigned there, a grumpy and absolute master, now so humble, with his eyes full of tears, that she told him everything.

"Don't make excuses for him, Uncle, I beseech you... He never loved Geneviève, he would have escaped earlier if you had wanted to hasten the marriage. I talked to him about it myself; he knew perfectly well what my poor cousin was suffering on his account, and you can see very well that that didn't prevent him from going... Ask Auntie."

Without opening her lips, Madame Baudu confirmed these words with a nod. At that the draper became even paler, his tears were now blinding him completely. He blurted out:

"It must be in the blood, his father died last summer from too much womanizing."

Mechanically his glance travelled round the dark corners, passed over the bare counters to the full shelves, and then returned to settle on his wife, still erect behind the cash desk, waiting in vain for the vanished customers.

"Well, it's the end," he went on. "They've killed our trade, and now one of their hussies is killing our daughter for us."

No one spoke any more. In the stagnant air, stifling beneath the low ceiling, the rumbling of carriages which from time to time set the tiles vibrating sounded like a roll of funeral drums. Then, in the dismal sadness of the old shop in its death throes, muffled knocks could be heard coming from somewhere in the house. It was Geneviève, who had just woken up, and who was banging with a stick which had been left close to her.

"Quick, let's go up," said Baudu, rising with a start. "Try to laugh, she mustn't know."

On the staircase he himself was rubbing his eyes hard in order to remove the traces of his tears. As soon as he opened the door on the first floor, a feeble voice, a frantic voice, could be heard calling:

"Oh, I don't want to be alone... Don't leave me alone... Oh, I'm afraid of being alone..."

Then, when she caught sight of Denise, Geneviève became calmer and gave a smile of joy.

355

"Ah! There you are! How I've been waiting for you, ever since yesterday! I was beginning to think that you too had abandoned me!"

It was pitiful. The girl's room looked over the yard, it was a small room lit by a livid glimmer of light. At first the parents had put the sick girl's bed in their own room, looking over the street, but the sight of the Bonheur des Dames opposite had upset her so much that they had had to take her back to her own room again. There she lay stretched out, so slight that one could no longer sense the form and existence of a body beneath the blankets. Her thin arms, wasted with the burning fever typical of consumptives, were perpetually on the move, searching anxiously and unconsciously for something, while her black hair, laden with passion, seemed to have become even thicker and to have a voracious life of its own, which was eating away her pathetic face – a face in which the ultimate degeneration of a long line grown in the dark, in that cellar of ancient Parisian commerce, was dying out.

Meanwhile Denise, her heart wrung with pity, was looking at her. She was not talking, for fear of shedding tears. In the end she murmured:

"I came at once... Is there anything I can do for you? You were asking for me... Would you like me to stay?"

Geneviève, short of breath, her hands still wandering over the folds of the blanket, did not take her eyes off her.

"No thank you, there's nothing I need... I only wanted to embrace you."

Her eyes were swollen with tears. At that Denise quickly bent down and kissed her on the cheeks, shuddering as she felt the fire of those hollow cheeks against her lips. But the sick girl had seized her, and was clasping her and holding on to her in a despairing embrace. Then she glanced towards her father.

"Would you like me to stay?" Denise repeated. "Is there something you wanted me to do?"

"No, no."

Geneviève was still looking steadily in the direction of her father, who was standing with a dazed look and a lump in his throat. Finally he understood, and withdrew without saying a word; they heard his footsteps going heavily downstairs.

"Tell me, is he still with that woman?" the sick girl asked immediately, seizing her cousin's hand as she did so, and making

356

her sit down on the edge of the bed. "Yes, I wanted to see you. You're the only person who can tell me... They're living together, aren't they?"

Denise, taken by surprise by these questions, had to admit the truth and blurted out the rumours which were going round the shop. Clara, bored by this lad with whom she found herself saddled, had already closed her door to him, and Colomban, in despair and with the humility of a beaten dog, was following her about everywhere, trying to obtain an occasional meeting with her. People affirmed that he was going to get a job at the Louvre.

"If you love him so much, he may still come back to you," the girl continued, trying to lull the dying girl with this last hope. "Get better quickly, he'll admit his mistake and marry you."

Geneviève interrupted her. She had been listening with her whole being, with dumb passion which had made her raise herself up. But she fell back again immediately.

"No, don't say any more, I know very well that it's the end... I don't say anything, because I hear Papa weeping, and I don't want to make Mamma more ill than she is. But you see, I'm going and I was calling for you last night because I was afraid I would go before daylight... My goodness! To think he's not even happy!"

When Denise protested, assuring her that her condition was not so serious, she cut short her words a second time, and suddenly threw back the blanket with the pure gesture of a virgin who in death has nothing more to hide. Uncovered to her waist, she murmured:

"Well, look at me! Isn't it the end?"

Trembling, Denise left the bedside as if afraid of destroying the girl's pitiful nakedness with a breath. It was the end of the flesh, a bride's body worn out with waiting, which had reverted to the slender childishness of its earliest years. Slowly Geneviève covered herself again, repeating:

"You can see for yourself, I'm no longer a woman... It would not be right still to want him."

They both fell silent. They were looking at each other once more, finding nothing more to say. It was Geneviève who went on:

"Come along now, don't stay here, you've got your work. And thank you, I was tortured by the desire to know – now

I'm content. If you see him again, tell him that I forgive him…
Farewell, my dearest Denise. Kiss me, it's the last time."

The girl kissed her, protesting as she did so.

"No, no, you mustn't lose heart like that, you need nursing,
that's all."

But the sick girl tossed her head obstinately. She was smiling,
she knew for certain. And, as her cousin finally went towards the
door she said:

"Wait a moment, knock with this stick for Papa to come up…
I'm too frightened when I'm alone."

Then, when Baudu was there in the cheerless little room where
he spent hours on a chair, she put on a gay air and called to
Denise:

"Don't come tomorrow, there's no point. But I'll expect you on
Sunday, you can spend the afternoon with me."

The next day, at six o'clock in the morning, Geneviève died,
after four hours of frightful agony. The funeral fell on a Saturday,
in murky weather and with a leaden sky weighing down on the
shivering city. The Vieil Elbeuf, draped with a white pall, lit up
the street with a patch of white, and the candles, burning in the
dim daylight, looked like stars submerged in twilight. Artificial
wreaths and a big bunch of white roses covered the coffin – the
narrow coffin of a little girl – which was placed beneath the dark
entrance passage of the shop, level with the pavement, and so
close to the gutter that carriages had already bespattered the
hangings. The whole ancient district was oozing with damp, exuding its musty smell of cellars, while on the muddy roadway
there was a continual bustle of passers-by.

Denise had been there since nine o'clock, in order to stay with
her aunt. But when the procession was about to leave Madame
Baudu, no longer weeping but with her eyes inflamed by tears,
asked Denise to follow the coffin and to watch over her uncle,
whose silent prostration and almost insane grief alarmed the
family. Downstairs, the girl found the street full of people. The
small tradespeople of the neighbourhood wanted to show their
sympathy to the Baudus, and their alacrity to do so was also a
kind of demonstration against the Bonheur des Dames, which
they held responsible for Geneviève's lingering death. All the
monster's victims were there: Bédoré and his sister, the hosiers
from the Rue Gaillon; the Vanpouille brothers, the furriers;

Deslignières, the fancy-goods dealer; and Piot and Rivoire, the furniture dealers; even Mademoiselle Tatin, the linen-draper, and Quinette, the glover, who had been swept away long ago by bankruptcy, had made a point of coming, the former from the Batignolles and the latter from the Bastille district, where they had had to take employment in the shops of others. While waiting for the hearse, which was held up by some mistake, this crowd dressed all in black, walking up and down in the mud, was aiming looks of hatred at the Bonheur. Its bright windows and displays bursting with gaiety looking across at the Vieil Elbeuf, which was giving the other side of the street a gloomy appearance with its mourning, seemed to them an insult. A few heads of inquisitive shop assistants were appearing behind the windows, but the colossus was maintaining the indifference of a machine going full steam ahead, oblivious to the deaths it may cause in its way.

Denise was looking round for her brother Jean. Finally she caught sight of him outside Bourras's shop. She went to join him in order to tell him to walk close to his uncle and support him should he have difficulty in walking. For some weeks now Jean had been solemn, as if tormented by an anxiety. On that day, squeezed into a black frock coat, now a made man and earning twenty francs a day, he seemed so dignified and so sad that his sister was struck, for she had not suspected he loved his cousin so much. She had wished to avoid pointless unhappiness for Pépé and so had left him with Madame Gras, planning to fetch him in the afternoon in order to bring him to embrace his uncle and aunt.

Meanwhile the hearse had still not turned up and Denise, feeling deeply affected, was watching the candles burning when on hearing the sound of a familiar voice talking behind her, she gave a sudden start. It was Bourras. He had beckoned to a chestnut-seller, who was installed opposite in a cramped booth forming part of a wine merchant's shop, and was saying to him:

"Look here, Vigouroux, will you do something for me? You see, I'm off… If anyone comes, will you tell them to call back? But don't let it worry you, no one will come."

Then he remained standing on the edge of the pavement, waiting like the others. Denise had glanced with embarrassment at the shop. He was letting it go now, in the shop window nothing could be seen but a pitiful helter-skelter of rotting umbrellas and walking sticks blackened by the gas. The improvements which he had made there, the light green paint, the looking glasses, the gilded signboard, were all cracking and getting dirty already, presenting a spectacle of the speedy and depressing decay of sham luxury plastered on top of ruins. Nevertheless, even though the old cracks were reappearing and the spots of damp had spread again beneath the gilding, the house was still stubbornly standing, stuck onto the side of the Bonheur des Dames like some shameful wart which, although it had cracked and come to a head, still refused to fall off.

"Ah, the wretches!" grumbled Bourras. "They don't even want to let her be taken away!"

The hearse, arriving at last, had just been run into by one of the Bonheur's vehicles which, its varnished doors scattering their starlike radiance in the mist, was vanishing at a brisk trot, pulled by two magnificent horses. The old shopkeeper was directing a sideways glance, burning beneath the undergrowth of his eyebrows, at Denise.

The procession moved off slowly, squelching through the puddles, in a silence made by cabs and omnibuses suddenly being brought to a standstill. When the coffin draped with white crossed the Place Gaillon, melancholy glances from the procession momentarily penetrated once more beyond the windows of the great shop, where only two salesgirls had rushed to look out of the window, glad of the distraction. Baudu was following the hearse with heavy, mechanical steps; he had refused with a sign to take the arm of Jean, who was walking close beside him. Then, after the people bringing up the rear on foot, came three funeral carriages. As they were cutting across the Rue Neuve-des-Petits Champs, Robineau, very pale, looking very much aged, ran up to join the procession.

At Saint-Roch a great many women were waiting, the small shopkeepers of the neighbourhood who had feared there would be a crush at the house of the deceased. The demonstration was turning into a riot, and when, after the service, the procession started off again, once more all the men followed, although from the Rue Saint-Honoré to the cemetery at Montmartre was a fair distance to walk. They had to go up the Rue Saint-Roch once more, and pass the Bonheur des Dames for the second time. It was like an obsession, the girl's pathetic body was carried round the big shop, as if she had been the first victim to fall under fire in time of revolution. At the door of the shop red flannel was flapping in the wind like flags, a display of carpets was bursting out in a blood-red blossoming of enormous roses and full-blown peonies.

Meanwhile Denise had got into a carriage, torn by such bitter doubts and her heart aching with such sadness that she no longer had the strength to walk. Just then there was a halt in the Rue du Dix-Décembre, opposite the scaffolding of the new shopfront, which was still obstructing the traffic. Then the girl noticed old Bourras lagging behind, limping along under the very wheels of the carriage in which she was sitting alone. He had raised his head and he looked at her. Then he got into the carriage.

"It's these damned legs of mine," he was murmuring. "Don't you draw back like that. It isn't as if it's you we detest!"

She sensed him to be friendly and furious, as he had been in the past. He was grumbling, declaring that that old devil Baudu was pretty tough to go on walking like that in spite of having suffered such blows. The procession had resumed its slow progress and, leaning forwards, she could see her uncle obstinately following the hearse with his heavy gait, which was setting the muffled, laborious pace of the procession. Then she sank back in her corner and listened to the endless words of the old umbrella dealer, to the accompaniment of the slow, melancholy swaying of the carriage.

"Really, the police ought to keep public thoroughfares clear! For more than eighteen months they've been cluttering our streets up with their new shopfront; only the other day another man was killed there. Never mind! In the future when they want to expand they'll have to throw bridges across the streets... They say you've got two thousand seven hundred employees, and that the turnover this year will reach a hundred million! A hundred million! My God! A hundred million!"

Denise had nothing to say in reply. The procession was just entering the Rue de la Chaussée-d'Antin, where conglomerations of carriages were holding it up. Bourras went on, his eyes vacant, as if he was dreaming out loud. He still could not understand the Bonheur des Dames's triumph, but he admitted that the old way of business had been defeated.

"Poor Robineau is done for, he's got the look of a drowning man. And the Bédorés, and the Vanpouilles, they can't stand up to it any more, they're like me, their legs are worn out. Deslignières will peg out from a stroke, Piot and Rivoire have had jaundice. Ah! We're all a pretty sight, what a lovely procession of carcasses we are for the dear child! It must be funny for the people watching to see this string of failures going past... What's more, it seems that the wiping-out process is going to continue. The rascals are going to make departments for flowers, for millinery, for perfumery, for shoes and I don't know what else. Grognet, the perfumer in the Rue de Grammont, might as well shut up shop, and I wouldn't give ten francs for Naud's shoe shop in the Rue d'Antin. The plague is spreading as far as the Rue Sainte-Anne, where Lacassagne, who keeps feathers and flowers, and Madame Chadeuil, whose hats, after all, are well-known, will be swept away before two years are out... And after them there'll be others, there'll always be others. Every trade in the neighbourhood will go the same way. When counter-jumpers start selling soap and galoshes, they're quite capable of getting an ambition to sell fried potatoes. The world's really going mad, upon my word!"

By then the hearse was crossing the Place de la Trinité and, from the dark corner in the carriage where Denise, lulled by the funereal pace of the procession, was listening to the old shopkeeper's incessant complaint, she could see the coffin already going up the slope of the Rue Blanche, as they came out of the Rue de la Chausée-d'Antin. Behind her uncle, who was walking blindly and dumbly like a felled ox, she seemed to hear the trampling of a flock being led to the slaughterhouse, the total collapse of the shops of an entire neighbourhood, small traders with the squelching sound of down-at-heel shoes trailing ruin through the black mud of Paris. Bourras, meanwhile, was speaking in an even more hollow voice, as if slowed down by the steep incline of the Rue Blanche.

"As for me, you can put paid to me... But I'm hanging on to him all the same, and I'm not letting him go. He's just lost another appeal. Ah! It's cost me a pretty penny: almost two years of lawsuits and solicitors and barristers! It doesn't matter, he won't go underneath my shop, the judges have decided that work of that sort doesn't at all come into the category of justified repairs. When you think that he was talking of creating there, underneath me, a specially lit room where people could see the colours of materials by gaslight and which would have connected the hosiery and the drapery departments! And he's like a bear with a sore head about it, he can't stomach it that an old wreck like me is barring his way, when everyone else goes down on their knees to his money. Never! I don't want to! They'd better get that straight. Of course I may be left high and dry. Since I've had to fight against the bailiffs, I know that the scoundrel is hunting up my debts, no doubt so as to be able to play a dirty trick on me. It doesn't matter, he says yes, I say no, and I'll always say no, by God! Even when they nail me up between four boards like that poor kid going on ahead there."

When they arrived at the Boulevard de Clichy the carriage went faster, the puffing of the crowd and the unconscious haste of the procession, in a hurry to get it over, was discernible. What Bourras did not mention outright was the dire poverty into which he had fallen, utterly beset as he was by the worries of a small shopkeeper going under yet persisting in holding out under a hail of protests. Denise, who knew about his circumstances, finally broke the silence, murmuring in a voice of entreaty:

"Monsieur Bourras, don't go on being difficult any longer. Let me settle things for you."

He cut her short with a violent gesture.

"Be quiet, it's no one else's business but mine. You're a good little girl, I know that you're making things difficult for him, for that man who thought you were for sale like my house. But what would you say if I advised you to say yes? Well? You'd tell me to go to hell... Very well! When I say no, don't stick your nose in."

As the carriage had stopped at the gate of the cemetery, he and the girl got out. The Baudus' family grave was in the first avenue, on the left. The ceremony was over in a few minutes. Jean had taken his uncle, who was staring open-mouthed at the hole in the ground, to one side. The tail of the procession was spreading out among the neighbouring tombs, the faces of all those shopkeepers, impoverished from living in the depths of their unhealthy ground-floor premises, were acquiring a sickly ugliness beneath the mud-coloured sky. As the coffin sank quietly into the ground, cheeks scarred with blotchiness grew pale, noses nipped with anaemia were lowered and eyelids yellow with biliousness and ravaged by adding up figures turned away.

"We ought all to go and jump into that hole," said Bourras to Denise, who had remained close to him. "That child is the neighbourhood being buried... Oh! I know what I'm saying, the old way of business might as well go and join those white roses they're throwing after her."

Denise took her uncle and her brother home in a carriage. For her it was a day of unrelieved sadness. First, she was beginning to worry about Jean's paleness: when she realized that some fresh affair with a woman was at the back of it, she tried to silence him by opening her purse, but he shook his head and refused; it was serious this time, the niece of a very rich pastry cook, who would not even accept bunches of violets. Next, in the afternoon, when Denise went to fetch Pépé from Madame Gras, the latter announced to her that he was getting too big for her to keep him any longer; if she had any more bother with him a school would have to be found for him, he would have to be sent away perhaps. And finally, when she took Pépé to visit the Baudus, her heart was torn by the bleak sorrow of the Vieil Elbeuf. The shop was closed, her uncle and aunt were at the back of the small dining room, in which they had forgotten to light the gas in spite of the utter darkness of the winter day. There was no one left but them, they were face to face in the house which ruin had slowly emptied, and the death of their daughter was making the dark corners seem even more cavernous; it seemed the ultimate cleavage which would make the old beams, eaten away with damp, fall to pieces. Crushed by the calamity, her uncle was walking blindly round the table all the time, without saying anything, unable to stop himself, with the same gait he had had during the procession; whereas her aunt, silent too, was sunk in a chair with the white face of a wounded person whose blood is running out drop by drop. They did not even weep when Pépé covered their cold cheeks with kisses. Denise was choking back her tears.

That evening, it so happened, Mouret sent for the girl in order to discuss a child's garment which he wanted to put on the market, a cross between a kilt and the broad trousers of a Zouave. Quivering all over with pity, shocked by so much suffering, she was unable to control her feelings; she ventured first of all to speak of old Bourras, of the poor old man they were going to strike when he was already down. But at the name of the umbrella dealer, Mouret lost his temper. The crazy old man, as he called him, was making his life a misery, spoiling his triumph by his ridiculous obstinacy about not parting with his house, that filthy hovel soiling the Bonheur des Dames, the only little corner of the vast block which had escaped conquest. The whole affair was becoming a nightmare; Mouret was so tormented by a morbid desire to kick down the hovel that anyone, apart from the girl, who spoke in favour of Bourras would have risked being thrown out. After all, what did they want him to do? How could he leave that rubbish heap on the Bonheur's flank? It would have to disappear in the end, the shop would have to pass over it. Too bad for the old madman! And he recalled his proposals, how he had offered him as much as a hundred thousand francs. Wasn't that a reasonable offer? He wouldn't haggle to be sure, he would give what was asked for it, but people should at least have a bit of intelligence, they should let him complete his achievement! Did people interfere by stopping locomotives on railways? She was listening to him, her eyes lowered, able to think only of sentimental reasons. The old fellow was getting on in years, they could at least have waited for him to die; if he went bankrupt it would kill him. At that Mouret declared that he was no longer even in a position to prevent things taking their course; Bourdoncle was dealing with it, for the board had decided to put an end to the matter. In spite of her tender-hearted and sorrowful compassion, there was nothing more she could think of to say.

After a painful silence it was Mouret himself who mentioned the Baudus. He began by saying how sorry he was for them about the loss of their daughter. They were excellent people, very worthy, and they were dogged by misfortune. Then he resumed his arguments: really, they had brought their troubles on themselves, people shouldn't remain obstinately like that in a worm-eaten hovel of old-fashioned business; there was nothing surprising about the house falling on their heads. He had foretold it scores of times; why, she must remember how he had told her to warn her uncle that it would be fatal for him to go on lagging behind with ridiculous outworn ideas. And the catastrophe had come, and no one in the world could prevent it now. They couldn't really expect him to ruin himself in order to spare the neighbourhood. In any case, if he had been so mad as to close the Bonheur, another big shop would have sprung up on its own next door to it, for the idea was in the air all over the world, the triumph of workers' and industrial estates had been sown by the breath of fresh air brought by the new century, which was sweeping away crumbling edifices of past ages. Little by little Mouret was warming up, gaining eloquent emotion with which to defend himself against the hatred of his involuntary victims, against the clamour of small, moribund shops which he could hear rising around him. One cannot keep one's dead, after all, they must be buried, and with a gesture he swept away the corpse of old-fashioned trade, the greenish stinking remains of which were becoming the disgrace of the sunny streets of modern Paris and threw it into a pauper's grave. No, no, he had no remorse at all, he was merely carrying out the task of his epoch, and she very well knew it, what is more, she who loved life and had a passion for bold business deals settled in the glare of publicity. Reduced to silence, she listened to him for a long time and then withdrew, her heart full of confusion.

That night Denise did not sleep at all. Insomnia interspersed with nightmares made her toss and turn under the blankets. She fancied she was quite small, bursting into tears in their garden at Valognes at the sight of warblers eating spiders who, in their turn, were eating flies. Was it really true then that death must fertilize the world, that the struggle for life propelled people towards the charnel house of destruction? Next she saw herself again beside the grave into which Geneviève was being lowered, she saw her uncle and aunt, alone in the depths of their dark dining room. In the deep silence, a muffled sound of something crumbling down was echoing through the deathlike air: it was Bourras's house caving in, as if undermined by floods. The silence began again, more sinister than ever, and a fresh collapse reverberated, then another, and another: the Robineaus, Bédoré and his sister, the Vanpouilles, were cracking up and collapsing one after another, the small trade of the Saint-Roch district was disappearing under an invisible pickaxe, with the sudden thunder of carts being unloaded. Then a feeling of immense sorrow woke her with a start. My God! What tortures! Weeping families, old men thrown on to the street, all the poignant tragedies of ruin! And she could not save anyone, she was even aware that all this was a good thing, that this manure of distress was necessary to the health of the Paris of the future. When morning came, she grew calmer; with immense, resigned sadness she remained there, her eyes open and turned towards the window which was growing lighter. Yes, that was the necessary sacrifice, every revolution demanded its victims, one could only advance over dead bodies. Her fear of being an evil genius, of having helped in the murder of her relatives, was not dissolving into heartbroken pity at those irremediable ills, the painful birth pangs of each fresh generation, with which she was confronted. She ended up by trying to think of possible alleviations; her kind heart mused for a long time over measures to be taken in order to save at least her own family from the final collapse.

Then a vision of Mouret rose up before her, with his passionate expression and his caressing eyes. Surely, he would not refuse her anything, she was certain that he would grant her all reasonable compensation. And her thoughts strayed, trying to sum him up. She was familiar with his life, the opportunism of his affections in the past, his continual exploitation of women, the mistresses he had taken in order to get on in the world, his liaison with Madame Desforges with the sole aim of keeping a hold on Baron Hartmann, and all the other women too, the Claras he picked up, the pleasure which he bought, paid for and threw back into the street. Only, these beginnings of a career of amorous adventure, which the shop joked about, blended in the end and disappeared in the man's streak of genius, his all-vanquishing charm. He was seduction personified. What she would never have forgiven him was falsehood in the past, his coldness as a lover beneath the sham gallantry of his attentions. But now that he was suffering because of her, she harboured no resentment. His suffering had made him a nobler man. When she saw him tormented, paying so dearly for his contempt for women, she felt he was redeemed of his shortcomings.

On that very morning Denise obtained from Mouret the promise of such compensation, on the day when the Baudus and old Bourras succumbed, as she should consider legitimate. Weeks passed, and almost every afternoon she would slip out for a few minutes to go and see her uncle, bringing with her her laughter and her brave girl's courage to brighten up the dark shop. She was principally worried about her aunt who, since Geneviève's death, had been in a listless stupor; it seemed as if her life was ebbing away all the time, and when questioned, she would reply with an air of surprise that she felt no pain, that she just felt overwhelmed with sleep. The neighbourhood shook its head: the poor woman would not pine for her daughter for long.

One day, Denise was coming out of the Baudus' house when at the corner of the Place Gaillon she heard a loud shriek. A crowd was rushing forwards, there was panic in the air, the breath of fear and pity which will suddenly stir up a street. The wheels of a brown omnibus, one of the vehicles plying between the Bastille and the Batignolles, were going over the body of a man at the corner of the Rue Neuve-Saint-Augustin, opposite the fountain. Standing on his box with a movement of fury, the driver was holding back his two black horses, which were rearing; and he was swearing, working off steam in strong words.

"Good God! Good God! Can't you look where you're going, you damned blunderer!"

By now the omnibus had stopped. A crowd was surrounding the injured man, a policeman by chance happened to be there. The driver was still standing, calling the passengers of the double-decker as witnesses – for they had also stood up in order to lean out and see the blood – and was giving his version of the story with gestures of exasperation, choking with increasing anger.

"Have you ever seen anything like it? Why the hell should I have got mixed up with an individual like that! I yelled at him, and he just went and jumped under the wheels!"

At that a workman, a house decorator who had rushed up with his brush from a neighbouring shop window, said in a piercing voice in the midst of all the uproar:

"Don't get so worked up! I saw him, honest he stuck himself under there on purpose! Why, he took a header just like that. Another person who was fed up, I suppose!"

Other voices were raised, people were concurring about the idea of suicide, while the policeman was taking down particulars. Ladies, quite pale, were getting out quickly from the vehicle without turning round, taking away with them the horror of the soft jolt which had made their stomachs turn over when the omnibus had gone over the body. Meanwhile Denise drew near, drawn by her constructive pity, which made her interfere in accidents of all kinds – dogs run over, fallen horses, workmen fallen from roofs. And she recognized the unfortunate man lying on the road, unconscious, his frock coat dirtied with mud.

"It's Monsieur Robineau!" she exclaimed in painful astonishment.

The policeman immediately questioned the girl. She gave Robineau's name, profession and address. Thanks to the driver's efforts, the omnibus had swerved, and only Robineau's legs had been caught under the wheels. But it was to be feared that they were both broken. Four volunteers carried the injured man to a chemist's shop in the Rue Gaillon, while the omnibus slowly resumed its journey.

"By God!" said the driver, cracking his whip round his horses. "I've had enough today!"

Denise had followed Robineau to the chemist's shop. The chemist, while waiting for a doctor who could not be found, declared that there was no immediate danger, and that the best thing would be to carry the injured man to his own home, since he lived nearby. A man had gone to the police station to ask for a stretcher. Then the girl had the bright idea of going on ahead so as to prepare Madame Robineau for this dreadful shock. But she had all the difficulty in the world in reaching the street through the crowd, which was making a dreadful crush at the door. This crowd, avid for sensation, was increasing from minute to minute; children and women were craning their necks, standing their ground against violent shoves, and each newcomer was inventing his own version of the accident; by that time it had become a husband whose wife's lover had thrown him out of a window.

In the Rue Neuve-des-Petits-Champs Denise caught sight of Madame Robineau in the distance, standing in the doorway of the silk shop. This gave her a pretext for stopping, and she chatted for a moment, while trying to think of a way of breaking the terrible news gently. The disorder and abandon of the final struggles of a dying business were writ large all over the shop. This had been the expected outcome of the battle of the two rival silks; following a further reduction of five centimes the Paris-Bonheur had crushed all competition: it was now selling at only four francs ninety-five, and Gaujean's silk had met its Waterloo. For two months now Robineau, reduced to trying all kinds of expedients, had been leading a nightmare existence in order to prevent being declared bankrupt.

"I passed your husband in the Place Gaillon," murmured Denise, who had finally gone into the shop.

Madame Robineau, whose glances seemed continually drawn towards the street as if by some secret anxiety, said sharply:

"Ah! Just now, wasn't it? I'm expecting him, he should be here. Monsieur Gaujean came this morning, and they went out together."

She was just as charming as ever, dainty and gay, but her pregnancy, already well advanced, was tiring her, and she was becoming more flustered, more out of her element in business than ever, for her affectionate nature found difficulty in grasping it, and now anyway it was going badly. As she often said, what was the point of it all? Wouldn't it be nicer to live peacefully in some little place on nothing but a crust of bread?

"My dear," she went on, her smile growing sad, "we've nothing to hide from you... Things aren't going well, my poor darling doesn't sleep any more because of it. Why today again Gaujean tormented him about some bills he's late with... I felt I would die of anxiety, all by myself here."

She was returning towards the door when Denise stopped her. The latter had just heard the noise of the crowd in the distance. She could imagine the stretcher which they were bringing, the stream of inquisitive people who had not left the accident for an instant. And then, her throat dry, unable to think of the consoling words she wanted she was forced to tell her.

"Now you mustn't worry, there's no immediate danger... Yes, I saw Monsieur Robineau, he's had an accident... They're bringing him, don't worry, I beseech you."

The young woman was listening to her, dead-white, without yet clearly understanding. The street had filled with people, cabbies who were held up were swearing, some men had set down the stretcher outside the door of the shop, in order to open the double glass doors.

"It's an accident," Denise was continuing, determined to conceal the attempt at suicide. "He was on the pavement, and he slipped under the wheels of an omnibus. Oh, just his feet. They're fetching a doctor. You mustn't worry."

A great shudder shook Madame Robineau. She made two or three inarticulate cries; then, no longer speaking, she swooped down on the stretcher and drew back its curtains with trembling hands. The men who had just been carrying it were waiting outside the house in order to carry it away when a doctor had finally been found. They no longer dared touch Robineau, who had regained consciousness, and whose sufferings at the slightest movement were agonizing. When he saw his wife, two huge tears flowed down his cheeks. She had kissed him, and she was weeping, looking at him with a fixed expression. There was still a mob in the street, faces were crowding together as if at a theatre, their eyes shining; some girls who had slipped out from their workroom were in danger of breaking the glass of the shop windows in order to see better. So as to escape from this fever of curiosity, and thinking in any case that it was not advisable to leave the shop open, Denise had the idea of lowering the roller shutters. She went herself to turn the crank handle, the gearwheels made a plaintive cry and the iron plates were slowly descending, like heavy drapery coming down on the close of a final act. When she came in again and had shut the little round door behind her, she found Madame Robineau still clasping her husband in her distracted arms, beneath the sinister half-light coming from two stars cut out of the metal. The ruined shop was seemingly slipping into a void; the two stars alone shone on that swift, savage catastrophe of the Paris streets. At last Madame Robineau found her voice again.

"Oh, my darling!... Oh, my darling!... Oh, my darling!..."

She could think of no other words, and he, seeing her kneeling like that, bending over, her stomach of an expectant mother crushed against the stretcher, could bear it no longer and, in an attack of remorse, confessed. When he did not move he could only feel the burning leaden weight of his legs.

"Forgive me, I must have been mad... When the solicitor told me in front of Gaujean that the notices will be served tomorrow, I seemed to see flames dancing, as if the walls were burning... And then, I don't remember any more: I was going down the Rue de la Michodière, I thought the people in the Bonheur were making fun of me, that great bitch of a shop was crushing me... Then, when the omnibus turned round I thought about Lhomme and his arm, and I threw myself under it..."

Slowly, in horror at these confessions, Madame Robineau sank down and sat on the floor. Goodness! He had wanted to die! She seized Denise's hand, for the girl, deeply moved by the scene, had leant towards her. The injured man, whose emotion was exhausting him, had just lost consciousness again. And still the doctor did not come! Two men had scoured the neighbourhood already, and now the porter of the house had gone off in his turn.

"You mustn't worry," Denise was repeating mechanically, and she too was sobbing.

Then Madame Robineau, sitting on the ground, her head on the level of the stretcher, her cheek against the webbing on which her husband was lying helpless, unburdened her heart.

"Oh! If I were to tell you... It's for me that he wanted to die. He was always saying to me: I've robbed you, it was your money. And at night he used to dream about those sixty thousand francs, he used to wake up in a sweat, saying that he was no use. When one hadn't more wits than that one shouldn't risk other people's fortunes... You know that he was always highly strung, harassed by nature. In the end he used to see things which made me frightened, he would see me in the street in rags, begging, me whom he loved so deeply, whom he wanted to see rich and happy."

But, turning her head, she saw that his eyes were open again; and she went on in her stammering voice:

"Oh, my darling! Why did you do it? Did you really think I was so mean then? I don't care if we're ruined, believe me. So long as we're together, we're all right... Let them take everything, do. Let's go off somewhere where you won't hear any more about them. You'll be able to work all the same, you'll see how good everything can be still."

Her forehead had dropped down close to her husband's pale face, in the emotion of their distress they were both speechless now. There was silence, the shop seemed to be sleeping, numbed by the pallid dusk which was flooding it; while behind the thin metal of the door, the din of the street could be heard – life passing by in the daylight, the rumbling of vehicles and the bustle of the streets. Finally Denise, who kept on going to glance out of the little door opening onto the hallway of the house, came back calling:

"The doctor!"

The house porter was bringing him, a young man with bright eyes. He preferred to examine the injured man before putting him to bed. Only one leg, the left one, turned out to be broken above the ankle. It was a simple fracture, there appeared to be no danger of complications. They were preparing to carry the stretcher inside the bedroom, when Gaujean appeared. He was coming to report a final step he had taken, which in any case had fallen through: the declaration of bankruptcy was certain.

"What's this?" he murmured. "What has happened?"

In a few words, Denise told him and he grew embarrassed. Robineau said to him feebly:

"I don't hold it against you, but all this is a bit your fault."

"Why, old fellow," Gaujean replied, "we needed to have stronger backs than ours were... You know that I'm in no better way than you are!"

They were lifting the stretcher. The injured man found enough strength to say:

"No, no, stronger backs would have bent all the same... I can understand that obstinate old men like Bourras and Baudu stay on – but as to us, who were young, who were accepting the new state of affairs! No, you know, Gaujean, it's the end of a world."

He was carried away. Madame Robineau kissed Denise with an impulsive gesture, in which there was almost joy at being at last rid of the worries of business. As Gaujean was leaving with the girl, he confessed to her that that poor devil Robineau was right. It was idiotic to wish to fight against the Bonheur des Dames. He personally knew he was finished unless he could get into their good graces again. Already the day before he had secretly approached Hutin, who was just about to leave for Lyons. But he was losing hope, and he tried to arouse Denise's interest, having no doubt heard about her influence.

"My word!" he was repeating. "It's too bad for the manufacturers. People would laugh at me if I ruined myself by battling in other people's interests, when the fellows are quarrelling over who will manufacture the cheapest... My goodness! As you used to say in the past, the manufacturers have only got to keep up with progress by better organization and new methods. Everything will turn out all right, so long as the public's pleased."

Denise was smiling. She replied:

"Just you go and say that to Monsieur Mouret himself... He'll be pleased to see you, he's not the man to bear you a grudge if you offer him a profit of so much as a centime a yard."

One bright, sunny afternoon in January Madame Baudu died. For a fortnight she had no longer been able to go down into the shop, which a charwoman was looking after. She was sitting in the middle of her bed, her back propped up by pillows. In her white face only her eyes were still alive and, her head erect, she directed them stubbornly through the little curtains on the windows towards the Bonheur des Dames opposite. Baudu, made ill himself by this obsession, by the despairing fixity of her gaze, would sometimes try to pull the big curtains. But, with a gesture of entreaty, she would stop him, she persisted in seeing it until her very last breath. Now the monster had taken everything from her, both her shop and her daughter; she herself had been gradually ebbing away together with the Vieil Elbeuf, losing her life as it was losing its customers; the day on which it was at its last gasp, she no longer had any breath. When she felt herself dying, she still had enough strength to insist on her husband opening both windows. It was mild, a stream of gay sunshine was gilding the Bonheur, whereas the room in the ancient dwelling was shivering in the shade. Madame Baudu remained with a fixed stare, filled with this vision of the triumphant building, of the clear glass behind which a rush of millions was passing. Slowly, her eyes were growing dimmer, invaded with darkness, and when they were extinguished in death, they remained wide open, drowned in great tears, still gazing.

Once more all the ruined small shopkeepers of the neighbourhood walked in the funeral procession. The Vanpouille brothers were there, pale from their December bills, paid by a crowning effort which they would not be able to repeat. Bédoré, leaning on a cane, with his sister, was worried by such anxieties that his stomach trouble was getting worse. Deslignières had had a stroke, Piot and Rivoire were walking in silence, noses to the ground, like finished men. And no one dared ask about those who had disappeared, Quinette, Mademoiselle Tatin and others who, from morning till night, were going under, being knocked down and swept away by the stream of disaster, to say nothing of Robineau lying in bed with his broken leg. But they were particularly pointing out to each other, with an air of interest, the new shopkeepers stricken by the plague: Grognet, the perfumer, Madame Chadeuil the milliner, Lacassagne the florist, and Naud the shoemaker, still on their feet, but filled with anxiety by the disease which would sweep them away in their turn. Behind the hearse Baudu was walking with the same gait of a felled ox with which he had accompanied his daughter, while from the depths of the first mourning carriage Bourras's glittering eyes could be seen beneath the undergrowth of his snow-white eyebrows and hair.

Denise was in great trouble. For a fortnight she had been worn out with worries and fatigue. She had had to put Pépé in a school, and she had her hands full with Jean, for he was so much in love with the pastry cook's niece that he had begged his sister to ask for her hand in marriage. Then there had come the death of her aunt, and these repeated catastrophes had completely overwhelmed the girl. Mouret had once more offered his assistance: what she was doing for her uncle and the others would be well done. One morning, hearing the news that Bourras had been thrown into the street and that Baudu was going to shut up shop, she had yet another interview with Mouret. Then after lunch she went out, in the hope of being able to make things easier at least for them.

Bourras was standing in the Rue de la Michodière, planted on the pavement opposite his house, from which he had been expelled the day before following a fine trick, a real gem which the solicitor had thought up: as Mouret had claims, he had without difficulty just had the umbrella dealer declared bankrupt and had then paid five hundred francs for the lease at the official receiver's sale; thus the obstinate old man had lost for five hundred francs what he had refused to part with for a hundred thousand. What is more, when the architect arrived with his demolition squad, he had had to resort to the police in order to get Bourras out. The goods were sold, the furniture removed from the rooms, and he stubbornly remained in the corner where he slept, from which, moved to pity at last, they did not dare turn him out. The demolition workers even attacked the roof over his head. They had removed the rotten slates, the ceilings were falling in, the walls were cracking, and there he remained in the middle of the rubbish, beneath the ancient beams which had been stripped bare. Finally, when confronted with the police, he had left. But from the very next morning he had reappeared on the pavement opposite, after having passed the night in a nearby hotel.

"Monsieur Bourras," said Denise gently.

He did not hear her, his blazing eyes were gazing intently at the demolition workers, whose pickaxes were starting on the front of the hovel. Now, through the empty windows, the interior could be seen, the wretched murky staircase to which the sun had not penetrated for two hundred years.

"Ah! It's you," he replied in the end, when he had recognized her. "They're making a job of it, aren't they, the robbers!"

Deeply moved by the woeful sadness of the old dwelling place, she no longer dared say anything, and was herself unable to drag her eyes away from the mildewed stones which were falling. Upstairs, on a corner of the ceiling of her old room she could still see the name "Ernestine" written in black shaky letters with the flame of a candle, and the memory of her days of poverty came back to her, tinged with pity for all suffering. The workmen, in order to pull down a section of wall all at once, had had the idea of attacking it at its base. It was tottering.

"If only it would crush them all!" Bourras was murmuring in a savage voice.

A terrible cracking sound was heard. The terrified workmen rushed out into the street. The wall was loosening and carrying away the whole ruin as it crashed down. It was clear that the hovel, with all its subsidences and cracks, was no longer standing the strain, one push had sufficed to split it from top to bottom. There was a pitiful landslide, the flattening of a mud hut sodden with rain. Not a wall remained standing, there was nothing left on the ground but a heap of rubbish, the refuse of the past being thrown out.

"My God!" the old man had cried, as if the blow had reverberated through the very depths of his soul.

He was standing there open-mouthed, he would never have thought it could be over so quickly. He stood looking at the open gash, the gaping hole on the flank of the Bonheur des Dames, which was now rid of the wart which had been disfiguring it. The gnat had been squashed, this was the ultimate triumph over the bitter obstinacy of the infinitely small, the whole block had been overrun and conquered. Passers-by who had flocked there were talking at the top of their voices with the demolition workers, who were losing their tempers over the old masonry, which was quite liable to kill people.

"Monsieur Bourras," repeated Denise, trying to draw him aside, "you know that you won't be deserted. All your needs will be provided for..."

He drew himself up.

"I haven't any needs... It's them who's sent you, isn't it? Well, tell them that old Bourras still knows how to work, and that he'll find work wherever he wants... Really, it's a bit too much of a good thing, to give charity to the people one murders!"

At that she entreated him:

"I beseech you, do accept, don't make me so unhappy." But he was shaking his white mane.

"No, no, it's all over. Goodbye. You're young, you go and live happily, do, and don't stop the old from going off with their own ideas."

He cast one last glance at the pile of rubbish, then he walked heavily away. She watched his back going through the scrimmage of the street. Then it disappeared round the corner of the Place Gaillon, and that was all.

For a moment Denise remained motionless, her eyes vague. Then she went into her uncle's house. The draper was alone in the dark Vieil Elbeuf. The charwoman came only in the mornings and evenings to do a little cooking, and to help him take down and put up the shutters. He passed hours deep in solitude, often without anyone coming to disturb him for the whole day, and when a customer did still venture in he became flustered and was no longer able to find the goods. He walked up and down continuously in the silence and half-light, still with his heavy funereal gait, giving way to a morbid need, to real paroxysms of forced marching, as if he wanted to lull and deaden his pain.

"Are you better, Uncle?" asked Denise.

He only stopped for a second, and then went off again, walking from the cash desk to a dark corner.

"Yes, yes, very well... Thank you."

She was trying to think of something comforting to say, of cheerful words, but was unable to do so.

"Did you hear that noise? The house is down."

"Why, so it is!" he murmured with an astonished air. "That must have been the house... I felt the ground tremble, I shut my door this morning when I saw them on the roof."

He made a vague gesture, as if to say that such things no longer interested him. Each time he came back to the cash desk, he looked at the empty bench, that bench covered with worn velvet on which his wife and daughter had grown up. Then, when his perpetual tramping brought him to the other end of the shop, he would look at the shelves drowned in shadow, in which a few pieces of cloth were being finished off by mildew. It was a widowed shop, those whom he loved were gone, his business had come to a shameful end, he alone remained, carrying his dead heart and his broken pride about with him through these catastrophes. He was looking up at the black ceiling, listening to the silence coming from the darkness in the little dining room, the family nook which he had loved in the past even down to its stale smell. There was not a breath left in the ancient dwelling, and his regular, heavy footsteps made the old walls echo, as if he was walking on the tomb of all he had loved.

Finally Denise broached the subject which had brought her there.

"Uncle, you can't stay here like this. You must make up your mind."

Without halting his walk, he replied:

"Certainly, but what's to be done? I've tried to sell, no one came. My God! One day I'll just shut the shop and go away."

She knew that there was no longer any danger of him being declared bankrupt. In the face of such relentless misfortune, his creditors had preferred to come to an agreement. Her uncle would simply find himself in the street, with everything paid.

"But what will you do then?" she murmured, trying to think of some way of coming to the offer which she did not dare put forward.

"I don't know," he replied. "I suppose someone will pick up my bits."

He had changed his course, and was walking from the dining room to the shop windows; each time he reached them, he contemplated the pitiful windows and their forgotten display with a dejected gaze. He did not even look up at the triumphant façade of the Bonheur des Dames, its architectural lines disappearing to the right and left at either end of the street. He was prostrate; he no longer had the strength to lose his temper.

"Listen, Uncle," Denise said finally in embarrassment. "Perhaps there might be a job for you..."

She began afresh, blurting out:

"Yes, I've been asked to offer you a job as a shopwalker."

"Well, where?" asked Baudu.

"Why there! Over the way... At our place... Six thousand francs, it isn't tiring work."

Suddenly he came to a standstill, facing her. But, instead of flying into a rage as she had feared, he became very pale, overcome with a painful emotion, with bitter resignation.

"Over the way, over the way," he muttered several times. "You want me to go and work over the way?"

Denise herself was overcome by the same emotion. She looked back on the long struggle between the two shops, was present again at the funeral processions of Geneviève and of Madame Baudu, she could see before her eyes the Vieil Elbeuf overthrown, massacred where it stood by the Bonheur des Dames. And the idea of her uncle going to work over the way, walking about there in a white tie, made her gorge rise with pity and resentment.

"Come now, Denise, my dear, how could I?" he said simply, folding his pathetic trembling hands as he did so.

"No, no, Uncle!" she exclaimed, with an upsurge of her whole upright, honest being. "It would be wrong... Forgive me, I beg of you."

He had started walking up and down again, once more his tread was shaking the sepulchral void of the house. And when she left him, he was still walking, walking with the obstinate restlessness of deep despair, which goes round and round in circles without ever being able to escape.

That night Denise once more could not sleep. She had now plumbed the depths of her impotence. She could do nothing to relieve the distress even of her own family. She had to witness to the bitter end the inexorable workings of life, which must have death in order that it may be continually renewed. She no longer fought against it, she accepted this rule of the struggle, but her woman's heart was filled with compassion, moved to tears and brotherly love for the whole of suffering humanity. For years she had been caught in the wheels of the machine. Had she not shed her own blood in it? Had she not been bruised, driven out, heaped with insults? Even nowadays she was sometimes panic-stricken at feeling herself singled out by a logical sequence of events. She was so frail, why should it be her? Why should her small hand suddenly carry so much weight in the monster's task? And the force which was sweeping all before it was carrying her away too, in her turn, she whose coming was to be a revenge.

Mouret had invented this mechanism for crushing people, the brutal working of which aroused her indignation; he had strewn the neighbourhood with ruins, he had despoiled some and killed others; yet she loved him in spite of it for the grandeur of his achievement, and each time he committed some fresh excess of power, notwithstanding the flood of tears which overwhelmed her at the thought of the misery of the vanquished, which was sacrosanct, she loved him even more.

14

THE RUE DU DIX-DÉCEMBRE, brand new, was stretching out with its chalk-white houses and the last scaffoldings of a few buildings which were behind schedule, beneath a limpid February sky; a stream, a broad conquering procession of vehicles was going along through the middle of the new opening, full of light, which was cutting through the dank shade of the ancient Saint-Roch district – and between the Rue de la Michodière and the Rue de Choiseul there was a regular riot, the crush made by a crowd of people which had been raised to fever heat by a month of advertisement, and was looking up and gaping at the monumental façade of the Bonheur des Dames. It was going to be opened on that Monday, on the occasion of a great exhibition of household linen.

There was a vast expanse of polychrome architecture, gay in its freshness and heightened with gold, which heralded the din and glare of business inside, attracting the eye as if it were a gigantic display blazing with the most brilliant colours. On the ground floor, so as not to kill the effect of the materials in the shop windows, the decorations were sombre: the base of the building was of sea-green marble – the corner piles and supporting columns were inlaid with black marble, the severity of which was lightened by gilded tablets – and everything else was of plate glass in a framework of metal – nothing but glass, which seemed to open up the depths of the galleries and halls to the daylight of the street. But as the storeys rose up, the tones lit up and became more dazzling. Mosaics stretched out in the frieze on the ground floor – a garland of red and blue flowers alternating with slabs of marble on which the names of various wares were carved – encircling the colossus, going on to infinity. Next, the base of the first floor, made of glazed bricks, was in its turn supporting the glass of the broad bay windows as far up as the frieze, which consisted of gilded shields bearing the coats of arms of French towns, and designs in terracotta, the glazing of which repeated the clear tones of the base. Finally, at the very top, the entablature burst out as if it was a flamboyant blossoming of the whole shopfront, the mosaics and ceramics reappeared in warmer colouring, the zinc of the gutters was cut in a pattern and gilded, statues representing the great industrial and manufacturing cities were lined up on the acroterium, their delicate silhouettes standing out against the sky. The sightseers were above all marvelling at the central door, which was as high as a triumphal arch; it too was decorated with an abundance of mosaics and ceramics, and surmounted with an allegorical group – Woman, being dressed and embraced by a laughing flight of little cupids – the fresh gilding of which was glinting in the sun.

As two o'clock approached, the police had to move the crowd on and keep an eye on the parking of vehicles. The palace was built, the temple to Fashion's madness for spending had been set up. It dominated a whole neighbourhood and cast its shadow over it. Already the wound left on its flank by the demolition of Bourras's hovel had healed so completely that one would have searched in vain for the place where that ancient wart had been; in superb isolation the four shopfronts ran the length of four streets without a break. On the opposite pavement the Vieil Elbeuf, which had been closed since Baudu's admittance into a home for the aged, was walled up like a tomb behind the shutters which were no longer taken down; little by little the wheels of cabs were bespattering them, in the rising wave of publicity they were drowned under posters which glued them together and which seemed to be the final nail in the coffin of the old way of business, and in the middle of that dead shop window, soiled and bespattered by the street, motley with the rags and tatters of the Parisian turmoil, an immense yellow poster was displayed like a flag planted on a conquered empire. It was brand new, and in letters two feet high it announced the great sale at the Bonheur des Dames. It was as if, after its successive extensions, the colossus had been seized with shame and repugnance for the murky neighbourhood into which it had been born without any pretensions and which it had later massacred, and was now turning its back on it, leaving the mud of its narrow streets behind it and looking out on the sunny thoroughfare of the new Paris with the face of one who had risen in the world. Now, as it was represented in the picture on the advertisements, it had swollen, like the ogre in the fairy tale whose shoulders threatened to break through the clouds. First, in the foreground of this picture, the Rue du Dix-Décembre, the Rue de la Michodière and the Rue Monsigny were shown full of little black figures and stretching out inordinately, as if to open up the way for customers from all over the world. Then, the buildings themselves, of which a bird's eye view was given, were of an exaggerated vastness, with their main roofs indicating the position of the covered galleries and their courtyards with glass roofs through which the halls could be discerned, a limitless lake of glass and zinc shining in the sunshine. Beyond, Paris stretched out, but a Paris which was dwarfed and eaten up by the monster: the houses surrounding it had the humility of thatched cottages, and were scattered beyond it in a dust of blurred chimneys; the monuments seemed to be melting away, two strokes of the pen on the left-hand side indicated Notre-Dame, there was a circumflex accent on the right for the Invalides, and the Panthéon in the background was lost and shamefaced, no bigger than a pea. The skyline was fading away in dust, it had become nothing but a frame to the picture to be treated with scorn, and its distant blurred outlines indicated that it too, as far away as the heights of Châtillon and the open country, was enslaved.

The crowd had been growing from the morning onwards. No other shop had stirred up the town with such a racket of publicity. Nowadays the Bonheur was spending nearly six hundred thousand francs on posters, advertisements and appeals of every kind each year; the number of catalogues sent out was reaching four hundred thousand, more than a hundred thousand francs' worth of materials was being cut up into patterns. Newspapers and walls were completely overrun with advertisements, the mass of the public were assailed as if by a monstrous brass trumpet relentlessly blazoning the hubbub of huge sales to the four corners of the globe. In future too, the shopfront itself, outside which people were crushing each other, would become a living advertisement, with its variegated and gilded luxury of a bazaar, its windows broad enough to display the whole gamut of women's clothes, its shop signs lavishly distributed everywhere, from the marble slabs of the ground floor right up to the sheets of iron arched over the roofs – shop signs which were painted, engraved, carved, uncoiling the gold of their streamers on which the name of the shop could be read in azure letters, cut out of the blue of the air. In order to celebrate the opening, banners and flags had been added as well; each storey was decked with banners and standards bearing the arms of the principal towns of France; while right at the top the flags of foreign nations, hoisted on flag poles, were flapping in the wind of heaven. Finally, downstairs in the shop windows, the display of household linen was of a blinding intensity. It was a strain on the eyes, there was nothing but white, a complete trousseau and a mountain of sheets on the left, and curtains forming chapels and pyramids of handkerchiefs on the right, and between the "hangings" at the doorway – lengths of linen, of calico, of muslin, tumbling in sheets like falls of snow – there were clothed figures made of sheets of bluish cardboard, a young bride and a lady in evening dress, both life-size and dressed in real lace and silk, smiling with their painted faces. A circle of gapers was ceaselessly forming and reforming, amazement mixed with desire was mounting in the crowd.

The Bonheur des Dames was also arousing curiosity because of a calamity which was the talk of Paris, a fire which had burnt down the Quatre Saisons, the big shop which Bouthemont had opened scarcely three weeks earlier near the Opéra. The newspapers were crammed with details: how the fire had been started by a gas explosion during the night, how the terrified salesgirls had fled in their nightdresses, how Bouthemont had been heroic and had carried five of them to safety on his shoulders. In any case, the enormous losses were covered by insurance, and the public was beginning to shrug its shoulders, saying that it had been a splendid advertisement. For the moment public attention, fired by the stories which were going round and occupied to the point of obsession by these emporiums which were acquiring such importance in public life, was flowing back to the Bonheur again. That fellow Mouret had nothing but luck! Paris was hailing his star and rushing to see him standing there erect, with all competition at his feet, swept there by the conspiring flames, and people were already calculating the season's profits, estimating how much the enforced closing of the rival shop was going to increase the flow of the crowd through the doors of the Bonheur. For a moment he had been a prey to anxieties, worried at feeling he had against him a woman, that same Madame Desforges to whom, to a certain extent, he owed his fortune. The financial dilettantism of Baron Hartmann, who had put money into both businesses, also irritated him. And he was, above all, exasperated at not having had the same idea of genius as Bouthemont, for that hedonist had just had his shop blessed by the vicar from the Madeleine, accompanied by all his clergy. It had been an astounding ceremony, religious rites were paraded through the silk and glove departments, God had landed up amongst women's knickers and corsets; it is true that this had not prevented the whole shop being burnt down, but it had had such an effect on society customers that it had been worth a million advertisements. Ever since then Mouret had been dreaming of getting hold of the Archbishop.

Meanwhile, the clock over the doorway was striking three. It was the afternoon crush, nearly a hundred thousand customers were suffocating in the galleries and halls. Outside, from one end of the Rue du Dix-Décembre to the other, carriages were waiting, and towards the Opéra another solid block of vehicles was occupying the blind alley where the avenue which was to be built would eventually start. Ordinary cabs were mingling with gentlemen's broughams, coachmen were waiting among the wheels, rows of horses were whinnying, shaking their glinting curbs, which were lit up by the sun. The ranks were endlessly reforming in the midst of summonses from the ostlers and the jostling of the animals which were moving closer to each other as fresh vehicles were incessantly arriving. Pedestrians were fleeing to street islands in startled bands and, in the vanishing perspective of the broad, straight thoroughfare, the pavements were black with people. Between the white buildings the clamour was mounting, and above that rolling human river there hung the soul of Paris, an enormous, gentle breath, the gigantic embrace of which could be felt.

Outside one of the windows Madame de Boves, accompanied by her daughter Blanche and Madame Guibal, was looking at a display of semi-made-up suits.

"Oh, do look!" she said. "Those linen suits for nineteen francs seventy-five!"

In their square cardboard boxes, the suits, tied up with a ribbon, were folded so as to show only the trimmings, embroidered with blue and red, and across the corner of each box a picture showed the garment already made up, being worn by a young lady looking like a princess.

"My goodness! It isn't worth any more," murmured Madame Guibal. "As soon as you get it in your hand you can see it's just rags!"

Nowadays, since Monsieur de Boves had become tied to an armchair by attacks of gout, the two women were on intimate terms. The wife tolerated the mistress, on the whole preferring that the affair should take place in her own house, for she made a little pocket money there by picking up sums of which her husband allowed himself to be robbed, for he knew he had need of indulgence himself.

"Well, let's go in," Madame Guibal resumed. "We must have a look at their exhibition… Didn't your son-in-law say he'd meet you inside?"

Madame de Boves did not reply, her eyes were vague, and she was looking with absorption at the line of carriages which, one by one, were opening their doors and releasing more and more customers.

"Yes," said Blanche in the end, in her lifeless voice. "Paul is going to pick us up at about four in the reading room, when he leaves the Ministry."

They had been married for a month, and Vallagnosc, following three weeks' leave spent in the Midi, had just returned to his job. The young woman already had the heavy build of her mother, her flesh had become puffier and had been somehow coarsened by marriage.

"Why, there's Madame Desforges over there!" the Countess exclaimed, her eyes on a brougham which was drawing up.

"Oh, do you think so?" murmured Madame Guibal. "After all that business… She must be still mourning the fire at the Quatre Saisons."

Nevertheless it was indeed Henriette. She caught sight of the ladies and came towards them gaily, hiding her defeat beneath the polished ease of her manners.

"Why yes! I wanted to get an idea... It's better to see for one-self, isn't it? Oh, Monsieur Mouret and I are still good friends, although they say he's furious since I've had an interest in the rival shop... So far as I'm concerned, there's only one thing I can't forgive him, and that's having encouraged that marriage, you know, that man Joseph and my protégée, Mademoiselle de Fontenailles..."

"What! Has it come off?" Madame de Boves broke in. "How awful!"

"Yes, my dear, and solely in order to put us in our place. I know him, he wanted to show that our society girls are only good for marrying his porters."

She was growing animated. All four of them were standing on the pavement, in the middle of the scrimmage at the entrance. Little by little, however, they were being caught up in the stream, and they could do nothing but abandon themselves to the current; they went through the door as if they had been lifted up, without realizing they had done so, talking more loudly in order to make themselves heard. Now they were asking each other for news of Madame Marty. It was said that poor Monsieur Marty, following some violent family scenes, had just been struck down with megalomania; he would draw out treasures by the handful from the earth, he would empty gold mines and load up tumbrels with diamonds and precious stones.

"Poor fellow!" said Madame Guibal. "He who was always so shabby-looking and humble, like the poor tutor he was! And what about his wife?"

"She's living on an uncle at the moment," Henriette replied. "A nice kind old uncle who went to live in her house when he lost his wife... In any case, she should be here, we'll see her."

The ladies stood stock still with surprise. Before them stretched out the shop, the vastest shop in the world according to the advertisements. By now the great central gallery ran from one end of it to the other, opening into the Rue du Dix-Décembre and the Rue Neuve-Saint-Augustin, while to the right and left, like the side aisles in a church, the Monsigny gallery and the Michodière gallery, which were narrower, also ran the whole length of the two streets without interruption. From place to place, amidst the metal framework of the hanging staircases and suspension bridges, the halls widened out into squares. The interior plan had been changed round: now the remnants were on the Rue du Dix-Décembre side, the silks were in the middle, the gloves occupied the Saint-Augustin Hall at the back, and when one looked up from the new main entrance hall one could still see the bedding, moved from one end of the second floor to the other. The enormous number of departments had risen to fifty: many of them, brand new, were being opened that day; others, which had become too important, had simply had to be split up in order to facilitate selling – and because of the steady increase in business, the staff itself had just been brought up to three thousand and forty-five employees for the new season.

It was the stupendous sight of the great exhibition of household linen which was holding up the ladies. First of all, surrounding them, there was the entrance hall, with light windows and paved with mosaics, in which displays of inexpensive goods were drawing the voracious crowd. Next there were galleries leading out, of a dazzling whiteness like a polar vista, a whole snowy region unfolding with the endlessness of steppes draped with ermine, a mass of glaciers lit up beneath the sun. The same whiteness as that in the outside windows was repeated there, but it was heightened and on a colossal scale, burning from one end of the enormous nave to the other with the white blaze of a conflagration at its height. There was nothing but white, all the white goods from every department, an orgy of white, a white star, the steady radiance of which was blinding at first and made it impossible to distinguish any details in the midst of this unparalleled whiteness. Soon the eyes grew accustomed to it: to the left in the Monsigny gallery there stretched out white promontories of linens and calicoes, white rocks of sheets, table napkins and handkerchiefs, while in the Michodière gallery on the right, occupied by the haberdashery, hosiery and woollens, white edifices were displayed made of pearl buttons; there was a huge set piece made of white socks, a whole hall covered with white swansdown and lit up from above by a shaft of light. But the main source of light was that radiating from the central gallery, where the ribbons and fichus, the gloves and silks were situated. The counters disappeared beneath the white of silks and ribbons, of gloves and fichus. Around the iron pillars froths of white muslin were twining up, knotted from place to place with white scarves. The staircases were decked with white draperies, draperies of piqué alternating with dimity, which ran all along the banisters, encircling the halls right up to the second floor – and the ascending whiteness was taking wing, thronging and disappearing like a flight of swans. From the domes the whiteness was falling back again in a rain of eiderdown, a sheet of huge flakes of snow: white blankets and white coverlets were waving in the air, hung up like banners in a church; long streams of pillow lace were interlaced and seemingly suspended like swarms of white butterflies, humming there motionless; laces were quivering everywhere, floating like gossamer against a summer sky, filling the air with their white breath. And over the silk counter in the main hall there was a tent made of white curtains hanging down from the glass roof, which was the miracle, the altar of this cult of white. There were muslins, gauzes, guipures, flowing in frothy waves, while sumptuous embroidered tulles and lengths of oriental silk and silver lamé served as a background to this gigantic decoration, which smacked both of the tabernacle and of the bedroom. It looked like a great white bed, its virginal whiteness waiting, as in legends, for the white princess, for she who would one day come, all-powerful, in her white bridal veil.

"Oh, it's fantastic!" the ladies were repeating. "Extraordinary!"

They did not tire of this hymn of white which all the materials in the whole shop were singing. It was the vastest exhibition Mouret had so far made, the crowning stroke of genius of his talent for display. All through this avalanche of white and the seeming disorder of the materials there ran a harmonic phrase, white sustained and developed in all its tones, which were stated and then grew and expanded with the complicated orchestration of some masterly fugue, the continued development of which carries the soul away in an ever-widening flight. There was nothing but white, yet it was never the same white, but all the different tones of white, one against another, contrasting and complimenting each other, achieving the brilliance of light itself. First came the mat whites of calico and linen, the dull whites of flannel and cloth; next came the velvets, the silks, the satins, a rising scale, the white little by little lighting up, finishing in little flames around the breaks of the folds, and in the transparency of the curtains the white took wing, in the muslins and laces it became untrammelled light, and the tulles were so ethereal that they seemed to be the ultimate note, vanishing into nothing – while at the back of the gigantic alcove the silver in the lengths of oriental silk sang out above everything else.

In the meantime, the shop was full of life, people were besieging the lifts, there was a tremendous crush in the buffet and the reading room, a whole multitude was travelling through those snowy spaces. The crowd looked black, like December skaters on a lake in Poland. On the ground floor there was a dark surge ebbing back, in which nothing but fragile, delighted women's faces could be seen. Through the fretwork of the iron frames, all up the staircases and on the suspension bridges, there was an endless ascent of little figures, seemingly straying among snowy peaks. The suffocating hothouse heat which confronted them on those icy heights came as a surprise. The buzz of voices made the deafening noise of a river full of drift ice. On the ceiling the lavish gilding, the glass inlaid with gold and the golden rosettes were like a burst of sunshine, shining on the Alps of the great exhibition of white.

"Come, come," said Madame de Boves, "we must move on, all the same. We can't stay here for ever."

Inspector Jouve, standing near the door, had not taken his eyes off her since she had entered the shop. When she turned round their glances met. Then, as she started to walk off again, he let her get a little ahead and then followed her at a distance, without appearing to take any further notice of her.

"Why!" said Madame Guibal, stopping once more at the first cash desk. "Those violets are a nice idea!"

She was speaking of the Bonheur's new free gift, little bunches of white violets, bought in their thousands in Nice and distributed to every customer who made even the smallest purchase; this was an idea of Mouret's which there was a great fuss about in the newspapers. Boys in livery were standing near each cash desk and handing out the free gifts, under the supervision of a shopwalker. Gradually the customers were becoming decked with flowers, the shop was filling up with these white bridal bouquets, all the women were carrying a penetrating perfume of flowers around with them.

"Yes," murmured Madame Desforges in a jealous voice, "the idea's all right."

But just as the ladies were about to move away, they heard two salesmen joking about the violets. One of them, tall and thin, was surprised: so it was coming off, was it, the chief's marriage with the buyer in the children's department? While the short, fat one was replying that no one knew for certain, but that they'd bought the flowers all the same.

"What!" said Madame de Boves, "Monsieur Mouret is getting married?"

"It's the first I've heard of it," Henriette replied, feigning indifference. "But anyway, everyone ends up by doing it."

The Countess had thrown a sharp glance at her new friend. Now they both understood why Madame Desforges had come to the Bonheur des Dames, in spite of the battles since the rupture between them. She was obviously giving way to an invincible urge to see and to suffer.

"I'll stay with you," Madame Guibal, her curiosity aroused, said to her. "We'll meet Madame de Boves again in the reading room."

"Very well, let's do that!" the latter declared. "There's something I want to see about on the first floor... Are you coming Blanche?"

And she went upstairs, followed by her daughter, while Inspector Jouve, still following her, took a neighbouring staircase in order not to attract her attention. The other two were lost in the dense crowd on the ground floor.

In the midst of the bustle of selling yet once more all the departments were talking of nothing but the governor's love affairs. The intrigue which had for months been giving the assistants, delighted by Denise's long resistance, something to talk about, had just suddenly come to a head: it had been learnt the day before that the girl was leaving the Bonheur, in spite of Mouret's entreaties, on the plea that she greatly needed a rest. Opinion was divided: would she or wouldn't she leave? From department to department bets of five francs were being laid that she would marry him the next Sunday. The crafty ones were staking a lunch on her marrying him in the end, and yet the others, those who believed that she would leave, were not risking their money without good reason either. Assuredly, the young lady was in the strong position of an adored woman who refuses to yield, but the director, on his side, was strong because of his wealth, his happiness as a widower and his pride, which some final unreasonable demand might provoke beyond measure. In any case, both factions agreed that the little salesgirl had conducted the affair with the skill of a courtesan of genius, and that she was playing her final card by giving him a choice: marry me or I leave.

Meanwhile Denise did not think of such things at all. She had never been either demanding or calculating. She had decided to leave precisely because of the opinions which, to her continual surprise, were being passed about her conduct. It was not as if she had willed it all, or had shown herself to be astute, flirtatious or ambitious. She had simply turned up there, and she was the first to be surprised that anyone could love her like that. And why, even now, did people see cunning in her resolve to leave the Bonheur? Yet it was so natural! She was becoming a nervous wreck, she felt unbearable anguish, surrounded as she was by the everlasting gossip of the shop, by Mouret's burning obsession, and faced with the struggle which she had to have with herself, and she preferred to go away, seized with the fear that she might give in one day and then regret it for the rest of her life. If these were skilful tactics, she was not aware of the fact, and she would ask herself in despair what she could do to avoid looking like a husband hunter. The idea of marriage now made her angry; she was resolved to go on saying no, always no, if he should carry his madness as far as that. She alone should suffer. The necessity for parting reduced her to tears, but, greatly courageous as she was, she repeated to herself that it was necessary, and that she would have no more peace or happiness if she were to act in any other way.

When Mouret received her resignation, in his effort to contain himself he remained silent and seemingly frigid. Then he curtly declared that he would give her a week to think it over before allowing her to do anything so silly. At the end of a week, when she brought the subject up again and expressed her categorical desire to leave after the big sale, he did not lose his temper any more than he had before, he affected to talk reason: she was ruining her fortune, she would never again get the same position anywhere else as she occupied in his shop. Had she got another job in view then? He was quite ready to give her the advantages which she was hoping to find elsewhere. When the girl replied that she had not yet looked for a job, but that, thanks to what she had already saved, she was hoping to have a month's rest at Valognes before doing so, he asked what would prevent her from coming back to the Bonheur after that, if it was only the care of her health which was obliging her to leave it. She remained silent, tortured by this interrogation. At that it occurred to him that she was going to rejoin a lover, perhaps a husband. Had she not confessed to him, one evening, that there was someone she loved? From that moment onwards he had carried the avowal he had dragged from her in a moment of distress deep in his heart, plunged in like a knife. If that man was going to marry her, she was abandoning everything in order to follow him – that explained her obstinacy. It was all over; he merely added in his icy voice that he would no longer detain her, since she could not tell him the real reasons for her departure. This callous conversation, which took place without anger, upset her more than the violent scene which she had foreseen.

During the week which Denise still had to spend in the shop Mouret remained pale and tense. When going through the department, he pretended not to see her, never had he seemed more detached, more buried in his work – and the bets began again; only the very brave dared risk a lunch on marriage. Meanwhile beneath this coldness which was so unusual for him, Mouret was hiding an appalling attack of indecision and suffering. Frenzy made the blood rush to his head: he saw red, he would dream of taking Denise by force, of keeping her by stifling her cries. Next he would try to reason, he would try to think of practical ways of preventing her from going out of the door, but he was always confronted with his own powerlessness, filled with fury by his useless money and might. Nevertheless, in the midst of these mad projects, an idea was growing, little by little making itself felt, in spite of his feelings of rebellion. After the death of Madame Hédouin he had sworn not to re-marry; having had his initial luck because of a woman, he was resolved from then on to make his fortune out of all women. It was a superstition with him, as it was with Bourdoncle, that the director of a big drapery store should be a bachelor if he wished to retain his male empire over the scattered desires of his nation of customers: once a wife was introduced there, the atmosphere would change, her smell would drive the others away. He was resisting the invincible logic

of facts, he would rather have died than give in; he was overcome
with sudden rage against Denise, sensing all too well that she
was the revenge, and he was afraid that, on the day he married
her, he would be broken like a straw by the Eternal Feminine.
Then he would gradually become faint-hearted again and would
argue his reluctance away: what was there to be afraid of? She
was so gentle, so sensible, that he could surrender himself to
her without fear. Twenty times an hour the struggle would begin
again in his torn being. Pride was irritating the wound, and he
was finally losing what little reason he had left at the thought
that, even after that last surrender on his part, she might say no,
still no, if she loved someone else. On the morning of the big sale
he had not so far come to any decision, and Denise was leaving
the next day.

On that day, so it happened, when Bourdoncle went into Mouret's office at about three o'clock as was his custom, he caught
him unawares, his elbows on the desk, his fists in his eyes, so
absorbed that Bourdoncle had to touch him on the shoulder.
Mouret raised his face wet with tears, they looked at each other
and held out their hands; these men, who had fought so many
commercial battles together, embraced each other abruptly.
For the past month, in any case, Bourdoncle's attitude had
been completely changed: he was giving way to Denise, he was
even secretly pushing his chief into marriage. Doubtless he was
manoeuvring in that way so as not to be swept away by a force
which he now acknowledged to be superior. But at the root of
this change there could also be discerned the awakening of a
long-standing ambition, a frightened hope which was little by
little growing, of devouring Mouret, to whom he had kowtowed
for so long, in his turn. Such a thought was in the very air, in the
battle for existence, the continual massacres of which boosted the
sales around him. He was carried away by the machine's motion,
seized by the same appetite as the others, by the voraciousness
which, from the lowest to the highest, was spurring the thin on
to exterminate the fat. Nothing but a sort of religious fear, the
religion of luck, had so far prevented him from taking his bite.
And now the director was becoming childish again, was slipping
into an idiotic marriage, was going to kill his luck, spoil the
charm he had for the customers. Why should he dissuade him
from it, when it would then be so easy for him to pick up the

inheritance of a man who was done for, who had fallen into the arms of a woman. Therefore it was with a feeling of farewell, with compassion for a comradeship of long standing, that he was shaking the hands of his chief, repeating as he did so:

"Come now, cheer up, confound it! Marry her and have done with it."

Mouret was already ashamed of his moment of weakness. He stood up, protesting.

"No, no, it's too silly... Come along, we'll go and make our tour of the shop. It's going well, isn't it? I believe it'll be a splendid day."

They went out and began their afternoon inspection, in the midst of the department congested with crowds. Bourdoncle was slipping side glances at him, worried by this last spate of energy, studying his lips in order to catch the slightest lines of pain.

The sale was indeed at full swing and gathering pace, making the shop shake like a great ship going full speed ahead. In Denise's department a mob of mothers were crushing each other, trailing gangs of little girls and boys who were drowning beneath the garments which were being tried on them. The department had brought out all its white things, and there, as everywhere else, there was an orgy of white, enough white to clothe a whole troupe of cupids feeling the cold: there were overcoats in white cloth, dresses in piqué and nainsook and white cashmere, sailor suits, and there were even white Zouave outfits. Although it was not yet the season, there were displayed in the centre as a decoration first-communion dresses and veils in white muslin, white satin shoes, a sparkling ethereal fluorescence, as if an enormous bouquet of innocence and guileless ecstasy had been planted there. Madame Bourdelais, facing her three children who were sitting in order of size – Madeleine, Edmond, Lucien – was losing her temper with the last named because he was struggling while Denise was striving to put a jacket made of nun's veiling on him.

"Keep still, can't you? Don't you think it's a little tight, Mademoiselle?"

With the straight look of a woman who cannot be taken in she was examining the material, criticizing the cut and looking at the back of the seams.

"No, it's all right," she went on, "it's quite a business when one has to dress these youngsters... Now I must have a coat for this big girl of mine."

The department was being taken by assault and Denise herself had had to start selling. She was looking for the coat which was required, when she gave a little exclamation of surprise.

"What! You! What on earth's the matter?"

Her brother Jean, his hands encumbered with a parcel, was standing in front of her. He had been married for a week, and on the preceding Saturday his wife – who was small and dark with a charming, anxious face – had paid a long visit to the Bonheur des Dames in order to make some purchases. The young couple were going to accompany Denise to Valognes; it was to be a real honeymoon, a month's holiday surrounded by memories of the past.

"Just fancy," he repeated, "Thérèse forgot masses of things. There are some to be changed and others to be bought... So as she's busy, she sent me with this parcel... I'll explain..."

But, catching sight of Pépé, she interrupted him.

"What! Pépé too! What about school?"

"Well, you see," said Jean, "after dinner on Sunday, yesterday, I didn't have the heart to take him back. He'll go back tonight... The poor kid's pretty sad at being left shut up in Paris while we have an outing over there."

In spite of her troubles, Denise was smiling at them. She handed Madame Bourdelais over to one of her salesgirls, then came back to them in a corner of the department which was fortunately thinning out. The children, as she still called them, had become great strapping fellows. Pépé, now twelve years old, was already taller than she was, and more solid too; he was still untalkative and thrived on affection, and in his school uniform he had a winning gentleness about him – whereas Jean was broad in the shoulder and towered over her by a whole head; with his fair shock of hair brushed back in the windswept style affected by artisans, he still had the beauty of a woman. And she, as thin as ever, no fatter than a sparrow as she said herself, had retained her authority over them like an anxious mother, treated them like little boys who needed looking after, and would rebutton Jean's overcoat so that he should not look like a tramp and make sure that Pépé had a clean handkerchief.

That day, when she saw the latter looking at her reproachfully, she gently lectured him.

"You must be sensible, my sweet. You can't interrupt your studies. I'll take you there in the holidays... Is there anything you'd like to have now? Perhaps you'd rather I left you a little money?"

She turned back to Jean again.

"You know, dear, you make him worked up by letting him think we're going to have a good time. Do try to have a little sense."

She had given her elder brother half her savings, four thousand francs, to enable him to set up house. Her younger brother was costing her a good deal at school and, as in the past, all her money was spent on them. They were her only reason for living and working, for she still swore that she would never marry.

"Well, look," Jean resumed, "first of all in this parcel there's the tan coat which Thérèse—"

But he stopped short and, on turning round to see what was awing him, Denise caught sight of Mouret standing behind them. For some little time he had been watching her standing between the two strapping lads, mothering them, scolding them and kissing them, turning them round like babies having their clothes changed. Bourdoncle had remained in the background, apparently absorbed in the sale, but he lost nothing of the scene.

"They're your brothers, aren't they?" asked Mouret after a silence.

He spoke in his icy voice, with the stiff manner with which he addressed her nowadays. Denise herself was making an effort to remain cold. Her smile faded, she replied:

"Yes, Monsieur... I've married off the elder one, and his wife has sent him to me about some purchases."

Mouret went on looking at the three of them. In the end he continued.

"The younger one has grown a great deal. I recognize him, I remember having seen him in the Tuileries one evening with you."

His voice, which was growing more hesitant, shook slightly. Completely taken aback, she bent down under the pretext of adjusting Pépé's belt. The two brothers, pink in the face, were smiling at their sister's employer.

"They're like you," the latter added.

"Oh!" she exclaimed. "They're better-looking than I am!"

For a moment he seemed to be comparing their faces. But he was at the end of his tether. How she loved them! He walked a few steps away; then he came back and said in her ear:

"Come up to my study after the sale. I want to talk to you before you leave."

This time Mouret did walk away and resumed his tour of inspection. The battle within him was starting again, for now he was annoyed that he had arranged a meeting. To what impulse had he yielded when he saw her with her brothers? It was insane, he no longer had the strength even to have a will of his own. Well, he'd get out of it by saying a word of farewell to her. Bourdoncle, who had rejoined him, seemed less anxious, though he was still studying him with sly glances.

Meanwhile Denise had gone back to Madame Bourdelais.

"Well, is the coat all right?"

"Yes, yes, it's very nice... Well, that's enough for today. These little fellows are really ruinous!"

Denise was then able to slip away and listen to Jean's explanations, and afterwards she accompanied him through the departments, where he would certainly have lost his head. First of all there was the tan coat which Thérèse, after thinking it over, wanted to change for a white cloth coat, same size, same shape. Having taken the parcel, the girl proceeded to the ready-made department, followed by her two brothers.

The department was displaying all its garments in pale colours, summer jackets and mantillas made of flimsy silk and fancy woollens. But the sale had moved elsewhere, and customers there were relatively sparse. Almost all the salesgirls were new. Clara had disappeared a month ago; according to some, she had been carried off by the husband of a customer, and according to others, she had sunk into debauch on the streets. As to Marguerite, she was at last going back to run the little shop in Grenoble where her cousin was waiting for her. Madame Aurélie alone remained there, unchanging in the bulging armour of her silk dress, and with her imperial mask which had the yellowish fleshiness of an antique marble statue. Nevertheless, her son Albert's bad behaviour had left its mark on her, and she would have retired to the country but for the holes made in the family savings by that good-for-nothing, whose frightful debts bit by bit were even threatening to eat away their little estate at Les

Rignolles. It seemed like a revenge for their broken home, for whilst the mother had started holding tasteful parties for women only again, the father, on his side, continued to play the horn. Bourdoncle already had a dissatisfied eye on Madame Aurélie, surprised that she had not the tact to retire: too old for selling! That knell would soon be tolling, sweeping away the Lhomme dynasty.

"Why, it's you!" she said to Denise with exaggerated graciousness. "You want this coat to be changed, do you? Of course, immediately... Ah! So there are your brothers. They've grown into real men now!"

In spite of her pride, she would have gone down on her knees to pay homage to Denise. In the ready-made department, as in the other departments, they were talking of nothing but Denise's departure, and the buyer was quite ill over it, for she counted on the protection of her erstwhile salesgirl. She lowered her voice.

"They say you're leaving us... Come now, it isn't really true?"

"Yes, it is," replied the girl.

Marguerite was listening. Since the date of her marriage had been fixed, she had been going about with a more supercilious expression than ever on her pasty face. She came up to them, saying:

"You're quite right. Self-respect is more important than anything else, isn't it? I bid you farewell, my dear."

Some customers were arriving. Madame Aurélie severely bade her attend to the sale. Then, seeing Denise take the coat so as to make the "return" herself, she protested, and called an assistant. It so happened that this was an innovation which Denise had suggested to Mouret; there were women whose duty it was to carry the goods in order that the salesgirls should be less tired.

"Kindly conduct Mademoiselle," said the buyer, handing the coat over to her.

And, returning to Denise she said:

"Do think it over, won't you? We're all very grieved at your departure."

Jean and Pépé, who were waiting, smiling in the midst of the overflowing stream of women, started once more to follow their sister.

They had now to go to the trousseau department to get six chemises just like the half-dozen which Thérèse had bought on

Saturday. But in the lingerie department, where a display of white was snowing from every shelf, there was a tremendous crush, and it was becoming very difficult to get through.

First of all, in the corsets, a slight disturbance was making a crowd collect. Madame Boutarel, who had arrived from the Midi, this time with her husband and daughter, had been scouring the galleries since the morning in quest of a trousseau for the girl, who was getting married. The father had to be consulted all the time, and the business was endless. The family had just finally come to grief in the lingerie department, and while the young lady was engrossed in a detailed study of knickers, the mother, having taken a fancy to some corsets herself, had disappeared. When in dismay Monsieur Boutarel, a big red-faced man, abandoned his daughter in order to go and look for his wife, he finally found her again in a fitting room, outside the door of which he was politely asked to sit down. These rooms were narrow cells shut off with frosted-glass doors and, because of the exaggerated prudery of the management, men, even husbands, were not allowed to enter them. Salesgirls were going in and out of them briskly, and each time they rapidly slammed the door they allowed a glimpse of visions of ladies in their chemises and petticoats, with bare necks and arms, of fat women whose flesh was fading and of thin women the colour of old ivory. There was a row of men waiting on chairs, looking bored: Monsieur Boutarel, when he grasped the situation, had simply lost his temper, and had shouted that he wanted his wife, that he intended to know what they were doing to her, and that he would certainly not allow her to undress without him. Vainly they tried to calm him down: he appeared to believe that something unseemly was going on inside. While the crowd debated the matter and laughed about it, Madame Boutarel was forced to reappear.

After that, Denise and her brothers were able to get through. Every variety of women's linen, all the white things which are hidden underneath, were displayed in a succession of rooms divided into different departments. The corsets and bustles occupied one counter; there were stitched corsets, long-waisted corsets, armour-like boned corsets, above all white silk corsets with coloured fan stitching on them, of which a special display had been arranged that day; there was an army of dummies without heads or legs, nothing but torsos lined up, their dolls' breasts flattened beneath the silk and with the disconcerting lewdness of the disabled, and on neighbouring stands there were bustles of horsehair and jaconet, their enormous taut rumps forming extensions to the long rods and giving them outlines which had the indecency of a caricature. But beyond them, there began a scene of wanton undress, garments littering the vast rooms as if a group of pretty girls had gone from department to department divesting themselves of their clothes as far as the very satin of their skin. On one side there were fine linen goods, white cuffs and scarves, fichus and white collars, an infinite variety of frills and furbelows, a white froth escaping from the boxes and rising in a snow. On the other side there were camisoles, little bodices, tea gowns, dressing gowns made of lawn, nainsook and lace and long white garments, loose and diaphanous, which conjured up visions of long-drawn-out lazy mornings succeeding nights of love. And the clothes underneath were appearing, being shed one after another; there were white petticoats of every length, petticoats tight across the knees and petticoats with a train sweeping the ground, a rising sea of petticoats, in which legs were drowning; then there were knickers of cambric, of linen and of piqué; broad white knickers in which the haunches of a man would have fitted loosely; lastly there came the chemises, buttoned up to the neck for the night and leaving the bosom bare for the daytime, held up only by narrow shoulder straps and made of plain calico, Irish linen and cambric, the seventh veil slipping down from the bosom and all down the hips. The display in the trousseau department was lavish and indiscreet; it was Woman – from the lower-middle-class woman in plain linen to the rich lady smothered in lace – turned inside out and seen from below, a bedchamber exposed to the public eye, and its hidden luxury, its tucks and embroideries and Valenciennes lace, became more and more of a sensual debauch as they overflowed in costly caprices. And as Woman dressed herself again, the white billows of this flood of linen once more were hidden beneath the quivering mystery of skirts; the chemise stiffened by the dressmaker's fingers, or the frigid knickers still folded as they had been in the box, and all that dead cambric and batiste lying dishevelled, strewn about and piled up on the counter, were soon to become alive with the life of flesh and blood, sweet-smelling and warm with the fragrance of love, a cloud of white which would become sacred, steeped in night, and of which the slightest flutter, the least bit of pink flesh of a knee glimpsed in the depths of the whiteness, played havoc with the world. Beyond that there was still one more room, the baby linen, where the voluptuous white of Woman led to the guileless white of children: innocence, joy, the sweetheart who wakes up a mother, infants' vests made of fluffy quilting, flannel hoods, chemises and bonnets no bigger than toys, and christening robes and cashmere shawls, white down like a rain of fine white feathers.

"You know, those are Empire-waist chemises," said Jean, who was entranced with delight at this unrobing, this spate of clothes into which he was sinking.

In the trousseau department Pauline ran up immediately on catching sight of Denise. And before she even asked what the latter wanted, she spoke to her in an undertone, very upset about the rumours which the whole shop was discussing. In her department, two salesgirls had even quarrelled, one insisting that she would leave, the other denying it.

"You're staying with us, I've staked my head on it... Why, what would become of me?"

And when Denise replied that she was leaving the next day, she said:

"No, no, you think you will, but I know you won't... Why! Now I've got a baby, you'll have to get me made assistant buyer. Baugé is counting on it, my dear."

Pauline was smiling with an air of conviction. Then she gave them the six chemises, and as Jean had said that they were now going on to the handkerchiefs, she also called another assistant to carry the chemises and the coat left by the assistant from the ready-made department. The girl who turned up was Mademoiselle de Fontenailles, who had recently married Joseph. She had just obtained this menial job as a favour, and was dressed in a big black overall marked on the shoulder with a number in yellow wool.

"Kindly follow Mademoiselle," said Pauline.

Then, coming back and once more lowering her voice, she said to Denise:

"I'll be assistant buyer, won't I? It's agreed!"

Joking in her turn, Denise laughingly gave her promise. Then she moved on and went downstairs with Pépé and Jean, the three of them accompanied by the assistant. On the ground floor they found themselves in the woollens, one corner of a gallery was entirely hung with white duffel and flannel. Liénard, whose father was vainly summoning him back to Angers, was talking there with handsome Mignot, who had become a broker, and who had the nerve to reappear brazenly in the Bonheur des Dames. Doubtless they were talking of Denise, for they both fell silent in order to greet her obsequiously. Indeed, as she advanced through the departments, the salesmen were growing excited and were bowing down before her, uncertain as to what she might be on the morrow. People were whispering, saying that she looked triumphant, and this had a fresh repercussion on the wagers, people began staking a bottle of Argenteuil wine and some fried fish on her. She had entered the household-linen gallery in order to reach the handkerchief department at the end of it. It was an endless procession of white: the white of cotton, of dimity, of piqués, of calicoes; the white of madapollam, nainsook, muslin and tarlatan; then, in enormous piles built of lengths of material alternating like stones hewn in cubes, came the linens, coarse linens and fine linens of every width, white or raw, made from pure flax bleached in the meadows; then the whole thing began all over again and departments for every kind of made-up linen succeeded each other; there was household linen, table linen, kitchen linen, an endless avalanche of white, there were sheets and pillow cases, innumerable different kinds of table napkins and tablecloths, of aprons and dishcloths. And as Denise passed through, people were lining her way and the salutations were continuing. In the linen department Baugé had dashed forwards to give her a smile, as if she was the well-loved queen of the shop. Finally, after having gone through the blankets department, a room decked with white banners, she went into the handkerchiefs, where the ingenious decorations were sending the crowd into ecstasies – it was all white columns, white pyramids, white castles, complicated architecture built up of nothing but handkerchiefs, handkerchiefs made of lawn, of cambric, of Irish linen, of Chinese silk, initialled handkerchiefs, handkerchiefs embroidered with satin stitch, trimmed with lace, hemstitched and with woven designs on them, a whole town of white bricks of infinite variety, standing out like a mirage against an oriental sky warmed to white heat.

"Another dozen, you say?" Denise inquired of her brother. "It's Cholets you want, isn't it?"

"Yes, I think so, the same as this one," he replied, showing her a handkerchief in the parcel.

Jean and Pépé had not left her side, but were still pressing close to her just as they had in the past when, worn out from the journey, they had arrived in Paris. This vast shop, where she was at home, was confusing them; they were taking refuge behind her and, their childhood instinctively reawakening, were once more putting themselves under the protection of the sister who was a mother to them. People were watching them, smiling at the two strapping lads – at Jean who was scared in spite of the fact that he had a beard, and at Pépé bewildered in his tunic – following in the footsteps of the slight, serious-looking girl, all three of them now with the same fair hair – fair hair which made people from one end of the department to the other whisper as they passed:

"They're her brothers... they're her brothers..."

While Denise was looking for a salesman, an encounter took place. Mouret and Bourdoncle were coming into the gallery, and just as the former was once more coming to a standstill facing the girl, without however saying a word to her, Madame Desforges and Madame Guibal passed by. Henriette repressed the tremor which had shaken her whole body. She looked at Mouret, then she looked at Denise. They too had looked at her; this was the silent fall of the curtain, a glance exchanged in the bustle of a crowd, the common end of violent emotional dramas. Mouret had already moved on, while Denise disappeared at the far end of the department, still searching for a free salesman and still accompanied by her brothers. Then Henriette, who had recognized the assistant following the three of them – with a yellow number on her shoulder and her masklike face coarse and ashen like that of a servant – to be Mademoiselle de Fontenailles, relieved her feelings by saying to Madame Guibal in an irritated voice:

"Just look what he's done to that poor girl. Isn't it a shame? A marchioness! And he forces her to follow the creatures he's picked up off the pavements as if she was a dog."

She tried to regain her composure, and putting on an air of indifference added:

"Let's go and have a look at their silk display."

The silk department was like a great room dedicated to love, hung with white by the whim of a woman in love who, snowy in her nudity, wished to compete in whiteness. All the milky pallors of an adored body were assembled there, from the velvet of the hips to the fine silk of the thighs and the shining satin of the breasts. Lengths of velvet were hung between the columns, and against that creamy-white background silks and satins stood out in hangings of metallic and porcelain whiteness, and there were silk poults and Sicilian grosgrains too, light foulards and surahs, falling in festoons and ranging from the pasty whiteness of a Norwegian girl to the transparent whiteness of a redhead from Italy or Spain warmed by the sun.

Favier was just measuring some white foulard for the "pretty lady", that elegant blonde who was a regular customer in the department and to whom the salesmen never referred except by that name. She had been coming there for years, and they still knew nothing about her, neither what sort of life she led, nor her address, nor even her name. No one, moreover, ever tried to find out, although all of them made guesses about it each time she appeared, just for the sake of talking. She was getting thinner, she was getting fatter, she had slept well, or she must have gone to bed late the day before, and each small occurrence of her unknown life – events outside, dramas at home – therefore had a repercussion which would be commented on at length. On that day she appeared to be very gay. And Favier, when he came back from the cash desk whither he had accompanied her, imparted his ideas to Hutin.

"She's probably getting married again," he said.

"Why, is she a widow?" asked the other.

"I don't know… Only, don't you remember the time she was in mourning… Unless perhaps she's made some money on the stock exchange."

Silence reigned. Then he concluded:

"It's her business. What would happen if we called all the women who came here by their Christian names…"

But Hutin appeared to be thoughtful. He had had, two days earlier, a sharp dispute with the management, and he felt himself condemned. After the big sale, his dismissal was certain. His job had been shaky for a long time; at the last stock-taking he had been reproached for not having reached the turnover fixed in advance – and above all, there was still the slow pressure of appetites devouring him in his turn, a whole secret war in the department throwing him out, forming part of the very motion of the machine. Favier's hidden work was making itself heard; there was a loud sound of hungry jaws, muffled underground. The latter had already been promised that he would be made buyer. Hutin, who was aware of all this, instead of going for his old friend, now considered him to be very clever. Such a cold fish, with such a docile manner, of whom he had himself made use in order to wear down Robineau and Bouthemont! He was overwhelmed with surprise mingled with respect.

"By the way," Favier went on, "you know she's staying on. Someone's just seen the director making sheep's eyes... I stand to lose a bottle of champagne, I do."

He was talking of Denise. Gossip was spreading more rapidly than ever from one counter to another, across the endlessly swelling stream of customers. The silk department, especially, was in an upheaval, for heavy bets had been laid there.

"Confound it!" Hutin blurted out, waking as if from a dream. "What a fool I was not to sleep with her! I'd be in clover today if I had!"

Then, seeing Favier laughing, he blushed at his confession. He pretended to laugh too, adding, in order to make up for what he had said, that it was that creature who had done for him in the eyes of the management. All the same, a need for violent action was overwhelming him, and he ended by losing his temper with the salesmen who had dispersed beneath the customers' assault. But suddenly he began to smile again: he had just caught sight of Madame Desforges and Madame Guibal slowly going through the department.

"There's nothing you need today, Madame?"

"No thank you," Henriette replied. "You see, I'm just walking round, I only came today out of curiosity."

Having stopped her, he lowered his voice. A whole plan was springing up in his head, and so he humoured her by running down the shop: he had had quite enough of it, he would rather leave than stay on any longer in such chaos. She was listening to him, delighted. It was she who, thinking she was stealing him from the Bonheur, offered to get him taken on by Bouthemont as buyer in the silk department, when the Quatre Saisons was refitted. The deal was clinched, both of them whispering in undertones, while Madame Guibal was investigating the displays.

"May I offer you one of these bunches of violets?" Hutin went on, pointing to a table where there were three or four gift bunches, which he had procured for his own personal presents from one of the cash desks.

"Oh no, what an idea! I don't want to join the wedding party!"

They understood each other. They separated, still laughing with understanding glances.

As Madame Desforges was looking for Madame Guibal, she gave an exclamation, for she had caught sight of her with Madame Marty. The latter, followed by her daughter Valentine, had spent two hours in the shop, carried away by one of those fits of spending which left her tired out and ashamed. She had combed the furniture department, which had been transformed by a display of white enamelled furniture into a young girl's bedroom; and the ribbon and fichu department, where there were colonnades covered with white awnings; and the haberdashery and trimming departments, where white fringes framed ingenious trophies painstakingly built up out of cards of buttons and packets of needles; and finally the hosiery department, where that year there was a tremendous crush of people wanting to see an immense decorative design: the glorious name of the Bonheur des Dames in letters three yards high, made of white socks against a background of red socks. But Madame Marty was fired up above all by the new departments; a department could not be opened without her going to inaugurate it: she would rush there, buying in spite of everything. She had spent an hour in the millinery department, which had been installed in a new salon on the first floor, having cupboards emptied for her, taking hats from the mushrooms made of Brazilian rosewood with which the two tables there were decked, and trying them all on, together with her daughter – white hats, white bonnets, white toques. Then she had gone downstairs again to the shoe department, beyond the ties at the far end of one of the downstairs galleries, a department which had been opened that very day; she had ransacked the showcases, seized with morbid desire at the sight of white silk mules trimmed with swansdown and shoes and boots of white satin on high Louis XV heels.

"My dear!" she stammered. "You really can't imagine! They have a marvellous array of bonnets. I've chosen one for myself and one for my daughter... and what about the shoes, eh? Valentine..."

"It's fantastic!" added the girl, as lacking in shyness as a mature woman. "There are boots at twenty francs fifty... Oh, what boots!"

A salesman was following them, dragging the inevitable chair on which a heap of goods was already piling up.

"How is Monsieur Marty?" asked Madame Desforges.

"Not too bad, I believe," replied Madame Marty, flustered by this sudden question which struck a jarring note in her fever of spending. "He's still away, my uncle was supposed to go to see him this morning..."

But she broke off and gave an exclamation of ecstasy:

"Do look, isn't that adorable?"

The ladies, who had advanced a few steps, were now standing facing the new flower-and-feather department, which had been installed in the central gallery between the silks and the gloves. There a vast blossoming lay under the bright light from the glass roof, a white sheaf as tall and broad as an oak tree. Clusters of flowers decorated the base – violets, lilies of the valley, hyacinths, daisies, all the delicate whites of a flower bed. Then, higher up, there were bunches of white roses softened with a touch of flesh colour, huge white peonies barely tinted with carmine, white chrysanthemums in delicate sprays starred with yellow. The flowers went up and up, there were great mystical lilies, branches of spring apple blossom, sheaves of fragrant lilac, an endless blossoming which, on a level with the first floor, was crowned with plumes of ostrich feathers, white feathers which seemed to be the breath flying away from this crowd of flowers. The whole of one corner was devoted to a display of trimmings and wreaths made of orange blossom. There were flowers made of metal, silver thistle and silver ears of corn. Amidst the foliage and corollas surrounded by muslin, silk and velvet, in which drops of gum were made to look like drops of dew, there flew birds of paradise for hats, purple tangaras with black tails and septicolours with shimmering breasts, shot with all the colours of the rainbow.

"I must buy a bunch of apple blossoms," Madame Marty went on. "It's delightful, isn't it... And that little bird, do look, Valentine. Oh! I'll get it!"

In the meantime Madame Guibal was getting bored at staying there motionless, in the swirl of the crowd. Finally she said:

"Very well! We'll leave you to your purchases. The rest of us are going upstairs."

"Oh no, wait for me!" the other exclaimed. "I'm going upstairs again too... the perfumery is up there. I must go to the perfumery."

This department, which had only just been created, was next door to the reading room. Madame Desforges, in order to avoid the crush on the stairs, talked of taking the lift, but they had to abandon the attempt, there was a queue of people at the door. They got there in the end by going through the buffet, where there was such a mob that a shopwalker had been obliged to curb people's appetites by only allowing the gluttonous customers to enter in small groups at a time. Even in the buffet the ladies began to smell the perfumery department, the penetrating scent of a sachet was making the gallery fragrant. People there were discussing a soap, the Bonheur soap, a speciality of the shop. Inside the glass counters and on the small crystal shelves of the showcases pots of pomades and creams were lined up, boxes of powder and rouge, phials of oils and toilet waters – while the delicate brushes, combs, scissors and pocket flasks occupied a special cupboard. The salesmen had used their ingenuity to decorate the display with all their white china pots, with all their white glass phials. People were enraptured by a silver fountain in the centre, a shepherdess standing in a harvest of flowers, from which a continuous trickle of violet water was flowing, tinkling musically in the metal basin. The exquisite scent was spreading everywhere, and as they passed the ladies soaked their handkerchiefs with it.

"There!" said Madame Marty, when she had loaded herself up with lotions, toothpastes and cosmetics. "Now, that's that, I'm at your disposal. Let's go and find Madame de Boves again."

But on the landing of the big, central staircase, she was brought to a halt once more by the Japanese department. This counter had grown since the days when Mouret had amused himself by taking a chance in the same place with a little auction stall, spread with a few shop-soiled trinkets, without himself foreseeing its enormous success. Few departments had had such modest beginnings, but now it was overflowing with old bronze, old ivory, old lacquer.

His turnover there was fifteen thousand francs each year, and he was turning the whole Far East, where travellers were ransacking palaces and temples for him, topsy-turvy. What is more the departments were still growing, they had launched two new ones in December, in order to fill the gaps during the winter off-season – a book department and a children's toy department – which would certainly also grow and sweep away more businesses in the neighbourhood. In four years the Japanese department had succeeded in attracting all the artistic clientele of Paris.

This time Madame Desforges herself, in spite of the grudge she bore which had made her swear not to buy anything, succumbed to an ivory of charming delicacy.

"Send it to me," she said quickly, at a nearby cash desk. "Ninety francs, isn't it?"

And seeing Madame Marty and her daughter deep in a selection of trashy china, she said, leading Madame Guibal away as she did so:

"You'll find us in the reading room... I really must sit down for a bit."

In the reading room the ladies had to remain standing. All the chairs round the big table covered with newspapers were taken. Portly men were reading, leaning back, displaying their stomachs, without it occurring to them that it would be polite to give up their places. A few women were writing, their noses buried in their letters, looking as if they were trying to hide the paper with the flowers on their hats. In any case, Madame de Boves was not there, and Henriette was growing impatient when she caught sight of Vallagnosc, who was also looking for his wife and mother-in-law. He greeted her, and finally said:

"They're certain to be in the lace department, one can't drag them away from it... I'll go and see."

He gallantly procured them two chairs before he disappeared.

In the lace department the crush was increasing from minute to minute. It was the crowning glory of the great display of white, the most delicate and costly whites were to be seen there. The temptation was acute, it gave rise to an insane wave of desire which unhinged every woman. The department had been transformed into a white chapel. Net and guipure lace were falling from above, forming a white sky, like a veil of cloud, its flimsy gossamer paling the early morning sun. Round the

columns flounces of Mechlin and Valenciennes lace were hanging
down like the white skirts of ballerinas, tumbling right down to
the ground in a shiver of whiteness. And everywhere, on all the
counters, there was a snow of white, Spanish blond lace as light
as a breath, Brussels appliqué with broad flowers on fine mesh,
needlepoint and Venetian lace with heavier designs, Alençon and
Bruges lace of a regal and almost religious richness. It seemed to
be the white tabernacle of the God of Fashion.

Madame de Boves, after having walked about with her daughter for a long time, prowling about in front of the displays and
feeling a sensual urge to bury her hands in the materials, had just
made up her mind to get Deloche to show her some Alençon lace.
At first he had brought out the imitation, but she had wanted to
see real Alençon, and was not content with little trimmings at
three hundred francs a yard, but insisted on the big flounces at a
thousand francs, and handkerchiefs and fans costing from seven
to eight hundred francs. Soon the counter was littered with a
fortune. In one corner of the department Jouve the shopwalker,
who had not lost interest in Madame de Boves in spite of her
apparent dawdling, was standing motionless in the midst of the
jostling, with an air of unconcern, his eyes still on her.

"And have you any berthas in needlepoint?" the Countess
asked. "Would you show them to me, please?"

She looked so distinguished, with her build and voice of a
princess, that the assistant, whom she had been monopolizing
for twenty minutes, dared not demur. He did, however, hesitate,
for salesmen were recommended not to pile up valuable laces like
that, and the week before he had let himself be robbed of ten yards
of Mechlin. But she was making him flustered, he gave way and
abandoned the pile of Alençon for a moment in order to take the
berthas for which she had asked from a shelf behind him.

"Do look, Mamma," said Blanche who, at her side, was rummaging through a box full of narrow inexpensive Valenciennes.
"You could get some of this for pillows."

Madame de Boves did not reply. Then her daughter, looking
round with her flabby face, saw her mother, her hands deep in the
lace and in the act of making some flounces of Alençon disappear
up the sleeve of her coat. Blanche did not seem surprised, she
was moving forwards with an instinctive movement in order to
hide her, when Jouve suddenly loomed up between them. He

was leaning down, murmuring in the Countess's ear in a polite voice:

"Would you be so kind as to follow me, Madame?"

She rebelled for a moment.

"Why should I, Monsieur?"

"Would you be so kind as to follow me?" the shopwalker repeated, without changing his tone.

She cast a rapid glance around her, her face stricken with anguish. Then, having recovered her haughty bearing, she submitted, walking beside him like a queen who deigns to entrust herself to the care of an aide-de-camp. Not a single one of the customers crowding there had even noticed the scene. Deloche, who had returned to the counter with the berthas, watched open-mouthed as she was led away: What? Her too! That lady who looked so aristocratic! One might as well have them all searched! Blanche, who was left at liberty, was following her mother at a distance, lingering in the midst of the surge of shoulders with a ghastly expression, torn between her duty not to abandon her and her terror of being detained with her. She saw her go into Bourdoncle's office, and was content to hover outside the door.

Bourdoncle, from whom Mouret had just succeeded in escaping, happened to be there. He usually pronounced sentence on thefts of this sort, committed by respectable people. Jouve, who had had his eye on Madame de Boves, had told him his doubts about her long ago; therefore he was not surprised when the shopwalker acquainted him with the facts in a few words; besides, such extraordinary cases passed through his hands that he was wont to declare that Woman, when carried away by her passion for clothes, was capable of anything. As he was aware of the director's social relations with the thief, he treated her with the utmost politeness.

"Madame, we forgive these moments of weakness... I beg you to reflect on where forgetting yourself like that might lead you. If some other person had seen you slipping that lace—"

But she interrupted him indignantly. She, a thief! For whom did he take her? She was the Comtesse de Boves, her husband, Inspector-General of Stud Farms, was received at Court.

"I know, I know, Madame," Bourdoncle was calmly repeating. "I have the honour to be acquainted with you... Would you first of all kindly return the lace which you have on you..."

She expostulated again, did not allow him to say another word; her violence made her look magnificent, and she even went so far as to venture the tears of a great lady who has been insulted. Anyone else but him would have been shaken, fearing some deplorable mistake, for in order to avenge such slander she was threatening to sue him.

"Take care, Monsieur! My husband will go to the minister himself!"

"Come now, you're no more sensible than the rest of them," declared Bourdoncle, out of patience. "If we must, we shall have to search you."

Still she did not flinch, but said with superb assurance:

"Very well, search me... But I warn you, you are jeopardizing your shop."

Jouve went to fetch two salesgirls from the corset department. When he came back he notified Bourdoncle that the girl who had been with the lady and had been left at liberty had not left the door, and he asked if he should arrest her too, although he had not seen her take anything. Bourdoncle, always correct in his behaviour, decided in the name of good morals that she should not be brought in, so that a mother should not be forced to blush in front of her daughter. Meanwhile, the two men retired to a neighbouring room while the salesgirls searched the Countess, even taking off her dress in order to inspect her bosom and hips. Apart from the Alençon flounces, twelve yards at a thousand francs, which were hidden in the depths of a sleeve, they found a handkerchief, a fan and a scarf hidden squashed and warm in her bosom, altogether about fourteen thousand francs' worth of lace. Ravaged by a furious, irresistible urge, Madame de Boves had been stealing like that for a year. The attacks had been growing more acute, increasing until they had become a sensual pleasure necessary to her existence, sweeping away all the reasonings of prudence and indulged in with an enjoyment which was all the more keen because she was risking her name, her pride, and her husband's important position, under the very eyes of the crowd. Now that her husband let her take money from his drawers, she was stealing with her pockets full of money, stealing for stealing's sake as people love for the sake of loving, spurred on by desire, unhinged by the neurosis which had been developed within her in the past by her unassuaged desire for luxury when faced with the enormous, ruthless temptation of big stores.

"It's a trap!" she cried, when Bourdoncle and Jouve re-entered. "Someone slipped this lace on to me. Oh! I swear it before God!"

Now she had fallen on to a chair and was weeping tears of rage, sobbing in her dress which had not been properly refastened. Bourdoncle sent the salesgirls away. Then he resumed in his calm manner:

"We are quite prepared to hush the matter up, Madame, out of consideration for your family. But, first of all, you are going to sign a paper worded as follows: 'I have stolen lace from the Bonheur des Dames', with particulars of the lace and the date... Moreover, I will give you back this paper as soon as you bring me two thousand francs for the poor."

She had risen to her feet again; once more rebellious, she declared:

"Never will I sign a thing like that. I'd rather die."

"You won't die, Madame. Only I warn you that I am going to send for the police."

At that there was a terrible scene. She insulted him, blurting out that it was cowardly of men to torture a woman like that. Her Junoesque beauty, and her buxom and majestic body were blended with the fury of a fishwife. Next she tried pity, she begged them in the name of their mothers, she talked of crawling at their feet. Then, since they remained unmoved, their hearts hardened from practice, she suddenly sat down, and with a trembling hand began to write. The pen was spluttering; at the words "I have stolen" she pressed with such fury that it almost broke through the carbon paper, and she kept on repeating in a choking voice:

"There you are, Monsieur, there you are, Monsieur... I yield to force..."

Bourdoncle took the paper, folded it carefully, and in her presence locked it in a drawer, saying as he did so:

"You can see that it won't be alone, for ladies, having talked of dying rather than signing, generally omit to come and collect their love letters... Well, I'll keep it at your disposal. You will think over whether it's worth two thousand francs."

She was finishing fastening up her dress; now that she had paid she was recovering all her arrogance.

"May I leave?" she asked in a curt tone.

Bourdoncle was already busy with other matters. On hearing Jouve's report, he decided on Deloche's dismissal: he was a stupid salesman, he was continually letting himself be robbed, and would never have any control over the customers. Madame de Boves repeated her question, and when they had dismissed her with an affirmative sign, she swept them both with a murderous glance. From the stream of coarse words which she was choking back a melodramatic exclamation rose to her lips:

"Villains!" she said, banging the door.

Blanche, meanwhile, had not moved from the door of the office. Her ignorance of what was taking place inside and the comings and goings of Jouve and the two salesgirls had completely overwhelmed her, making her conjure up visions of the police, the assizes, prison. But suddenly she stared open-mouthed: her husband of a month's standing, whom she was still used to addressing as "sir", was standing before her; surprised at her dazed state, he was questioning her.

"Where's your mother? Did you lose each other? Come now, answer me, you alarm me…"

She could think of no plausible lie. In her distress, she told him everything in a whisper.

"Mamma, Mamma… She's stolen something…"

"What? Stolen?" At last he understood. His wife's bloated face, that livid mask ravaged with fear, terrified him.

"Some lace, like this, in her sleeve," she went on blurting out.

"Then you saw her do it, you were watching?" he murmured, chilled at the thought that she had been an accomplice.

They had to stop talking, people were already turning round to look at them. For a moment Vallagnosc remained motionless, paralysed by agonized hesitation. What was to be done? He was just making up his mind to go in to see Bourdoncle, when he caught sight of Mouret who was crossing the gallery. He told his wife to wait for him, and seized the arm of his old friend, whom he acquainted with the facts in disjointed phrases. The latter hastened to take him to his office, where he put his mind at rest about the possible consequences. He assured him that there was no need to intervene, and explained the way in which things would certainly turn out, without appearing to be disturbed about the theft himself, as if he had foreseen it for a long time.

But Vallagnosc, once he no longer feared an immediate arrest, did not react to the incident with such praiseworthy calm. He had thrown himself into an armchair and, now that he was able to reason, was launching into lamentations about his own lot. Could it really be true? So he had entered a family of thieves! It was a stupid marriage into which he had rushed in order to please her father! Surprised by this violence, which was like that of a sickly child, Mouret watched him weep, recalling the pessimism he had affected in the past. Had he not heard him discoursing on the ultimate pointlessness of life a hundred times? Had he not considered only misfortune to be slightly amusing? And so, in order to take his mind off his troubles, Mouret amused himself for a moment by preaching indifference to him, in a tone of friendly bantering. At that Vallagnosc lost his temper: he was quite unable to regain his now compromised philosophy, the whole of his middle-class upbringing was recoiling from his mother-in-law in virtuous indignation. As soon as he experienced something personally, at the slightest contact with human misery at which he had pretended to sneer, the braggart sceptic in him came a cropper and was wounded. It was abominable, the honour of his ancestry was being dragged through the mire, and the world seemed to be cracking up as a result.

"Come along now, calm down," Mouret, overcome with pity, concluded by saying. "I won't tell you that everything happens and nothing happens, since that doesn't seem to console you at the moment. But I think you ought to go and offer your arm to Madame de Boves, which would be more sensible than creating a scandal... Confound it! You who used to profess to be contemptuous and unmoved by the universal baseness of mankind!"

"Well, yes!" exclaimed Vallagnosc naively. "When it's in other people's families."

However, he had got to his feet and he followed his old school friend's advice. They were both going back to the gallery, when Madame de Boves came out of Bourdoncle's room. She graciously accepted her son-in-law's arm, and as Mouret bowed to her with an air of courteous respect, he heard her say:

"They offered me an apology. Really, mistakes like that are appalling."

Blanche had rejoined them, and was walking behind them. They slowly became lost in the crowd.

Then Mouret, alone and thoughtful, went through the shop once more. This scene, which had taken his mind off the conflict which was rending him, was now increasing his fever, bringing the final struggle within him to a head. In his mind he felt that everything was vaguely connected: that unfortunate woman's theft, the final act of madness of his clientele which lay vanquished, prostrate at its tempter's feet, evoked for him the proud avenging image of Denise, whose victorious heel he could feel trampling on him. He stopped at the top of the central staircase, looked for a long time at the immense nave, at his multitude of women crushing each other.

Six o'clock would soon be striking; the light which was waning outside was retreating from the covered galleries which were dark already, and was fading in the depths of the halls flooded with lingering shadows. In this still not properly extinguished daylight, electric lamps were lighting up one by one, and their opaque white globes were spangling the distant depths of the departments with bright moons. They shed a white brightness of blinding fixity, like a reflection from some colourless star which was killing the dusk. Then, when all the lamps were alight, the crowd gave a murmur of rapture; beneath this new lighting the great display of white took on the fairy-like splendour of a transformation scene. It seemed as if the colossal orgy of white was burning too, was becoming changed into light. The white poem was taking wing in the blazing whiteness of a dawn. A white gleam was sparkling from the linens and calicoes in the Monsigny gallery, like the first bright streak which whitens the sky in the East, while the haberdashery and the trimmings, the fancy goods and ribbons all along the Michodière Gallery, were casting reflections of distant slopes – the white glitter of mother-of-pearl buttons, of silvered bronze and of pearls. In the central nave, above all, there was a glory of white bathed in flames; the froth of white muslin round the pillars, the white dimities and piqués which were draping the staircase, the white coverlets hanging like banners, the guipures and white lace floating in the air – all this opened up a dream firmament, a glimpse into the dazzling whiteness of a paradise, where the marriage of the unknown queen was being solemnized. The pavilion in the silk hall, with its white curtains, white gauzes and white tulles, formed a gigantic bedchamber, and the glare of its hangings was sheltering the white nudity of the bride from onlookers. There was nothing left but a blinding dazzle, a whiteness of light in which every tone of white was dissolving, a dusting of stars snowing in the white luminosity.

Amidst all this blaze Mouret was still looking at his multitude of women. Against the pale backgrounds, black shadows were being carried along by force. Long eddies were breaking through the mob, the fever of that day of immense sales was passing away like a delirium, swaying the disordered swirl of heads. People were beginning to leave, a havoc of materials was littering the counters, gold was tinkling in the cash desks; while the customers, despoiled and violated, were going away dishevelled, their sensual desires satisfied and with the secret shame caused by yielding to temptation in the depths of some shady hotel. And it was he who possessed them all like that, who by his continual piling-up of goods, by his price reductions and his returns, by his compliments and his publicity, held them at his mercy. He had even conquered the mothers themselves, he reigned over them all with the brutality of a despot, whose whim could wreck families. His creation was producing a new religion; churches, which were little by little being deserted by those of wavering faith, were being replaced by his bazaar. Woman came to spend her hours of idleness in his shop, the thrilling, disturbing hours which in the past she had spent in the depths of a chapel, for such expenditure of nervous passion was necessary; it formed part of the recurring struggle between a god and a husband, the ceaselessly renewed cult of the body, with the divine future life of beauty. If he had closed the doors, there would have been a rising in the street, a desperate outcry from the devout, whose confessional and altar he would have abolished. In spite of the lateness of the hour he could see them still in their luxury, which in the last ten years had increased so much, persistently lingering beneath the enormous metal framework, and all along the staircases and suspension bridges. Madame Marty and her daughter, swept up to the very top, were wandering about among the furniture. Madame Bourdelais, her children holding her back, could not drag herself away from the fancy goods. Then came the pack: Madame de Boves, still on Vallagnosc's arm, was followed by Blanche, and was stopping in every department, still having the nerve to examine the materials in her arrogant manner. In the crush of customers, the sea of bosoms bursting with life, palpitating with desire, all decked with bunches of violets as if the nuptials of some sovereign were being celebrated by the populace, he could, in the end, no longer distinguish anything but the bare bosom of Madame Desforges, who had stopped in the glove department with Madame Guibal. In spite of her jealous rancour, she too was buying, and once more for the last time he felt himself the master; under the dazzle of the electric lights they were all at his feet, like cattle from which he had extracted his fortune.

Mechanically Mouret went along the galleries, so deeply absorbed in his thoughts that he let himself drift with the pressure of the crowd. When he looked up again he was in the new millinery department, the windows of which looked out on the Rue du Dix-Décembre. There his forehead pressed against the glass, he made a fresh halt and watched the people leaving. The setting sun was gilding the summits of the white houses, the blue sky of the beautiful day that it had been was paling, cooled by a strong fresh breeze, while in the dusk which was already flooding the thoroughfare, the electric lights of the Bonheur des Dames were casting the steady brilliance of stars lit up on the horizon at the decline of day. Towards the Opéra and the Bourse the motionless carriages in triple lines were sunk in darkness, although the harness still reflected glints of bright lights – the gleam of a lantern, the spark from a silvered bit. Calls from liveried ostlers were ringing out all the time, and a cab would advance, a brougham would come forwards and pick up a customer, then move away at a resounding trot. The queues were growing smaller now; in the midst of the banging of doors, the cracking of whips, the buzz of pedestrians overflowing between the wheels, there were six vehicles travelling abreast from one end of the street to the other. There seemed to be a continual thinning-out of customers who were dispersing and being carried away to the four corners of the city, emptying the shop with the roaring noise of a sluice gate. While the roofs of the Bonheur, the great golden letters on the signboards and the banners hoisted up in the sky were still flaming with the reflection of the sunset and looked so colossal in that oblique lighting that they conjured up the monster on the advertisements, the phalanstery with its endlessly multiplied buildings, which were devouring whole districts as far away as the distant woods of the suburbs. The soul of Paris hovering over it like an enormous, gentle breath, was falling asleep in the serenity of the evening, flowing over the last vehicles in long, soft caresses, escaping down the street which was gradually being cleared of the crowd and disappearing in the darkness of the night.

Mouret, his gaze lost in the distance, felt that something immense had just taken place within him; and, in the thrill of triumph with which his flesh was trembling, faced with Paris devoured and Woman conquered, he experienced a sudden failing, a weakening of his will by which he was being overthrown in his turn as if by a superior force. In his victory he felt an irrational need to be conquered; it was the meaningless action of a general yielding on the morrow of his conquest to the whim of a child. He who for months had been struggling, who only that morning had still been swearing he would stifle his passion, had suddenly given in, overcome with vertigo, and happy to do something which he believed to be silly. His decision, so rapidly taken, gathered such momentum from one minute to the next that he no longer considered anything else in the world to have any importance or to be necessary.

That evening, after the last meal service, he waited in his study. He was trembling like a young man whose whole happiness is at stake, and could not remain in one spot, but kept on returning to the door in order to listen to the vague din from the shop, where the assistants, up to their shoulders in the havoc from the sale, were folding up the goods. His heart beat at the slightest sound of footsteps. Then, on hearing in the distance a muffled murmur, which was gradually swelling, he felt a thrill and rushed forwards.

Lhomme was slowly approaching, loaded with the takings. On that day the weight was so great, there was so much copper and silver in the cash taken, that he had made two porters accompany him. Behind him, Joseph and one of his colleagues were bending under the sacks, enormous sacks thrown over their shoulders like sacks of cement, while Lhomme was walking ahead and carrying the notes and the gold in a wallet bulging with paper, and in two bags hanging round his neck, weighting him down on his right-hand side, the side on which he had lost an arm. Slowly, sweating and puffing, he had come from the far end of the shop, through the growing excitement of the salesmen. Those in the gloves and silks had laughingly offered to relieve him of his burden; those in the cloths and woollens had wished him to take a false step which would have strewn gold all over the department. Then he had had to go up a staircase, cross a suspension bridge, go up again, turning through the girders, followed by the gazes of the salesmen in the household linen, the hosiery and the haberdashery, who stood gaping with ecstasy at the sight of such a fortune travelling through the air. On the first floor the gowns, the perfumes, the laces and the shawls had lined up with devotion, as if God himself was passing by. With every step he took the hubbub was increasing, becoming the uproar of a nation bowing down to the golden calf.

Mouret, meanwhile, had opened his door. Lhomme appeared, followed by the two porters, who were staggering, and although he was out of breath, he nevertheless still had sufficient strength to shout:

"One million, two hundred and forty-seven francs, ninety-five centimes!"

It was a million at last, a million collected in one day, the figure of which Mouret had dreamt for so long! But he made a gesture of anger, and with the disappointed air of a man disturbed in his vigil by an unwelcome intruder, he said in an irritated way:

"A million? Very well, put it there."

Lhomme knew that he liked to see big takings on his desk, before they were deposited in the central counting house. The million covered the desk, crushed down the papers on it and almost upset the ink, and the gold, silver and copper, flowing from the sacks and bursting out of the bags, made a great heap, a heap of raw takings, just as they had left the customers' hands, still warm and alive.

Just as the cashier was withdrawing, cut to the heart by his employer's indifference, Bourdoncle arrived, exclaiming gaily:

"Well! We've got it this time! We've reached a million!"

But noticing Mouret's restless preoccupation, he realized the cause of it and recovered his composure. His gaze had lit up with joy, and after a short silence, he resumed:

"You've made up your mind, haven't you? Upon my word, I think you're right."

Suddenly Mouret planted himself squarely in front of him, and in the terrifying voice he had on days of crisis, he said:

"I say, my good fellow, you're a bit too gay... You think I'm finished, don't you, and you're sharpening your teeth. You beware! People don't eat me up!"

Disconcerted by this blunt attack by that diabolic man who always guessed everything, Bourdoncle blurted out:

"What's that? You're joking! I who've got so much admiration for you!"

"Don't lie!" Mouret went on more violently. "Listen, we were stupid to have that superstition that marriage would sink us. After all, isn't it the health necessary to life, its very strength and order. Well! Yes, my dear fellow, I'm going to marry her, and I'll kick you all out if you lift a finger. Yes, precisely! You'll proceed to the pay desk just like anyone else, Bourdoncle!"

He dismissed him with a gesture. Bourdoncle felt himself condemned, swept away by the victory of Woman. He left the room. Just then Denise was coming in, and he saluted her with a deep bow, having lost all his self-possession.

"It's you at last," said Mouret gently.

Denise was pale with emotion. She had just suffered a final grief, for Deloche had told her of his dismissal, and when she had tried to keep him back by offering to intercede for him he had clung to his misfortune, saying he wanted to disappear: what was the good of staying? Why should he stand in the way of more fortunate people? Denise, overcome with tears, had bade him a sisterly farewell. After all, was she not herself hoping to forget? Soon it would all be over, and all she asked of her exhausted powers was courage for the separation. In a few minutes, if she had sufficient valour to break her own heart, she would be able to go away and weep somewhere far away, alone.

"Monsieur, you said you wished to see me," she said in her calm way. "In any case, I would have come to thank you for all your kindness."

As she came in she caught sight of the million on the desk, and the display of all that money grated on her. Above her, as if watching the scene, the portrait of Madame Hédouin in its golden frame had its eternal smile on its painted lips.

"You're still resolved to leave us?" asked Mouret, whose voice was trembling.

"Yes, Monsieur, I must."

Then he seized her hands and, his tenderness bursting out after the coldness he had forced himself to have towards her for so long, he said:

"And if I was to marry you, Denise, would you still leave?"

But she had withdrawn her hands, she was struggling as if stricken by some great sorrow.

"Oh! Monsieur Mouret, don't say more, I beg of you! Oh! Don't make me more unhappy!... I can't! I can't! God is my witness that I was going away so as to avoid a misfortune like that!"

She went on defending herself in broken phrases. Had she not already suffered enough from the gossip of the shop? Did he want her to seem a trollop in other people's eyes as well as in her own? No, no, she would be strong-minded, she would prevent him from doing anything so silly. He was listening to her in torment, repeating passionately:

"I wish it... I wish it..."

"No, it's impossible... And what about my brothers? I've sworn never to marry, I can't bring you two children, can I?"

"They'll be my brothers too... say yes, Denise!"

"No, no. Oh! Leave me, you're tormenting me!"

Little by little he was losing heart, driven mad by this final obstacle. What! Even at that price she still refused! In the distance he could hear the uproar of his three thousand employees, shifting his regal fortune about by the armful. And before him lay that idiotic million! He could not bear the mockery of it, and would gladly have thrown it all out into the street.

"Well then, go!" he exclaimed in a flood of tears. "Go and rejoin the man you love... That's the reason, isn't it? You warned me, I ought to have known and not tormented you any longer."

She was staggered at the violence of this despair. Her heart was bursting. Then, sobbing herself, with the impetuosity of a child she flung her arms round his neck, blurting out as she did so:

"Oh! Monsieur Mouret, it's you I love!"

A last confused murmur, the distant acclamation of the crowd, rose from the Bonheur des Dames. The portrait of Madame Hédouin was still smiling with its painted lips. Mouret had collapsed onto the desk, where he was sitting in the middle of his million which he no longer even noticed. He was holding Denise to him, clasping her distractedly to his breast, telling her that she could go away now, that she could spend a month at Valognes, which would put an end to gossip, and that then he would go there himself to fetch her, to bring her back, all-powerful, on his arm.

Note on the Text

The text in the present edition is a revised version of the 1957 John Calder edition. The spelling and punctuation have been standardized, modernized and made consistent throughout.

Notes

p. 4, *AU BONHEUR DES DAMES*: "The Ladies' Delight" (French).

p. 33, *the Folies*: The Folies-Bergère, a famous variety theatre in Paris which opened in 1869.

p. 114, *Delacroix*: Eugène Delacroix (1798–1863), the famous French Romantic painter.

p. 208, *the Halles*: Paris's main market place, revamped in the 1850s with large glass and iron structures.

p. 243, *the Moniteur*: *Le Moniteur Universel* was founded during the French Revolution in 1789, becoming the official government newspaper until 1901.

p. 318, *Aux Quatre Saisons*: "The Four Seasons" (French).

Extra Material

on

Émile Zola's

Ladies' Delight

Émile Zola's Life

Émile Zola was born in Paris on 2nd April 1840, the son of Francesco Zolla, an Italian civil engineer from Venice, and Émilie Aubert, from a small town near Chartres. Zola spent his early life in Aix-en-Provence. His father, in charge of the construction of a canal to supply Aix with drinking water, died in 1847, and the Canal Zola was only completed in 1854. The young Émile was deeply affected by the death of his father, which seems to have resulted in an increased sense of attachment to his mother. She faced great difficulties raising him on her own, although she did have the support of her parents, who had also moved to Aix two years previously. The Zola household was now quite impoverished, which led Émilie in 1849 to embark on an ultimately fruitless decade of legal wranglings with the Société du Canal Zola in order to keep the modest pension they paid her and receive due compensation for her shares.

Despite this loss, Zola's childhood appears to have been an idyllic and happy one. His mother allowed him much freedom, although she was also very protective of her young son, who was small and sickly and stuck out in southern France with his Parisian accent. But by the time Émile was eight, it became clear to her that he needed schooling, which was beyond her means at the time. After a term spent at the Pension Notre-Dame, Émile was enrolled on a scholarship at the Collège Bourbon, a Jesuit school where Aix notables and rich farmers sent their children. On the one hand, the Collège Bourbon was austere to the point of extreme discomfort, renowned for terrible food and the absence of heating, but on the other it was remarkably lax compared to most Jesuit establishments and offered beautiful premises. Zola was one of the top students during his six years there, when he won prizes in French narration – he later claimed he was spurred on by the shadow of his father and the fact that he knew he would later in life be dependent on his own efforts – but he was also fond of camaraderie and the countryside. Despite initially suffering the harassment reserved for beneficiaries of bursaries, he made long-standing friends there, the most famous of them being the future Impressionist painter Paul Cézanne. During this period, he read widely, especially authors such as Dumas, Sue, Féval, Hugo, Lamartine and Musset.

Move to Paris   When her mother Henriette died and things came to a head in her legal action, requiring her to be in Paris, Mme Zola moved to the capital at the end of 1857, with Émile and his grandfather joining her in February of the following year. Through a connection, his mother managed to secure a place for him at the prestigious Lycée Saint-Louis, where the shy, provincial and impecunious eighteen-year-old Zola again found it difficult to fit in. He missed Aix-en-Provence and his friends there, and found it difficult to keep up academically in Paris, although he did win the second prize for narration. That autumn he fell gravely ill for several months, and failed his *baccalauréat* in science twice in 1859.

Hardship   This scuppered his plan to become an engineer and, in 1860, faced with the increasing impoverishment he and his mother were experiencing, he briefly took on a clerk's position at the customs house of the Canal Saint-Martin. The drudgery of this occupation made him miserable. In 1862, after various office jobs and periods of unemployment – which did however enable him to read extensively and start moving in artistic circles – Zola began work, thanks to a family friend, with Hachette and Company, France's most important publishing house. Initially placed in the post room, he was soon promoted by his employers to the publicity department, where he eventually became the manager. Working in this department provided him with the platform to launch a literary career, as it enabled him to learn how the milieu operated and meet many established authors on Hachette's books, as well as journalists and new talent. He began to write short stories: 1863 saw the publication of two of them, which appeared with several more in the collection published in November 1864, *Stories for Ninon*. In 1865 appeared *The Confession of Claude*, an autobiographical novel written in the first person, recounting a young man's (illicit) initiation into the ways of love. At this early stage, a key feature of Zola's career was already in evidence, namely the parallel output in the fields of literature and journalism: Zola had regular articles and columns in the press, and in 1866 was able to leave Hachette to take up a position as columnist with *L'Événement*. It is worth stressing that Zola – though clearly a highly original, distinctive and extraordinarily prolific writer – is somewhat symptomatic of a phenomenon which, though by no means unprecedented, became the norm over the course of the nineteenth century as publishing and the press became mass industries, and culture as well as society became increasingly democratized. This was the phenomenon of the professional author who lived from writing, as opposed to the gentleman of leisure, whose private income allowed time for literary pursuits. The dual character of Zola's early activities also foreshadows another distinctive aspect of his career: the involvement of the writer in the domain of public affairs. As for his private life, he began a relationship with Alexandrine Meley, who would become his wife in 1870.

After the publication in 1867 of his successful but controversial novel *Thérèse Raquin*, Zola sent a plan to its publisher Albert Lacroix for a series of ten novels – which was to become known as the *Rougon-Macquart* cycle – about various members and generations of a family living during the social transformations and political upheavals of the previous two decades. This was not an altogether unusual project for a politically engaged journalist contributing to a number of opposition newspapers on matters of political actuality. Nor was Zola, on the literary front, necessarily doing anything particularly original per se in writing a series of novels about contemporary French society: this type of totalizing social vision had also been expressed some decades previously in Balzac's *Human Comedy*, a cycle of novels containing numerous recurring characters and depicting the panoply of human activity in Restoration France. Zola himself had written a series of interlinked stories about urban life, *The Mysteries of Marseille* (1867), its title alluding to Eugène Sue's melodramatic serial work *The Mysteries of Paris* (1842–43).

What was strikingly original about Zola's planned series was that it combined this preoccupation with depicting the

The Rougon-Macquart Series

totality of the modern world with what he referred to in the plan sent to Lacroix as "questions of blood and milieux". That is, there was to be an underlying theme founded on the rapidly developing science of heredity, the key aspect of a broadly deterministic scientific basis for the motivation of fictional characters living in various modern environments. Zola's stated intention was to "rummage around in the very heart of the human drama, in those depths of life where great virtues and great crimes come into being, and to rummage there in a methodical fashion, led by the guiding thread of new physiological discoveries". This would facilitate the other broad aim, namely "to study the Second Empire, from the *Coup d'État* to the present day". In 1869, Zola finished the first novel in the series, *The Fortune of the Rougons*, charting the origins of his fictional family and its involvement in major political upheavals, and Lacroix offered him a contract for the whole series, which developed from the originally planned ten-volume work into a cycle of twenty novels published as separate volumes – usually after their appearance in serial form – between 1871 and 1893.

Height of Success   In 1870, in the middle of the Franco-Prussian conflict, Zola worked for the war-time government in Bordeaux. After another brief spell away from the capital during the bloody Paris Commune episode the following spring, Zola began enjoying unprecedented success as a novelist and public figure. He published novels in his *Rougon-Macquart* series at the rate of almost one a year. As well as the various artists he had been associating himself with and whom he often defended in his articles, he established friendships with many of the most important authors of the time, such as Flaubert, Daudet, Maupassant, Turgenev and Mallarmé. The seventh *Rougon-Macquart* novel, *L'Assommoir*, was a commercial and critical sensation, although – like most of his novels – it polarized readers and reviewers, with some left shocked by its graphic depictions of poverty and alcoholism. The sales of that book meant that he was able to afford a villa in Médan in 1878, to which he had several extensions made in subsequent years. In 1881 he was elected as a local councillor to the town of Médan, and on 14th July 1888 he was awarded the French Legion of Honour. To his great annoyance, however, he failed in successive bids, from 1889 onwards, to be voted into the prestigious Académie Française.

This successful period had its difficult moments, such as the death in October 1880 of his beloved mother, which came shortly after the passing away of Flaubert, who had become a kind of father figure as well as a friend. He was also periodically beset by ill health, suffering mostly from complaints of a nervous nature.

During this period, there was a major twist in his domestic *Jeanne Rozerot* situation: much like the protagonist in the final *Rougon-Macquart* novel, *Doctor Pascal* – the story of the ageing documenter of the Rougon-Macquart family rejuvenating himself in the arms of a young woman – Zola found a new love in his life. He had been married to Alexandrine Meley since 1870, and indeed remained with her for the rest of his life, but in 1888 he began a long-term affair with Jeanne Rozerot, a twenty-one-year-old Burgundian who had entered into service in the Zola household. Very soon Zola had installed her in an apartment in Paris, to which he would make frequent visits, and in 1889 she gave birth to a daughter, Denise, followed by a son, Jacques, in 1891. After Alexandrine discovered the affair in 1892 thanks to an anonymous letter, there was a mutually accepted arrangement, whereby Jeanne and the children lived as part of the Zola family.

It has been written that this new-found romantic and family bliss, although fulfilling Zola the man, somewhat took the edge off Zola the author – indeed his subsequent novel cycle, *The Three Cities*, failed to capture the public's imagination in the same way his previous series did, and has received less acclaim – perhaps somewhat unfairly – to this day. Zola also felt that he was the subject of unjust criticism, as he was sometimes portrayed as being insensitive, hard-hearted and excessively motivated by financial gain. Partly, perhaps, in order to dispel this image, he consented to be the first subject of Dr Édouard Toulouse's "medico-psychological" study, which aimed to investigate the pathologies of intellectually gifted individuals. Toulouse concluded that Zola was mentally stable and well balanced, and the author himself claimed in the preface to the published report that he had always been spurred on by the pursuit of truth above everything else.

Zola soon had a chance to demonstrate his commitment to *The Public Intellectual:* truth and justice. No event illustrates better the engagement *the Dreyfus Affair* of the writer in public life than the Dreyfus affair, which created, or rather perhaps exacerbated, a political chasm in

431

French society during the 1890s and still has repercussions today. Captain Alfred Dreyfus, a Jewish army officer, was falsely accused of passing French military secrets to Germany, and in 1894 was found guilty, forced to undergo a military degradation ceremony and sentenced to life imprisonment on the penal colony of Devil's Island.

After the acquittal at the beginning of 1898 of Commandant Ferdinand Walsin Esterhazy, for whose involvement in the initial passing of information there had been compelling evidence (pointing by implication to Dreyfus's innocence), an open letter from Zola to Félix Faure, President of the Republic, which has come to be known – after its banner headline – as 'J'Accuse!', was published in the newspaper *L'Aurore* on 13th January. In the letter, in fact quite a lengthy article, Zola took to pieces the case against Dreyfus and catalogued the deceit of individuals within the military high command in doing their best to keep an innocent man in prison, exile and ignominy, for the sake of shoring up the authority of the army and the state. The following month Zola was tried for having accused the court-martial of knowingly acquitting a guilty man, and sentenced to a year in prison. The conviction was quashed on appeal, but a further writ emerged, and in July 1898 Zola fled to England for a year – during which time he was stripped of his Legion of Honour – remaining in exile until, in June 1899, a review of the case was ordered, vindicating Zola and allowing him to return. The sequence of events arising from 'J'Accuse!' meant that the details of the case were aired fully, and a retrial was ordered: Dreyfus's sentence was cut down to ten years' hard labour in 1899, and he was subsequently pardoned and released.

The End   After the Dreyfus affair, Zola's stamina was undiminished, and he launched himself into his next project, a four-volume series entitled *The Four Gospels*. He managed to complete the first three, *Fecundity*, *Work* and *Truth*, but the fourth volume of this Utopian cycle, to be entitled *Justice*, never materialized. Zola died on 29th September 1902 of asphyxiation, after inhaling carbon monoxide fumes from a blocked fireplace in his Paris apartment. The circumstances of Zola's death were suspicious, and there has been speculation ever since that he may have been poisoned. Zola certainly had many enemies, not least over his role in the Dreyfus affair, which had still not been brought to its definitive conclusion, so such conjecture cannot be dismissed lightly as conspiracy theory. Whatever its cause, precisely because of the controversy it continues to arouse, Zola's death is further testimony to the power and significance of the figure of the writer in the public domain. Buried initially in Montmartre cemetery, Zola's remains were removed to the Panthéon in 1908 – a clear and unambiguous acknowledgement of his contribution to French national life.

Émile Zola's Works

Since Zola was a professional writer and journalist, the extent of his writings is vast to say the least. From an early age, he composed poetry, and later in his career he made attempts to write for the theatre as well. He was also a prolific letter-writer throughout his life. By necessity, this section focuses on Zola's major works of fiction, but it should be borne in mind that these form part of a much larger body of work.

Zola's work from the late 1860s onwards begins to engage not only with history, politics and the modernity of a society undergoing rapid urbanization and industrialization, but also with philosophical, sociological, medical and technological ideas and developments. And present from the outset is a spirit of specifically scientific, empirically observational enquiry, which later comes to play a significant role in the literary movement associated with Zola, known as Naturalism. *Thérèse Raquin and Naturalism*

Although Naturalism did not immediately declare itself as such and was not comprehensively formulated until many years later, one of the movement's key features, that of a certain kind of scientific determinism, is already to be found in Zola's 1867 novel, *Thérèse Raquin*, in which the title character and her sweetheart kill her husband (who is also her cousin) in order to be together, only to find that their horror and guilt over their action prevents them from enjoying their life together as lovers. The initial action prompts a logical development: a psychological decline in both characters which leads to the seemingly inevitable conclusion of insanity and suicide, which are presented not as supernaturally ordained moral just deserts, but as *naturally* determined consequences as physiological as they are psychological. *Thérèse Raquin* is in some sense a prototype for the Naturalist novel, though there are others, such as Zola's next book, *Madeleine Férat*,

433

the Goncourt brothers' *Germinie Lacerteux*, or – as Zola would later claim himself – Flaubert's *Sentimental Education*. However, *Thérèse Raquin* and *Madeleine Férat* are rather one-dimensional works. It is Zola's next project which develops Naturalism's remarkably wide-ranging scope as a form of literature which deals with all aspects of modern life and is underpinned by modern ideas from varied fields.

The Rougon-Macquart Cycle

The Rougon-Macquarts, subtitled *Natural and Social History of a Family under the Second Empire*, is the story of two branches, one legitimate (Rougon), the other illegitimate (Macquart), of a family from Plassans, a town in the South of France usually held to be a fictionalized version of Aix-en-Provence. However, it is also the story – or indeed set of stories – of the wider context of the period in which it is set, namely the Second Empire, the authoritarian regime of Louis-Napoléon Bonaparte, Napoleon III, which styled itself on the Empire of his uncle, Napoleon I. The Second Empire began with Bonaparte's *coup d'état* against the faltering Second Republic on 2nd December 1851, and ended in his ignominious defeat by Prussia at Sedan in September 1870, ushering in the Third Republic. The period was a time of great social and political change, most notably in infrastructural and economic terms. Under the direction of Baron Eugène-Charles Haussmann, Prefect of the Seine, Paris was transformed from a labyrinth of narrow medieval streets to an efficient network of boulevards facilitating circulation between all parts of the city and rapid movement to the new railway terminals and beyond; through state support the railways expanded massively, especially after 1860, to the extent that by 1870 all major cities were within twenty-four hours of Paris, and passenger numbers had increased within twenty-five years from 6 to 100 million. The economy – not least because of the developments in Paris – shifted to a model based on property speculation and capital investment in industry.

During this period, characterized by unprecedented capitalist growth subordinated to massive state intervention and control, France, though still at this stage a rural nation over much of its territory, acquired all the characteristics of a modern industrialized country. And it is France's adjustment to urban modernity, industry and capitalism that represents a significant element of Zola's novelistic project. As well as charting the political birth pangs and death throes of the period, the *Rougon-Macquart* cycle depicts – in a highly systematic way – modern social and industrial trends and institutions, as the following examples illustrate.

The second novel in the series, *The Kill* (1871), examines the mad rush for property in the new Paris being constructed by Haussmann. *The Belly of Paris* (1873) shows in intimate detail the workings of the central food markets in Paris, and exploits the metaphorical potential of the idea of digestion, showing economic competition as a struggle between fat and lean (a theme taken up elsewhere in the series, notably in *Germinal*). *L'Assommoir* (1876) provides a tragic account of alcoholism among the urban poor in a transforming city, which was a major breakthrough in making Zola a household name. His reputation for crude realism was enhanced by the publication of *Nana* (1880), a novel about the oldest profession in its most up-to-date Parisian context, in which the eponymous anti-heroine's prostitution – seen as poisoning the entire social body during the build-up to war and the collapse of the regime – is attributed to her forebears' drunkenness. The modern workplace is also a major theme: *Ladies' Delight* (1883) – discussed in detail below – is a story set in one of the new Parisian department stores selling mass-produced consumer goods, while *Germinal* (1885) deals with industrial unrest in a mining community in northern France. *The Masterpiece* (1886), over which Cézanne – on whom the central character Claude Lantier was allegedly based – fell out with Zola, is a novel about the world of art (and its relationship with writing) in an age when, at last, modern representational techniques could represent modern life. Another recurrent feature in Zola's work is that of the network: *The Human Beast* (1890) is a crime novel centred on the railway, represented as a body spreading its interconnected tentacles throughout the national territory; *Money* (1891) represents the world of high finance as a circulatory system (as indeed does Karl Marx – regularly alluded to in the novel – in *Capital*). These two novels also have in common a sense of impending catastrophe, metaphorically figuring the collapse of the Second Empire, a collapse given concrete and literal expression in *The Debacle* (1892), a novel about Jean Macquart's experience in the Franco-Prussian war. Although each of the novels just cited has its own specific focus, they are all, in their representation of the workings of various systems (social, bodily, technological, institutional, economic), in some way about the mechanisms of society as a whole: not only do they illustrate how the system functions, they also typically show what happens when it falls into dysfunction – a dysfunction implicitly presented as being inherent in the system rather than brought about through external intervention. So, on the one hand, there is a totalizing depiction of the society of the middle of the nineteenth century (and in some sense also of that of the Third Republic, during which Zola wrote most of the novels); on the other hand, this is intimately connected with the "family" aspect of Zola's fictional cycle, itself informed by the novelist's engagement with new developments in science, medicine and technology.

As the cycle developed, the main features of Naturalism began to cohere: extreme and profuse detail, scientific determinism, the hereditary underpinning, the incorporation of knowledge from various fields and engagement with the modern world. Two elements in particular are worth bearing in mind. Firstly, documentary exactitude based on research and empirical observation. Naturalism is sometimes – with some justification – portrayed as an extreme offshoot of earlier Realism, in its concern for accuracy and its refusal to spare any information, no matter how gruesome or shocking. But it is perhaps in the area of documentary precision and the research necessary for it that Zola's Naturalism most impressively fulfils the Realist brief to represent the modern world as it is. While preparing *Germinal*, for example, Zola went down a mine in northern France, and observed the labour and living conditions of the miners and their families; for *The Human Beast*, he arranged to travel on the footplate of a locomotive, engaged in lengthy correspondence with railway employees and read several technical works on the railways. And the novel to which we shall shortly turn our attention, *Ladies' Delight*, presents detailed analysis of the various mechanisms involved in the functioning of the modern department store; the store in the novel is based on two Parisian department stores – Le Bon Marché, which still exists, and Le Louvre – where Zola carried out research, involving interviews with staff. No stone was left unturned in the mission to represent reality accurately, and in accordance with "natural" (rather than metaphysical or idealistic) principles.

Naturalism, however, was not as coherent a system as Zola's rhetoric – deployed in *The Experimental Novel, Naturalism in the Theatre* (1881) and elsewhere – might have liked to claim, and a number of Naturalist features were more prominent in some novels than in others. If we consider *Germinal*, for instance, the stress is on the heredity theme, expressed by generations of miners inheriting obeisance and resignation to a miserable life, and the fantastical "machine-monster" metaphor of the mine as devouring ogre. In *The Human Beast*, we have perhaps the closest thing to "total" Naturalism, in which the character of a psychopathic engine driver whose uncontrollable urge to kill, inherited – like his sister Nana's tendency to prostitution – from his alcoholic forebears, is paralleled in the relentless, unstoppable, mathematical inexorability of his locomotive's functioning. Other novels are Naturalist in the sense that they deal with the natural cycles of the earth, in particular *The Joy of Life* (1884) and *Earth* (1887), which have both rural settings. Others are concerned explicitly with the family history – such as *The Fortune of the Rougons, The Conquest of Plassans* (1874) and *Doctor Pascal* (1893). Others have a more institutional emphasis, focusing on politics – such as *His Excellency Eugène Rougon* (1876), in which the hero scales the commanding heights of the Bonapartist regime – or religion, such as *Abbé Mouret's Transgression* (1875), addressing the problematic question of celibacy, and *The Dream* (1888), set around an ancient cathedral.

Doctor Pascal (1893) brings to an end the *Rougon-Macquart* cycle in a highly self-referential way: Pascal Rougon drafts the family tree from a series of dossiers which he has built up on his relatives from both sides of the extended family. The final version of the family tree is presented with the last novel, which updates the versions provided with *The Fortune of the Rougons*. The cycle ends with the death of Pascal and simultaneously the birth of his child with his niece Clotilde, identified only as "the unknown child" on the family tree. This child is symbolic of the ultimate optimism of the *Rougon-Macquart* series, which does nevertheless have some very gloomy moments.

The eleventh novel in the series, *Ladies' Delight*, is as much about the rise of a certain type of commerce as of its central male character, Octave Mouret. In it, we have a detailed representation of a modern institution – the department store

Ladies' Delight

437

– networked into a completely new commercial, industrial and urban infrastructure, and at the same time the depiction of the archetypally Naturalist "machine-monster": the store is represented as a devouring beast, crushing all opposition in its path, extending its reach throughout the metropolitan territory and gobbling up goods, money and, most of all, women, victims of its sensual appeal to their consumer sensibilities.

Octave Mouret, descended on his mother's side from the Rougons and on his father's from the Macquarts, is ruthlessly ambitious and has an intuitive commercial sensibility. His mother, Marthe Rougon, has a history of hysteria and nervous ailments; his father knows how to watch his money. But unlike in novels such as *Nana*, *Germinal* and *The Human Beast*, the inherited traits are not to any great extent pathologized. Octave is clearly just someone with sound business instincts, honed in the previous novel in the series, *Pot-Bouille* (1882), in which he is one of the residents of the apartment block – the novel's subject and central narrative device – behind the immaculate façade of which the often less than immaculate activities of a cross-section of Parisian society are represented. At the end of *Pot-Bouille*, set in 1865, Octave – a reformed ladies' man – marries Caroline Hédouin, owner of Ladies' Delight, which started in the 1820s as a *"magasin de nouveautés"* (literally, a "novelty shop", and in practice a shop which sold ladies' fashions and fabrics), and which, having been left to Octave in her will by the prematurely deceased Caroline, is now poised, in its manifestation as a modern department store selling mass-produced goods within the price range of a whole new class of consumers, to conquer Paris commercially and topographically.

Complaining at Mouret's continued expansion, Baudu, the owner of a small, old-style fabric shop and the uncle of Denise, the heroine of the novel and object of Mouret's affection, denounces him as "a dangerous troublemaker who'll turn the whole neighbourhood topsy-turvy if he's allowed to". Baudu's outburst is telling in that it expresses unease at Mouret's way of doing business, and fear that it will supplant his own business, but it also accurately predicts what will literally happen in the part of Paris in question, that is, the area known today as the Grands Boulevards. This area is the *locus classicus* of the process which has come to be known as "Haussmannization", consisting in the "piercing" of wide boulevards which would facilitate rapid movement of goods, people and troops within the city, and, via the new railway termini with which the boulevards were connected, beyond. This area – home also to two other major Haussmannian icons, the Gare Saint-Lazare and Garnier's Opera – was central to the representation of modern urban life by Impressionist artists such as Manet, and has been the site of Paris's major department stores since the Second Empire.

The department store resembles two other key urban structures of the period, namely the railway station and the exhibition palace, both also concerned with circulation. It is perhaps in the novel's representation of the part of the store concerned with direct circulatory interaction with the city beyond it that we can best see an intersection of the Naturalist concerns in the novel. The loading and dispatch bays, despite not being seen by the consuming public, are however witnessed by the narrative, uncovering (through the eyes of Mouret surveying his domain) what lies beneath the sales galleries' overt manifestation of modernity. Here we see not only the running of another microcosmic department in the interconnected series of departments constituted by the store, but also the functioning of a machine with beastlike qualities, swallowing up manufactured goods and regurgitating them into the metropolitan infrastructure of which the store itself is a microcosm, and at the same time alchemically producing gold from the process. What is striking in the descriptions of the store is the combination of the efficiently mechanical and the fantastically organic, the imagery of the machine running at full capacity and that of the digesting and egesting creature.

The store is an ogre nourished through the payment of tribute in the form of fabrics, but also (like the coal mine in *Germinal*) in the form of human flesh. For the store's running depends on two specific groups of human beings. First of all, there are the (almost exclusively female) consumers, integrated into what one critic of the novel has referred to as the "economy of female desire". The other major group essential to the machine are the workers – shopgirls, drivers, post-room employees – who are, like the customers, in some sense transformed, to the extent that they become mere cogs in the workings, losing their individual identities. Although the store, which houses a considerable proportion of its staff under its own roof as if it were a military barracks, is full of young people of both sexes, there is little interaction between them, least of all amorous interaction, because, as Denise, who has by now climbed up the rungs of the store's hierarchy, realizes, "those who worked there had become nothing but cogs, caught up by the impetus of the machine, surrendering their personalities, merely adding their strength to the mighty common whole of the phalanstery". The phalanstery was a particular form of idealized industrial system associated with the utopian socialist Charles Fourier (1772–1837), and it is no surprise that the term should arise here. Mouret's store is in fact a kind of utopian ideal city, of which all the components play a specific and essential – though by no means equally rewarded – role in making the system work perfectly.

Mouret however is not satisfied by the system's perfection: he is "secretly getting exasperated by the perfect running of the machine which he had himself regulated". The reason? The continued indifference of Denise to his advances. What finally brings the two together is a kind of compromise whereby Mouret acknowledges her concerns regarding the running of the store, to do primarily with the provision of better conditions for the employees. Importantly, Denise's concerns are not with the essential business principles on which the machine operates: but she believes it is possible to "improve the system", rather than to abolish it. It is on this basis that she speaks up for the workers, "imagining a huge, ideal emporium, a phalanstery of trade, in which everyone would have his fair share of the profits according to his merits, and his future assured by a contract". This is miles away from Zola's other major novel of the workplace, *Germinal*, written two years later, in which, far from coming to a compromise, labour and capital perpetuate an age-old struggle which ends in bloodshed.

In a sense, despite the presence of a representative range of typically Naturalist features, *Ladies' Delight* is unusual in that it is a Naturalist novel in which the system represented does not fall into complete disarray, but rather goes from strength to strength after some minor alterations are made. Philippe Hamon observes that out of the *Rougon-Macquart* series, it is the "only novel with a happy ending". It certainly does have a happy ending in the classic sense – but essential to this happiness, and to the triumph of the store, is the triumph over Mouret of Denise, who, having conquered a system that Mouret has set up to exploit women, is, in the last words of the novel, an "all-powerful" woman.

Zola's later novels continue in the life-affirmingly opti- *The Three Cities* mistic, quasi-religious vein of *Doctor Pascal*, the final instalment of the *Rougon-Macquart* series. His next project was a trilogy, *The Three Cities*, consisting of *Lourdes* (1894), *Rome* (1896) and *Paris* (1897). Inspired initially by a visit to Lourdes – which, after Bernadette Soubirous claimed to have seen the Virgin Mary there in 1858, had become a major pilgrimage centre and rallying point for religious fervour in the face of an emboldened rationalism – the trilogy deals with questions of faith, doubt and reason in the modern age. Its central character, a priest called Pierre Froment, has a crisis of faith and at the same time warms to a progressive Catholic socialism, on which grounds he is summoned to Rome to account for himself. Froment's development might be seen in the light of a sea change in the Vatican under the pontificate of Leo XIII, under whom the Church began to accommodate itself with modernity in a way unimaginable under his ultraconservative predecessor Pius IX. Ultimately, Pierre loses his faith, is defrocked and finds redemption in work, love and the fight for social justice.

As with the earlier trilogy, the *Four Gospels* cycle raised *The Four Gospels* the possibility of a secularized replacement for Christianity in an age of reason and progress. *Fecundity* (1899), as its title suggests, celebrates the remarkable extent of the progeny of Pierre Froment's son and his wife Marianne, and articulates the potential for French civilization to spread itself throughout a fertile and receptive world. *Work* (1901) depicts a religion of humanity trumping both Christianity and capitalism in an ideal worker-owned neo-Fourierist workplace which Luc Froment has created from an abominable steelworks. *Truth* (published posthumously in 1903) relates the Dreyfus Affair in disguise, in a small-town setting. As we have seen above, the fourth volume of the series, *Justice*, was never completed.

– Larry Duffy, 2008

Select Bibliography

Standard Edition
Au Bonheur des Dames, in volume III *Les Rougon-Macquart, Histoire naturelle et sociale d'une famille sous le second Empire*, edited by Henri Mitterand, (Paris: Gallimard, Bibliothèque de la Pléiade, 1960–67) is the most authoritative edition to date.

Biographies:
Brown, Frederick, *Zola. A Life* (London: Macmillan, 1995)
Hemmings, F.W.J., *Émile Zola* (Oxford: Clarendon Press, 1965)
Mitterand, Henri, *Zola*, 3 vols. (Paris: Fayard, 1999–2002)
Richardson, Joanna, *Zola* (London: Weidenfeld & Nicolson, 1978)
Wilson, Angus, *Émile Zola: An Introductory Study of His Novels* (London: Secker and Warburg, 1952)

Additional Recommended Reading:
Baguley, David, *Napoleon III and his Regime: An Extravaganza* (Baton Rouge, LA: Louisiana State University Press, 2000)
Baguley, David, *Naturalist Fiction: The Entropic Vision* (Cambridge: Cambridge University Press, 1990)
Benjamin, Walter, *The Arcades Project* (Cambridge, MS: Belknap Press, 1999)
Bowlby, Rachel, *Just Looking: Consumer Culture in Dreiser, Gissing and Zola* (London: Methuen, 1985)
Clark, T.J., *The Painting of Modern Life. Paris in the Art of Manet and his Followers* (New York, NY: Knopf, 1985)
Duffy, Larry, *Le Grand Transit Moderne: Mobility, Modernity and French Naturalist Fiction* (Amsterdam: Rodopi, 2005)
Hamon, Philippe, *Expositions. Literature and Architecture in Nineteenth-Century France* (Berkeley, CA: University of California Press, 1992)
Miller, Michael, *The Bon Marché. Bourgeois Culture and the Department Store, 1869–1920* (London: George Allen and Unwin, 1981)
Nelson, Brian, *Zola and the Bourgeoisie: A Study of Themes and Techniques in* Les Rougon-Macquart (London: Macmillan, 1983)
Nelson, Brian, ed., *The Cambridge Companion to Zola* (Cambridge: Cambridge University Press, 2007)

Niess, Robert J., *Zola, Cézanne and Manet: A Study of* L'Œuvre (Ann Arbor, MI: University of Michigan Press, 1968)

Christopher Prendergast, *Paris and the Nineteenth Century* (Oxford: Blackwell, 1992)

Juliet Wilson-Bareau, *Manet, Monet, and the Gare Saint-Lazare* (New Haven, CT: Yale University Press, 1998)

On the Web:

abu.cnam.fr/BIB/auteurs/zolae.html

gallica.bnf.fr/classique

www.chass.utoronto.ca/french/sable/collections/zola/

Appendix

The Opening Pages of
Ladies' Delight in French

1

Denise était venue à pied de la gare Saint-Lazare, où un train de Cherbourg l'avait débarquée avec ses deux frères, après une nuit passée sur la dure banquette d'un wagon de troisième classe. Elle tenait par la main Pépé, et Jean la suivait, tous les trois brisés du voyage, effarés et perdus, au milieu du vaste Paris, le nez levé sur les maisons, demandant à chaque carrefour la rue de la Michodière, dans laquelle leur oncle Baudu demeurait. Mais, comme elle débouchait enfin sur la place Gaillon, la jeune fille s'arrêta net de surprise.

« Oh ! dit-elle, regarde un peu, Jean ! »

Et ils restèrent plantés, serrés les uns contre les autres, tout en noir, achevant les vieux vêtements du deuil de leur père. Elle, chétive pour ses vingt ans, l'air pauvre, portait un léger paquet ; tandis que, de l'autre côté, le petit frère, âgé de cinq ans, se pendait à son bras, et que, derrière son épaule, le grand frère, dont les seize ans superbes florissaient, était debout, les mains ballantes.

« Ah ! bien ! reprit-elle après un silence, en voilà un magasin ! »

C'était, à l'encoignure de la rue de la Michodière et de la rue Neuve-Saint-Augustin, un magasin de nouveautés dont les étalages éclataient en notes vives, dans la douce et pâle journée d'octobre. Huit heures sonnaient à Saint-Roch, il n'y avait sur les trottoirs que le Paris matinal, les employés filant à leurs bureaux et les ménagères courant les boutiques. Devant la porte, deux commis, montés sur une échelle double, finissaient de pendre des lainages, tandis que, dans une vitrine de la rue Neuve-Saint-Augustin, un autre commis, agenouillé et le dos tourné, plissait délicatement une pièce de soie bleue. Le magasin, vide encore de clientes, et où le personnel arrivait à peine, bourdonnait à l'intérieur comme une ruche qui s'éveille.

« Fichtre ! dit Jean. Ça enfonce Valognes… Le tien n'était pas si beau. »

Denise hocha la tête. Elle avait passé deux ans là-bas, chez Cornaille, le premier marchand de nouveautés de la ville ; et ce magasin, rencontré brusquement, cette maison énorme pour elle, lui gonflait le coeur, la retenait, émue, intéressée, oublieuse du reste. Dans le pan coupé donnant sur la place Gaillon, la haute porte, toute en glace, montait jusqu'à l'entresol, au milieu d'une complication d'ornements, chargés de dorures. Deux figures allégoriques, deux femmes riantes, la gorge nue et renversée, déroulaient l'enseigne : *Au Bonheur des Dames*. Puis, les vitrines s'enfonçaient, longeaient la rue de la Michodière et la rue Neuve-Saint-Augustin, où elles occupaient, outre la maison d'angle, quatre autres maisons, deux à gauche, deux à droite, achetées et aménagées récemment. C'était un développement qui lui semblait sans fin, dans la fuite de la perspective, avec les étalages du rez-de-chaussée et les glaces sans tain de l'entresol, derrière lesquelles on voyait toute la vie intérieure des comptoirs. En haut, une demoiselle, habillée de soie, taillait un crayon, pendant que, près d'elle, deux autres dépliaient des manteaux de velours.

« *Au Bonheur des Dames*, lut Jean avec son rire tendre de bel adolescent, qui avait eu déjà une histoire de femme à Valognes. Hein ? c'est gentil, c'est ça qui doit faire courir le monde ! »

Mais Denise demeurait absorbée, devant l'étalage de la porte centrale. Il y avait là, au plein air de la rue, sur le trottoir même, un éboulement de marchandises à bon marché, la tentation de la porte, les occasions qui arrêtaient les clientes au passage. Cela partait de haut, des pièces de lainage et de draperie, mérinos, cheviottes, molletons, tombaient de l'entresol, flottantes comme des drapeaux, et dont les tons neutres, gris ardoise, bleu marine, vert olive, étaient coupés par les pancartes blanches des étiquettes. À côté, encadrant le seuil, pendaient également des lanières de fourrure, des bandes étroites pour garnitures de robe, la cendre fine des dos de petit-gris, la neige pure des ventres de cygne, les poils de lapin de la fausse hermine et de la fausse martre. Puis, en bas, dans des casiers, sur des tables, au milieu d'un empilement de coupons, débordaient des articles de bonneterie vendus pour rien, gants et fichus de laine tricotés, capelines, gilets, tout un étalage d'hiver, aux couleurs bariolées, chinées, rayées, avec des taches saignantes de rouge. Denise vit une tartanelle à quarante-cinq centimes, des bandes de vison d'Amérique à un franc, et des mitaines à cinq sous. C'était un déballage géant de foire, le magasin semblait crever et jeter son trop-plein à la rue.

L'oncle Baudu était oublié. Pépé lui-même, qui ne lâchait pas la main de sa soeur, ouvrait des yeux énormes. Une voiture les força tous trois à quitter le milieu de la place ; et, machinalement, ils prirent la rue Neuve-Saint-Augustin, ils suivirent les vitrines, s'arrêtant de nouveau devant chaque étalage. D'abord, ils furent séduits par un arrangement compliqué : en haut, des parapluies, posés obliquement, semblaient mettre un toit de cabane rustique ; dessous, des bas de soie, pendus à des tringles, montraient des profils arrondis de mollets, les uns semés de bouquets de roses, les autres de toutes nuances, les noirs à jour, les rouges à coins brodés, les chairs dont le grain satiné avait la douceur d'une peau de blonde ; enfin, sur le drap de l'étagère, des gants étaient jetés symétriquement, avec leurs doigts allongés, leur paume étroite de vierge byzantine, cette grâce raidie et comme adolescente des chiffons de femme qui n'ont pas été portés. Mais la dernière vitrine surtout les retint. Une exposition de soies, de satins et de velours, y épanouissait, dans une gamme souple et vibrante, les tons les plus délicats des fleurs : au sommet, les velours, d'un noir profond, d'un blanc de lait caillé ; plus bas, les satins, les roses, les bleus, aux cassures vives, se décolorant en pâleurs d'une tendresse infinie ; plus bas encore, les soies, toute l'écharpe de l'arc-en-ciel, des pièces retroussées en coques, plissées comme autour d'une taille qui se cambre, devenues vivantes sous les doigts savants des commis ; et, entre chaque motif, entre chaque phrase colorée de l'étalage, courait un accompagnement discret, un léger cordon bouillonné de foulard crème. C'était là, aux deux bouts, que se trouvaient, en piles colossales, les deux soies dont la maison avait la propriété exclusive, le Paris-Bonheur et le Cuir-d'Or, des articles exceptionnels, qui allaient révolutionner le commerce des nouveautés.

« Oh ! cette faille à cinq francs soixante ! » murmura Denise, étonnée devant le Paris-Bonheur.

Jean commençait à s'ennuyer. Il arrêta un passant.

« La rue de la Michodière, monsieur ? »

Quand on la lui eut indiquée, la première à droite, tous trois revinrent sur leurs pas, en tournant autour du magasin. Mais, comme elle entrait dans la rue, Denise fut reprise par une vitrine, où étaient exposées des confections pour dames. Chez Cornaille, à Valognes, elle était spécialement chargée des confections. Et jamais elle n'avait vu cela, une admiration la clouait sur le trottoir. Au fond, une grande écharpe en dentelle de Bruges, d'un prix considérable, élargissait un voile d'autel, deux ailes déployées, d'une blancheur rousse ; des volants de point d'Alençon se trouvaient jetés en guirlandes ; puis, c'était, à pleines mains, un ruissellement de toutes les dentelles, les malines, les valenciennes, les applications de Bruxelles, les points de Venise, comme une tombée de neige. À droite et à gauche, des pièces de drap dressaient des colonnes sombres, qui reculaient encore ce lointain de tabernacle. Et les confections étaient là, dans cette chapelle élevée au culte des grâces de la femme : occupant le centre, un article hors ligne, un manteau de velours, avec des garnitures de renard argenté ; d'un côté, une rotonde de soie, doublée de petit-gris ; de l'autre, un paletot de drap, bordé de plumes de coq ; enfin, des sorties de bal, en cachemire blanc, en matelassé blanc, garnies de cygne ou de chenille. Il y en avait pour tous les caprices, depuis les sorties de bal à vingt-neuf francs jusqu'au manteau de velours affiché dix-huit cents francs, La gorge ronde des mannequins gonflait l'étoffe, les hanches fortes exagéraient la finesse de la taille, la tête absente était remplacée par une grande étiquette, piquée avec une épingle dans le molleton rouge du col ; tandis que les glaces, aux deux côtés de la vitrine, par un jeu calculé, les reflétaient et les multipliaient sans fin, peuplaient la rue de ces belles femmes à vendre, et qui portaient des prix en gros chiffres, à la place des têtes.

« Elles sont fameuses ! » murmura Jean, qui ne trouva rien d'autre pour dire son émotion.

Du coup, il était lui-même redevenu immobile, la bouche ouverte. Tout ce luxe de la femme le rendait rose de plaisir. Il avait la beauté d'une fille, une beauté qu'il semblait avoir volée à sa sœur, la peau éclatante, les cheveux roux et frisés, les lèvres et les yeux mouillés de tendresse. Près de lui, dans son étonnement, Denise paraissait plus mince encore, avec son visage long à bouche trop grande, son teint fatigué déjà, sous sa chevelure pâle. Et Pépé, également blond, d'un blond d'enfance, se serrait davantage contre elle, comme pris d'un besoin inquiet de caresses, troublé et ravi par les belles dames de la vitrine. Ils étaient si singuliers et si charmants, sur le pavé, ces trois blonds vêtus pauvrement de noir, cette fille triste entre ce joli enfant et ce garçon superbe, que les passants se retournaient avec des sourires.

Depuis un instant, un gros homme à cheveux blancs et à grande face jaune, debout sur le seuil d'une boutique, de l'autre côté de la rue, les regardait. C'était là, le sang aux yeux, la bouche contractée, mis hors de lui par les étalages du *Bonheur des Dames*, lorsque la vue de la jeune fille et de ses frères avait achevé de l'exaspérer. Que faisaient-ils, ces trois nigauds, à bâiller ainsi devant des parades de charlatan ?

« Et l'oncle ? fit remarquer brusquement Denise, comme éveillée en sursaut.

– Nous sommes rue de la Michodière, dit Jean, il doit loger par ici. »

Ils levèrent la tête, se retournèrent. Alors, juste devant eux, au-dessus du gros homme, ils aperçurent une enseigne verte, dont les lettres jaunes déteignaient sous la pluie : *Au Vieil Elbeuf draps et flanelles, Baudu, successeur de Hauchecorne*. La maison, enduite d'un ancien badigeon rouillé, toute plate au milieu des grands hôtels Louis XIV qui l'avoisinaient, n'avait que trois fenêtres de façade ; et ces fenêtres, carrées, sans persiennes, étaient simplement garnies d'une rampe de fer, deux barres en croix. Mais, dans cette nudité, ce qui frappa surtout Denise, dont les yeux restaient pleins des clairs étalages du *Bonheur des Dames*, ce fut la boutique du rez-de-chaussée, écrasée de plafond, surmontée d'un entresol très bas, aux baies de prison, en demi-lune. Une boiserie, de la couleur de l'enseigne, d'un vert bouteille que le temps avait nuancé d'ocre et de bitume, ménageait, à droite et à gauche, deux vitrines profondes, noires, poussiéreuses, où l'on distinguait vaguement des pièces d'étoffe entassées. La porte, ouverte, semblait donner sur les ténèbres humides d'une cave.

« C'est là, reprit Jean.

– Eh bien ! il faut entrer, déclara Denise. Allons, viens, Pépé. »

Tous trois pourtant se troublaient, saisis de timidité. Lorsque leur père était mort, emporté par la même fièvre qui avait pris leur mère, un mois auparavant, l'oncle Baudu, dans l'émotion de ce double deuil, avait bien écrit à sa nièce qu'il y aurait toujours chez lui une place pour elle, le jour où elle voudrait tenter la fortune à Paris ; mais cette lettre remontait déjà à près d'une année, et la jeune fille se repentait maintenant d'avoir ainsi quitté Valognes, en un coup de tête, sans avertir son oncle. Celui-ci ne les connaissait point, n'ayant plus remis les pieds là-bas, depuis qu'il en était parti tout jeune, pour entrer comme petit commis chez le drapier Hauchecorne, dont il avait fini par épouser la fille.

« Monsieur Baudu ? demanda Denise, en se décidant enfin à s'adresser au gros homme, qui les regardait toujours, surpris de leurs allures.

– C'est moi, » répondit-il.

Alors, Denise rougit fortement et balbutia :

« Ah ! tant mieux !... Je suis Denise, et voici Jean, et voici Pépé... Vous voyez, nous sommes venus, mon oncle. »

Baudu parut frappé de stupéfaction. Ses gros yeux rouges vacillaient dans sa face jaune, ses paroles lentes s'embarrassaient. Il était évidemment à mille lieues de cette famille qui lui tombait sur les épaules.

« Comment ! comment ! vous voilà ! répéta-t-il à plusieurs reprises. Mais vous étiez à Valognes !... Pourquoi n'êtes-vous pas à Valognes ? »

De sa voix douce, un peu tremblante, elle dut lui donner des explications. Après la mort de leur père, qui avait mangé jusqu'au dernier sou dans sa teinturerie, elle était restée la mère des deux enfants. Ce qu'elle gagnait chez Cornaille ne suffisait point à les nourrir tous les trois. Jean travaillait bien chez un ébéniste, un réparateur de meubles anciens ; mais il ne touchait pas un sou. Pourtant, il prenait goût aux vieilleries, il taillait des figures dans du bois ; même, un jour, ayant découvert un morceau d'ivoire, il s'était amusé à faire une tête, qu'un monsieur de passage avait vue ; et justement, c'était ce monsieur qui les avait décidés à quitter Valognes, en trouvant à Paris une place pour Jean, chez un ivoirier.

« Vous comprenez, mon oncle, Jean entrera dès demain en apprentissage, chez son nouveau patron. On ne me demande pas d'argent, il sera logé et nourri... Alors, j'ai pensé que Pépé et moi, nous nous tirerions toujours d'affaire. Nous ne pouvons pas être plus malheureux qu'à Valognes. »

Ce qu'elle taisait, c'était l'escapade amoureuse de Jean, des lettres écrites à une fillette noble de la ville, des baisers échangés par-dessus un mur, tout un scandale qui l'avait déterminée au départ ; et elle accompagnait surtout son frère à Paris pour veiller sur lui, prise de terreurs maternelles, devant ce grand enfant si beau et si gai, que toutes les femmes adoraient.

L'oncle Baudu ne pouvait se remettre. Il reprenait ses questions. Cependant, quand il l'eut ainsi entendue parler de ses frères, il la tutoya.

« Ton père ne vous a donc rien laissé ? Moi, je croyais qu'il y avait encore quelques sous. Ah ! je lui ai assez conseillé, dans mes lettres, de ne pas prendre cette teinturerie ! Un brave coeur, mais pas deux liards de tête !... Et tu es restée avec ces gaillards sur les bras, tu as dû nourrir ce petit monde ! »

Sa face bilieuse s'était éclairée, il n'avait plus les yeux saignants dont il regardait le Bonheur des Dames. Brusquement, il s'aperçut qu'il barrait la porte.

« Allons, dit-il, entrez, puisque vous êtes venus... Entrez, ça vaudra mieux que de baguenauder devant des bêtises. »

Et, après avoir adressé aux étalages d'en face une dernière moue de colère, il livra passage aux enfants, il pénétra le premier dans la boutique, en appelant sa femme et sa fille.

« Élisabeth, Geneviève, arrivez donc, voici du monde pour vous ! »

Mais Denise et les petits eurent une hésitation devant les ténèbres de la boutique. Aveuglés par le plein jour de la rue, ils battaient des paupières comme au seuil d'un trou inconnu, tâtant le sol du pied, ayant la peur instinctive de quelque marche traîtresse. Et, rapprochés encore par cette crainte vague, se serrant davantage les uns contre les autres le gamin, toujours dans les jupes de la jeune fille et le grand derrière, ils faisaient leur entrée avec une grâce souriante et inquiète. La clarté matinale découpait la noire silhouette de leurs vêtements de deuil, un jour oblique dorait leurs cheveux blonds.

« Entrez, entrez », répétait Baudu.

En quelques phrases brèves, il mettait au courant Mme Baudu et sa fille. La première était une petite femme mangée d'anémie, toute blanche, les cheveux blancs, les yeux blancs, les lèvres blanches. Geneviève, chez qui s'aggravait encore la dégénérescence de sa mère, avait la débilité et la décoloration d'une plante grandie à l'ombre. Pourtant, des cheveux noirs magnifiques, épais et lourds, poussés comme par miracle dans cette chair pauvre, lui donnaient un charme triste.

« Entrez, dirent à leur tour les deux femmes. Vous êtes les bienvenus. »

ONEWORLD CLASSICS

ONEWORLD CLASSICS aims to publish mainstream and lesser-known European classics in an innovative and striking way, while employing the highest editorial and production standards. By way of a unique approach the range offers much more, both visually and textually, than readers have come to expect from contemporary classics publishing.

CHARLOTTE BRONTË: *Jane Eyre*

EMILY BRONTË: *Wuthering Heights*

ANTON CHEKHOV: *Sakhalin Island*
Translated by Brian Reeve

CHARLES DICKENS: *Great Expectations*

D.H. LAWRENCE: *The First Women in Love*

D.H. LAWRENCE: *The Second Lady Chatterley's Lover*

D.H. LAWRENCE: *Selected Letters*

JAMES HANLEY: *Boy*

JACK KEROUAC: *Beat Generation*

JANE AUSTEN: *Emma*

JANE AUSTEN: *Pride and Prejudice*

CONNOISSEUR

THE CONNOISSEUR list will bring together unjustly neglected works, making them available again to the English-reading public. All titles are printed on high-quality, wood-free paper and bound in black cloth with gold foil-blocking, end papers, head and tail bands and ribbons. Each title will make a perfect gift for the discerning bibliophile and will combine to make a wonderful and enduring collection.

❧

GIFT CLASSICS

HENRY MILLER: *The World of Sex*

JONATHAN SWIFT: *The Benefit of Farting*

ANONYMOUS: *Dirty Limericks*

NAPOLEON BONAPARTE: *Aphorisms*

ROBERT GRAVES: *The Future of Swearing*

CHARLES DICKENS: *The Life of Our Lord*

CALDER PUBLICATIONS

Since 1949, John Calder has published eighteen Nobel Prize winners and around fifteen hundred books. He has put into print many of the major French and European writers, almost single-handedly introducing modern literature into the English language. His commitment to literary excellence has influenced two generations of authors, readers, booksellers and publishers. We are delighted to keep John Calder's legacy alive and hope to honour his achievements by continuing his tradition of excellence into a new century.

Antonin Artaud: *The Theatre and Its Double*

Louis-Ferdinand Céline: *Journey to the End of the Night*

Marguerite Duras: *The Sailor from Gibraltar*

Erich Fried: *100 Poems without a Country*

Eugène Ionesco: *Plays*

Luigi Pirandello: *Collected Plays*

Raymond Queneau: *Exercises in Style*

Alain Robbe-Grillet: *In the Labyrinth*

Alexander Trocchi: *Cain's Book*

To order any of our titles and for up-to-date information about our current and forthcoming publications, please visit our website on:

www.oneworldclassics.com